A Spell to Unbind

A Spell to Unbind

Spellbound Book One

Victoria Laurie

Copyright @ 2021 by Victoria Laurie

TABLE OF CONTENTS

Chapter One 1
Chapter Two 29
Chapter Three 46
Chapter Four 67
Chapter Five 79
Chapter Six 102
Chapter Seven 114
Chapter Eight 132
Chapter Nine 151
Chapter Ten 168
Chapter Eleven 182
Chapter Twelve 201
Chapter Thirteen 214
Chapter Fourteen 228
Chapter Fifteen 246
Chapter Sixteen 270
Chapter Seventeen 285
Chapter Eighteen 303
Chapter Nineteen 323
Chapter Twenty 347
Chapter Twenty-One 368

CHAPTER ONE

All things considered, the interview seemed to be going well. So far, I'd met with several of Elric's underlings, each of them oozing power but very little charm, and the fact that none of them had managed to kill me yet suggested that I might actually land this job.

To be specific, I'd made it through six rounds of tête-à-têtes, and each underling had left the interview looking furiously murderous at my very-much-alive self. It seemed like no one would be getting a bonus today, at least not over my dead body.

Still, I couldn't afford to be either cocky or confident. Yes, I'd dodged everything they'd thrown at me—from fire to ice, from poison to sharp instruments and projectiles, from wild beasts to birds of prey, from things that slithered, crawled, bit, chomped, and stung to a few even *less* fun things than those—but I certainly didn't have this new job in the bag. I mean, I'd survived—but barely.

Yet, by 4:45 in the afternoon, I was in far better shape than any of the other applicants. At the start of the day, there'd been ten of us: three ladies and seven guys. Assessing the competition, I'd noted that, judging by appearances alone, I was maybe one of the youngest in the group. That'd given me a bit of a pause when I'd traded looky-loos with a guy who could've easily been pushing three hundred. He was a mean-looking character—formidably intimidating for even the most hardened among us—with his long, jagged scar, creasing lengthwise across a weathered face, and deep-set eyes that reflected suspicion and confidence. The rest of him was equally menacing: tall, broad-framed, and wrapped in a bulging network of muscles, covered almost humorously by a skintight cotton black T-shirt and camo pants. If I'd been a betting woman, which, on occasion I am, I would've laid money on him as the winner. So my confidence was bolstered when I saw that he hadn't even made it through to the third round.

By noon we'd been down to just four: two men and two ladies. None of us had spoken to each other. It was better that way, but secretly I'd been pulling for the girls' team.

That's a bet I would've won, actually, because I'd come out of the fourth round and saw only one other applicant—the remaining woman—crumpled in a chair. It'd been pretty obvious then that she wasn't likely to last to the end, or, for that matter, the next hour. Her barely conscious form was puddled in a chair, missing a section of her upper left arm, three of her right fingers, and much of her left foot.

Comparatively I'd fared considerably better, with only a black eye, bloody lip, broken wrist, a few cracked ribs, talon marks down my left arm, and a somewhat hobbled right leg. Oh, and my head was pounding in such a way as to make me think that a marching band had taken up residence in my cranium. Still, I wasn't missing any *pieces*, and that put everything else into perspective.

When I emerged as the lone applicant after the sixth round, I felt a swell of relief that was decidedly short-lived the closer the clock ticked to 5 PM. The hard part was not knowing what I'd have to face next.

I figured Elric was the kind of man who saved the best for last, and I had no expectation of success. Just because I'd survived longer than the others didn't mean I was about to be employed. It only meant I'd outlived the other applicants going into the seventh and final interview. The odds were still against me, and I'd probably leave the building in a body bag, or garbage pail, depending on what deadly creature Elric threw at me next.

Still, I'd long ago made my peace with dying here, and I'd accepted that it was the price I'd have to pay for failure. So I sat alone again in the waiting area in one of the only chairs that wasn't smeared with blood.

The lobby was located in an eighteen-story office building devoted entirely to Signature Property Enterprise, Limited Liability Solutions Inc.

SPELLS Inc.

You'd think that someone of Elric's stature would be a bit cleverer. Then again, flaunting their talents right under the noses of the unassuming, ignorant-to-our-magical-ways mortals—the unbound, as we usually refer to them—is a particular delight to most mystics. At least it is to all of the ones I've stolen from over the years.

At some point maybe the acronym was too on the nose, though, so the official logo had been reduced to simply SPL Inc.

Either way it was still one of the most exclusive mystic enterprises in the world. Once an employee joined the organization, they're almost always there for life.

Literally.

SPL has no pension plan or 401(k). No, it only has the kind of retirement that comes from six feet under.

Knowing that, however, did little to dissuade me from wanting to join its forces. And it'd taken me nearly a decade for my application to be accepted and land an interview. The things I'd had to do to gain the skills to be able to even qualify as an applicant would make your hair curl. But desperation has a way of driving one to believe that every obstacle is merely an invitation for creativity. The more formidable the obstacle, the bigger the reward. And I'd obtained a substantial number of rewards in my fairly short time as a thief. Several pieces of that cache had already been turned over to Elric—the price of admission, so to speak. I suspected that a few more pieces would also have to be given up later. Assuming I survived, of course.

A door on my left opened, and Elric's secretary, Sequoya—a dark-skinned vision of beauty with almond-shaped eyes, high arched brows, broad forehead, and a long mane of white, braided hair—beckoned me forward with a simple crook of her finger. I swallowed hard, braced myself, and rose as smoothly as my cracked ribs and swollen knee would allow.

Sequoya's lips parted seductively as I came close. With my one good eye, I held her gaze and refused to blink. The slight smirk on her face hinted at approval, and she waved me into a grandiose room with golden textiles, emerald accents, high ceilings, and the distinct aroma of power.

"Sit," she ordered. I made no move to do so, and she dipped her chin demurely, that quirk to her lips lifting a bit. "Or stand. You won't have long to wait. But try not to bleed on the carpet. Or anything else."

With that she closed the door, and I waited a beat or two before relaxing my posture and shuffling painfully over to a wing chair, but I didn't sit down just yet. Instead, I used the chair to steady myself while I appraised the room.

The setting, honestly, was a bit unnerving. All of the other rooms I'd been led into had been bare. Even the floors had been stripped down to the concrete—probably to make cleanup a breeze.

This particular suite, however, was carpeted with a luxurious weave, and the elegant furnishings were probably costlier than my entire net worth. Clearly, whatever the seventh round entailed wasn't going to be messy.

Neat meant *quick*. Quick took power. And that's what made me nervous.

I strongly suspected that this was Elric's office, so my final interview would be with him. A thought that both terrified and excited me.

The heartbreak spell that bound and protected me was itself immensely powerful, but there was no way to test its limit without subjecting myself to this kind of trial. At some point the spell had to fail because, in my opinion, there was no mystic in the world as powerful as Elric Ostergaard. Not even his wife Petra.

And certainly not the old hag who'd cursed me.

At least I hoped that was the case.

Still, if Elric wanted to kill me, he would. Simply. Deliberately. Efficiently. I'd never have a chance. But if the spell that bound me could withstand even a bit of his effort, then I might pass the test—he might find me worthy enough to make me his newest employee. And that was the key to everything. If I had any chance at a life free of perpetual, soul-crushing heartbreak, a life open to the possibility of finding true love, then Elric Ostergaard was my only hope.

"Game on," I whispered, easing myself slowly into the chair. The effort cost me a grunt or two, but I managed it without getting the chair dirty or bloody, or falling to the floor. I figured I'd take my victories where I could.

Glancing at the large mahogany clock mounted on the wall to my left, I watched the minutes tick down with nervous excitement.

The terms of the job application were specific. Anyone left standing by 5 pm was an automatic hire. So either I had ten minutes left before starting my new job, or I had ten minutes left to live.

My gaze traveled from the clock to the door, then back again, but no one entered, and there were no sounds outside to indicate that someone was about to. I took a moment to focus my breathing, which was difficult. My ribs screamed in pain at every inhalation. I kept my breathing shallow but steady, and with effort I managed to slow the rate of my heartbeat using a technique taught to me by a Buddhist monk.

While I waited, I held as still as possible, focusing only on breathing, my heartbeat, and that clock. Nine minutes melted into eight, which gave way to seven, which demurred to six, which bowed to five, which headed to four. I bit my lip with anticipation as the big hand rounded the turn toward the twelve. Would Elric simply let the clock run out? Had I already passed his final test by making it through all the others?

Abruptly, the door opened, and the man himself walked in. "Hello, Esmé," he said, his wonderfully silky voice hypnotic and inviting.

I steeled myself, not out of fear, but out of my intense reaction to Elric, who was as tall, lithe, and eminently beautiful a man as ever I'd seen. He had dark mahogany hair that fell to his collar, a perfectly shaped goatee of a richer color, sharp light-blue eyes, and angularly European features.

His shoulders were broad, his waist small, and there was an erotic quality about him that I physically responded to even though I did my absolute best to cover it.

"Elric," I said, adding a small nod. "A pleasure to finally meet you."

My host studied me intently, his hand still resting on the handle of the door. I couldn't tell if he'd noticed my reaction to him or if I'd managed to hide the instant attraction I'd felt quickly enough, but I suspected he'd noticed, and I also suspected he was amused by it. I wanted to tell him there was no reason to feel flattered. The more dangerous the man, the more attracted I became. But that was one secret I'd take to my grave.

Elric crossed the room silently, the only sound the loud ticking of the clock, which I was now refusing to look at because I knew we had only two minutes to go and I couldn't afford to appear eager.

At last, the most powerful man in the world sat down across from me and we locked eyes.

My physical reaction to him rose up and washed over me for a second time. Despite my best efforts to quell it, I felt my face flush, my heartbeat quicken, and my palms become slick. Against my will, my lips parted and my chin lifted lustfully.

Elric crossed his legs and relaxed into his chair, no doubt pleased by his effect on me. I forced myself to take a deeper breath than was comfortable, and the pain helped me focus again. I'd never make it out of the room alive if I didn't curb my lustful attraction.

"You're more attractive in person than I'd anticipated," I said, hoping to cover the spell's influence.

Elric sat there studying me, with a hint of a smile. "Jacquelyn would like to have another go at you," he said, referring to the mystic from Round Three.

"Would her second attempt involve a bigger dragon?"

"Oh, I'd count on that," he replied. Neither one of us was joking. "I've waited two years to find someone skilled enough to make it through all six rounds. I've had to promote from within to fill the last few vacancies."

"How long have you waited for someone to make it through the seventh round?" I asked, referring to our present little meet and greet.

Again, Elric's lips quirked. "Considerably longer."

"Ah." I felt oddly calm as I sat there—my life in the balance. It was then that I allowed my gaze to travel to the clock. Surely it was five o'clock by now, wasn't it? My breath caught when I spied it. The second hand was locked at fifteen seconds to five, and the clock itself had stopped ticking.

"Time can be such a nuisance, don't you agree, Esmé?" Elric said softly. "I find that it's sometimes necessary to halt its progress entirely."

I understood then that he meant to kill me. There'd be no running out the clock. I hadn't succeeded. As well as I'd performed through the interviews with his underlings, I hadn't impressed him enough to get the job, and he wouldn't be sparing my life.

Reluctantly I pulled my gaze away from the clock and back over to Elric. Our eyes met again, and I could see the cold-blooded amusement there. He liked that I'd just realized the truth of things. There was something I could offer him to perhaps change his mind, but it angered me that he'd so quickly dismissed me. I'd made it through all of his trials only to have the prize pulled unfairly away from me at the last fifteen seconds?

Fuck that.

My chest burned with the injustice of it.

Denying him a prize suddenly felt like something I wanted to do, so I settled my expression into one of neutrality. I wasn't going to give him the satisfaction of a reaction. I simply waited.

One of his brows arched.

Still, I stared at him blankly. It was over. All I had left at my disposal was to die with grace and withhold something he would surely have coveted.

We sat like that for what felt like an eternity. I focused only on my breathing and the pain in my ribs. I knew he was waiting to see me crack, to break down, to dissolve into a weeping puddle, pleading for mercy, but that wasn't my style. I don't crack. I don't regret. And I certainly won't beg.

Elric inhaled deeply and closed his eyes. I kept my gaze on him steadily, waiting to black out, or see a shining light, or simply wink out of existence, but for a long time, absolutely nothing happened.

When my host at last opened his eyes again, I made sure to keep the triumph out of mine. If the mystic truly wanted to kill me, I thought he wouldn't hesitate to resort to "other" measures.

"That's a powerful binding," he said, resting his elbows on the arms of the chair as he posed his elegant fingers into a steeple at his chin. "The spell protects you well."

I was a little stunned to realize he'd been assessing the spell that bound me, and I allowed myself the smallest nod as I felt my simmering anger at him falter. The fact that I wasn't dead yet meant there *was* still a chance he'd hire me.

"What are your terms?" he asked.

A little thrill went through me. "The standard contract you offered Welker plus fifty percent of what I bring in."

Elric's eyes narrowed. "Twenty."

I leaned forward slightly, like a moth to a flame. God, I wanted him. "Forty."

The mystic drummed his fingertips together. I'd just taken a hell of a chance, and clearly, I'd displeased him. But then he did something unexpected. He paused the drumroll and leaned forward himself. "What are your *real* terms?"

I dipped my chin demurely. Elric was indeed as clever as his reputation suggested. "Welker's contract, thirty-percent and, at the end of five years of loyal service, I want one favor from you and to be released from the contract."

Elric barked out a laugh. "You really think you're that special, Esmé?"

I held his gaze. "I made it here, didn't I? All in one piece, I might add."

He nodded, and his amused expression lingered. "What's the favor?"

I took a deep breath. I might as well go for broke. "I want the name of the mystic who bound me, and I want to know where she is."

My host seemed pleased. Or maybe he was simply toying with me. It was hard to tell. "You don't know who bound you?"

What I did next was hard for me. Really hard. Admitting to Elric that I didn't know the name of my binder was like admitting a personal failure. "No," I said stiffly. "Even after searching the globe, I haven't been able to either identify or locate her."

Mystics almost always know who binds them. It's part of our culture, similar to how a vampire might absolutely know the name of who had first turned him or her.

But the mystic who'd bound me had been a total stranger. She'd never made her identity known in the five minutes it took her to murder my father and uncle right in front of me before cursing me into a living hell.

A Spell to Unbind

She'd come like a thief in the night to commit these terrible crimes, and then, rather than killing me too, she'd bound me by the cruelest of spells. One I couldn't escape or hide from. I lived under its dark skies and craved nothing but sunshine. More than anything in the world I wanted to find the elusive mystic who'd killed my family and cursed me so that I could kill her in turn and free myself from her spell. A spell that haunted my dreams and my everyday thoughts:

Beauty, beauty with eyes of green
All those men will watch you preen
Bound to love only those who leave you
Never catch the one you need
To mend your heart and unbreak the tie
With these words I cast the die
Those of true hearts will elude
The strings that help you set the mood
Lethal ones, they'll be the worst
Hear me now and know you're cursed!

Such a simple, silly poem. Sung by a mortal, it was powerless. Sung by a powerful mystic, it was as binding as prison cell. I'd only figured out its meaning as I grew up and began to fall in love. Over and over I'd had my heart broken, and at last I began to see the pattern: Every man I desired was of despicable character, and yet, I could think of nothing else but them. Eventually, they all left me utterly devastated. Broken. Alone.

An even worse aspect to the curse was that every man worthy of my heart couldn't capture it. I felt no attraction at all to brave, beautiful men who would've made any other woman the happiest person alive. And no matter how hard I tried, I couldn't feel anything beyond friendship for them.

And yet, I'd attempted courtship with them all the same, but I always ended up cheating on them with someone despicable.

In other words, in matters of love, I was cursed to always, always fail. And all because of a hateful mage with the power to invoke a binding spell.

For the record, only a fraction of us are talented enough to cast a binding spell. The only cure is death. In other words, when a mystic binds a mortal, making them a mystic too, should the binder die, the binding curse begins to fade away like a foul odor carried off by a breeze. They remain mystic, but are no longer bound by the nuisance tethers of their bindings.

Eventually, I'd be free, but only if I outlived the mage.

"Interesting," Elric replied to my admission about not knowing my binding mystic's name. His eyes danced with amusement when he saw me flush, but there was also something else reflected there...something that gave me pause.

As I looked at him, I swear I could see an element of recognition in his expression. I realized in that moment that he knew *exactly* who'd bound me.

Whether he'd known before assessing the spell or after was unclear, but I had no doubt he knew, or at least strongly suspected who'd bound me to my cursed life.

"You know who bound me," I said.

He shrugged one shoulder. "I do. And I'm curious what you plan to do once you find her?"

"Convince her to lift the spell," I said, hoping my answer was vague enough that he'd let it pass.

But Elric was no fool. He laughed lightly and said, "I'd love to watch you try, child. You'd be dead before you finished your plea. But maybe I can help you. Tell me the elements of your curse."

It was clear in that moment that, even though Elric wasn't a fool, he mistook me for one.

The elements of a binding curse are the specific words used to cast it. Even though I couldn't identify my binder, I remembered her spell like it was a song long ago memorized that replayed on a loop in my mind nearly every day. Giving the elements of my binding to a mystic as powerful as Elric Ostergaard was akin to committing myself to be Elric's personal slave—for life.

"Thank you for the offer," I said carefully, "but at this time, I'm going to decline and simply request that the name of my binder be provided to me at the end of the contract."

Elric smiled, however this time his smile wasn't so amused. As he stared at me, a certain mercilessness crept back into his eyes, and my blood ran cold.

"No deal," he said. Not even a second later I was pinned to the back of the chair by an unseen force. It was so sudden and so violent that I felt another rib crack, but I was powerless to cry out. I couldn't breathe, move, twitch, or blink. The force of the pressure being applied to every single inch of me was so intense that it was impossible to think beyond the scream in my mind. I felt the weight of the ocean on top of every millimeter of my skin. I was being crushed, slowly but surely against the back of the chair. Three fingers snapped, and then my toes, and the pain was more excruciating than anything, *anything* I'd ever even imagined.

I wanted desperately to black out, to vanish into an unconscious abyss as Elric flattened my body like a tin can, but there was no such relief. I suspected that the mystic had a hand in that too.

And in that moment where I knew he intended to break every bone in my body before he'd actually allow me to die, I found a tiny spark of resistance, and with it a small surge of adrenaline coursed through my veins, briefly numbing the pain and allowing me to move my lips enough to gasp out a whispered, "The... egg."

Elric, who'd been sitting back in his chair with that same smug, reptilian smile as he watched me die from the inside out, cocked his head slightly and squinted at me. The pressure on my skeletal structure never let up. I felt my right wrist snap and I jerked in silent agony, shutting my eyes against the unbearable pain.

And then... abruptly the pressure halted, and all I could hear was the pounding of my own heartbeat in my ears and my ragged struggle for breath.

Panting against the pain, I waited to see if the pressure would return, but after several seconds when it hadn't, I risked opening my eyes.

Elric seemed to be considering me now with interest. "What egg?" he asked.

With significant effort, I unclenched my jaw and didn't give in to the muted scream that was currently threatening to burst from my lungs. I've experienced—and endured—*terrible* physical pain in my life, but never anything on a scale of what was currently rippling through my bones. Still, I managed to stammer out the words, "Gri... Gri... Grigori's egg... I know... where it... is, and I... can get it... for you."

I hoped that was enough to save my life.

"Where?" Elric asked me simply.

I shuddered with the effort to tamp down a scream while I tried to adjust my position in the chair, and it resulted in two broken ribs grinding against each other. If I told Elric where the egg was, he'd very likely carry on with the crushing spell. But if I didn't tell him, if I negotiated the job for its location, there was a tiny chance he'd let me live.

There was also a chance (a much bigger chance) that he'd find an even more painful way to dispatch me, but I tried not to think about that.

It took me a moment to answer him, and even then I was taking a huge risk. "J-j-job?"

Elric tapped the arm of his chair with one slender finger. "If you're lying to me...."

I managed to bare my teeth in something I hoped was close to a grin. "Who... would... dare lie... to you?"

He made a casual motion with his hand. "Indeed."

At that moment I heard a small tick. Then another. Then a third and a fourth. It was coming from the direction of the clock on the wall. I held Elric's gaze and took a short, shallow breath for every tick that came after that, until fourteen total had metered out.

Just when I thought I'd made it, silence once again filled the room.

Across from me, Elric stared into my eyes with a coldness that was terrifying. Without a doubt he could kill me in the only second that remained between death and clemency. It was there in his eyes: his power, his will, his incredible force. I took tiny, shallow breaths and barely managed not to faint. I was completely and totally at his mercy, but I hadn't yet surrendered. Nor would I. And as I stared back at him, I wanted him only to know that.

The moment dragged on for eternity, or at least that's how it felt. Finally, though, and with no discernable change in Elric's expression, there was one final tick from the clock on the wall, and I knew that my life had been spared.

"Fail me and I will kill you, Esmé," Elric said next. It was both a promise and a reprieve delivered in a smooth silky voice that—were I not in agony—would've sent a shiver of pleasure down my spine.

"I know," I replied. "How long do I have to deliver the egg to you?"

Elric got up, casually buttoning his suit coat before shooting each cuff. He pointedly ignored my question, turning away from me to move to the door. "Sequoya will fill you in on the details," he said before departing.

I sagged in the chair, which proved to be a mistake when I had to hiss air in and out through gritted teeth so as not to pass out. There wasn't a part of me that didn't feel broken, bruised, cut, or beaten on. *Everything* hurt, and by hurt, I mean a level of pain that few people ever experience without being set on fire or trampled by elephants.

It was so intense, actually, that I think I blacked out for a while. I can't be sure, but I do know that when I managed to lift my head high enough to eye the clock again, it was nearly 6:25.

Dex was going to be insane with worry.

Blearily I gazed around the room again. My mind felt hazy and unfocused, so I spent some time simply trying to clear the clouds from my mind, and then I spent a little more time trying to wrap my head around everything I'd already been through and everything I still had to do. "Solve the problem in front of you, Esmé," I muttered.

That'd been a favorite mantra from my mentor, and one that'd always served me well when in a tough spot.

With a sigh, I looked around the room again, wondering if I was supposed to stay in here until Sequoya came to fetch me to go over the details or if I needed to exit and meet her somewhere out in the hallway.

Thinking on it, I realized that Elric hadn't specified. I glanced again at the clock. It was now 7:15 PM.

That jolted me into full alertness. *How the hell is time moving so quickly?* It occurred to me that I must still be moving in and out of consciousness, and the longer I stayed in the chair, the more I risked sinking into a deep unconsciousness, which would be bad. Probably lethal given my surroundings and Jacquelyn's thirst for revenge.

So I inhaled as deeply as I could without overly upsetting my broken bones and focused on gathering the strength to get up from the chair. It would definitely be the most difficult obstacle I'd faced today. Several of my fingers looked and felt broken. My toes and feet were throbbing in a way that signaled significant injury, but I thought that both femurs, kneecaps, tibias, and fibulas were intact. If I could just get to my feet, I might be able to shuffle out the door.

"Okay," I whispered. "Time to go." Very carefully I eased little increments of my weight onto my feet, which screamed in protest, until I managed to stand. Sort of. My posture was bent and sagging, but at least I was out of the chair.

Hissing through gritted teeth, again I took a few steps, each like walking on cut glass, while excruciating bolts of lightning shot up both legs all the way to my hips.

With tears leaking down my cheeks, I finally made it to the door. I stood there for an extra moment panting, sweating, and trembling from head to toe while eyeing the handle. I'd have to turn it to get it to open, and neither hand seemed up for such dexterity.

Still, I'd made it this far. Gingerly I tried six times to get the knob to turn, a nearly impossible task given the broken state of my hands and right wrist.

Please, I thought, resting my forehead against the doorframe. *Just let me make it through this door.* It was the only time all day I'd allowed myself even a little prayer.

With three more shallow breaths for courage, I regrouped, curled two fingers around the handle, rotated my elbow outward and pulled. With a satisfying click, the knob gave way and the door swung inward.

I shuffled forward again, slowly and painfully, until I came to the lobby where I'd been sitting before being shown into Elric's suite.

I didn't venture farther into the lobby, however, mostly because I needed a moment to rest against a wall and get my breathing under control.

While I waited to recover, I was surprised to see a bustle of foot traffic passing by. Men and women dressed in business attire walked purposefully across the marble floor, right past me and the bloodstained chair where I'd last seen the female applicant—who'd no doubt lost her life somewhere in the building.

I wondered where her body would be taken. If there even *were* a body to be taken away. If her luck with Jacquelyn's dragon hadn't been as good as mine, there'd be nothing left of her but a bit of ash.

Then I considered that they might've fed her remains to the dragon anyway, just to dispose of them. The other bodies too. At least I'd avoided being lizard lunch.

Leaning hard against the wall, I gathered as much resolve as I could and gingerly took a step forward, but my knee buckled, and I grunted in pain as I fought to stay on my feet. Nobody stopped to help me or see if I was okay. Not that I'd expected them to, but it was pretty remarkable that not a soul cast even more than a passing glance my way given that I was clearly beaten, bloody, and in distress.

Welcome to SPL Inc., I thought.

Clenching my jaw, I took a more careful step forward and then another, and another.

"Ms. Bellerose," I heard a voice say when I was almost to the chair I'd previously sat in.

I recognized the voice, and with effort, I stood up a little taller as Elric's assistant moved toward me with elegant, nearly liquid strides. "Sequoya," I said. "Surprised to see me?"

"A bit," she admitted, stopping in front of me. Then she gestured toward a door on the other side of the hallway. "Let's go over your paperwork in there."

I eyed the door. It seemed so very far away, and by now my body was shivering violently from the effort to remain standing. No doubt shock was finally settling in. "After you," I said to her.

Her brow rose with amusement, or maybe skepticism, before she stepped in front of me without comment.

I allowed myself a two-second pity party in the middle of that busy, bustling hallway, and then followed after her. Sequoya led me into a large conference room with black walls, a massive ebony table, and white leather chairs. Mounted to the walls were the encased spoils of war: weapons of destruction that Elric had claimed when he vanquished various legendary mystics over the years. I recognized the Axe of Ungar, the Saber of Cissé, and the Bow of Anubis.

Obviously, Elric took pleasure in reminding anyone entering the conference room of how very powerful he must be to have acquired such an intimidating collection of trophies.

Sequoya led the way to the head of the table, where a thick binder had already been placed. With a wave of her hand she indicated the chair next to her, taking her seat in front of the binder.

I moved forward to the chair but didn't sit down. "Maybe it's better if I stand," I said.

"As you wish," she replied. Flipping open the cover of the binder, she began to go over the contents with me. Belatedly I realized that the paperwork was my new contract of employment.

Sequoya covered all the many, many, *many* ways Elric could and would kill me if I ever betrayed him. "For the next one hundred hours, your employment will be conditional upon providing SPL Inc. the trinket known as Grigori's egg. At midnight on the sixteenth, if you do not provide SPL Inc. with that trinket, this contract shall be revoked."

Sequoya paused here to look meaningfully at me. "And so will you, Esmé Bellerose."

"Got it," I said crisply. That'd give me four days and four hours. Plenty of time. "What else?"

She smirked and looked back to the paperwork. "Elric has reviewed your trinket buy-in, and he's found it…" her voice trailed off.

I rolled my eyes. "Yes?" I asked.

I'd given up a treasured level-six trinket to gain entrance into today's proceedings. The rules had stated that only a level-four was required for buy-in, but higher-level offerings were encouraged, and besides, everybody knew that you didn't give Elric Ostergaard a fucking level-four trinket. You either ponied up something good, or you'd be summoned here to get your ass *literally* chewed off by one of Jacquelyn's dragons in the first round—not the third.

I suspected that most of my peers had offered up a level-five, which are hard for junior thieves to come by. Maybe one or two had offered him a level-six, like me, but I doubted anybody had been able to pony up anything above a level-seven.

I had several level-seven trinkets at home, but I certainly wasn't going to go advertising my skills to Elric before I'd secured gainful employment. Being too eager to show off could've ended my interviewing process as surely as insulting him with a level-four buy-in.

And, in my defense, my level-six offering had been a long-held prize of mine, and giving it up had been hard, so I was put off that Sequoya was hinting that I'd somehow missed the mark.

"He'd like to encourage you to offer up something a little more...memorable," Sequoya said, with a slight shrug.

"I see," I said tersely.

It was well-known that Elric collected trinkets in order to grant favors and gain loyalty from other powerful mystics. It was a way of keeping the more powerful mystics who gathered here in his territory in check. I was fairly certain that Elric had a whole cache of magical trinkets somewhere in the building to draw upon should the need arise.

"Would Grigori's egg do for more memorable?" I asked, trying to sidestep the obligation.

"He'd like that *plus* another offering, Esmé," she said—like I was stupid.

A long stretch of silence spread out between us. Essentially Elric was asking me to either cough up a more valued or powerful trinket of my own or steal him something in the seven to eight range, along with the egg, both of which would be required to be handed over without any compensation on my part. Well, save for my life. It was an end run around the verbal terms we'd agreed to in his office, and I resented it.

And while it was true, I'd been willing to die here to get the job, Elric knew damned well that most of the trinkets that thieves like me didn't unload on the mystic black market were the very things that made it easier to thieve. By asking me to give up yet another trinket, he'd be making my job of collecting the egg all that much harder.

But what choice did I really have? I wasn't exactly in a position to bargain.

"Fine," I said at last, reaching into my pocket to withdraw a silver, diamond-studded ballpoint pen. Handing it to Sequoya, I asked, "Will this work?"

Sequoya took the pen and studied it for a moment before clicking the trigger. Instantly she disappeared from view, and the only way I knew she was still in the room was because of the light chuckle coming from her chair. "Clever," she said. "How long does it last?"

"Exactly one hour," I said, hating the loss of the pen. It'd saved my life at least twice that very morning. "You can break up that hour as much as you like within a twenty-four-hour period, but if you use it up in the first go, then you'll have to wait a day to use it again. But another mystic can use it immediately, so tell Elric that it's best to keep an eye on it or it'll end up in hands you won't be able to easily track."

I heard another click and Sequoya appeared again, her eyes gleaming with greed as she looked again at the pen. I felt certain she'd find a way to ask Elric to give it to her, and it made me mad all over again because she'd probably use it for something stupid like spying on her boyfriend. Or girlfriend. Or both.

After a moment Sequoya set my pen aside and picked up another, which she used to make a notation in the binder. "I can't speak for Elric," she said as she wrote, "but I believe he'll be satisfied with your additional offering."

"Awesome," I sneered, still bitter.

Sequoya either didn't notice or didn't care about my irritation because she got on with the rest of the contents in the binder without even looking up.

While she spoke I took a moment to temper the irk I felt at being forced to give up another one of my hard-earned trinkets. Especially after I'd sweated giving up my initial offering, which was a tiny treasure box, no larger than a cigarette case, but into which one could hide almost any object of any size as long as one could fit even a small section of the object into the opening. Over the years I'd stuffed it full of numerous trinkets on my way out the door after a night of thieving.

I reminded myself that I still had a nice cache of trinkets that I could use to get the job done, and even though Elric now had two of my most valuable toys, he didn't have a clue about what else I had. And he certainly didn't know that I had in my possession the mother lode of all magical objects—a level-fifteen. Something so magical that most mystics believed it to be pure myth. Excluding me, only two other people in the world knew that I possessed it. One, I was desperate to kill. The other, I was desperate to love.

"Do you agree to the terms and conditions as laid out in this contract?" Sequoya asked, interrupting my thoughts.

I shook my head, realizing I'd been only half paying attention. "Not before reading the fine print," I told her. I had a feeling she'd been counting on the fact that I was a little out of it. It seemed to me that she'd skimmed over a lot of the details.

She pushed the contract toward me and took up the ballpoint pen again to play with it.

While she vanished and appeared again and again, I read the contract cover to cover, pausing to scrutinize the compensation package. Should I survive the week, Elric would pay me handsomely. There was a housing and clothing allowance, a car from one of his fleets, access to a wonderful array of magical weapons (not that I needed any of his castoffs, but his variety was likely to be much better than mine), immediate reservations to all the posh restaurants in town, access to the corporate gym (which I was hoping would pale in comparison to mine) membership to the best country club in Virginia, and a travel allowance for those times when business took me afield.

There was also a considerable stock option and signing bonus, and it was the signing bonus I was really after. It was more than enough to pay off the mortgage on the warehouse I'd moved into, and I personally needed that space to be free and clear of any financial obligation.

Plus there'd be enough left over to give Dex—my partner, best friend, and the man I wanted to spend my life with—a well-deserved and long-overdue bonus of his own. He might not take it, but I owed him at least the offer of something substantial.

Once I was finished reading the contract and making a dozen small changes in the wording so that it was less biased toward Elric, et al., I handed it back to Sequoya. "I agree," I told her.

She lazily took the contract, noted all the changes, and initialed next to them. Then she reached down to her lap to retrieve a small stone crucible and to her belt to pull out a green dagger made of jade. It looked sharp as hell and definitely lethal.

"Your hand," she said.

I tensed. There are two ways to bond a mystic to an agreement. A simple handshake could meld together both mystics' energies and hold us to the bonds of our agreement while withstanding all but the most intense effort to break it. The other—more archaic method—was by blood.

A blood contract was impossible to break. Even if I tried to break from the employment agreement my subconscious would always lead me back to this building and force me to carry out the terms of the deal.

A blood contract was obviously also more painful, and I was already in enough pain to make remaining conscious a struggle.

Still, I didn't hesitate beyond that half-second and extended my right hand, palm up.

She was quick about it at least, but the cut into the center of my palm was deep. I felt the tip of the knife strike bone, and I couldn't hold back the small yelp of pain. It was a weakness that I regretted showing to Sequoya. No doubt she'd report it back to Elric.

With watery eyes, I turned my palm down and allowed several drops of blood to drip onto the stone dish. Sequoya then handed me a quill pen with a large white plume.

I dipped the tip into the blood, scribbled my name on the dotted line, and waited.

Heat erupted at my fingertips before spreading out through my hands, wrists, arms, shoulders, chest, neck, and so on, until even the tips of my toes felt hot.

The effect lasted only a few moments, but the indication was clear: Elric now owned me, body and soul.

Sequoya got up and gathered the binder and the ballpoint pen. She started to reach for the crucible of blood, but I quickly snatched it, and put it and the feathered quill into the inside of my leather jacket before also stuffing my still-bleeding hand into my pocket, wincing with each jerky movement. I didn't trust Sequoya. Once my back was turned, she could've easily signed my name to another contract assigning all of my earnings and worldly possessions over to her, and it would've been perfectly legal.

At least, under mystic law.

She chuckled as she got up and brushed past me. "Use the back stairwell as you exit," she told me, clicking the ballpoint and disappearing again. "Those stairs empty into the alley behind the building. You'll attract attention if you're not careful...and *do* be careful, Esmé," she warned. "Elric doesn't like attention. Especially from the unbound. Remember that if you want to live."

With that the door to the conference room opened, then closed, and I suspected that Sequoya had left me.

For a long moment I eyed the chair she'd vacated. I wanted to collapse into it and rest more than I'd ever wanted anything. But if I let myself ease into that chair, I doubted I'd get back out of it for the next ten to twelve hours, and this wasn't a place you'd ever want to spend the night, especially if you were unconscious.

So I took several deep breaths and whispered, "Come on, Esmé. Pull it together." When I felt ready, I edged toward the door.

It took forever, but at last I reached the first floor of the back stairwell I'd been told to exit from. Trembling violently from the effort, I stood in front of another door, which took almost all that I had left in me to open, but at last the door gave way, and I stumbled into the alley that Sequoya had promised would be there.

It was already dark out, and the alley was unlit. Something skittered to my right, but I ignored it and kept my sights on the end of the alley. I had no cellphone or means to communicate with Dex, but I was hoping he'd be circling the block.

Ten meters from the end of the alley, a yellow Mustang with tinted windows cruised past before there was a screeching of brakes.

The Mustang came back into view and the window rolled down, revealing a guy with dark-blond hair, square jaw, prominent nose, and thick full lips. He smiled at me, and it instantly turned his somewhat heavy-faced features into boyish charm. That smile could melt ice.

Seeing it gave me an extra boost, and I wanted to smile back, but the most I could manage was a forced grimace.

Rolling the window back up, Dex pulled to the curb and parked while I kept awkwardly gimping down the alley. A second later, all six-feet-three-inches of him appeared in the entrance to the alley.

He took a moment there to gaze up and down the street before hastily making his way to me.

"Gaw blimey, Esmé," he whispered as I collapsed against him. "You look half-dead."

"You should see the other guy."

Dex lifted me into his arms. "Was the other guy a tiger?"

"Dragon."

"Huh... then I'm surprised you're only half-dead."

"Could've gone either way," I admitted, settling my head onto his shoulder.

"When you didn't come out and the clock kept ticking..." he said next, letting the rest of that sentence fade away.

"What about the other seconds-in-command?" I asked as we reached the car.

"They've all gone home, except for Raider's girl. She just went through the front entrance."

I winced when Dex shifted my weight to rest me against his chest while squatting down to open the passenger-side door.

"She'll be as dead as he is in less than ten minutes," I hissed through gritted teeth as Dex adjusted my weight to ease me into the car.

The rules clearly stated that no applicant's second could enter SPL headquarters. It was one additional test that Elric had set up, and I'd heard about a guy, years earlier, who'd made it to the five o'clock hour, only to be slain by Elric in the front lobby when the applicant's second had come rushing into the building to look for him.

"Poor dumb girl," Dex said. "Still, I'll admit to almost giving in to the urge to follow her and find out what happened to you."

My eyes widened as he settled me carefully so that I could pivot into the seat. I took a moment to gingerly touch his arm. "Thank the gods you didn't. If I'd died, Elric would've loved to pit you against Raider's girl, then make sure no one left the Thunderdome."

His expression was grim as he belted me into the seat, and I grunted in pain. "How bad is the pain?" he asked.

I closed my eyes. "I'm ready to pass out."

I heard Dex close my door, then felt the breeze when he opened his and got in. "I'll get you home as quick as I can."

I sighed with relief and then did indeed black out.

CHAPTER TWO
DAY 1

I woke up just before dawn, curled around Ember. Em is a Hungarian vizsla (pronounced *VEEZ-luh* in the US or *VEESH-luh* in Europe). Vizslas are one of the oldest dog breeds in the world, with roots dating back to the ninth century. Like most V's, she's a medium-size dog (just forty-eight pounds), with a square muzzle, floppy ears, long graceful legs, olive-green eyes, and a short smooth coat that's the color of a hot ember.

Ember's specific roots aren't entirely known to me, but I suspect she's roughly one millennium old. You'd never know it to look at her; I mean, she's simply beautiful and youthful in every way—bouncy, happy, fast as lightning, and loyal to me like no other. Which is saying a lot, because I know that Dex would give his life for me.

Em and I are bonded by magic, entirely of her own making. Her bond to me is as strong as the curse I myself am bound by. Maybe it's even stronger because it's entirely encased in love. Believe it or not, that's a hard thing for me to admit, because of what it means.

A major reason why I'm so desperate to rid myself of the curse that binds me is complicated exponentially by Ember's love for me and mine for her.

As long as she's near my side, I cannot die. Like, I *literally* can't. For all intents and purposes, she's rendered me immortal. If I'm grievously injured, or even if I'm stone-cold dead, once she lays down next to me, within a few hours, or sometimes just a few minutes, every wound, every injury—be it a lost limb, venomous sting, broken bone, snapped spine, lethal virus, water-filled lungs, or crushed skull—becomes completely healed and/or restored. I'm made whole again no matter how grievous the injury, and in healing me, Ember suffers no noticeable ill effects.

It's a profound power that she extends only to me, or on occasion, someone close to me. (She's brought Dex back from the brink four or five times now.)

The benefits of her magic extend beyond simply healing me. I age much more slowly than even the most powerful among us. By mystic standards, I'm fairly young, but Ember's company ensures that I'll outlast even the likes of Elric and Petra.

And while immortality sounds cool, the fact is that living a life that promises only soul-crushing heartbreak isn't much of a life. I should know. I've lived it for ninety-three years and counting.

In that time, I've been devastated by heartbreak sixteen times. Sixteen. I tried committing suicide three times, and in each instance, Ember managed to find me and bring me back.

Ironically, the only wound that Ember cannot heal is a broken heart.

Now, certainly, if I really, really, really wanted to end it all, I could throw myself into the pit of the nearest volcano, or simply allow Elric to feed me to one of Jacquelyn's dragons, and I'd be beyond Ember's reach. But that would also leave her vulnerable. Sure she could and likely would bond with Dex, and he'd do everything in his power to protect her, but the trouble is that while Dex is physically formidable, as mystics go, he's not nearly as powerful or skilled as he'd need to be to protect her, and at some point in the future, that would no doubt expose Ember to forces that would make her life unbearable.

Every mystic in the world and probably most mortals would give anything to get their hands on my pup. She would assure them immortality. She would also assure them unquestionable power. And once they captured her, I had no doubt they'd put her someplace where no one could ever get to her. Someplace far away from open skies, sunshine, green grass, and trees. She'd be imprisoned in a dungeon and left there to suffer for the rest of her days, which would no doubt be eons long.

If the unthinkable happened and Elric discovered her (and I had no doubt that if I weren't around to keep watch over her that he would), he'd not only make himself immortal, but he'd also use her to heal an army of mystics in a war I was certain he'd start against the six other rivals he faced in various territories around the globe, who, collectively with Elric, made up the group known as the Seven.

While it's true that Elric is probably the most powerful mystic in the world, the word "probably" is key, because no one is really certain he is. To my knowledge, he hasn't been challenged in several centuries, so there's no surefire way to tell how he'd fare against one of his rivals on any given day. This uncertainty keeps his power in check, and it brings balance to the world, keeping lower-level mystics and mortals generally out of harm's way.

Of course, Petra also helps to keep her husband in check. She's the less powerful of the pair by only the smallest fraction, which allows both sides to coexist in relative peace, with each of them leading a large following of loyal mystics who routinely square off but are also careful never to start a war.

Ember, however, would present Elric with a game-changer. There'd be no stopping him. I knew the man to be calculating and cold-blooded, so instilling that kind of additional power in someone with a psychotic tendency would leave the world in chaos. Hundreds of millions, if not billions, of mortals and thousands of mystics would perish—of that I was certain.

And if, God forbid, Petra or one of the other remaining five got hold of Ember, I had no doubt the world would end, because Elric would stop at nothing to acquire her magic. The war would be far worse than if he found Ember first, and the world would absolutely end in a raging, terrible, bloody, horrific ball of fire. It would literally be hell on Earth until there was nothing left but a burnt-out husk.

So the risk I took by seeking employment from Elric was a calculated one. I knew myself well enough to understand that the next time I fell in love and got my heart good and broken, I'd find a way to kill myself beyond Ember's ability to bring me back. Sixteen times I've crawled out of that dark hole, and each time it's been exponentially harder to make that climb. I didn't try to kill myself the first three times I got my heart broken; I tried to take my life with the most recent breakups, and I came closer to getting the job done each time.

It's been an unsettling trend.

So, while I put myself and Ember at considerable risk by seeking to join the ranks of SPL Inc., the alternative was equally as bad, because the next time I fell in love and suffered through that inevitable loss, it would be lights out for me. No doubt about it.

Had I perished during my interview, Dex's instructions were to take Ember back to his homeland and hide her as best he could for as long as he could, until he either gained enough power and skill to protect her or aligned himself with someone like me. Someone adept at wielding their magical essence and someone he could trust. As I'd left for the interview, I'd tried not to think about how unlikely the second scenario would be because, as a whole, mystics are the most untrustworthy group of misfits ever created.

It was less of a worry now, though, because I'd made it through with only some internal bleeding and several broken bones, which were now almost completely healed thanks to Ember.

As I moved to sit up, my sweet pup yawned, stretched, and laid her head on my shoulder in an effort to keep me close. "I know, lovey, but I have to get up," I whispered, still feeling fatigued from all the battles waged the day before.

She sighed, and I knew she thought it was too soon, but I had only four days to get Elric his damned egg, and I certainly couldn't take the morning off.

Still, when I looked down into her big olive-green puppy-dog eyes, I said, "Okay, maybe just five more minutes."

Five minutes turned into thirty, which would've normally made me crazy, but I realized at the end that I'd needed them. Getting out of bed at last, I left Ember to continue sleeping there and padded to the bathroom for a shower and an assessment.

Gazing into the mirror while the water heated, I smiled in relief. I'd had a quick glimpse of myself in one of the mirrors at SPL and I had looked *rough*.

But this morning, I appeared fine. Even the tangles in my long, black hair had seemed to smooth out. Turning my face from side to side I could see none of the telltale bruises put there by dragons and fiends the day before. My pale skin was clear and smooth. I blinked at my reflection, studying my image for a moment. It'd been a while since I'd taken a long hard look at myself, and this morning it seemed appropriate.

My light green eyes shown with purpose and determination—which was a good sign, and the set of my jaw in my heart-shaped face was firm. The only thing that didn't look determined and ready for battle was my nose, which is my best feature.

My father told me I had my mother's nose. I took his word for it as she died in childbirth and there'd been no pictures or portraits of her in our home. But I could imagine she was there, present with me in the thin, delicate shape of my nose, which took otherwise common features and turned them into something more memorable and pleasing.

Satisfied with both my mindset and my now unmarred appearance, I hopped into the shower and was ready for battle just twenty minutes later.

Clad in black leggings, a white V-neck t-shirt, calf-length leather boots, and a matching leather jacket, I moved out of the bedroom, making my way onto the catwalk that overlooked the large open warehouse, which was home sweet home for me and Dex.

I'd acquired the place two years earlier when I'd first come to the Eastern Seaboard. Before then I'd been in Europe, slowly gaining the skills and tools I'd needed to make a play for Elric's team.

The warehouse was in a section of Alexandria, Virginia known as Old Town North, not on the water of the Potomac River, but not far away either. Ember and I go running along the river most days, and it's especially lovely each spring when the cherry blossoms are in bloom. Listed in the low seven figures, I'd won the three-story five-thousand square-foot warehouse in a game of chance from a chronic gambler and lowlife mystic.

I hadn't cast a single spell to get my hands on the deed either. Still, there'd been considerable work needed to bring the place into a livable state, and that had cost me a quarter-million and change. Lucky me, I had a high FICO score and a bank willing to lend out a lot of cash on a property valued at six times the mortgage amount. Unlucky me, I hadn't had any income coming in the previous two years, and I was down to my last couple thousand. I was either going to get Elric his egg and secure myself some gainful employment, or die trying (literally).

Peeking over the railing, I saw Dex at the ground-floor level, shimmying up a twenty-five-foot rope using only his arms.

He was bare-chested and glossy with sweat, muscles bulging with every pull, his six-pack abs rippling with definition.

Were I a woman free of the shadow of the spell I'd been cursed with, I'd have met him at the top of the rope and ridden him all the way down.

But for almost the entire time we've been together (save one glorious and memorable night), Dex has done absolutely nothing to stir my home fires, as it were.

He and I have been together for a couple of decades now. We'd met during the Mystic Games on a tropical oasis that's as magical a place as any on Earth.

The games are held each year on an island in the South Pacific called Celeo, which can't be found on any map. It's rumored that Amelia Earhart crash-landed there and was eaten by one of the island's many monsters. (A rumor I wholeheartedly believe.)

For six days at the height of winter, forty of the world's most athletic, skilled, and perhaps suicidal mystics come to Celeo to compete against one another and the native flora and fauna. Most entrants don't make it to the end, but the top ten competitors (assuming there're ten left; sometimes there aren't) come away with sizable cash prizes and some potential name recognition.

I'd entered the games for the money and to prove myself as a skilled mystic. Like most sporting events, the top contestants are always sponsored, and the reason for my entering at all, beyond the cash, was to get noticed by one of the sponsors—specifically, by Elric Ostergaard. His mystics almost always won, but the year I entered, all three members of his team were killed. The death toll on Elric's team included a mystic known only as Maverick—an absolute legend given his performance at previous games. In the last event of the games, Maverick had been stung by a wicked scorpion six feet tall and eighteen feet long, with a stinger as thick as my arm.

As it happened, I'd killed that very scorpion, but I'd had some help in the form of another contestant named Dexter Valerius.

The way it went down was, after killing Maverick, the scorpion had come at me, and I'd fended it off—rather well, I might add—until its mate had come at me from behind. Now normally in a competition like the games, that would've been lights out for me because nobody there is gonna have your back given the cutthroat vibe of the competitors, but I was saved when Dex launched himself from an overhang above us to drive a stake right through the head of the scorpion on my flank. It was a move that completely confused me because Dex had had the clear advantage of gaining the overhead where the scorpions couldn't reach him. All he'd had to do was fend off any other mystics trying to take that spot, and he would've won the event. He'd taken a huge risk and saved my ass, and in the process, he'd put himself in mortal jeopardy because, once it'd seen what Dex had done to its mate, the bigger arachnid had suddenly stopped its assault on me to go after him.

The second I was freed from the attentions of the larger scorpion, I could've simply scrambled up the rock to the now-vacant ledge and waited to see what happened between the two, but that's not what I did. Instead, I returned the favor when Dex was pinned by the scorpion, and killed it with the same stake he'd used on its mate. And because I'd killed the bigger of the two, I'd come out the victor, earning myself some major points once the results were in.

At the end of the games, I'd come in a very respectable sixth place and Dex had come in seventh. During the award's ceremony, we'd caught the other's eye, and that's when the real magic happened—well, at least for me.

You see, on the island of Celeo, although regular spells themselves do work, no mystic's binding curse will hold. In other words, for the first time in about seven decades, and for the six days of the games, I'd been completely free from the curse that bound me. It was the most liberating sensation I'd ever felt. For once I was completely in charge of my own reactions to a member of the opposite sex, and the afternoon that Dex had saved my life I'd felt my first *real* attraction to another man. That night we'd made love, and it'd been glorious—so natural, so sweet, so filled with possibility.

Afterward, in the dark as we lay together, I can remember so distinctly not feeling that desperate empty fear that always took hold in the pit of my stomach at the beginning of every love affair—that sinking feeling that soon I'd be untethered and reeling from the loss of someone I was desperate to hold onto. It hadn't been there to fill me with doubt, to throw me off balance, and push me to cling to him in needy, desperate ways.

As dawn blossomed on the horizon and we prepared to leave the island, he'd kissed me, and I'd felt...happy. Something so simple, so normal, but for me, something supremely rare.

I hadn't known how I'd react to Dex once we boarded the ship to leave the island, allowing our binding curses to take root again, but after he invited me to join him on a trip back to his native Australia—or Oz, as he refers to it—I'd been surprised to find myself saying yes. At the time, I'd reasoned that I'd need a good second once I got closer to applying for a post at SPL, and Dex had already proved himself to be a skillful and reliable backup in tight situations, so getting to know him a little better was probably a good thing.

And then the moment my curse had taken hold again, I'd known he was in fact a good guy, because when I looked at him, I felt no attraction whatsoever. My binding curse is particularly cruel that way—I'm attracted to the worst of men and totally romantically uninterested in men who're of good heart.

In fact, the higher the moral character of a man, the more likely I am to be repulsed by him.

With Dex my reaction to the notion of being intimate with him makes my stomach turn. It's awful, because more than anything I want a thousand more nights like the one we had on that island decades before. If not for the curse, he'd be my one and only.

Still, even though I'm not physically attracted to him, I do enjoy his company very much. And deep down I know him to be a truly good friend. At least he's good to me. He knows the curse I'm bound by, and still he's unflinchingly loyal to me. All this time I've known he's wanted more, but he never asks for what I can't give him, which makes me fiercely loyal to him in return.

But beyond even all that, Dex is earnest, smart, funny, and even thoughtful. These aren't qualities you normally find in a mystic. The life calls for a certain edge to one's personality, but Dex seems to float above the typical stereotype.

He's not especially skilled or even very good at using his magical essence, but what he lacks in talent, he more than makes up for in other ways. His ability to take the hit of a spell is one of them. I've seen Dex get hit with a solid punch from a powerful bundle of energy cast by a deadly mystic that would normally leave a guy unconscious, paralyzed, or even dead, and get up to walk it off like it was nothing more than a pesky shove to the shoulder.

Physically he's insanely strong and one of the fittest men on Earth. I've witnessed him lift the front end of a car before. I've seen him pick up a refrigerator, push over an eighteen-foot-tall tree, and run a mile in under five minutes.

I've also seen him wrestle an alligator, fend off sharks, and punch a dragon in the nose. He's physically formidable and courageous in every sense.

He has other skills that I admire too; as in, he might not be good at casting a spell, but he's a genius for sussing out how a trinket might work. Some of the prizes I bring home are loaded with obvious magic layered on top of more powerful magic. Dex almost always discovers their secrets. That alone is a highly prized skill. If we can't figure out how to make the trinket work for us, then they're as good as junk.

And it's something I remind myself about every time he brings home yet another yellow object.

My second's binding curse was done to him out of spite by an irresponsible, drunken douchebag of a mystic aptly nicknamed Weasel, who picked a fight with Dex in a bar and had his ass handed to him in three quick punches—by a mere mortal.

After losing face to my friend, Weasel cursed Dex with a ridiculous but surprisingly strong binding curse that he left activated—meaning he gets no downtime from it, and which makes it impossible for Dex to resist his attraction to the color yellow. The poor man can't walk by anything painted or dyed any shade of yellow without making an attempt to acquire it. It's why I now do all of the thieving; more than once I've sent Dex out on a job and he's come back not with the intended prize, but rather with a yellow vase, paperweight, or bowl that soon proved to hold no magical value at all.

In fact, in all the years we've known each other, the only time I've ever seen him dressed in a color other than yellow was at the Mystic Games. He'd worn lots of bright blue, red, and aqua back then, and he'd been stunning in those colors.

The true shame is that yellow is a terrible color on Dex. His skin tone is all wrong for it, but that never stops him from adorning himself from head to toe in the color.

And it's everywhere in our warehouse too, from the throw pillows on our loveseat and couches, to the salt and pepper shakers, coffee maker, Dex's office chair, area rugs, Ember's dog bed—you name it; if it comes in yellow, he's made a play to try to decorate our home base with it.

Anyway, I can put up with the color thing as long as it keeps him protected from most death curses. That's what good binding spells do. They offer at least some protection against other spells. The more powerful the binding spell, the more difficult it is to kill or harm a mystic by unleashing a deathly curse or mass of energy. It's how I knew my binding spell was incredibly powerful. Through the years I've faced down several notoriously deadly mystics who'd thought to dismiss and dispel me with a few whispered words or lobbed essence only to be shocked when I'd barely flinched.

Of course, it's also how I now knew that Elric was even more powerful than I'd originally given him credit for. I hadn't even detected that he'd launched a death curse at me until I was being crushed to death.

"You're up?" I heard Dex call, and I realized I'd been staring off into space, lost in thought.

I smiled. "I am."

Dex, wearing bright yellow shorts and matching shoes and socks, gripped the rope with his legs, arched his back, and got himself some momentum to swing over to the railing of the catwalk. With a nimble leap, he made it to the railing and climbed over to me. "You should get back to bed and curl up with Ember for a while longer," he said. "I felt a lot of broken bones before putting you to bed last night."

I smirked. "You'll look for any excuse to feel me up."

Dex rolled his eyes playfully, but then he focused a pointed look at me like I should make a U-turn and head right back to bed.

I gave him a gentle pat on the shoulder. "I'm fine."

He arched a skeptical eyebrow.

I matched his expression, and we stood there with arching brows for a few beats.

"I guess there's no stopping you then," he finally said.

"No. I gotta get to Tic."

Dex frowned. "I hate that little prick."

That made me chuckle. "I'm pretty sure the feeling's mutual."

"Tic" was the nickname given to one of my regular informants. His nickname stems from his binding curse, which, when recited verbatim, activates a small tic somewhere on his body. Left unchecked—i.e., without the countercurse being cast—the tic eventually spreads to the rest of his body and ultimately sends him into convulsions. The curse has the very real power to kill him within about twenty-four hours.

"I thought you believed the little bug was lying when he bragged to you that he knew where Grigori was hiding," Dex said.

"It's hard to tell with Tic. He could've been lying or he could've been trying to save himself from a flinch-filled afternoon."

Dex grunted and crossed his arms. "What's going to happen when you find out the little shit made up the whole thing?"

"I'm going to hand Ember over to you and tell you to hit the bricks, bud."

"Seems harsh."

"Elric won't stop at killing just me if he thinks I've conned him."

Dex swept a hand through his hair and blew out a sigh. "I know you were a bit desperate in your interview with him yesterday, Ezzy, but you're taking a helluva chance with this whole Tic angle."

"I've been taking chances my whole life, D."

He considered me solemnly. "But the stakes were never this high, were they, luv?"

I shrugged. "I knew what I was getting into when I applied for the job."

Dex didn't have a counterargument to that, but I could tell he didn't like any part of my current plan—which, admittedly, wasn't all that great. Still, this was the corner I'd painted myself into, so I had no choice but to keep pushing forward.

"Will you run Ember for me?" I asked as the silence between Dex and me began to feel awkward. "She'll want some exercise soon."

"You can run with her later. Right now, I'm coming with you."

"No, you're not."

"Esmé, I'm bloomin' well going."

"Dex," I said on a heavy sigh. We'd discussed—at length—my initiation into SPL, and how important it was to show Elric that *I* was the right person for the job, and not my insanely physically powerful second. While I knew that Dex would never intentionally show me up, I also knew that Elric preferred men over women when employing thieves. I couldn't afford to have Dex tag along with me on this first crucial mission and risk having Elric jump to the conclusion that Dex was the better fit for his organization than me. If Elric had spies reporting back to him about my progress, and no doubt he did, those spies might report back that Dex was with me every step of the way. That feedback could influence Elric into thinking Dex was the real leader of our team, and provoke him to extend the position to Dex rather than to me. If Elric offered Dex the job, there was no way Dex could turn him down...and live. Elric Ostergaard wasn't someone to whom you said, "Golly gee, thanks for the offer and all, but Imma pass."

So even though I knew Dex's heart was in the right place, I still couldn't give in to the impulse to bring him with me. "This isn't a job for us," I said gently. "This is a job for *me*. I've got to prove myself to Elric, and I have to do it alone, and I know that you know that."

Dex scowled. "You can't trust Tic, Ezzy. He's as likely to send you into a trap as he is to lie to you about Grigori's whereabouts. Just let me be your lookout. If I have to stay hidden, I will."

I reached for his arm and gave it a squeeze. "I'm so sorry, Dex, but no." I waited for him to process that before I added, "Trust me when I tell you that I'll definitely need your help once I get my hands on the egg. I'll need to know how many more times it can heal before it becomes a dud, and only you'll be able to tell me that."

A trinket as powerful as Grigori's egg had a limited shelf life. It was rumored that the egg could be used magically only twelve times before it crumbles into bits of eggshell and becomes useless. "There's no telling how many lives Grigori has already used up with it," I said when Dex didn't reply.

At last he gave a soft pat to my hand, which was still on his arm, and said, "Keep your eyes open and me in the loop."

I beamed at him. "Don't I always?"

"No, and by that, I mean, never."

I rolled my eyes. "I'll call. Promise."

"I'll make sure I'm sitting down when the call comes in," he said. "The shock's likely to keel me over."

"Ha-ha," I said flatly, already heading toward the stairs.

Jogging down them, I was so thankful for my magical pup. Sure, I was still a little sore in places, but at least every step wasn't sheer agony. Plus, Tic wasn't anyone you'd want to meet on an off day. I'd need to rely heavily on both my wits and agility if past encounters with him were any predictor.

The hard part was going to be getting the jump on him; if I didn't, he'd go into hiding and I'd have a helluva time finding him again.

Grabbing a protein bar and a bottle of coffee-flavored almond milk on my way out the door, I paused only to assess the arsenal of magical trinkets I might need. After selecting just a few items, I left to hunt down my source.

Chapter Three
Day 1

Like all mystics, Tic has a compulsive personality. I think it must be something that happens in the binding process because we're all the same in that. Each and every one of us is addicted to something. Sometimes we're addicted to several things.

Most of the mystics I know are addicted to gambling. It's safer than drugs, of course, but if you're going to live longer than a few years as a mystic, then drugs and/or alcohol are not the compulsion to have. Any newbie mystic that becomes addicted to intoxicants winds up overdosing within the first few months. The compulsion to use can be even more consuming than the actual addiction.

Somehow I'd managed to avoid the more troublesome vices, although admittedly I'm a *very* good gambler, I still never developed an actual compulsion for it.

My vice is exercise. I work out religiously sometimes for hours a day. I do a mix of cross-training and martial arts, with the occasional run thrown in.

Dex has the same compulsion, thank God. It's nice to have a companion in the gym who doesn't think it's freakish to work out for two to three hours straight.

Truth be told though, there're a fair number of us out there who get addicted to the gym. It's an absolute must for anyone thinking about trying out for the Mystic Games. And for the role of thief, being in top physical shape should be a job requirement because you've got to be fast, strong, nimble, and at times, able to endure considerable discomfort.

But some thieves aren't willing to do the work, and they get by on tricks and sleight of hand. Tic is one of those people, and he makes more money trading information for a cut of the take than he makes trying to pilfer anything away from a fellow mystic.

When he steals or gambles with the unbound, he cheats by using an assortment of spells that don't require much talent, or even finesse, which is what I figured he was doing at the park playing speed chess with a guy who looked to be in his seventies. The older gentleman didn't appear to be the kind of person who had a lot of cash to spare on a bet against Tic, who, in turn, looked like he had money to burn.

Tic is a pretty stylish guy—a total clotheshorse, he's enamored with the idea of reinventing himself every few weeks by wearing a different stereotype. Today he was dressed like a posh member of the British elite, in a charcoal blazer with matching silk slacks, leather loafers, maroon dress shirt, and a silver ascot. He'd also grown a beard and mustache, which gave his long face an intriguing quality.

I'm not really attracted to him, which is a relief because there are times when I'm forced to do some particularly mean things to Tic. But he almost always has it coming. Almost.

He's a nervous guy, as are most mystics, especially the less-powerful ones, and Tic is definitely in the less-powerful category.

But he knows things, and he sees things, and he's been a convenient source of information for me over the years. I was hoping today was going to be the day our association really paid off, but I had to be careful, because I was positive Tic had heard that I'd applied for the job at SPL, and he very likely also knew that, because I was still alive, I'd gotten the job, and as the newest agent of SPL, fencing stolen trinkets wasn't something I was allowed to do anymore.

So, if he saw me coming, he'd know I'd be looking to him for info about the egg, and that I wouldn't think twice about forcing its location out of him without the promise of something for him in return.

True, he'd come to me first with the tip about the egg two days before my interview with Elric and his underlings, and of course I hadn't told Tic I'd applied at SPL, and that was all fairly deceitful, but deceit is a requirement for surviving in the mystic world. It's how I've made my living all these years, after all.

For sure, Tic could easily consult another mystic about a deal for the egg, and I had no doubt he would—it's worth a king's fortune if it were retrieved in good condition and had at least one life left in it. I, on the other hand, being cash poor at the moment, wouldn't be able to pay Tic anything up front—something he hated—and even after retrieving the prize, I'd be able to offer him only a tiny fraction of what he might be able to earn otherwise. Which was all the more reason for him to take off at a sprint the second he saw me.

Lucky me I had a trinket in my pocket in the form of a rare gold coin that allowed me to approach him head-on without him being any wiser. I simply had to activate the coin using a bit of my essence and approach Tic head-on.

A Spell to Unbind

All trinkets require a bit of a mystic's essence—our energy—to become activated. Some require a little something extra, such as a twist or a turn or a click, but many can simply be activated by willing some of our energy into the core of the trinket.

The way it works is that, basically, when we're bound, our physiology changes. The electromagnetic current that all living beings generate—some people call this an aura—gets energized like a thousand percent. Once we're bound, we're able to activate that current in ways that help us live longer, recover from injury faster, and turn everyday objects into magical devices—or trinkets.

Most trinkets are small and can fit in your pocket. Most are also made of metal, but quite a few are made of glass or other natural materials such as crystals, gems, and even wood.

Plastic doesn't hold a current, like, at all, so it's the one material almost nobody uses.

Now, most mystics are able to create trinkets, but it takes a lot out of us—especially if we want a prized trinket that can allow us to do fairly impossible things. So, being the lazy schmucks that we are, we like to steal the good ones and pump only a little bit of our essence into them anytime we need to use them.

The most prized trinkets—those that're already infused with a significant amount of power—are in turn collected by the most powerful among us. These are the trinkets that can actually enhance and amplify our individual essences. Elric and Petra have both spent millennia collecting a treasure trove of the world's most powerful trinkets.

And even though their coffers are filled with all sorts of magical goodies, Elric and Petra still don't have the power to pump out a trinket worth risking your life to steal.

Those trinkets are crafted by a special and exceptionally rare group of mystics. So special and so rare that there've been only a few dozen in all the history of our magical world.

These mystics are named after the most legendary of their kind: Merlin the Enchanter.

Upon their binding, merlins don't simply have an electromagnetic current that's a thousand times normal. They have a current that is a *hundred* thousand times normal.

In other words, what these merlins are able to do that no other mystics can is harness the electromagnetic current that hums among every living being on the planet, and direct a portion of that current into an object that gives it magical properties.

It was one such merlin who created Grigori's egg. Peter Carl Fabergé was a merlin of amazing talent and ability. He enchanted thousands of trinkets with a wide range of magical powers, but he was unique even among merlins because he was also able to bind a couple of mortals and turn them into merlins too.

That'd never been done before, but both Mikhail Perkhin and Henrik Wigström—two once-mortal craftsmen that Peter bound and who worked in the Russian Fabergé's trinket shop—could definitely kick out some incredibly powerful toys and were made rich, rich, rich for it.

But the story doesn't have a happy ending. Fabergé was killed by Petra's brother in a dispute over Fabergé's refusal to create a merlin just for him—his own personal slave.

After Fabergé's death, Mikhail and Henrik went into hiding, and no new trinkets bearing their signature have come to market in the hundred years since.

Still, the three of them left behind an absolute treasure trove of trinkets that were highly sought out on the black market, and I'd made a killing as a thief over the decades stealing and fencing their creations. Thieving is an art that takes great skill, because not only can most mystics turn deadly when faced with losing one of their most prized possessions, but trinkets themselves can also be infused with other protective powers on top of the ones that are at their core's purpose. These are usually protective spells which, in theory, would prevent a thief like me from either taking them or using them after I'd stolen them. And that's where Dex comes in.

My second is a master in deactivating protective spells—especially the ones that pack a punch. He simply absorbs the blow and figures out how to strip down the trinket to its core purpose. We then put our own layer of protection on the trinket so that it can't be easily stolen back.

The coin in my pocket is a good example of this. It'd been a hard-won prize for me because the mystic I'd taken it from had been clever and quick.

Once I'd managed to steal it, however, I'd nearly lost it three times on the way back to the Paris apartment I shared back then with Dex. The coin had been layered with more than one comeback spell—a spell that would return it to its rightful owner—and I'd had a hell of a time holding onto the damn thing in the two miles it'd taken to hike it back home.

The moment I came through the door I'd handed it over to Dex, and he'd gotten to work, managing to use his own essence to strip the coin of the three comeback spells, but the second he'd stripped those off, the damn thing had surprised us both by having a *fourth* layer of protection that'd punched Dex clear across the room. Poor guy. Luckily he'd shaken it off and managed to strip the coin down bare, and it'd become an immensely useful tool for us for almost twenty years.

I'd only put it in storage when I'd gotten my mitts on the ballpoint pen that I'd had to cough up to Sequoya. So, after discovering Tic playing chess in the park, I was relieved to feel the warmth of the coin beginning to work its magic in my palm.

Once the heat had spread through me, I made my way across the park, moving steadily toward Tic until I was about fifteen feet away from him, and that's when I heard the sound of running feet charging toward me from behind. Without thinking, I dropped low to the ground and spun in a tight circle while extending one foot, sweeping it under my attacker and tripping him. He went down with a loud, rather unmanly shout, just as something else flickered into my peripheral vision.

Launching upward, I leaned back and raised my extended foot high, knocking a brown, oblong object right out of the air that would've otherwise hit me hard in the head.

Standing tall again, I realized that the man I'd tripped had been running to catch a football, thrown by another man a good twenty meters away who was looking in my direction with no small measure of confusion.

"Dammit!" I muttered, whipping my head around to see if Tic had noticed the commotion.

Of course he had, and I growled low in my throat when I saw him get to his feet and stare right at me. I knew he couldn't see me, but he could see the man I'd tripped now trying to pick himself up. Tic moved his gaze between the guy getting to his feet and that man's buddy who was squinting oddly in our direction, as if he couldn't understand what had tripped his friend up.

Focusing back on Tic, I saw that he was wise to me, because he was now turning his head to the side. He'd spot me for sure in his peripheral vision, so I did the only thing I could: I began to sprint toward him as fast as I could.

He saw me coming when I was just five feet away, and he took off like a rocket. He got probably ten paces before I tackled him to the ground, throwing him hard onto his side before rolling him over to his back. I had to scramble to pin down his arms before he could shove the special earplugs he'd created into his ears. Once those were in, he'd be deaf for at least a week.

"Stop it!" he shouted. "Get *off* me, Esmé!"

"Hiya, Tic," I replied. "Or should I say, *tick-tock, tick-tock, big hand on the clock starts the tics and lets them toc, tick-tock, tic-toc, one tick-tock.*"

The second I finished the little rhyme, Tic went completely limp except for the tiny tic of his now glaring right eye. "You stupid bitch."

"Hey!" I heard behind me. Chancing a look over my shoulder, I saw the young guy who'd thrown the ball my way approaching us cautiously. "Are you guys just playin'? Or do I need to call the cops?"

"Call the cops!" Tic yelled.

I frowned at Tic first, then at the guy approaching. Why could he see me? And then I noticed the gold coin had come out of my jacket pocket when I'd tackled Tic, and it was lying on the ground about five feet away. Getting to my feet, I reached down to haul up Tic and moved both of us strategically over to the coin, hiding it with my boot. Its magical effect was no longer functioning, of course. Once it'd broken contact with my energy, the coin had gone back to neutral, but I sure as hell didn't want the stranger approaching us to see it and think about playing a game of finders keepers with me.

Facing the stranger while holding firmly to Tic, I said, "We're just playing. Right, Tic?"

Tic became stubbornly silent. Perhaps he needed a little encouragement. "I'm waiting," I whispered into his ear. "Much like you'll be doing for an extra hour or two if you don't go along with me on this."

"We're cool," he said stiffly.

For a moment, the stranger simply stared at us, unsure what to do, but then a sort of dopey smile came over his face, and he began to give me the up-down. When his eyes met mine again, I knew he liked what he saw. "Whoa," he said. "You're freaking *gorgeous*!"

Poor guy didn't yet understand that he had no chance with me because I wasn't even remotely attracted to him. And that told me he was probably a decent enough man.

"Go," I said, pointing back to his friend and making sure my tone left no room for either flirtation or argument.

He seemed confused by the cold shoulder and went with ignoring the hint. "Feel like hanging out later?"

Mentally I rolled my eyes. Why was it always when I had no time for this kind of crap that it always came up? Taking a calming breath, I pushed a smile to my lips. "Okay, sure. Name the place and I'll meet you."

"Yeah?" he asked. I nodded. "Cool. How about Bulldog's in Georgetown?"

"I know it well. Meet you there around seven."

"Awesome!" he said with a little too much enthusiasm. Catching himself, he cleared his throat and added, "I mean...yeah. That'd be good."

A slightly awkward silence followed until I made an impatient waving motion and he finally seemed to get the hint. "Uh, okay, see you later then."

I waited until he moved off before focusing back on Tic. "Are you going to come along peacefully? Or do I have to resort to more physical motivation?"

Tic didn't answer. Instead he stood there glowering at me, and I had no doubt he was mentally weighing his options.

"*Tick-tock, tick-tock, big hand ticks one more tock,*" I sang.

Immediately Tic's right pinkie began to twitch, and the ticking of his right eye continued to pulse. I looked pointedly at Tic's little finger and shrugged.

Tic's brow furrowed furiously. But still, he refused to speak.

I'd have to call his bluff. "Okay," I said, turning away. "Have fun finding me when you can barely manage to walk tonight."

I got about ten feet before the stubborn fool gave in. "Wait," he growled. "Esmé, wait."

Just to show him who was in charge, I kept walking.

"Esmé!" he yelled. "Dammit, woman. Don't be like that."

Pausing briefly, I glanced over my shoulder and took in that the tic under his eye had grown slightly more exaggerated. It was subtle, and I could tell he was working hard to fight it, but within a few hours, his face and entire right hand would become a storm of misfiring synapses that would both continue to spread, rendering him a convulsing mess before midnight. The saddest thing of all was that Tic's painful affliction was purposely cast on him by his own mother, Petra. It was one of the many reasons why I'd never applied to work for her; she was petty and cruel. Elric might be ruthless but at least he wasn't petty.

Tic was the product of what was rumored to have been a passionate love affair, but it hadn't been between Petra and her husband, Elric. By mystic royalty tradition, Petra should've killed Tic the second he was born; instead, she bound him from birth with the compulsive muscle twitch which would spread throughout his body until he either died or was given the counterspell. Petra herself employed the curse whenever Tic disobeyed her. It was said that she had actually given him the nickname, and although no one was willing to call him "Tic" within her presence, it was well known that she encouraged its use.

Thus, Petra raised and mentored her son, often cruelly, right under Elric's nose, which was only part of the reason the pair loathed each other.

And yes, I'd just taken advantage of Tic's binding spell, and also only referred to him by the insensitive moniker which might also mark me as someone cruel, but I can assure you, I won the knowledge and language of Tic's binding fair and square in a poker game where he'd known exactly what the stakes had been. He would've been no less cruel to me had the tables been turned.

"You know what I want," I said to him.

His head gave an involuntary jerk and he closed his eyes for a moment, frustration and anger written all over his features. "We need to talk about the terms," he said, opening his eyes again.

I shrugged. "I'm working for Elric now, Tic. I've got nothing to offer you."

"Then give the counterspell!"

"Sorry, can't do that. You have information I want."

"This is beyond the pale, Esmé. You can't do this to me!"

"Ah, but I can. And you knew that I would someday when you set the terms, played the game, and lost."

"I still think you cheated," he said, his eyes narrowing.

I shrugged again. "I didn't, but you would completely ignore the fact that we played the game in Madame Solange's parlor, which made cheating impossible."

"I had an unbeatable hand!"

"Au contraire. You had a hand that was beatable by only one other. Royal flush beats straight flush every time, my friend."

Tic's right cheek began to twitch along with his eye, and a vein in his temple throbbed with the effort to both keep his cool and control the tics. "You've taken advantage of me."

"Of course I have. As would you if you'd learned my binding spell that night."

Tic glared at me for several more seconds, and I arched an eyebrow expectantly.

But he continued to stand stubbornly mute, so I took it to the next level. "Time's a-wastin', Tic. *Tick-tock, tick-tock, big hand ticks one more tock.*"

As I lit up Tic with the spell again, he made a sound deep in his throat right before his left leg gave a small involuntary jerk. "*Stop it!*"

"Tell me what I want to know," I said, standing casually and crossing my arms.

Tic clenched his teeth and curled his hands into fists. He wanted to kill me, I could tell, but he wasn't sure he could take me on and win, and that doubt was revealed in his eyes. There was also the troublesome problem that if he didn't manage to kill me and survived my counterattack, if I got away without releasing him from the tics, he'd essentially be sentencing himself to a long, slow, agonizing death.

"If I have to ask again," I warned, "I'll increase the spell tenfold before I leave the park."

A little color drained from Tic's face. "That would kill me."

"I'm sure it would."

After just another moment's consideration, Tic finally said, "414 Wolfe Street. In Old Town."

A slight smile tugged at my lips. "And what else?"

Tic's face flushed with anger again. "No. Absolutely not! Not before you agree to compensate me!"

"I won't be fencing the egg, Tic. There'll be nothing to compensate you with."

Tic's face reddened with rage. "Elric always gives his new thieves considerable signing bonuses. That's the least you owe me for the information."

"Bold words for someone in no position to take advantage and make bargains."

"I'm not the one taking advantage, Esmé. You know what that egg is worth. Any of my other contacts would pay me part of the cut."

"That's true," I said. "But how many of them know your binding spell?"

He ground his teeth together and glared at me for all he was worth. "I wish I'd known you were applying for a job with Elric. I would've told Jacquelyn to use her blue dragon over that lazy ruby-throated one."

I smiled wickedly. So Tic was privy to more details than even I'd assumed. And he was right; if Jacquelyn had unleashed her blue at me, I likely wouldn't have made it out of the room.

I clapped him hard on the back. "It's nice to know you were rooting for me, you spiteful toad."

He jerked away and rubbed the spot where I'd just whacked him. "When it comes to Elric adding to his despicable forces, I *always* root for the dragon, you negligibly talented hag."

I inhaled a deep breath and considered him. We could stand here all day and trade insults or I could try to find a way to compromise with the little turd. "This isn't getting either of us anywhere. Let's negotiate."

Tic clenched his right fist, attempting to stop the tremors that were slowly inching their way across his whole hand. "You first," he said.

"Fine. *Stop the clock by one tick-tock.*"

Tic sucked in a breath of surprise, and the jerking emanating from his leg abruptly halted. The other tics remained, however.

Shaking out his leg a little, he said, "Thank you, Esmé." But then he remained stubbornly silent again.

"You have ten seconds before I reverse that effect and add ten more," I warned. I wasn't playing. My life depended on Tic's information being both accurate and forthcoming.

"It's not fair that you should reap all the benefits and I end up with nothing," he complained. "All I ask is for some minor compensation. That's not unreasonable, given the value of the information I'm passing on to you."

I hated to admit it, but he was absolutely right. While I didn't have any available cash to offer him, I did have something I knew Tic might consider valuable. "Okay," I said, reaching into the folds of my leather jacket to pull out a brown feather, the end of which was tipped in red.

Tic's eyes widened. "Is that…"

"It is." The feather was a trinket I'd picked up only the week before. It wasn't an especially powerful trinket in that it really only worked on the unbound, but it allowed the bearer to scrawl a signature at the bottom of any contract and have it accepted as valid. Mostly it was intended to be used to sign forged checks, and I'd considered using it to sign away the debt on my mortgage, but it was actually more valuable if I traded it to Tic for the information he held. With it, Tic could walk into any bank run by mortals and withdraw as much as he liked as often as he wanted and, using another trinket I knew he possessed, obscure his features for the security cameras.

The quill had twenty-six uses still in play before it ran out of juice, enough for Tic to get by for a nice stretch.

Giving it up wasn't especially hard, because while my own morals were a bit loose by mortal standards, I hadn't yet needed to use the quill, although I wouldn't have hesitated if things had gotten desperate before I was granted the interview with SPL.

My informant's head jerked involuntarily as the tic that'd begun under his eye continued to spread, only his attention was so focused on the feather that he didn't even seem to notice. "I accept," he said greedily. "Grigori takes his tea every Wednesday at noon in the Empress Lounge. He meets a group of friends for a boisterous game of Durak."

"Durak?"

Tic pulled his gaze away from the feather to consider me with a petulant look. "It's a Russian card game. Grigori is very good, but not quite as good as I am."

"Ahhhh," I said, suddenly understanding how it was that Tic had come to discover Grigori's whereabouts in the first place. No doubt the long-sought-after Russian had no idea he'd been found out. Tic played the fool very well. He was constantly being underestimated.

"How long will he be at the card game?" I asked. I'd need time to search Grigori's residence thoroughly.

"At least an hour. The commute will add forty minutes each way."

"You're sure he doesn't carry the egg on his person?"

"I'm not sure at all," Tic said. "He very well could, and if he does, you'll never get it away from him unless you kill him, which, as you know from your Russian history lessons, is next to impossible."

That was true enough. Grigori Rasputin had evaded death at the hands of the tsar's cousin at least four times, possibly five, all because of a certain enchanted Fabergé egg given to him by the tsarina herself. She probably couldn't have guessed that she'd one day have a desperate need for it when her entire family was brutally executed. Had she simply held onto it, she could've lived, and brought back to life her loved ones.

That was the power of Grigori's egg. It gave the holder a second chance—even twenty-four hours after death, it had the power to bring one back to life fully restored, no matter how grave the injuries.

The egg was similar to Ember in its power to heal, but unlike her, the egg had its limits. If a person had been dead longer than twenty-four hours it wouldn't work, and if the egg reached the end of twelve uses, it would crumble into small bits of useless shell.

The merlin Fabergé had created the charmed trinket in the early 1900s, and had always intended for it to go to the Russian royal family, whom he greatly admired, but they were quite mortal, and the tsarina had received the charmed relic without knowing anything about how to use it, although of course she knew of its mystical powers. She had been one of the few thousand mortals in the world privy to mystics and our magic, and it was likely she was brought into the fold only because she was royalty.

To assist her, Fabergé had introduced her to a fellow mystic who was down on his luck at the time, none other than Grigori Rasputin. And he did in fact help the tsarina by using the egg twice to save the life of little Alexi.

However, shortly after that, the tsarina became convinced that her son was fully cured of his "royal disease"—hemophilia—and in gratitude she'd offered the precious egg to Rasputin. It was largely believed that Grigori had knowingly deceived the tsarina about the state of her son's health, something for which Fabergé never forgave him. Meanwhile, relatives of the tsar plotted to do away with the meddling mystic and attempted to kill him a few times over. Each time Grigori rose from the dead, ultimately fleeing the country.

Just months later, the tsar, tsarina, and all five of their children were summarily executed, while Grigori Rasputin slid into exile and anonymity, taking all knowledge of the egg's whereabouts and available offerings with him.

So at most, the egg, if it hadn't already been used up, had five or six offerings left before it could never be used again. And even if it had only one offering left, it would've been unthinkable for Grigori to leave the egg behind whenever he left his house.

Then again, traveling around D.C. with an enchantment that powerful in a city ruled by arguably the two most powerful mystics in the world could also be quite reckless. But then I had to consider that the egg might be too precious for him to take into the city and risk being mugged by a fellow mystic—I was certain the man could more than hold his own against an unbound, but that egg was incredibly valuable on the mystic black market. Any mystic thief wouldn't think twice about using violence to obtain it.

Well, except maybe me. I draw the line at physically attacking someone for their magical charms. If I'm attacked first, all bets are off, but I prefer to poach my trinkets honestly—from behind, when no one's looking.

And I had to wonder again what had brought Rasputin to the US, and to this city specifically, in the first place. He was certainly tempting fate by being here. Everyone knew he possessed the egg, and I was sure that Elric and Petra had been hunting Europe for him for a hundred years, which gave me a bit of pause.

"You're sure you've identified him?" I pressed. The last thing I needed was for Tic's information to come up false. "*The* Grigori Rasputin?"

"Positive," he said confidently, adding, "Although Grigori doesn't remember it, I met him in 1915 when my father was invited to stay with the tsar and tsarina on our way back to Italy from Prussia. Of course I was only seven at the time, so it's not surprising he doesn't recognize me, but I remember the crescent scar on the side of his thumb, which he told me he got when he'd been a lad about my age. He said he'd gotten it when a parrot his mother kept as a pet bit him and nearly broke the bone. He told me that his mother had refused to get rid the bird, claiming she preferred the company of the parrot over that of her children. As you can imagine, I could relate to that."

I studied Tic curiously. It was sometimes easy to forget how difficult it'd been for him growing up. Everyone knew about the time, in a jealous rage, his mother had murdered his father right in front of their young son. Petra had then brought Tic to the US and had forced him to live in a place where his life was constantly threatened by her estranged husband, Elric, who wouldn't hesitate to kill Tic—if he could avoid a war in doing so, that is. Meanwhile Petra appeared to relish dangling her bastard son right under Elric's nose. Never mind how her son felt about it.

Petra was a serious bitch.

Tucking the feather back into my jacket, I heard Tic click his tongue in irritation. "Relax," I said. "Once I recover the egg, you'll get the feather." And then as a show of good faith I added, *"Stop the clock by one tick-tock."*

A slight sigh passed Tic's lips as the tremor moving up his arm subsided. "It should be mine for simply giving you the information, Esmé," he said stubbornly. "Why do I have to rely on your thieving skills to get paid?"

"Because I don't trust you, Marco," I said, using his given name and trying to make peace.

He didn't appear mollified. He glared at me angrily, but what could he do? I had him at a serious disadvantage, and he knew it. "Fine," he groused. "Enter through the smallest window at the rear of the house. That's a bathroom. Grigori has a fetish for goulash, but his bowels don't handle it well. That bathroom window is nearly always open at least a crack."

"Got it," I said. "I should be finished by four o'clock."

Tic's eyes widened. "You can't leave me like this all afternoon!"

I considered that. *"Stop the clock by one tick-tock."*

Tic sighed in relief, shaking out his hand before pointing to his face. "Thank you. Now how about this last one as a show of good faith?"

I laughed lightly. "No deal. And if your info comes back as false or you sent me into some kind of a deathtrap, then know you'll be signing your own death warrant."

"I'm aware of the consequences," he snapped. "And my information is accurate, but I shouldn't be held responsible for whatever mess you blunder into. Grigori's house will have an assortment of enchantments standing guard. If you step into one of his traps, why should I end up paying for it?"

"Sorry," I said without an ounce of sympathy. "That's just how this has to play out today, Tic. If I let you go, you could head to your mother, and she'd send an army of minions to cut me off at the pass."

"I could've gone straight to Mommy Dearest with my intel, Esmé, but instead I sent word to *you*."

"True, but she wouldn't have given you a thing for the info, and that's the real reason you came to me first."

"I'm still not getting anything for it."

"You'll get the quill, Marco. I promise. As long as I get the egg."

"This is the worst deal I've ever struck."

I gave him a much friendlier pat on the back this time. "Buck up, little camper. The day is still young. There might be time to strike up a worse deal before the sun sets."

Tic stared furiously at me, and the tic under his eye was now taking command of his cheek muscle. "I hate you, Esmé Bellerose."

"Aww, and here I thought we were gonna be besties."

For a long moment we simply stared hard at each other, but then Tic said, "You'll need to remove the last tic no later than four o'clock."

"Yeah, yeah," I said with a lazy wave of my hand. "Where can I find you? Here?"

"I'll leave word with that goon you insist on keeping company with," he said.

I eyed Tic curiously. "You've got his number?"

Tic snickered. "We're friends on Facebook."

That actually gave me a chuckle. No mystic would ever risk having a profile on social media, because no mystic would ever allow any of their personal thoughts or information anywhere they believed another mystic could easily access it. In the mystic world, personal information was power, which again made me wonder how Tic planned on getting ahold of Dex. I wanted to press him on it, but then I realized I didn't really care. By four o'clock, Tic was going to be a mess of misfiring synapses. He'd be lucky to get his fingers to work well enough to send a text message, let alone speak into a phone. If he wanted to keep me in the dark about his whereabouts until then…fine. It was his risk to take.

"Have it your way," I said, turning away.

"Wait!" Tic called.

"No time," I told him, quickening my pace to an easy jog.

"I'll be here, Esmé!"

I waved casually over my shoulder, but there was a slight smirk on my face.

I'd left him with one tic, which would grow in magnitude over the course of the next few hours. It was the only way to ensure that he wasn't sending me into a trap.

Of course, Grigori Rasputin's home was guaranteed to be loaded with traps, but I didn't need any extra set out just for sweet little ol' me.

Heading to the car, I glanced at the clock on my dash. I had just enough time to get my butt over to Wolfe Street in Old Town and hunt for the egg for an hour or so before I'd have to get out of there to avoid the risk of running into Grigori.

Of course, if Tic's information was incorrect, and the house I'd be searching wasn't owned by *the* Grigori Rasputin or, if he'd taken the Fabergé egg with him, I was likely a dead woman.

I tried not to focus on that.

Chapter Four
Day 1

Soon after leaving the park, I was cruising down a street in Old Town, which is the most historic part of Alexandria. It's a quaint if crowded place, and homes here are arranged in the most efficient manner possible. The structures themselves tend to be deeply narrow rectangles with no surrounding yard to speak of, and space between homes was down to a mere few feet.

Grigori's house was typical in style, with parking at the side of the house rather than the front, and an iron gate at the walkway leading to the front door. There was no car in the drive, and the gate was closed and probably locked.

Parking across the street and down a few houses from his, I got out of the car and reached into my jacket for my gold coin, only to discover it missing. And then I remembered with horror that I'd forgotten all about it when I was arguing with Tic, and it was either still lying in the grass at the park or in someone else's pocket.

Growling low and muttering some choice expletives, I sent a text to Dex to ask him to invoke the comeback spell on the coin, then made sure no one was around and approached the gate leading to Grigori's house.

Once there, I pulled out a handy little gadget that resembled a corkscrew. Holding it in my hand, I pushed a little of my essence into it before inserting it into the lock. There was a rush of warmth along my fingertips, and the lock clicked open—and that gave me pause.

The lock had required very little energy from my handy trinket to open. It should've left my entire arm burning. Maybe my entire right side, and it should've taken at least three tries...which could only mean that the lock hadn't been secured by magical means.

Feeling the first tinges of frustration, because no way would Grigori Rasputin have forgotten to secure his own gate against intruders like me, I slipped through the entry anyway and headed up the walk, almost certain I was being set up after all.

Still, I'd need to see it through before I could hunt down Tic and beat the crap out of him. It was just like him to play me like this, only I was in a game for my life and no way could I afford to waste time on a hassle like this.

Tamping down my anger, I eased my way carefully along the edge of the home, avoiding the windows. I didn't know if anyone was inside, and it was best not to take any chances. Moving beyond the front door and over to the back of the property, I quickly discovered the portal window that Tic had described. What was odd was that there was indeed a foul odor coming from inside. "Huh," I whispered. Tic had lied about who the house belonged too, obviously, but he'd given me a truthful detail that would've required him scoping out the residence. I wondered why?

Reaching again into my jacket pocket, I took out a trinket crafted by Henrik Wigström, the merlin. It was an absolutely beautiful thing, made of a thin round piece of nearly perfectly clear crystal, encased in a ring of gold studded with topaz.

It resembled a monocle, and it essentially was, but with a twist. By looking through it I was able to literally see any enchantments that might be present. Holding it up to my right eye, I looked through it to the window and saw nothing obstructing the view.

"Yep," I growled. "Wild goose chase." There were no spells or curses across the open window. It was unarmed, so to speak. It was also open a crack, meaning, it was likely unarmed from a mortal perspective too. No interior alarm was going to sound if a window wasn't securely shut.

I very nearly gave up and left the property. I was so mad at being played that I wanted to find Tic as soon as possible and exact my revenge. The *only* reason I was still alive after my interview with Elric was because I'd had inside info on the whereabouts of Grigori's egg, and I'd come across that information from Tic himself when he'd bragged to me that he knew where Grigori Rasputin was currently hiding.

Still, I'd come this far, and this house was large enough, and in a neighborhood exclusive enough to be worth a considerable fortune. Maybe there was some peace offering inside that Elric might desire. It wasn't likely to spare my life, but maybe it'd make Elric a bit more merciful when he brought down the deathblow.

Creeping close to the window, I peered inside. The smell hit me like a hammer. It was as foul a smell as anything I'd ever whiffed, and it set off my gag reflex. With effort, I managed to keep it together without losing my breakfast and held my breath while opening the window to crawl inside.

Once in the lavatory, I waited and listened for any signs or sounds of someone moving about inside. But there was only silence.

Covering my nose and mouth with my left hand, I crept forward a few steps, pausing in the doorway to peer out into the main hall.

The house was a tasteful mix of colors and textures. Lots of greens and yellows, with antique rugs, vintage furniture, and portraits of Southern ladies from a bygone era adorning the walls.

It looked nothing like an old Russian mystic's place...more like something that belonged to a Southern grandmother of means.

After listening and watching from the lavatory doorway for a few moments, I moved into the hallway, placing my feet very carefully so as not to have them make a sound. And that's when I realized that the God-awful stench wafting in the air inside the lavatory wasn't actually coming *from* the lavatory, but from somewhere else in the house.

Immediately every single hair on my arms and the back of my neck stood up on end. A force permeated the home that had nothing to do with the noxious smell. A *bad* energy slithered in and around the environment, staining the very air of the place and letting me know that something seriously wicked this way had come.

For several seconds I stood there, frozen and unsure what to do. I sensed that no one was in the home, but I was also fairly positive that whoever had been here was an evildoer of unspeakable things. His or her essence clung to the very air like a dank cologne and it made me shiver.

Alarmed and unnerved, I turned my head to look back toward the window I'd come through; should I stay and investigate or get my ass out of this place before whatever had been here came back?

The decision came down to one thing: Whatever had been here had enough power to leave an imprint on the atmosphere, and that told me that someone from my world had in fact been here. Whether that someone was Grigori Rasputin or someone else was what I didn't yet know.

If it did belong to the mystic, then I needed to do a thorough search, and I needed to do it quickly.

Keeping my nose and mouth covered, I stepped away from the wall and proceeded slowly and cautiously toward the source of the smell. I had to find out what was causing it before I searched the rest of the house.

Passing the staircase, I turned my head with each step, ready to bolt or produce an enchanted weapon in an instant. I had a few tricks up my magical sleeve, but nothing that would necessarily stop a mystic significantly more powerful than me. All my defenses would buy me only a little time.

Still, it was better than nothing, and I moved steadily toward the overpowering odor, at last identifying that it was coming from the dining room, which was off the central hallway just past the main stairway.

When I arrived at the door to the dining area, I came up short and had to clamp both hands over my mouth to keep that gag reflex from kicking in again.

Apparently I'd interrupted a dinner party. Seated at the table was a fat man with bushy brown hair, full beard, and eyebrows so big and thick that they all but obscured his eyes. None of that detracted from the fact that his head was lolled back at an odd angle and his mouth hung open as if frozen in midscream.

He wore a blood-spattered dinner jacket made of the finest silk, completely ruined now. His hands were frozen in a fierce grip, clinging to the armrests of the dining chair, and there was an indentation around the cuff of his blazer—as if his wrists had been secured there by invisible rope. The bottom of his trousers wore a similar indentation, and I couldn't help but notice as I took in the scene that his calves were pressed tightly to the legs of the chair.

Something had bound him there as sure as iron chains, and it was easy to see that he would've needed to be restrained while he was being eviscerated and his entrails placed on the fine china plate in front of him.

"Holy mother of God," I whispered, fighting hard to choke back the bile at the back of my throat. I'd seen some truly nightmarish things in my life, but this… this was an unimaginable horror made all the worse by the fact that the fat man had not been alone.

Also at the ghoulish dinner party was a woman with long, wavy blond hair, spattered with her own blood and a similar entrée in front of her. She too appeared bound by invisible rope, and her mouth was also as wide as her eyes, forever frozen in abject agony. To her right was another man, and to his right another woman, each one with the same expression and gruesome serving in front of them.

A terrible shudder racked my whole body and I shut my eyes against the scene, but what wouldn't leave me was the thought that they likely hadn't been murdered all at once; any killer capable of such a macabre scene would've intended to maximize the fear and agony, and he would've worked his way around the table, slicing open one after the other.

I morbidly wondered if Grigori had been the first or last in the queue, and decided he'd likely been the last. The killer would've wanted him to see what was happening to his friends before delivering the fatal wound.

Tears sprang to my eyes in the face of such suffering. How long had it taken these four to die? It hadn't been quick, that's for sure, but it had been unbearable given the frozen scream on each of their faces.

A Spell to Unbind

Turning my back to them, I fled to the bathroom, barely making it in time to give up my breakfast. Cold sweat snaked its way down my spine and droplets formed at my temple, and yet, I felt colder than I could ever remember. I shuddered, shivered, and trembled, unable to get any part of myself to cooperate and hold still because the scene from the dining room kept flashing over and over in my mind's eye like a loop from a horror movie.

Soon I was breathing erratically. I couldn't seem to get enough air into my lungs. Moving over to the window, I shoved it up as high as it would go and hung my head out, gulping for air. I desperately wanted to run away from this house as fast as I could and never look back, but if I did—if I left this place without discovering the Fabergé egg—then I was as dead as anyone in that dining room. And my death wasn't likely to be nearly so pleasant.

"Shit!" I hissed. "Shit! Shit! Shit!"

Reluctantly I pulled my head back inside and sat on the floor for a moment, trying to work up the courage to get up and go back into that hallway to begin the search. It took a bit of time, but at last I felt I could stand and not have my legs give out from underneath me.

I no longer doubted that this was the home of a mystic. It might not be Grigori Rasputin at the head of that table, but I had no doubt that whoever he was, he'd been murdered by magical means. A spell had bound his hands and feet; I could feel the trace of it still lingering even all these hours later. Plus, there was no fiber evidence of tape or rope on the cuffs of his jacket or trousers, and the fine silk he wore was unmarred where he'd been bound. Rope would've cut or frayed the fabric as he'd struggled.

No, a mystic had done that to him, and if that actually was Rasputin in there, then he'd been overpowered by someone significantly more talented than he. Which was an unsettling thought.

Now I also knew why his house was essentially wide open to thieves. Grigori wouldn't have locked it up tight if he'd been at home entertaining.

I had no idea how long the four had been dead, but I suspected from the god-awful stench that they'd been murdered sometime in the past two to three days.

I wondered if the murderer had already taken the egg, and I could only hope that it might still be here somewhere in the house. Regardless, I couldn't leave without checking.

On shaky legs, I hedged back into the hallway and avoided looking directly down the length of it toward the dining room. Taking a deep breath I pulled out the monocle from my pocket, beginning my scan of the area.

The monocle is a little something I lifted off a fairly powerful mystic about a quarter-century ago in Bangladesh. I'd trailed him relentlessly for almost two years, waiting and watching from the shadows until I finally got the chance to take it from him, and for the next year I'd had to remain on the run, fearing for my life, until I'd heard he'd been assassinated by one of Elric's henchmen.

That'd been one lucky day for me. It was the moment I knew I could finally stop living in fear and settle down to focus on a plan to get hired by SPL Inc.

The monocle had quickly become one of my most prized possessions, and if Elric knew I had it, he'd take it from me without a moment's hesitation. If I even thought to resist his effort to take it, he'd no doubt kill me on the spot. The monocle was that valuable.

While there were other trinkets out there that might have similar magical properties, nothing could compare to how perfectly adapted the monocle was for the purpose of seeing what couldn't otherwise be seen or even often felt. It gave me an unequaled advantage that couldn't be thwarted by any magical means meant to obscure it.

In short, looking through the monocle allowed the possessor to clearly distinguish magical energy. Through it, I could gaze at any object and see the faint green glow pulsing around it, which clearly indicated that it housed an enchantment. The more powerful the enchantment, the brighter the green of the light surrounding it.

The aura emanating from Ember was so green that it was turquoise. No other object I'd ever seen using the monocle—including a certain ring on Elric's left hand—had even come close to the intensity of her brilliant, beautiful light.

Without a doubt, she's the most enchanted thing in the world.

It's why I guard the monocle so diligently. I can't risk having anyone look through it and see Ember in her true magical form. And I would throw the monocle down a deep, deep hole and cover it with cement so that no one could ever discover its powers, but I couldn't have made a play for Elric's team without it, and it'd proved itself an absolutely invaluable tool for me over the years. I'd gained both a reputation as an excellent thief and some very, very powerful trinkets to sell on the mystic black market.

So I kept the monocle under wraps at all times except during expeditions like this, where I was pressed for time, and, more important, when I needed to avoid any magical traps.

Looking through it, I was now convinced that I was in the home of a great mystic because such a collection would never belong to anyone of average rank.

Flashes of green abounded in the spacious home. Most of them were of a soft pulsing light, meaning that the various trinkets he'd had on hand weren't especially powerful, and were likely only there as decoys but there was an interesting piece on the mantle in the shape of a small green glass cruet with a swirl of white on the base and a golden stopper. To the naked eye the cruet looked a bit blurry, meaning that it had once been hidden from view by a concealing spell. That was super common in homes where mystics had things to hide.

I looked at the cruet through the monocle again and saw only a hint of green smoke coming from around the stopper. "Hmmm," I whispered. The hint of green smoke wasn't any stronger than any of the other objects I could detect in the room, but the fact that Grigori had tried to conceal it either made it a good decoy or something that he'd actually wanted to keep hidden.

The concealing spell had all but worn off so there was no way to know how powerful it'd been when he'd been alive.

I walked over to the mantle to have a closer look, picking it up to inspect it. The cruet itself could've been vintage, but it wasn't anything you wouldn't spot at any neighborhood flea market.

I was tempted to pull the stopper but decided to have a look around first, lest there be a powerful punch loaded in the trinket ready to knock me on my ass.

As I set it down, however, I wondered at the likelihood that the egg was held inside. Some magical trinkets can give off a distortion of appearance—I have a pocket in my leather jacket that can mask any object I manage to tuck into it, no matter how bulky, but I still doubted the cruet's ability to hide a Fabergé egg. I decided to ignore it for the time being and began an earnest search, using the monocle to guide me to all the spots in the house, which, by their green light, called my attention.

The one place I knew I didn't need to search was the dining room. If the egg had been within ten feet of anyone in that room, they'd still be alive. That was the magic of the egg. It was that powerful.

I figured if it was somewhere in the house, I'd find it. Heading up the stairs to the third floor, I started in the small guest bedroom and searched every corner and crevice, looking through the monocle as I went.

There was no sign of the egg on the third floor, and not much in the way of magical trinkets either. The second floor held a bit more promise, and I discovered a key on Grigori's dresser that hummed with green energy. Not having a clue what it was for, I pocketed it—I am a thief after all—and silently vowed to hand it over to Dex to see what he could tease out of it.

As I was pocketing the key, the doorbell rang. The sound—a hard bong that reverberated off the walls—was enough to freeze me in place.

Holding my breath, I waited, ears straining to hear anything that might indicate entrance into the house. But nothing else came to either my ears or eyes. Relaxing a fraction, I took note of the angle of the sunlight peeking through the windows. I'd been in the house about an hour and a half. It was time to wrap it up and go.

Making my way back down to the main floor, I scanned each room quickly but methodically, until only the parlor and the kitchen were left. Drawn to the mantle and that glowing smoke wafting around the cruet, I did something seriously stupid. I lifted the stopper and peered inside.

For a moment the world spun, and I heard someone, with a melodic voice, call out something. It sounded like a name, but it was so faint and so foreign that I couldn't quite catch it. "What?" I whispered, only now aware that I was so dizzy that I had to sit down. Rather than being alarmed, my focus was on the voice once again calling out a name. "Invi—" And then I saw her. The face of the hateful mystic who'd bound me. It was a face I'd never forget, seared into my memory.

"You!" I shouted, but it came like a hoarse whisper. She smiled wickedly before turning to walk away.

I wanted to go after her, to hunt her down and kill her, and I had the very real sense that if I simply let go, I'd learn exactly who and where she was, but as I was trying to decide what to do, I felt a violent tug on my essence that sent alarm bells clanging through my head.

The cruet was quickly absorbing all of my energy—like a vampire, it was trying to suck me dry. I recoiled violently, pulling as hard as I could to get out of its clutches, but the effort cost me, and no sooner did I feel all of my energy come crashing back into me than I lost all consciousness.

The next thing I knew, I was on the floor staring up into the bright sunshine, which was shining directly into my face from the window.

As I shielded my eyes, I realized several things at once: The sun should not have been that low on the horizon, because, last I'd checked the time, it'd been a little after noon. The monocle was still gripped tightly in my fisted right hand, but there was no sign of the cruet. And footsteps from inside the house were coming from the central hallway.

Clearly, I was no longer alone.

Chapter Five
Day 1

For several seconds, I didn't know which was louder: the sound of those footsteps on the bare wood floor or my hammering heart.

Blinking to full alertness, I scrambled up to my feet, but I was shaking all over, and my limbs felt weak and slow to respond. I was woozy and nauseous, and even with the surge of adrenaline, I still felt muddle-brained.

Surveying the room, I realized I'd have to either crawl out the window in the parlor or make my way across the hallway to the bathroom where the window was still open from when I'd come inside.

The window in the parlor looked older. Hauling it up would make noise and alert my presence to whomever was inside the house. But to get to the water closet across the hall I'd have to tiptoe over squeaky floorboards and make my way across the central hallway without being seen or heard.

Without my coin, I was totally exposed. Hiding was an option, but if whomever had entered was even half as powerful as me, then I'd be discovered rather quickly. And then I had to question whether the person in the house had perhaps been the killer. Suddenly I didn't just have to worry about being discovered. I had to worry about ending up like a guest at the dinner party.

If it wasn't the killer but a caretaker, then the police would certainly be alerted, and I'd be stuck here while the authorities searched the premises and hopefully missed discovering me. Mortals don't usually worry me, but given the scene in the dining room, I knew that I'd have far more than just one or two cops to contend with. The whole place would be crawling with the unbound in no time.

I thought about all of this in the span of just a few seconds, doing my best to control my racing heart and rapid breathing. I decided that the window off the bathroom was the best of the bad choices in front of me, so I began to creep toward the entrance of the parlor, keeping in time with the fall of the footsteps out in the hallway. It was a miracle the visitor hadn't yet seen me, but I'd been sprawled out on the floor near the wall, hidden from anyone advancing from the front door, which was definitely the way I thought the stranger had come in. He or she would certainly notice me if they decided to turn around, so I had to be quick and hope that the scene in the dining room was shocking enough to root them in place and allow me to get across the hall and out the window unseen.

As I neared the entrance to the hallway, however, I heard the footfalls pause, and someone sucked in a breath before whispering a string of expletives.

The voice, although hushed, was decidedly male, and it was obvious that he'd discovered the dinner party.

Flattening myself against the wall, I gathered my courage. I had one shot, and it needed to be now. Bracing myself for the dash, I poked my head around the corner to peek at where the stranger was standing and found myself looking down the barrel of a pistol big enough to take off my head.

"Don't. Move," the intruder said. He needn't have worried. I had no intention of moving even to blink. Or to breathe.

We stood like that, him facing me, me facing his gun for several seconds, and I began to realize that I'd shocked him by poking my head out from the doorway like that. He'd had his pistol drawn as he'd moved through the hallway to investigate, probably tipped off by the smell, and my timing had been such that I'd stuck my head out at the exact moment he'd begun turning back toward the door.

Sometimes, I have the *best* luck.

Chancing a deep, much needed inhalation, I lifted my gaze from the barrel to his face and was honestly shocked at the sight of him. He was absolutely beautiful.

With thick black hair, an absolutely straight, almost elegant nose, the most perfect square jaw, gorgeous hazel eyes, and lashes so long I was envious, I drank in the sight of him. There was such symmetry to his features, the right side of his face looking like an exact replica of his left—he seemed almost unnatural in his perfection.

And although he was holding his gun tensely as he stared at me, I imagined that his well-muscled arms and legs were lithe when in motion. He stood like someone who'd had a lot of practice holding a firearm. There was a confidence in the set of his shoulders, and he practically oozed virility.

In other words, I found him... breathtaking.

And yet... he ignited not a single spark in my home fires, even though he was, without question, the most gorgeous man I've ever laid eyes on.

Which meant that, were I not bound by the spell I'd been cursed with, he could've even been the love of my life.

Well, except for the fact that at his waist he wore a bronze shield, he'd just caught me at the scene of a grisly quadruple murder, and he could at any moment pull that trigger and take off my head.

It was hard to imagine that after hobbling out of Elric's offices last evening I could've been any more screwed, and yet here I was, a day later, with a cop's gun in my face and four dead bodies at the end of the hallway.

"Get on the ground," the cop ordered, his voice never rising above a conversational tone. My mind tried to search for an option that didn't include prostrating myself. "*Now*," he added, when it was clear I was stalling.

My gaze flickered over to the door of the bathroom. "Don't even think about it," he warned.

But I was thinking about it. I was thinking about it hard. "I want to show you my ID," I said to him.

"The only thing you're going to show me is your face on that floor."

"Okay," I said, lowering myself a little to demonstrate that I'm a good sport. "I'm getting down, but you're gonna be sorry when you cuff me and realize I'm a fed."

There was a flicker of doubt in those gorgeous hazel eyes, and I thanked my lucky stars that I'm a practiced and convincing liar.

"What agency?" he asked.

I continued to crouch down slowly, my palms raised. "The bureau. I'm a brick agent." I purposely used the slang word for a field agent, working an investigation for the FBI.

I thought I now detected a hint of interest in the cop's eyes. I couldn't tell if it was for me or for the fact that I'd verbally identified myself as a field agent. "Who's your SAC?" he asked, using the abbreviation for special agent in charge.

"Ted Kedzierski." I said the name without pause or stumbling over the difficult surname's pronunciation. Throwing out the lie that I worked for the feds wasn't something I did lightly; I've researched a whole division down at the Hoover Building, and I know enough to make myself sound credible, even without the badge.

My captor squinted at me. He seemed to recognize the name. "I know him," he said. "Who's his ASAC again?"

"John Fell," I told him, identifying Kedzierski's second in command, also without hesitation.

"Know him too," the cop said. "Helluva guy."

I offered up a crooked smile. "Helluv an asshole," I corrected. "But we bricks put up with him because Kedzierski is even worse."

One of the things I'd discovered in my research was that the number of field agents revolving through Kedzierski's division was twice that of the normal rate. I figured it had to be because Kedzierski was a prick, and Fell either was afraid to stand up to him or he was also a prick.

The cop chuckled, but he didn't relax his grip on the gun. "Okay, show me your badge, but do it slow."

I stood tall again and lowered my hands, then reached into the pocket of my leather jacket and withdrew one of my favorite trinkets. The object looks like nothing more than a bit of scrap metal, but when I hold it up to someone and place a suggestion around it, it transforms in their eyes to whatever they expect to see. "Here's my badge," I said. Making a flipping motion to activate the spell, I added, "And my ID. See? I'm Agent Courtney McMahon."

The detective peered at my palm, and his brow furrowed. "What the fuck is that?"

A whisper of alarm traveled across my shoulders. "My ID and badge," I said, giving the trinket another slight flick, feeling the warmth from the scrap within my palm. The spell on the charm was active.

The cop looked from my palm to my face and then back again before lines of anger creased his brow. "That some kind of joke? You think showing me a piece of trash when I ask to see your ID is funny?" Motioning over his shoulder with his chin in the direction of the dining room, he added, "You think *that's* funny?"

I glanced at my palm. The trinket was there, splayed out and warm against my skin. The magic was still present, and it should've worked to convince the cop that I was a fed, unless...

The trinket I carried wasn't especially powerful. It would work only on someone unbound. Mystics with almost any talent would be able to see right through it.

"You're bound..." I whispered.

Those beautiful hazel eyes widened for a moment before narrowing again. "*What* did you say?"

I pocketed the trinket and got down on the ground. I could've easily lied to a regular cop, but I had no chance with one who was a mystic. "It's not how it looks," I said, laying my cheek on the floor and lacing my fingers together over the back of my head. "They were dead when I got here."

Hours later, I sat handcuffed to a metal loop in an interrogation room, wondering how the hell I'd ended up here.

For most of my life, I'd put all of my focus into one objective: Find the mystic who'd bound me and kill her. That's it. Simple enough. Just that.

But for all of my life, that'd proved ridiculously hard. The woman was a ghost. It's like one of the world's most powerful mystics wasn't known within any circle of influence. How she'd gotten so powerful and yet had managed to fly so low under the radar was beyond me, but no one I'd ever questioned or interviewed had heard of her or recognized my description—except for one person.

A beautiful Nigerian mystic named Ndidi, who'd once been quite kind to me, had suggested that, fifty years earlier, during a long summer tryst with Elric Ostergaard, he'd once told her a story about an old mystic hag dressed in rags that he'd come across in Hungary. He told her the old woman was noteworthy because she was so incredibly talented, and yet, he'd never heard of her.

Elric had insulted the hag, and she'd given him a good wallop when she cast a bundle of essence at him. Things had escalated to traded punches of energy between them until the pair had come to an exhausted stalemate. It was at that moment that the hag had confessed to him that they both shared an interest in eliminating a mutual rival—a mystic who'd been attempting to control an area along the Romanian boarder. She suggested they form an alliance and Elric had agreed, although he was quite suspicious of the crone.

The next day a great battle had taken place, and the pair's mutual rival was soundly defeated. Afterward Elric sought to celebrate with the old woman, but when he went in search of her, he discovered that she'd simply walked back into the shadows without so much as a goodbye.

Elric had then remarked to Ndidi about the oddity of someone so powerful and yet so obscure, and he'd further hinted that the hag was one mystic he'd never forget, and the only one he might legitimately fear.

As I'd listened to Ndidi, I'd known immediately that Elric had encountered the very mage who'd cursed me, and that had set a whole new plan into action.

The plan would no doubt be challenging, but there was an orderliness to it and even a simplicity.

Step one: Gain the attention of Elric Ostergaard.

Step two: Win an interview.

Step three: Land the job.

Step four: Work off five years of contracted service.

Step six: Have Elric fulfill the contract by telling me who and where to find the hag.

Step seven: Find the hag, exact my revenge, and be free of the curse that bound me.

In all the planning and time that'd gone into steps one and two, I never thought I'd get so hung up on step three. I'd figured I'd either bomb the interview and die, or get the job and start working off my time.

This whole "bring me the egg and we'll see about a job" thing was something I'd only loosely strategized for, and all this additional stuff with Grigori's murder was further turning something complicated into a giant fucking mess.

Shaking my head ruefully, I considered that I've been in tricky spots before, but I don't know that I've ever been in a situation where I had four days to produce a mythical magical trinket or my life was forfeit, and I'd likely have to spend what was left of those days in jail watching the clock tick down because I'd been caught at the scene of a gruesome murder by perhaps the *only* mystic ever to enlist in the police academy.

And in the hours and hours of sitting here and wasting even more time that I didn't have, I hadn't yet been formally charged. Or interviewed. Or offered a phone call. Or a bathroom break. I'd simply been stripped of my leather jacket, parked in this interrogation room, handcuffed to the table by the hazel-eyed detective, and told to sit tight.

The charge of murder was only a matter of time, though. And I doubted I'd get any shot at bail—not once they correctly identified me, which was probably happening as I sat. If they'd just let me make a call, I could alert Dex and have him figure out a plan. Maybe he could spring me from the city lockup and grant me a few days on the run while I searched for the egg. But where could I even begin to search for it? Grigori's house had been a bust, and the mystic's killer had likely stolen it after he or she had done the deed.

I was coming to the realization that I had no play, no plan, and no chance.

It was enough to bum a girl out.

Just when I felt myself starting to give in to my own personal pity party, the door to the interrogation room opened, and in walked the star of the show: my gorgeous buddy from Grigori's house. He slapped my jacket on the side of the table and a folder down next to it, lifted the back of the chair opposite mine, and twirled it around to straddle it. He then took his time considering me with a steely, determined expression.

I returned the favor and once again admired his face, features, and especially his physique. He'd taken off his black blazer and now wore a charcoal gray V-neck sweater, which clung tightly to his well-muscled arms and broad shoulders. By the looks of things, he worked out perhaps almost as much as I did.

I appreciate that in a person.

"Detective," I said with a hint of mirth. I'd never heard of a mystic passing himself off as a cop before. Most of us figure out ways to make far better livings.

He lifted his chin in slight challenge. "Esmé Bellerose." My full name slipped off his tongue like a piece of milk chocolate—smooth and seductive. I liked it, but that twinge—that hint of something sexual taking place between us—wasn't happening for me.

Oddly, I was a little disappointed.

Shrugging my shoulders, I said, "I think it's hardly fair that you know my name when I still don't know yours."

"Kincaid," he said simply.

"Kincaid…" I prompted, waiting for him to tell me his full name.

My question sparked an amused expression. "That's it," he said. "Just Kincaid."

"Really?"

"Yep."

"It suits you."

Kincaid placed a hand on the folder he'd brought with him and flipped it open. Inside was a mug shot taken of yours truly more than twelve years before from the town of Nanterre, France, where I'd been caught by local authorities with some stolen merchandise on my person. Of course, I'd stolen the objects from a local mystic who'd been practically begging to have his house robbed, but I was able to convince the authorities that I'd come across the items innocently enough—by way of a stranger selling trinkets in the park. The charges were dismissed, and I was encouraged to leave town quickly, which I did.

I had to give some props to Kincaid for discovering the mug shot. As I said, it was more than a decade old and from a foreign law enforcement agency, no less.

He held the photo up for me. "Nice profile."

I smiled. "It's my good side."

"You're a thief."

"And you're a liar."

I wondered what he had to gain by passing himself off as an unbound rather than the mystic he so clearly was.

Kincaid narrowed his eyes. "Aren't we all?"

I offered him that one-shoulder shrug again. "I'm not."

"Really, Agent McMahon?"

"That wasn't so much a lie as a fib."

"Ah," he said, leaning back in his chair. "And, what's the next fib, Esmé?"

I shook my head and raised my palms up to him, the metal of the handcuffs clanking against the table. "Ask me anything, and I'll tell you the absolute truth."

"Did you kill those people?"

I stared levelly at him. "No."

"Did you have anything to do with their murders?"

"No."

He tapped his index finger on the table, considering me. Even without saying so, I could tell that he believed me. "Why were you in that house?"

"I was looking for something."

"What?"

"Something that, by rights, didn't belong to the Russian. Something he swindled away from someone else."

"Who?"

I sighed. There was no point to this conversation. We'd sit here for hours and hours going round and round. Kincaid would ask me a pointed question, I'd deflect and give him a nonsubstantive answer, he would press, I would deflect and on and on until it ate up hours of time and energy, and, while I do enjoy flirting, I just wasn't that into him.

So I said, "It doesn't matter. Now how about you formally charge me so I can call my attorney and you can book me into your city lockup before dawn."

Kincaid worked his jaw from side to side. I'd given the magic word, as good as any spell to a mystic working in a mortal's world: "attorney." He couldn't ask me even one more question, and he knew it. The interview was over.

And yet he continued to sit there and stare at me as if he knew me but couldn't quite place from where we might've encountered each other. I could've saved him the time; I would've remembered a man who looked like Kincaid. I suspect nearly any woman would. And a fair share of men.

"I'm not going to charge you," he said, closing the file and moving it to the side.

That took me by surprise, but I didn't want to react or respond until he showed his hand. He had something up his sleeve. I could tell. "Okay," I said after a long period of silence. "Then I'm free to go?"

"Nope."

"Shocker."

"I'm not going to charge you with murder, Esmé. Those four people were dead long before you showed up. At least forty-eight hours according to the ME, but that doesn't mean that you didn't have something to do with their murders."

I shook my head. "I had nothing to do with it. Like I said, I was there on a fact-finding mission."

"Right," he said, obviously not taking me at my word. "You were there looking for something that belonged to someone else."

"Again, Detective, I don't think I should speak until I've consulted *my lawyer.*"

Kincaid lifted up my jacket and reached into the pocket like he knew what he was looking for. I stiffened when he pulled out my monocle. Next, he retrieved the patch of scrap metal I'd tried to pass off as the FBI badge. "You know what I find curious?" he asked.

I didn't answer. Instead, I worked hard to keep my expression flat and unaffected, even while my heart hammered away.

"I think it's curious that you tried to convince me that this," he said, wiggling the scrap of metal, "was a badge. I told the story to my commander and showed it to him, and do you know what he said?"

I held very still and gave no answer.

"He said he was pretty impressed by the fake badge. He said he'd never seen a copy that good before, and then he held it in his hand and inspected it up close. I thought he was pulling my leg until he gave it back to me and asked if I was going to notify the feds about you, because they'd definitely want to know about a badge floating around out there that looked so much like the real deal."

I met Kincaid's gaze. Certainly, he'd known when he handcuffed me in Grigori's home that I was a mystic, right? But I could tell that he hadn't. That as he was telling me the story, he'd been shocked by the fact that the bit of scrap metal had had that kind of effect on someone else. And I realized too that he didn't even understand that when he was telling his commander about me and my magical piece of scrap metal, he'd inadvertently pushed his own essence into the trinket, which was why the other man had fully believed the scrap was a badge.

Only a mystic could harness a trinket's power. And this man didn't seem to fully grasp either what I was or what he was. And *that*...was stunning.

Kincaid picked up my monocle and looked through it. "What does this do?" he asked.

I said nothing, but I could feel myself about to do something desperate. Like slap the shit out of him. But then I realized that unless he looked down at the scrap metal, there was nothing to see through the monocle. So I sat there silently.

Kincaid waited for me to respond, and when I didn't, he set down the monocle, pulled the file with my mug shot close again and took out the photo. "You know what else is weird?" he said. "You don't look a day over thirty, and yet this was taken over a decade ago, when you didn't look a day over thirty."

My gaze slid to the mug shot, then back up to meet his. "You know what I am, right?"

He shook his head. "No," he said. "I know what Grigori was, but you're something of a mystery."

My brow furrowed. If he'd known that Grigori was a mystic, why was he surprised to discover someone like me?

Kincaid glanced at the two-way mirror across the room. "No one's watching us, Esmé," he said. "It's just you and me."

I arched an eyebrow. I didn't believe him.

The corner of his mouth quirked. "Yeah," he said. "I'd think I was full of shit too, but it's the truth. You and I are having a private chat right now."

I glanced up at the camera in the corner of the room. "Right. Private chat. I'll look for it on YouTube."

It was Kincaid's turn to sigh. Getting up from his chair, he reached again into his pocket and pulled out a set of keys. After unlocking my handcuffs, he took me by the elbow and said, "Come with me."

We exited the interrogation room and made our way to the stairs. It was very late by now, and there weren't many cops around. No one seemed to take notice of us.

As we headed down two floors, I thought about pulling out of the detective's grasp and making a run for it, but then what? Would he shoot me in the back? I hadn't been charged, but I knew I was still a suspect in custody, so I thought he might technically be able to shoot me if provoked. Playing along, at least for the moment, seemed like the better option.

We reached the street, and Kincaid motioned me over to a black SUV.

"In," he ordered, after unlocking the doors.

I did as he asked, and he got in on the other side, started the engine and turned up the heat. "Nobody's listening," he said at last. "It's just me and you."

"Okay," I said, not at all assured. "Now what?"

"Now I tell you that you need to cooperate with me."

"I thought I *was* cooperating with you." I was playing coy, but Kincaid had yet to reveal what he was really after, and that was making me increasingly nervous. I didn't have time for this shit.

"No," he said, his voice going soft. "You're not telling me anything. You're ready to call your lawyer and clam up, while whoever did that to my friend goes free."

"Wait, what?" I said. "Your *friend?*"

Kincaid nodded.

I stared at him in shock. "You're trying to tell me that Grigori Rasputin was *your friend?*"

"Yeah."

I studied Kincaid. There was no hint of a lie in either his voice or his expression. In fact, there was now something about him, something sad that tugged at me. "I think I need more information."

Kincaid shook his head and looked out the windshield. "As you've already figured out, I'm bound," he began.

"You're a mystic," I corrected.

Kincaid's expression darkened, as if he didn't like the term, but he acknowledged it by giving a slight nod. "I've never been mentored," he confessed. "Grigori had agreed to become my mentor."

His confession further stunned me. He didn't look like a newbie. He looked like someone who'd been bound for a while. Don't ask me how I can tell; it's a subtle shift, a tingling in the atmosphere. Mystics who've been bound the longest give off a powerful energy. Elric, for example, could silence a room on the top floor of his headquarters just by entering the building. The man sitting next to me in the car gave off more power than any newbie should.

"How long have you been bound?" I asked.

He considered me. It's no secret among our kind that knowing how someone is bound is the ace in the deck to be used against them. The details of our bindings are the ultimate details we all work *very* hard to keep secret, because if someone knows the spell by which you're bound, you can easily become their slave. In some ways, Tic was mine. And I've got a few others. No secret here; I'm always looking to add a few more. Creating a group—and ultimately, a small army—of allies is how we survive against each other. It's how less-powerful mystics live in a world with the likes of Elric, Petra, and the rest of the Seven who make up the most powerful mystics on the planet.

"I've been bound long enough to know not to share any of the details about it with you," Kincaid said.

Okay, so he wasn't a newbie, and he hadn't been mentored, but he'd clearly been made aware of how the game was played.

In truth, I could see why he hadn't been mentored. As a whole, we mystics are a pretty unscrupulous lot; we're careful to avoid the notice of mortals so that we can continue to take advantage of them. A mystic cop, on the other hand, would live and work immersed in their world, and if he truly had a sense of justice—as this guy seemed to—then he'd be a dangerous man to have around. No way would your average mystic sign up to mentor someone like him.

I turned up my palms to show him I'd meant no harm and no foul in the asking, even though we both knew I had. "Sorry," I said. "You were saying that Grigori had agreed to mentor you, and you've clearly been bound for a while, so may I ask: Why now? Why didn't you seek out a mentor earlier?"

Kincaid turned his face away from me to stare out the windshield again. "Let's just say it hasn't been my choice to stay out of the mystic world. I've been kept out. I've tried to find a mentor for decades and couldn't until Grigori agreed to take me under his wing."

That gave me pause. Only someone immensely powerful could command other mystics not to take on a protégé. Like I said, we're all looking to gather underlings who can help us stay alive, and in this town, the only two mystics who could've given that kind of directive were Elric and Petra. I couldn't imagine anyone crossing either of them if they'd been the ones to issue the order. It'd be a death sentence.

And maybe it was.

"Your kind—" Kincaid continued.

"*Our* kind," I corrected.

He rolled his eyes. "That's one I won't give you, Esmé. I'm not a thief or a power-hungry mystic, but I am sick and tired of watching the likes of Elric and Petra use their powers against the people in this town for their own personal gain. The more powerful they get, the more mystics come here to ride their coattails, and they use whatever trinkets they've collected to swindle, steal, manipulate, and corrupt the regular citizens of this city that I call home. Somebody needs to stand up against that. And I can't do it if I'm continually kept on the outside."

Goosebumps erupted along my arms. Kincaid didn't understand how dangerous his little speech was. Talk like that was sure to get him killed. Hell, *I* could be killed for simply listening to it.

"So, you've got a death wish," I said.

He adopted a crooked smile. "Maybe. Or maybe I'm the kind of newly mentored plebian that nobody'll even notice until I cut off the head the snake."

"You'll never get close enough to do that," I warned. I held no real allegiance to Elric. He was a means to an end for me, but Kincaid was dangerously naive to assume he even had a chance against the likes of Elric or Petra.

"We'll see," he insisted.

I rolled my eyes. I couldn't help it. This was a stupid conversation that was going to lead to somebody being made into dragon kibble.

Probably me.

Definitely Kincaid.

"Detective, how much of a real threat to Elric and Petra could you be?" I scoffed. "You have unharnessed power that you have no idea how to use. You also appear to have been totally unsuccessful in teaching yourself how to use it for all of the time since you've been bound. Other than knowing the two biggest names in the mystic world, I'm guessing you know next to nothing, and now, you don't even have anyone willing to mentor you."

Kincaid turned his head slowly back to me, and that crooked smile widened. "Don't I?"

He had to be kidding. "And here I was willing to believe you didn't have a sense of humor."

"Do you feel like laughing?"

"Nope. And something I feel even *less* like doing is mentoring you, Detective Kincaid-just-Kincaid." There was no way in hell I was going to even consider mentoring a mystic cop. It'd be the end. Of my career. Of my life. You pick, because you'd be right both ways.

"Well then, I guess today really ain't your day, Esmé, because you either mentor me and help me solve Grigori's murder or—"

"Whoa, whoa, whoa! *Nobody* said *anything* about helping you solve a murder."

Kincaid tapped his chin. "Didn't I mention that just now?"

I shook my head in disbelief. This guy wasn't just arrogant; he was fucking crazy. "I am so outta here," I said, reaching for the door. Before I could even pull on the handle, I felt something metallic slap across my left wrist and then the sound of a sharp *click*.

I didn't even need to look over my shoulder to know that Kincaid had just put the cuffs on me.

Again.

The bastard.

"Esmé Bellerose, you are under arrest for the murders of Grigori Rasputin, his girlfriend, Rachel McQueen, and Sara and Rob Murphy," said bastard proclaimed.

I turned my head to glare at him and yanked hard on the cuff, but Kincaid held tight.

"You're an asshole!" I spat.

"The choice is yours," he said calmly, reaching forward with his free hand to palm my left hand. As he grasped it, I felt our energies intertwine. "Mystic to mystic, you can either agree to mentor me and help solve this case, or I can book you on four counts of murder and two counts of B&E. I can also haul both Petra and Elric down here to interview them about why one of their employees was found at the scene of a murder with sticky connections leading back to them. I'm not sure which one you work for, but I know you're employed by one of them."

My breath caught. Was he *serious?!* Hauling either of those two downtown for questioning would definitely end in disaster. It wasn't just me who'd be fed to the dragons; it'd be the whole city block.

Looking into Kincaid's eyes, however, I could see that he was, in fact, serious. No fucking wonder he'd been left completely out of the mystic loop. It went beyond all logic that Grigori had even considered mentoring someone so obviously nutso. "You. Are. So. *Stupid!*" I yelled. "You don't know *anything* about what you're getting yourself into!"

"True," he said. "Which is why I need you."

I shook my head; no way was I going to help him. No. Way. And if he forced me to agree to help him, then I'd lie just to get out of the cuffs and disappear. If I didn't want to be found, no way was Kincaid going to find me.

But the detective seemed to read my mind because he squinted at me slightly before withdrawing my monocle. Holding it delicately between his thumb and index finger, he lifted it to eye level and asked, "What's the code among thieves like you, Esmé? Finders keepers?"

My blood boiled. I'd as soon kill him as allow him to keep that trinket, but something told me that getting rid of the stubborn lawman was going to be a whole lotta effort and a whole lotta time which, at present, I didn't have. Even if I managed to disappear from Kincaid and Elric, without the monocle, I'd be dead in the water. No way could I return to thieving without it, and I doubted highly that I'd ever be able to find Grigori's egg without it too. Plus, with the monocle out of my control, it would always represent a very real threat to Ember, and I simply couldn't have that.

So I sat back in the seat and turned my head away from the detective for a minute. I needed to think of a way out of this mess. But I couldn't come up with a single angle to try to get him to see reason. Well, other than the truth. "Listen," I said. "You don't get it, okay? If someone in my position were to agree to mentor someone like you in your position, it'd get me killed. My boss wouldn't stand for it, and by that, I mean, he'd kill me without a moment's hesitation."

Kincaid rolled his eyes. He wasn't buying it. "I'm guessing by your use of pronoun that Elric is your boss."

Shit. I'd said that without thinking. Still, I didn't confirm or deny it. "I'm serious, Kincaid."

"Me too. And when I look at you, this leggy, green-eyed beauty, who looks like she just walked off a photo shoot for Victoria's Secret, I gotta believe that Elric Ostergaard—who's never seen in this town without a solid ten on his arm—isn't about to feed *you* to the dragons no matter who your friends are. Of course, if you'd hinted that you worked for Petra, then maybe I could've believed you."

My jaw dropped. He was so clueless it was shocking. "You have no idea what Elric's capable of," I said.

"And you have no idea what *I'm* capable of, Esmé."

I turned my head away again because I couldn't look at him and resist the urge to punch him in the face, and that wasn't likely to get the cuffs off no matter how hard I hit him. Plus, he still had my monocle. And, he was also still holding tight to my hand, which meant that he obviously knew enough about mystics to understand that by doing so, he was intertwining our energies, which bound me to him until he let go.

As long as he palmed my fist and intertwined our energies, I couldn't say I'd mentor Kincaid and then not do it. The joining of our energies would activate the compulsive part of my personality, which would demand that I fulfill the obligation, and I'd be trapped by my own will.

The flipside was to turn his offer down, get tossed into jail, and brace myself for the wrath of either Elric or Petra. Briefly I wondered who'd be worse, but then I considered that I might never live long enough to even know which one ultimately dealt with pesky, little me.

Sure, Kincaid wouldn't live out the day either, but that was little compensation given that I was probably going to die first. "Son of a bitch!" I hissed. I was totally backed into a corner. My only play was to agree. I hate being forced into anything, but this... this was bullshit.

And then I had another thought. One that perhaps my own irritation hadn't initially allowed me to consider. If I assisted Kincaid on his investigation into the murders of Grigori and his dinner guests, I might be able to use him to help me locate the egg. If the egg still existed, then I was certain the mystic who'd killed the members of Grigori's dinner party had been after it, and he or she had stolen it upon exiting the premises. My only shot at locating it now was to perhaps stick close to Kincaid as we worked through the case and figured out who now had the egg and how I could steal it from them.

The other plus was that I'd also have my freedom back, which would allow me the opportunity to keep up the pretense that I was still being a model employee for SPL. If word got back to Elric that I'd been picked up by the police, he might not think I was worth the extra time to locate the egg and dispense with me sooner rather than later.

Turning back to Kincaid I said, "I'll agree to mentor you and help with your investigation on three conditions."

A triumphant look sparked a gleam in Kincaid's eyes. "And they are?"

"One, you give me back my monocle and my scrap of metal and you never, *ever* mention them to anyone else. Two, you also don't mention that I'm mentoring you. That'll be done in total secrecy. You don't tell your wife, your family, friends, or *anyone* else about it."

"Done," he said. "What's the third condition?"

"You look the other way when I continue on with my career."

"You mean, as a thief."

"Yes."

"You ever steal from mortals?"

"I do," I said bluntly. It was rare, but on occasion I'd needed to poach some necessity from an unbound.

"Then no deal."

I sighed. I was *really* beginning to dislike this man. "What if I promise not to steal from the unbound?"

"You'd agree to rob only mystics?"

"Yes. Unless it's an absolute emergency, then yes." As far as I knew, Elric didn't poach from mortals, and I knew he looked down on those in his rank and file who did. He'd tolerate it, but only as long as it never brought his organization under the notice of law enforcement.

"Whatever you take from them you'd have to pay back, Esmé," Kincaid insisted.

Sweet Jesus, this idiot was a stickler for details. "Agreed," I said with an exasperated sigh.

"Agreed," he said.

My fist warmed against his palm, and a sensation like liquid silk being wrapped around our hands snaked its way over my skin. The binding spell uniting our energies was already taking place.

"Okay then," I said when my fist began to cool. "Hand over my trinkets, and let's hash out some details."

Chapter Six
Day 1

I got back to the warehouse just before 11 pm. Dex met me at the door, his face a mask of concern. "Ezzy," he said in his most I'm-about-to-lecture-you voice. "Luv, they make these very handy instruments these days called *cellular phones*. Perhaps you've heard of them?"

I kept my expression neutral. Experience had taught me that it was easier if I simply allowed Dex to vent, then apologized to him and got on with my life.

My partner held up his smartphone and wiggled it at me. "They look a bit like this. Seem familiar?"

I sighed. This was going to be a long one, and I had too much on my mind and my plate to deal with Dex's irritation right now.

"I was in jail," I said simply, hoping he'd drop it.

Dex opened his mouth, but no words came out. He seemed thoroughly confused. "How'd *you* get arrested?" he finally said.

"The cop was bound."

Dex appeared even more taken aback. "You were arrested by a *mystic*?"

"I was," I said, breezing past him to the kitchen. I was famished.

"Why on earth would a mystic join the police force?" Dex asked, trailing after me.

After dropping my keys on the counter, I went to the fridge, pulled open the door, and peered inside. "Dunno, Dex. Maybe he was attracted to the low pay, long hours, and criminal element."

Behind me I heard the scrape of a barstool at the counter. Meanwhile, I reached for a plate of grilled chicken and felt Ember press against the backs of my legs.

"A mystic cop," Dex repeated, as if he could hardly believe it. "That's unheard of. Unless of course he's new. Is he new?"

Bringing the chicken to the counter, I stroked Ember's head and said, "I got the distinct impression he's not new, but he is unmentored."

Dex blinked. "He's not new and he's unmentored? How the bloomin' hell does that happen?"

"Would *you* mentor a cop?"

"Never," Dex said. "Wouldn't be able to trust him. He's either using the post to line his pockets, or he'd use his badge to make trouble for us."

I nodded, withholding the worst news for a moment longer. "Still, he's managed to figure out a few things," I said casually. "There're small things he's learned about that only someone bound for a while would have heard. I get the feeling he's been bound for at least a couple of decades, maybe longer. For whatever reason, though, he never aggressively sought out a mentor until now."

Dex cocked his head and eyed me critically. "Until now?"

I offered Ember a piece of chicken. She took it gently from my fingertips and moved away to devour it. "Yeah. He wants me to mentor him."

"Ezzy," Dex said softly. "Why don't you look like you told him to buggar off?"

I sighed again. "Because I agreed to do it."

Dex's jaw dropped, and for several moments he simply stared at me. "What the bloomin' hell did you do that for?"

"Trust me, I had very little choice in the matter."

"How's that?" he demanded.

I took the next twenty minutes to tell Dex everything that'd happened from the time I'd entered Rasputin's house to the conversation with Kincaid in his car.

"Tic," Dex spat when I was finished. "That crooked bastard set you up. And he's been texting me all day wondering where you are."

At the mention of Tic's name, I took a step back and covered my mouth with my hand. "Oh, my God! I forgot to stop the tick-tocks for Tic!"

"Oh, let him twitch," Dex said when I reached for my keys. "The little shit deserves it."

I shook my head. There was no way I was going to let Tic suffer any longer than he already had. By now he'd be a mass of involuntary shudders and twitches. He had to be in agony, and he'd likely been miserable for several hours. I then thought of something else and asked, "Did you retrieve the coin?"

"It didn't come back," he said with a frown.

"Son of a bitch," I growled.

"I bet Tic found it and he's keeping it," Dex said.

I nodded. Of course he had. It'd been right next to hm when I left for Grigori's.

Hurrying to our trinket room off the kitchen, I said, "I'm just gonna grab another trinket or two and run over to Tic's. Once I free him, I can force him to give up the coin."

Dex pointed a finger gun at me. "Good plan."

Grabbing two of my favorite trinkets, I said, "Did he text you where he is, Dex?"

"His last text was a bit knackered. I think he's at his girlfriend's place."

I rolled my eyes. I hated Tic's on again/off again girlfriend. "Thanks for holding down the fort," I said to Dex, leaning in to give him a kiss on the cheek. "I'll be back soon."

Tic was a little hard to hunt down, his girlfriend lived in a section of town where all the apartment buildings looked the same. Still, I finally managed to locate the right apartment and knocked urgently on her front door.

"Holy shit!" she yelled when she opened it and saw me on her welcome mat. "Where the fuck have you been?!"

"Bree," I said calmly. "I take it he's here?"

She looked mad enough to kill me, and if she thought she could've taken me on, we both knew she would've. "In the bedroom," she said through clenched teeth.

I waited for her to back up into the apartment before I crossed her threshold. It was a risky maneuver because I wasn't positive that Tic was actually there, and entering another mystic's domain—even a lower-level one like Bree—was a dangerous endeavor on the best of days.

Any mystic with a place of residence has the advantage of time to erect whatever traps they can think up, and while Bree was considerably less clever and less powerful than most, and definitely less skilled than me, she still wasn't a person to underestimate. Her petty jealousies made her someone to handle warily.

I was also at a disadvantage because I'd have to keep my monocle safely tucked away in my pocket. No one else could know that I had the little trinket. Not even someone as inconsequential to me as Bree. Motioning to her after crossing the threshold, I said, "After you, please."

She rolled her eyes and shut the door, then led the way through the kitchen, past the living room, and into the hallway leading to the bedroom.

I could hear the rattle of something as we approached, and I braced myself for the hard truth of what I was about to see.

Tic was lying on the king-size bed, his body splayed, his clothes soaked with sweat, and his face a contorted mask of agony.

Every inch of him was in motion—shuddering, twitching, trembling, convulsing. His eyes roved the ceiling as if his mind were desperate to find a way out of his tortured body. The sight gave me a nanosecond's pause before I moved past Bree to Tic's ear and bent low.

I was about to whisper the counterspell when I noticed that Bree had come up behind me, and she too was bent low. I stood up quickly and backed away from Tic, taking up a defensive stance as I did so. "Step away, Bree," I said firmly.

She glared hard at me. "Help him!"

I pointed to the door. "Leave." No damned way was I revealing any part of Tic's spell to her. Even knowing the counterspell was a dangerous prospect for someone like Bree. Certainly, she could release Tic from the tremors if a day came when I set the spell in motion again, but she could also kidnap and imprison him in order to gain other information from him while he was twitching and vulnerable. And low-level Bree was someone fully capable of double-crossing her lover. She'd done it several times before, in fact.

Bree stood her ground and crossed her arms. She wasn't leaving, and I couldn't help Tic with her in the room. It occurred to me that the couple might've currently been in the midst of a more "off again" arrangement than "on."

This put me in a dilemma, because Bree was clearly calling my bluff. I had a lot to lose by walking away. It wouldn't be long before Tic's mind succumbed to the pressures of the torture currently wracking his body.

He seemed to understand this too, because his eyes shifted from me to Bree, and in between convulsions, his lip snarled. With significant effort he managed to gurgle out the word, "G-g-g-g-go!"

Bree puffed out an annoyed bit of air before turning on her heel and stomping out of the bedroom. Reaching into my pocket, I took out a single die. It was yellow with age, and much of the black in the divots had long been rubbed clean. I'd often wondered what had happened to its twin, curious to know if it had also been infused with a magical energy, but the mystic I lifted it from was hardly going to tell me, especially since I was the thief who had seduced him and stolen his riches.

Careful to hide the die in my palm and out of sight from Tic, I gave it a rub and pushed a bit of essence into it. There was a tiny charge of heat that sprouted from the die, which made its way up from my fingertips to the nape of my neck, then looped around to cover my lips. I bent my head to Tic's ear, brushing my lips against his skin, confident that anything I said now would be for his ears only. As I opened my mouth to speak the counterspell, however, I felt a dramatic shift in the energy of the room.

It was as if the hum of a thousand volts of electricity had just come alive all around us. Every hair on my body stood up on end, and goosebumps lined my arms. I lifted my face away from Tic's ear to stare down at him. His eyes were impossibly wide. He'd felt it too.

And he seemed terrified.

I opened my mouth to ask him, "What the f—?"

BOOM!

The sound and force of the explosion was like nothing I'd ever experienced. I was launched forward with such frightening speed, I barely got my arms up in time to cushion the violent collision with Bree's headboard. What followed was a pummeling of debris that rained at me sideways and down. I crumpled to the bed, my whole body vibrating with pain, and my back felt the sting of several dozen cuts from splintered material and broken glass.

There was also a terrible ringing in my ears, which was so loud that it drowned out every other sound. My head throbbed in beat to the ringing, and my eyes were pinched shut from the shock and pain of the blast.

And then something jerked beside me, and I opened one eye. Tic was leaning against me, his body in a ball, but sticking out of his chest, just under his right collarbone, was a splinter of wood that was frightfully thick. His face was more than a mask of pain; it was chaotically contorted—the epitome of agony. He twitched and seized, and the splinter in his chest shivered with each tremble.

I realized as I watched him pant for air that I wasn't. Breathing, that is. There was a convulsion as my lungs tried to collect oxygen, but nothing moved past my open mouth. The wind had been knocked right out of me, and my diaphragm was seizing—that much I knew from experience, but it did little to ease the ripple of panic that was starting to overtake my brain.

Tic jerked again, and my other eye opened to see him lock onto my gaze, the plea reflected in the irises. He needed me to free him from the clutches of the curse, but without air, I could do little to help him.

Closing both lids again, I fought back against the panic and did my best to ignore the insanely loud ringing in my ears. I called up the image of my father holding a small, fragile puppy. "I want to call her Ember," I'd told him. And he'd smiled with such love and wonder in his eyes.

It was the sweetest, clearest, most treasured memory I had. One of the very last one's I'd had with him before he was murdered. The memory calmed me like nothing else, and after pulling it forward into my mind, only a moment or two passed before I felt my diaphragm release the seizure, and I was able to suck in a ragged breath. I took two more before I was able to stutter, "*T-t-tick-tock, tick-t-t-tock,... stop... the... c-c-clock at... all Tic's tocks!*"

When I opened my eyes again his body had stopped jerking and his face was less contorted, but he was quite obviously still in agony. I saw him try to speak, but if he made any sound, I couldn't hear past the ringing, which had actually intensified since I'd started sucking oxygen again. The pain in my head was nauseating, and the world began to spin underneath my helpless form.

I tried to lock my gaze on Tic again, hoping that would stop the spins, but it did little to help. And then I saw Tic lift up his head slightly to look toward the doorway as if he had seen a movement or heard a noise.

I tried to lift my own head, but the world took another dizzying turn and I had to shut my eyes against it. Feebly I reached both hands forward and placed them flat against the mattress, swallowing back the bile threatening to escape my throat.

A cold sweat broke out across my brow, and I knew I was starting to lose consciousness. *No, no, no!* my mind yelled. I had to stay alert; Tic appeared to be gravely wounded, and if he didn't get help soon, I thought he might die.

But the dizziness was overwhelming, and that ringing sound in my ears was rattling my brain against the inside of my skull. I couldn't think beyond it, the dizziness overpowering every one of my senses. Try as I might, I also couldn't stop it, make it lessen, or battle against it. I began to sink into an abyss. It washed over me like an inky pond. I was drowning in it, and I couldn't get out.

And then, everything faded to black.

I have no idea how much time had passed before I regained consciousness. I remember that the ringing in my ears had lessened by several degrees, and the world felt stable underneath me again. For a few seconds, I forgot where I was and what'd happened, and then it all came back to me in a rush and I jolted fully awake, pushing myself up from the mattress, my thoughts only of poor Tic.

But when I opened my eyes, what I saw utterly confused me. Tic had been right next to me, pinned by a splinter of wood and bleeding profusely, but what I saw next to me wasn't him. And I knew that by the fact that the torso was naked, but that's all there was to it, just a woman's naked torso. No head. No legs. And much of her left arm was gone.

But the right arm held a tattoo of a two-headed serpent.

"Holy shit!" I swore, scrambling away from what was left of Bree. I scrambled a little too hard though, and fell off the bed onto a pile of pillows. And thank God for that, because the last thing I needed was another hard surface to crash onto.

Especially given how dizzy I still was. Placing a hand to my head, I sat there for the count of five before struggling to my feet and taking in my surroundings.

The room looked like it'd been hit by a wrecking ball. Twice.

There was debris and clothing and broken furniture everywhere. Somehow the bed had stayed in place and intact, but literally *everything* else in the room had been toppled over, broken, or strewn about the room.

The other thing I noticed? Blood. *Lots* of blood. It was pooled on the bed, splattered on the walls, and had left a trail on the carpet. I leaned against the doorframe to the closet as I took it all in. And then I realized that much of my left side was covered in red as well.

But other than the blood on the bed, which could at least partly be attributed to Tic, there was no sign of him.

Pushing away from the closet door, I took a few staggering steps and fell when my foot got tangled in the debris littering the floor. My hearing was slowly returning by now, and faintly I could just make out the sound of sirens.

"Dammit!" I snarled, pushing to my feet again. The *last* thing I needed was to be caught up in several more wasted hours with the police. Willing myself to a somewhat erect posture again, I made my way more carefully out of the bedroom, down the hall toward the living room. But about five feet into the hallway, I stopped. Not because I wanted to, but because I *had* to.

In front of me was a giant hole. The entirety of Bree's living room and kitchen were now just open space. As was the apartment below hers. And the one above. I didn't know if anyone had been in the other two apartments when the explosion occurred, and I really couldn't wait around to find out. Tic was gone, and I had no idea where he was or how he'd gotten out of the building. In fact, at present, I had no idea how *I'd* be getting out of the building.

And getting out was a major concern, because those sirens were closing in...fast.

Looking around the massive hole in the side of the building, I decided that the only way out was down, and that meant picking my way across the edge of what was left of the floor and hoping to find a soft spot to land when I jumped.

There wasn't much below where I stood that looked like it might soften the blow, but then I noticed a couch cushion lying within jumping distance from the far left of the edge of the hallway. Wasting no more time, I went for it, leaping the ten feet down and landing on the cushion with more ease than I would've expected. Picking my way across the rest of the destroyed room, I made my way out to the street, where a crowd was already starting to gather.

"Ohmigod!" yelled a woman near me. "Were you *in* there?"

I shook my head, pulled up the collar on my jacket, and moved away from her. A wave of dizziness caught me off guard, though, and I staggered a little as I went.

"Honey!" she called to me. "Don't go! You're hurt!" She pointed to my bloody clothes for emphasis. "You're probably in shock, but you need to wait here for the paramedics." She then reached for me, her face a mask of concern.

"I'm fine," I said, twisting away. But she reached again and latched onto me. In desperation I said, "Listen, I think there's another bomb in there. We need to get away from this building!"

She let go of me instantly. "Ohmigod!" she cried again, before looking over her shoulder and then breaking into a run. "*There's another bomb!*" she screamed as she ran. "Everybody! Get clear!"

The crowd of fifteen or so took off like a herd of lemmings, dashing forward, and swallowing me up in their wake. I started to trot with them for about fifteen or twenty meters before I reached my car, stopped, and got in.

In front of me were the strobe lights of a dozen emergency vehicles quickly approaching, and I waited until they'd passed by my car before starting the engine and pulling away from the curb, purposely keeping the headlights on the car off until I was well down the street.

Rounding the first corner I came to, I pulled over and shrugged out of the white T-shirt I wore under my black leather jacket. The shirt was wet and sticky with blood, but I managed to find a clean corner of it and used the fabric with a little water from a bottle I had in the car to wash the worst of the blood off my face and hands. Throwing the T-shirt in the back seat, I zipped up my jacket and then pulled away from the curb again, zigzagging a few blocks over from the scene until I got to the highway and made my way quickly back to the warehouse, wondering the whole time what the fuck I'd gotten myself into now.

Chapter Seven
Day 2

"What the fuck did you get yourself into now?" Dex barked the second he laid eyes on me.

His reaction suggested I probably didn't look my usual glamorous self.

"Hey," I said, moving past him into the kitchen. I was thirsty as hell. And not for water.

Ember was at my side from the moment I entered the warehouse. She leaned against me as I reached for a glass tumbler and the bottle of twelve-year-old Lagavulin single-malt scotch we keep on hand for things such as entertaining important guests, big celebrations, and really, really, *really* bad days—like today.

And yesterday.

And probably tomorrow.

Twisting off the cap, I poured a very generous two fingers into the tumbler and eyed Dex like I double-dog-dared him to protest.

His initial alarm transformed to surrender. Palms up, he said, "Cheers, mate."

I tilted the glass toward him in silent toast and downed the contents. The aged liquid filled my nose with an aroma of sweet fruit and peppercorn before it glided across my tongue, dancing with notes of citrus and smoke. I closed my eyes for a moment, savoring the taste and feel of the heat the brew incited. Sweet Jesus, I loved the stuff.

"Ez," Dex said softly. "Talk to me."

Opening my eyes with a sigh and thinking that I might need another two fingers to get through this conversation, my gaze lingered on the Lagavulin. I was undecided about tempting my currently fairly clear head into inebriation.

With another sigh, I lifted the cap to the bottle and secured it in place. Two fingers of liquid gold would have to do for tonight.

Moving around the island, I pulled out a chair next to Dex, took a seat, and began my tale. "Tic was at his girlfriend's place. He was in a bad way. Before I could release him, there was an explosion."

"What kind of explosion? Like a bomb? Or a gas leak?"

I shook my head. "I don't think it was either. There was no fire. No smoke. Just a buildup of energy and then... *boom!*"

"From a mystic?" Dex asked.

"Undoubtedly. It obliterated Bree's apartment, and Bree, for that matter."

"What happened to Tic?"

Again, I shook my head. "He had a nasty piece of wood sticking out from under his collarbone the last time I saw him. I was able to release him from the spell right before I passed out."

"Where is he? Is he dead?"

"I have no idea. When I woke up, he was gone, and in his place was what was left of Bree. The bed was soaked with blood; I'm pretty sure it was Tic's. I have no idea if he survived or where he is, but no way did he leave on his own power. And given the state of that apartment, it's hard for me to imagine how somebody could've gotten him out of there in the two or three minutes that I was unconscious."

Dex's face was a mask of alarm. "You're telling me that Marco Sigourney Astoré—Petra's only son—has been mortally wounded and removed from the site of an explosion, and you have no idea if he's dead or alive or where he might be?"

I tucked a lock of hair back behind my ear. My fingers came away tinged in red. I wasn't even sure if it was Tic's blood or mine. "Yes, that's what I'm telling you."

"Did anyone see you there?"

I rubbed my temples as it began to dawn on me how much shit I was in. "Plenty of people."

"Bloody hell, Esmé!" Dex hissed. "We're in the shit now, given who his mother is."

"After the day I've had, Dex, I'd say that's probably the least of my worries."

Dex shook his head, and I knew him well enough to know he was thinking up ideas for an exit strategy. But there weren't any exits for us. At least not for me. It was, I guess, knowing this that made me say, "You should consider heading home."

Dex cocked his head. "What?"

I tried keeping the tremor out of my voice, but I couldn't. "I think it might be best if you packed your gear and got on the first plane back to Oz."

Dex squinted at me, and I could see the anger in his eyes when he replied, "I think you took a bigger hit to the noggin tonight than you might realize if you think I'm going to cut out on you, Ezzy."

I swallowed hard and stared longingly at the bottle of Lagavulin again. "You know I'm right," I insisted.

"I know you're talking like a nong if you think I'll squib out just because you're having yourself one helluva *Moan*day, Esmé Bellerose."

That got me to smile. But it was short-lived. "The odds are getting shorter and shorter that I'll survive this."

Dex crossed his arms and spread his feet wide in a stubborn stance. "Still doesn't make me want to pack my gear and leave you."

I nodded solemnly and laid my head down on the counter. I heard a rustle at my feet and felt Ember's warm weight against my shins. Almost immediately my headache eased. Still, I was exhausted from all the stress of the past two days. "I don't even know how this got so complicated," I admitted. "Someone got to the egg before me, killed Grigori, and I'm left holding the bag for it. Then someone blew Bree and her apartment to kingdom come and likely murdered Tic, and again, I very well could be left holding the bag for it."

"You think they're related?" Dex asked me.

I lifted my head from the counter. Dex had asked the one question that'd been bothering me the whole way back from Bree's apartment. "It's too big of a coincidence, isn't it?"

"Seems like it," he said gravely. "Except that Grigori and his dinner guests were carved up, while Bree's apartment was blown up and Tic was taken from the scene. Different method and different magic usually mean different mystics."

"That's true," I said, considering the point, before adding, "The magic used to blow up Bree's apartment like that was insanely intense. I swear it was on a level of someone like Petra or Elric. Maybe Jacquelyn could've managed it too."

"There're probably three or four others in this town who're as strong as Jacquelyn," Dex pointed out. "There's

Clepsydra, she's definitely as powerful as Jacquelyn and then there's Petra's new lieutenant."

I frowned. "Petra has a new lieutenant?"

"She does. Calls himself 'the Flayer.'" Dex rolled his eyes for effect.

"He sounds nice," I quipped. "Maybe we should invite him over for brunch."

Dex chuckled. "My point is that you don't rise to the level of lieutenant without some mad skills."

"Agreed, but Dex, both of them work for Petra."

"Maybe Mumsy ordered the hit."

I shook my head. Petra was certainly capable of killing her own son without a single regret, but I suspected she liked flaunting him in front of Elric too much to get rid of him. Still, I had to at least consider the possibility that Mommy Dearest was behind the explosion. "If Petra wanted to make it look like Tic was murdered, she'd make damn sure it looked like Elric had done it."

"Or someone who worked for him," Dex said, pointing at me.

I sighed and shook my head again. It didn't make sense for the hit to come from her. "If Petra even knows who I am, *and* knows that I'm working for Elric, then she'd also know that I'm on probation. Killing Tic would be something Elric would assign to one of his own lieutenants, not to a lowly new employee like me, and for sure Petra would've thought that through."

"True," Dex said. "But I still say two mystics violently murdered and another one abducted within a forty-eight-hour period is too big of a coincidence to ignore."

"I agree, but right now I can't focus on Tic. If I want to live past Saturday night, I have to keep my head in the game and focus on the prize."

"The egg," he said.

"Yes. And that's where this new association with Kincaid might help us."

Dex nodded, he could see the advantage now too. "All right, so where do we start?"

I rubbed my temples and noted that I no longer had a headache. Ember's presence against my legs was healing me quickly, thank God. "Well," I said. "The place to start is probably by seeing what Grigori has to say."

"Luv," Dex said with a side grin. "He's dead. He won't be able to tell you anything."

"Oh, really? I bet you're wrong."

"How's that?"

"He's no doubt been taken to the morgue, right?"

"Likely," Dex agreed.

"And the mortals will be conducting an autopsy…"

"Yeah, so?"

"So, as far as we know, the egg only brings a person back to life and heals what's either killed or is killing them. But it doesn't completely erase the scars of those injuries, right?"

Dex wiped his face with his hand impatiently. "I'm still not following you."

"We know that Rasputin used the egg twice for Alexi, and then maybe three more times to recover from the poisoning, stabbing, and bludgeoning done to him by the tsar's cousin, before they ripped off his coat where he'd hidden the egg, shot him and tossed his body into the river, which takes the egg's uses down to seven. Any additionally healed life-threatening injuries the ME finds would tell us about the remaining power of the egg."

"And his first autopsy takes the egg down to six," Dex said with a shudder.

I made a face, remembering that story. While undergoing an autopsy, Grigori's coat, hiding the egg, had been recovered from the bridge where his dead body had been tossed into the Neva River. The coat was brought to the morgue and set on a table next to the mystic, and it was that very fortunate act that had brought him back to life. Supposedly Grigori had come back to life while the coroner was weighing his liver, and the poor doctor had been so undone by the incident that he'd spent the rest of his life in a sanitarium.

"Right. Which means the egg could be down to six uses or less."

"He'll be the only man in history to have two autopsies," Dex said. "But I see where you're going with this. Count the scars, count the number of lives the egg has left to save."

"Exactly. And even if, at some subsequent point in the past hundred years, Grigori used the egg to thwart off another poisoning, or some illness like pneumonia, we probably won't be able to see that in the report, but anything else should have left a physical trace, and if the physically mortal wounds add up to ten or eleven, then we should consider that the egg might be useless. It could already be dust."

Dex's expression was grave. "That would be very bad news for us."

"It'd be very bad news for me, my friend. You would continue to draw breath. You'd just need to do it far away from here."

Dex shook his head. "Don't know what I have to do to convince you that life without you isn't much of a life, luv."

That broke my heart a little, and I could feel myself getting choked up, so I swallowed hard and waited until I could speak without my voice cracking. "It's what we agreed to, D."

"Yeah, I know, and I'd take Ember and head home to Oz, but it still wouldn't be much of a life."

I reached out and laid my hand on top of his. "We've had some fun, haven't we?"

He grinned, but there was so much sadness in his eyes. "No one I'd rather be thieving and scheming with than you, Ezzy."

"Ditto."

"Right," Dex said, giving my hand a squeeze. "Tonight, let's think positive and assume the egg's got some offerings left to give, and that it's out there somewhere. You'll be getting the autopsy report from Kincaid, I assume?"

"Yes. We're going to meet tomorrow—" I turned to look at the clock on the stove. "Correction, *today*, and swap information to develop some leads."

"Do we need to wait until then?" Dex asked. "Seems to me like a murder investigation's a bit like what we do when we select a new target. We dig into their life, find out as much as we can about them, and use it to our advantage."

I nodded. "Exactly what I was thinking. Obviously we're not going to be following Grigori around to study his habits, but Tic already did some of that heavy lifting for us." I told Dex about how the Russian used to play cards and have a cup of tea at the Empress Lounge. "Maybe you can use those Aussie good looks and all that beefcake at the Empress Lounge to gain us some intel on who Grigori might've taken tea with. Or who he played cards with."

Dex grinned back and flexed one arm. "I'll wear my tightest T-shirt," he promised.

I laughed and shook my head. "Those poor waitresses. Oh, but you should wear that black T with the yellow script on it." I had to make sure Dex didn't go for one of the neon yellow shirts he loved to wear. The color, which was way too loud for the Empress, also washed him out and made him look a little less charming.

"Right," he said, winking at me. He knew. "Maybe while I'm in the city I'll put my ear to the ground to see if anyone's heard about what might've happened to Tic."

I pointed at him. "That's a great idea. The explosion was either connected to this whole mess with Grigori and we've got someone new to be nervous about, or it was all on Tic and I was just at the wrong place at the wrong time."

Dex jotted himself a note on his phone. "Got it. I'll work that angle while you work the detective."

I sighed. "This is one time I really wish we could trade places."

Dex smiled slyly. "He's a charmer, is he?"

"He might be able to charm his way out of brown paper bag, but I suspect he'd be winded from the effort."

Dex laughed. "Any attraction?" he asked carefully.

"You know I only have eyes for you."

Dex looked skyward and placed his hand over his heart melodramatically. "*If* only."

I sighed. It was a joke we tossed back and forth quite often, but the truth was we both wanted nothing more than for me to feel for Dex what he so obviously felt for me. To spare his feelings, I said, "No attraction for the man whatsoever. He's pretty but not my type."

"As in, he'd be perfect for you."

"Oh, I think he'd bore me to tears, my friend."

I could see my words had a pleasing effect. At least they seemed to mollify Dex's fears that I'd leave him for another man. No chance of that happening, I told myself. With significant effort, I'd learned to somewhat control the worst aspects of my binding curse so that I could focus on getting the job with Elric's organization, but it'd often required me to pack up and leave town when my feelings started to get away from me.

That was a tricky edge to ride, especially now, because I couldn't quit this town. Knowing that made me extra careful to dance lightly where matters of the heart were concerned. All I had to do was avoid too much contact with someone I found myself attracted to. Dex could act as a buffer if need be. Elric was the only man I'd encountered in quite some time who'd even tempted me. I hoped that future contact with him would be relegated to emails and such. He didn't strike me as the kind of man who met regularly with the staff. He had other staff with higher pay grades than mine for that.

"When's the mentoring ceremony?" Dex asked.

All mentoring agreements were done in the form of a ceremony with a simple yet powerful spell. Typically these were done at night, and a lot of them involved a celebration like coitus...not my ceremony, of course—I'd been mentored by a castrated monk—and lovemaking of any kind definitely wouldn't follow the detective's ceremony. The thought of getting naked with Kincaid made me a bit nauseous.

"We'll do the ceremony tomorrow," I said with a wicked smile, "after he selects his gift."

Protégés were required to bring their mentors a gift—a trinket—and the binding spell in the agreement phase of the mentor/protégé arrangement gave the protégé the unique magical ability to seek out and be drawn to the gift that would become most useful to their mentor. In other words, for the first few days before the ceremony, protégés had special sight to see which trinket of any they were presented would be the most valuable to their mentor.

I took a moment to picture Kincaid: nervous and sweaty, meeting some low-life fencer in a dark alley and attempting to choose the trinket least likely to give him a guilt trip but that still served the purpose of being of significant value to me. The image made me want to grin.

"Mentoring can take years, Ezzy," Dex reminded me, pulling me from my thoughts.

I blew out another sigh. "Yeah, I know. Here's hoping Kincaid is a quick study."

Dex grunted an agreement. "We'll have enough on our plate once Elric officially hires you."

I nodded and blinked heavily. I was nearly asleep on my feet, with no adrenaline left to keep me upright and moving. The scotch hadn't helped matters, but I didn't regret it. I'd needed that drink.

"Hey," Dex said.

I forced my eyes to widen. "Yeah?"

"Get upstairs and fetch yourself some Zs. You need it."

I nodded again and got up from the chair at the counter. "Fine, but only a few hours, okay? Wake me at four."

"Of course, luv," he said.

True to his word, Dex got me up at exactly 4 AM. I was curled around Ember, who also startled awake when Dex called up the stairs to me. "I'm up," I called back, but then laid back against the pillow, still feeling exhausted.

A few minutes later, Dex appeared in the doorway wearing his favorite banana-yellow pajama bottoms.

"Coffee's on," he said.

I took a whiff and could just make out the wonderful scent of ground coffee beans percolating. "I'll be right down."

I got out of bed slowly, mindful of the many injuries I'd suffered in the past twenty-four hours alone. But being close to Ember all night had banished every wound, ache, and pain.

Stroking the top of her velvety head before leaving the sleepy pup, I whispered, "I love you," and headed straight to the shower.

After making myself presentable, I met Dex in the kitchen. He'd already preheated my mug and set out the cream. "Cheers, mate," I mimicked from the night before as I took my first sip. The coffee warmed my belly and woke my mind even more than the shower.

I moaned with pleasure. God, I love coffee.

"Have you called Kincaid?" Dex asked me, sipping from his bright yellow smiley-face mug.

"Not yet," I said, setting down my own cup to add more cream. "I'm pretty sure he had a late night too, so I'll give him until six before I call him."

"He could've pulled an all-nighter," Dex said. "With a hot case like Rasputin's, I'll bet he's still at it."

I immediately felt shitty about taking a four-hour nap. Bringing out Kincaid's card from my jacket's pocket, I considered the two numbers before choosing his office line, just in case he had actually gone home for some shuteye and was still asleep. I didn't mind rousing him at this early hour, but I'd taken note of the wedding ring on his left ring finger; no way did I want to wake his wife if I didn't have to.

To my surprise, the line was answered on the first ring. "Detective Kincaid," he said.

"Hello," I began, caught a little off-guard by the quick answer. "It's me. Esmé."

Silence.

I sensed confusion. "Esmé Bellerose," I clarified. Could he know more than one Esmé?

"Hello, Esmé Bellerose," he replied smoothly. "What can Detective Kincaid do for you?"

I felt my brow furrow. Was he serious? Or maybe drunk? "Well," I said, still a bit flustered. "I'd like to get a look at Grigori's autopsy report."

"Would you, now?" he asked, almost playfully.

Why was he being so weird? "Yes."

"And why would you like to look at Grigori's autopsy report?"

Shit. Did I have an answer to that other than "so I can tell how many times he might've died and was brought back to life by this incredibly valuable trinket I'm after"?

I took a steadying breath. "I'm hoping it can reveal something we didn't know before."

"Such as?"

"I won't know that, Detective, until I look at the autopsy report."

"Ah," he said.

That was it. Just, "Ah." I almost asked him why he was being so difficult but thought better of it. Deciding to go a different route and hoping to distance myself a little from what'd happened at Tic's place, I said, "I'm sure you heard about that bomb that went off across town last night."

"I did. Was that your doing?"

"No," I replied testily. God, this guy was seriously pushing my buttons. And, further irritatingly, it was turning me on a little. "Listen, I just wanted to let you know that I may have known one of the victims."

"Do tell."

Ignoring the sarcasm, I said, "He's an acquaintance of mine. Marco Astoré. He has a connection to Grigori."

I heard the creaking of a chair and imagined that I'd just gotten Kincaid's full attention. "What kind of a connection?"

"Marco was the one who told me where to find Grigori."

"How did Marco know anything about Grigori?"

I thought that was an odd question for Kincaid to ask. If it weren't for the distinct trace of smoky hoarseness in his voice, I'd have sworn I was speaking to someone else. "I don't know. Tic knows things."

"Tic?"

"Marco's nickname. Anyway, that's not important. What is important is that someone has now targeted two men who knew each other."

"Is Marco dead?" Kincaid asked next.

Again, I thought that a weird question, but then I remembered that Tic's body had been nowhere to be found when I regained consciousness. "I don't know. But I hope not."

Kincaid took a deep breath before saying, "Anything else you want to tell me, Esmé Bellerose?"

I really disliked the way he kept using my full name. It was condescending. Still, I needed to keep up the conversation if I was going to get anything useful out of him. "Two things. One, we should discuss what might be an appropriate gift for the ceremony—or in your case, what might *not* be an appropriate gift, and second—"

"Gift?" Kincaid said. "For what ceremony?"

I sighed. Man, dealing with the unmentored was a pain in the ass. "For your mentoring ceremony…. Did Grigori not mention this to you when he agreed to mentor you?"

There was a pause, then a crisp, "No."

"Well, it's customary to procure a trinket for your mentor. I'd start with Delphine Lefebvre. She has the best assortment of quality trinkets, and her stall down at the market is easy to find. Plus, she can be trusted. Well, to a point. But you'll need to bring cash, and don't go against your instincts. You'll want to simply let your gut tell you which trinket to choose for me."

There was dead silence on the other end of the phone, but then Kincaid said, "Got it. What else?"

"We should discuss next steps on the case sooner rather than later. Also, something I thought of this morning, I think we should go over all of your conversations with Grigori."

Again, Kincaid paused before replying. "Why would you think that?"

"Well, if it's true that Rasputin had agreed to mentor you, it's likely he would've talked about himself with you. He might've mentioned something that could help us identify some possible suspects."

The chair creaked again in the background while Kincaid considered that. "That's a fair point," he said at last. "Are you hungry, Esmé Bellerose?"

I blinked. "Excuse me?"

"Are you hungry?"

Sweet Jesus. The way he kept saying that, all low and throaty, made me think that Kincaid was being inappropriate. "For food?"

"Sure," Kincaid said with that same smooth, sexy tone.

Good, God. Was my face flushing? Before I could even answer, he added, "Meet me at Big Mike's in twenty. It's a diner two blocks west of the station on the south corner."

With that the line went dead.

I took my time getting to Big Mike's. And even then, I sat across the street staring at the diner for five minutes before I finally got out of the car and headed to the entrance. Pushing open the door caused a small bell to jingle, announcing my presence to an almost deserted restaurant that'd definitely seen better days from two or three decades ago judging by the worn upholstery, dusty shelves, and sun-faded interior.

My gaze instantly went to the two occupied booths, but Kincaid wasn't in either of them.

Next I scanned the counter. An elderly man sat hovered over a bowl of oatmeal and a steaming cup of coffee; otherwise, the counter was as empty as the rest of the place.

A carrot-haired woman wearing a dark brown polyester waitressing uniform poked her head out of the double-doors leading to the back and said, "Sit anywhere, hon. I'll be right with you." She then disappeared into the back again.

I glanced around the diner, feeling exposed. The place, for all its lack of charm, was brightly lit, and as it was still dark outside, this posed a bit of a dilemma. If I took a seat anywhere in the diner, I'd be visible from outside without being able to see who might be watching me. That was a situation I rarely put myself into.

Glancing at my phone, I took note of the hour. It was 5:15 AM. Kincaid had said to meet him here in twenty minutes, which made me ten minutes late.

Maybe he'd come here, hadn't seen me, waited five minutes, and left.

Again, I glanced at my phone. There'd been no texts to ask where I was, or to alert me that he'd be late, so if he'd come and gone, he hadn't even tried to contact me.

"Who leaves after only five minutes of waiting, though?" I muttered.

Behind me I heard the jingle of the bell above the door. My back stiffened, and I felt the hair rise on the back of my neck. Very slowly I turned around and saw Detective Kincaid standing in the doorway, looking at me.

For an instant I felt relieved. And then... *boom!* A wave of desire like I'd *never* felt, hit me like a blow to the body. My balance faltered, and I even took a step back. Heat rose from the pit of my stomach to flood through my veins and steal my breath in a gasp of surprise, or desire. Maybe both.

In that instant, the detective who'd arrested me the day before became the most attractive, desirable man I'd ever laid eyes on. My senses were flooded with him: his black hair, hazel eyes, broad shoulders, small waist, muscular physique, and lips so inviting I could hardly resist the urge to taste them.

I was so keenly aware of him, I felt I could hear his heartbeat from ten paces away.

And more than anything I'd ever wanted in my life—I wanted him.

I wanted to tear off his clothes and have him tear off mine. I wanted to feel my skin pressed against his, caress his lips, feel his tongue, be devoured by him in the way that true lovers do...

For several panicky moments, I could think of nothing else, and my breathing quickened with the effort to hold myself back from rushing to him and having my way with him right there in the diner on that filthy floor; I didn't even care.

And for his part, he seemed as surprised as I was by my obvious reaction. The confident smirk he'd worn upon entering faded quickly from his face, and he now stood rigid in that same doorway, his knuckles white on the handle of the door he still gripped.

"You two want a booth?" I heard behind me. It was the waitress.

I took a ragged breath and forced myself to turn away from Kincaid. "No," I said hoarsely. "I…won't be staying."

And then I willed my legs to move, to take one step, then another, and another, each one coming quicker than the next, but not in Kincaid's direction. My sights were set on the double doors leading to the kitchen, to where I knew a back exit must be.

I didn't stop until I'd run past the surprised cook, or the shocked busboy, who was taking a smoke break on the other side of the door leading to the back alley. Once I gained the street, I ran for my life.

Literally.

Chapter Eight
Day 2

I drove like a crazed person, constantly checking the rearview for any sign that the detective had followed me. Rolling down the window, I breathed in the crisp air hungrily. I couldn't seem to get my heart rate back to normal, and every nerve in my body felt on fire. *What the hell was that?* I asked myself.

I had no doubt that my binding spell was one hundred percent responsible for the nearly uncontrollable urge to mount Kincaid in a dirty diner where anyone and everyone could've seen us. After all, the spell had never cared about dignity or discretion. In the early days, I'd had plenty of openly public passionate moments, but I'd never, ever, in all of my one hundred-and-four years, felt such raw desire for another human being.

And that could only mean that Kincaid was the deadliest person I'd ever encountered. If he didn't represent a violent danger to me, then he surely represented a future heartbreak that I wouldn't survive. He was the embodiment of my worst fear come to life. A heartbreak so deep and so lasting that I'd find it impossible to go on living. I'd had a taste of that in Paris three decades before. It'd been unbearable.

But even that man hadn't evoked anywhere near the passionate response that Kincaid had.

What I couldn't understand was why there'd been a delayed response. Less than a day before I'd felt absolutely nothing for him. Not the smallest spark of desire.

What'd changed?

I drove aimlessly for a long time, waiting to regain my senses fully, but it was so difficult. The memory of him standing so gorgeous in that doorway kept replaying over and over in my mind, and with it the echoes of the desire I'd felt.

Finally I pulled into the parking lot of a strip mall and spent ten minutes doing nothing but taking in deep lungfuls of air, holding that breath for a count of ten, and releasing it slowly again. It was a meditative technique, and it helped more than anything.

After coming fully back to my senses, I considered what to do next. Kincaid was a link to discovering more about Rasputin. Now I'd have to proceed without his input. But I'd also have to come up with a reason never, *ever* to see him again.

No way could I mentor him now, and I said that to myself, even though I'd agreed to do it in a moment when our energies had been intertwined. Panic coursed through me then because I had no idea how to break a bounded promise. Running felt like it might work for a while, but that wasn't an option I could take, because if I didn't deliver Elric his egg, he'd hunt me down and kill me; if I did deliver his egg and I lived, then the contract would be in place, and it would hold me here even more firmly than the promise I'd made to Kincaid.

And then a dark thought occurred to me. It was possible to free myself of the promise bond to Kincaid, but he'd have to die in order for me to escape it. I didn't think my luck was anywhere near good enough to wish for a bus to hit him the next time he crossed the street, which meant that I'd probably have to murder him.

Sure I was capable; I'd killed one or two attackers in my day, but this would be different. This would be in cold blood, and in my heart, I knew I wasn't someone who could simply murder another human being that way.

So, Kincaid would live, and I'd have to face him again, and I knew I wouldn't survive any kind of continued interaction.

"I am so screwed," I muttered, putting my head in my hands. The minute I leaned against the steering wheel, my phone rang, and I jumped.

Grabbing the phone I looked at the display and didn't recognize the number. Tentatively I answered it. "Hello?"

"Esmé," said that familiar husky voice. "We need to meet." His tone suggested it was more of a command than a request.

"Listen, Detective," I said as my heart started to race again. "I'm sorry about the diner, but I...I had to go."

There was a pause, then, "What the hell are you talking about?"

My brow furrowed. "The diner," I repeated. "I know my exit was abrupt, but as I said, I had to go. It was an emergency."

Again, there was that distinctive pause before he answered. "I still don't know what the hell you're talking about. What diner?"

I pulled the phone away from my ear and stared at it. Was he toying with me? On the off chance that he was being serious, I said very slowly, "Big Mike's Diner."

"Okay," he said. "I know the place. What about it? Are you there now?"

"What the hell do you mean, what about it?!" I snapped. I wasn't into this little game. I didn't have time for it.

Kincaid sighed audibly into the phone. "Esmé, I just got to the station. There was an explosion at an apartment complex last night, two people were killed, and there's a description of a suspicious person fleeing the scene that sounds a lot like you."

I shook my head, wanting to push away everything he'd just said. "What do you mean, you *just* got into the station?!" I knew seeing him at Big Mike's had had a crazy effect on me, but it hadn't actually made me crazy. "I *just* saw you at Mike's!"

"What do you mean you—?" And just like that, Kincaid's voice cut off as if he'd caught himself before saying anything more. A moment later there was a muffled sound against the microphone of his phone, and I could hear some garbled words as he spoke to someone in the background. Then I clearly heard a string of expletives before he came back on the line. "That son of a bitch!" he groused. "I'll arrest him myself as soon as I see him."

I sighed wearily, and maybe with a little relief. I didn't seem to be having nearly the same reaction to the sound of his voice that I'd had earlier. In fact, as I listened to him, all I really felt was annoyed.

"You know what?" I said. "While you're out making arrests, how about you let me go so I can continue to work this case for you?"

"You don't understand," he said. "Esmé, that wasn't me at Big Mike's."

I rolled my eyes. Here comes some line, I thought. "Really," I said flatly. "It sure looked like you. It sure sounded like you when I called your office line and you said to meet you there."

"Not surprised," he said. "I have an identical twin brother. Finn." Kincaid cleared his throat before continuing, as if it was hard for him to talk about his brother. "We haven't spoken in a while, and I think he was trying to check up on me. He was the one who asked you to meet him at Mike's."

My mouth fell open because I completely believed Kincaid's explanation. Nothing else could account for the sudden insane desire I'd felt for him other than that it hadn't been the same man who'd arrested me the day before.

"You... you have a twin?"

"Yes. Identical. He's four minutes older."

A thousand questions exploded into my mind. "Is he a cop too?"

"No."

Just that. No further information.

"Is he also a mystic?"

Kincaid cleared his throat again, obviously uncomfortable with this line of questioning. "He is," he said. "And now I know for sure that you're working for Elric."

I blinked again, still trying to take all that in. "Why do you think you know that?"

"Because Finn works for Petra. If you worked for her, you'd definitely know about him. He's her new lieutenant."

My hand went to my forehead as a bead of sweat broke out across my brow. "You're telling me *the Flayer* is your twin brother?"

"Yes."

I took the phone away from my ear and held it between my clasped hands while I growled out a long stream of expletives.

When I felt I could speak calmly again, I put the phone back to my ear and said, "That would've been *very* useful information to share prior to muscling me into mentoring you, Kincaid."

"If I'd told you, would you have agreed to mentor me?"

"Fuck no," I said bluntly. Because it was the truth. The last thing I needed of all the other bullshit I didn't need right now was to have a kin connection to Petra's lieutenant. If Elric found out, he'd immediately assume Kincaid was a spy, and he'd kill me, Kincaid, and anyone else within a ten-foot radius. And if Petra found out, she'd assume the same thing about me, and while Kincaid might be spared, I sure as hell wouldn't be.

"Then I guess it's a good thing I didn't tell you, huh?" Kincaid said.

I desperately wanted to punch him in the throat.

"Kincaid," I said hoarsely, once I'd had time to consider all the many ways this new alliance could get me killed.

"Yeah?"

"You're right. We need to meet. Now."

Kincaid hesitated, then, "Fine. But I should warn you, Esmé, that assaulting a cop is a felony."

"Least of my worries, pal. Least of my worries."

Kincaid and I met up at a bar called Gert's near the warehouse. It was a place Dex and I often frequented because it was open twenty-four hours a day and run by a mystic who, for some reason, liked me. Or she just liked that I brought Dex around. It was hard to tell.

"Gert," I said, entering the empty establishment to find the owner behind the bar with a clipboard, taking inventory.

"Esmé," she sang, then immediately looked past me. "Sexy Dexy around?"

"Not today," I told her, taking a seat at a booth away from the bar. Gert pouted, and I softened. "Hey, don't be like that. There's still some eye candy coming in."

She brightened. "Usual?" she asked.

"Coffee," I said. My usual was a single-malt scotch, and, at six-thirty in the morning, even I felt it was a little too early in the day for hard liquor.

Gert brought over a steaming cup of joe and set it down, her gaze wandering back to the door as it opened, and Kincaid came strolling in.

Even though we'd had the conversation about his twin on the phone, I still braced myself against the back of the booth when he entered, fearful that my binding spell would act up again, but as he came forward, the only one turned on was Gert.

"Hello, gorgeous," she cooed.

Kincaid stopped in his tracks and looked over his shoulder, thinking she was speaking to someone behind him. This made Gert and me laugh.

When Kincaid realized his mistake, his face flushed, and that made us laugh all the more.

He sat down, with a roll to his eyes, and Gert elbowed him good-naturedly. "What'll it be?"

Kincaid pointed to my coffee. "That."

Turning to me she asked, "Anything to eat?"

My stomach gurgled. "Two eggs, over easy, and a couple of slices of rye toast, please."

Gert raised her eyebrows at Kincaid expectantly.

"Got a menu?" he asked.

She reached into her blouse and pulled out a folded piece of paper from her bra. "Thought you'd never ask," she said, sauntering off with a chuckle to get the detective his coffee.

Kincaid frowned, but he unfolded the menu and began to look it over. "What's good here?"

"The scotch," I said, pouring a large measure of cream into the coffee to soften the bite. (Rabid dogs were tamer than Gert's coffee.)

Kincaid sighed and looked at me in irritation.

I ignored him and stirred in some sugar.

Gert appeared with Kincaid's coffee, and he ordered a farmer's omelet and a side of wheat toast.

After Gert left our table to head into the kitchen, I made eye contact with Kincaid and decided not to mince words. "Spill it."

"My brother?" he asked.

"Yeah."

Kincaid sighed again, this time in resignation. "He's Petra's right hand. And he's the reason I've never been mentored."

"How could he prevent you from becoming mentored?"

"We were bound young—"

"How young?" I interrupted.

"Eleven."

"Huh," I said, sitting back in my seat.

"What?"

"Me too."

Kincaid's brow furrowed, as if he'd never imagined more children than he and his brother could be bound. It was common knowledge that binding children was a pretty despicable act, and both Petra and Elric forbade it within their respective camps. It just wasn't done, and until Kincaid confessed to me that he'd been bound at such a young age, I'm the only mystic I'd ever known—besides Tic—who'd been bound so young.

"What're the odds?" he asked, and I could tell he was partially joking.

"You were saying," I said, rolling my hand to remind him to continue.

"Right. Finn and I were bound young, and we didn't even know it for a couple of years. But you know how it is: The power grows, and you think you might be crazy, but for us, we knew it was real because we were each watching the other affect physical objects just by thinking about them."

"Or touching them," I said.

"Exactly," he agreed. "Anyway, it freaked me out more than it did Finn. I tried to bury it, while he went looking for answers. He found them in a mentor who had connections, and he introduced Finn to Petra. Around the time that I began coming to terms with the magic and wanted to be mentored too, Finn blocked me."

"He blocked you? Why would he do that?"

Kincaid shifted his gaze away from me, as if the question made him uncomfortable. "I think he was trying to protect me. Finn got in with Petra early, and by the time I expressed an interest in getting mentored, he was in deep. She owned him, and I think he was forced to do things that he later regretted. He also knew that if I became a mystic, anyone could come after me to manipulate him. Petra wouldn't stand for her right hand having a weakness like that."

I shook my head in awe of the utter idiocy that had led Kincaid to the conclusion that I should mentor him. "She's right, you know," I said.

"Who?"

"Petra. You would be a weakness for the Flayer. She'd demand your execution, and she'd demand that her lieutenant carry out the act in order to reaffirm his loyalty to her."

Kincaid tried to cover it, but I saw the way the color drained from his face. "Then I guess it's a good thing we're going to be keeping this on the down-low."

I wagged a finger at him. "You're forgetting something."

"What?"

"The Flayer and I have already had a conversation where he pretended to be you. Not knowing you had a twin, I felt free to remind him that he needed to procure a gift to me prior to our mentoring ceremony."

The rest of the color drained from Kincaid's face. "Fuck."

"Uh-huh," I agreed. "So no way can we go through with the mentoring ceremony now."

Color rushed back into Kincaid's complexion. "No way can we *not!*"

I sighed and rolled my eyes. This was my one chance to get out of this prickly-pear agreement, and I wasn't going to waste it. "I'll still help you with the investigation, Kincaid, but mentoring you is a death sentence for both of us now that your brother knows."

"He would never tell Petra, and he would never kill me," he said.

Gert came by with a pot of coffee to refill our mugs, and her brow arched as Kincaid blurted that out. I didn't say a word and avoided Gert's gaze while she topped off my coffee. Waiting until she left again, I said, "Your brother might not whisper a word of it to Petra, but he sure as hell would kill me. I'm the one putting you in the most jeopardy by bringing you into the mystic world, where you'll definitely draw notice."

Kincaid shook his head. "He won't kill you if you're already my mentor. If we go through with the ceremony, then we're bound to protect each other and, if one of us is killed by another mystic without just cause, then we're bound to seek revenge for the killing, right? Finn wouldn't kill you because he knows that I'd be bound to kill him in revenge."

Dammit. He'd done his homework. "Would you?" I asked him, still trying to convince him that the price he'd pay would be too high. "Would you really kill your twin?"

"How could I avoid it?" he answered in return. "The bond between us as mentor and protégé would compel me, right?"

"It would," I said, irritated that he still seemed to have the upper hand in this. "How long have you and your brother been estranged?" I asked next. I needed to understand the dynamics of their relationship because I still wasn't convinced—at all—that Finn the Flayer would just ignore the fact that an employee of SPL was mentoring his brother.

"A while," he said, twisting his wedding ring.

Mystics who married each other rarely wore symbols that announced such bonds, so I pointed to his ring and asked, "Are you married to a mortal?"

Kincaid covered the ring with his right hand. "I am."

"Ah," I said. "That's gotta be tough."

"It's not," he said curtly.

I knew he didn't want to talk about it, but I couldn't help probing the topic a bit. If I was going to mentor this man I needed to know his vulnerabilities. "Hasn't your wife noticed that you're not ageing and she is?"

Kincaid shrugged. "A little," he said.

"What happens when she turns fifty and you still look like you're in your early thirties?"

He looked up at me with a tinge of anger. "If there're spells that can keep you young, then there are spells that can make you to age."

My brow shot up. Now I understood more about what was motivating his sudden immersion into the mystic world. He held some romantic notion that he could grow old with his wife. And maybe he could. There were spells to affect all sorts of physiology, so why not something to age a mystic who didn't want to remain young?

I moved off the topic of Kincaid's wife but was still curious about the detective's background. "Why didn't the mystic who bound you offer to mentor you?" I asked.

"She wasn't the nurturing type."

I took a sip of coffee. "You're pretty defensive for a guy who's about to commit himself to a mentor."

Kincaid frowned. "Force of habit. I'm protective of my family and my past."

"I get it. To survive straddling both worlds like you've been doing, you'd have to be. Does your wife know you're a mystic?"

"Hell no," he said. "I cover it pretty well whenever it shows up."

"That must be hard," I said, because it had to be.

But Kincaid merely shrugged. "I've had a lot of practice at it. What other choice have I had?"

Gert came by again to deliver our breakfasts, and I wanted to laugh. She handed me a plate of two poached eggs and a cinnamon bun, gooey with glaze, and Kincaid got a bowl of oatmeal and a cup of fruit.

He looked down at the offering as if he couldn't understand how Gert had screwed up his order so badly when we were the only patrons in the place. "This isn't what I ordered," he said.

"No," she agreed. "It's what you need."

"What I *need*?" he asked, looking at me as if I could explain.

Gert reached down and patted Kincaid's midsection. "Fiber," she said. "The oatmeal should do the trick."

I stifled a laugh, and Gert padded away.

Kincaid just stared at me, then Gert's retreating form, then me again. For my part, I picked up the cinnamon bun and took a big bite. My eyes rolled up and I moaned, it was so good.

"Care to tell me what the hell she means?" Kincaid asked.

I chewed for a second and said, "As you might've already sensed, Gert's a mystic..."

"Yeah, I picked up on that, but what does that have to do with oatmeal and a fruit cup?"

"Her particular talents lie in being able to read people. It's how she knows when trouble enters the bar, and she usually knows, even before the troublemakers do, that they're gonna start something."

"Cops have a similar sense," he said.

I held back the urge to roll my eyes—but barely. "Anyway, Gert's senses go deep, sometimes into health, sometimes into feelings." I lifted the cinnamon bun high for emphasis. "She can read that I've had a bitch of a week so far and needed a little comfort food." Pointing then to Kincaid's oatmeal, I added, "She can also obviously tell you've got a giant stick up your ass, and she's just trying to do her part in helping you remove it."

Kincaid's expression flashed to angry, but I just laughed. "Okay, okay, I'll stop. You were saying about how you've tried to live as a mortal..."

Kincaid shrugged and dipped a spoon into his oatmeal. Gert had softened the blow by sprinkling it with cinnamon, maple syrup, bananas, and walnuts, which was a nice touch. "There's not much to tell beyond that, after Finn blocked me from being mentored, I immersed myself in the mortal world. I went to the police academy and worked my way up to detective. I got married, got a mortgage, live in a quiet suburban neighborhood, and lead a pretty normal life, but sometimes, when I'm stressed or tired, the magic just…gets away from me."

I nodded. I could only imagine how an unmentored mystic left to his own devices might wreak havoc in his own world because he couldn't control either the impulse to manipulate everyday objects or control the side of himself who wanted to manipulate the mortals all around him.

I mean, there's a reason we're a secretive fringe group who seeks out one another's company and try very hard to keep from calling attention to ourselves.

"But why now?" I pressed. "Why try to find someone to mentor you now, after all this time?"

Kincaid wiped his mouth with his napkin without looking me directly in the eye. "I came across some information that confirms a suspicion I had, and I want to take apart the power structure ruling the mystic world."

"What information?"

Kincaid lifted his gaze to look me directly in the eye. "I won't tell you that."

My brow rose. "Not even if I pinkie swear to keep it just between us?"

"I'm not kidding, Esmé. I won't tell you. Ever."

I shrugged, pretending I didn't really care, but the truth is, I did care. I cared a lot because this guy was so obviously insane if he thought he could take on Elric and/or Petra and live to talk about it. And I, as his mentor, didn't particularly want to be associated with some cocky newbie who thought he was in the same league as Elric Ostergaard. The dude wasn't even on the same planet, much less ballpark.

For now, however, there was no point pressing him. He wasn't going to tell me. Period.

"Fine," I said. "But at least tell me why your brother is going around impersonating you."

"I have no idea, but it wouldn't be the first time Finn came sniffing around my desk. Usually it's because there's something in it for Petra, so it's likely that's why."

"Oh, shit," I said.

"What?"

"I told your brother about my association with Tic."

"Tic?"

"The source who told me where to find Grigori. Last night he was at his girlfriend's apartment when it exploded."

"The one off Seminary."

"Yes. That's the one."

"Why would my brother care?"

"Tic is a nickname. His given name is Marco Astoré. You may have heard of his mommy dearest. Your brother works for her."

Kincaid gaped at me. "Astoré is Petra's kid?"

"'Fraid so."

"Shit," Kincaid said. "Is he okay?"

"Doubtful," I said grimly. "His girlfriend definitely didn't survive."

"Where is he now?"

"I have no idea."

"What does that mean?"

"It means I have no idea. The last time I saw Marco, he had a giant piece of wood sticking out from under his collarbone, and then I blacked out. When I came to, he was gone, and his girlfriend's torso was in his place."

"Jesus," Kincaid said. "I heard one of the vics was found in pieces. Could Tic have walked out of there?"

"No. Definitely not."

"So someone took him."

"Definitely yes."

"And left you," Kincaid said, pointing to me for emphasis. I nodded.

Kincaid ran his hand through his hair in a worried gesture. "So Petra's kid was in an explosion, badly wounded, and is now missing. That'd be enough to lure Finn into snooping around my desk. The explosion involved mortals, and he knew he could get info on it by impersonating me."

I felt another jolt of alarm. "When you called me earlier, you said that you had a report that identified a suspicious person leaving the scene who resembled me."

"Yeah. The report was on my desk this morning. I wondered why it was there—the case has already been assigned to another detective, but now I think that Finn pulled it from the network when he went to the station to snoop around."

I leaned my head against the back of the booth and closed my eyes. "So Finn knows that I was there."

I heard Kincaid hiss in a breath. "Yeah. Yeah, he probably does."

We sat in silence for a minute or two when Kincaid said, "But hey, you also told me you met him at Big Mike's, right? And he let you live, so how did you talk your way out of there?"

"I didn't. I just...left."

"You just *left?*"

"Yep."

"And he *let* you go?"

"He did. Of course, I left rather abruptly. He probably didn't even register that it was me before I ran outta there."

"Why didn't you speak to him?"

"I wasn't feelin' it," I said, careful not to reveal the real reason. "Something felt off."

Kincaid sighed heavily. "We're gonna need to speed up the timetable. If Finn gets to you before we complete the ceremony, he'll have two reasons to kill you."

"Like he needs more than one," I scoffed. "Which reminds me, you'll need to pick up a gift for me. It's part of the ceremon—"

"I've already picked out a token," he said.

I blinked. "When did you have time for that?"

"When my brother was busy impersonating me," he said.

I frowned. No way could he have gotten anything good in the middle of the night from the mystic market. The place was open 24/7, but only the good venders showed up during the day. The night was for paupers and peddlers of mostly trinket throwaways, so his selection was likely to be the most valuable trinket from a pile of crap.

"Great," I said woodenly, not even trying to hide my disappointment. "That's just great."

"It's not a piece of junk," Kincaid snapped, and I could tell he was offended.

I eyed him moodily, miffed that he'd rushed the process. Protégé's were supposed to take great care with the gift-selection process. Mentoring a newbie was a royal pain in the ass, and the gift was intended to make the task a bit more palatable. "If you got it from the market last night or early this morning, it's not likely to be a treasure, Kincaid."

"It's a good gift, Esmé," he insisted. "I got it from the same place I got the one for Grigori, and believe me when I tell you that it was a place of top quality."

My brow furrowed. "What'd you do with the trinket you were going to give to Grigori?"

"I gave it to him."

I shook my head. "Hold on, you *gave* it to him? *Before* the ceremony?"

Kincaid shrugged, but I could tell he was embarrassed for being called out for such a novice act. "I wanted to show him I was serious, and I hoped it'd prevent him from backing out of our deal. Besides, we were scheduled to do the ceremony the day I found you, breaking and entering."

"Ah," I said, making a face as I recalled the grisly scene.

"How soon can you be ready to do the ceremony?" Kincaid asked next, glancing at his watch.

"As soon as you are, but first we'll need a safe space to conduct the ceremony."

"What about your place?"

"No. My place is out."

"Why?"

"Because where I live is a coveted secret, and I don't trust you enough yet to allow you entrance. We can do it at your place."

"Nope," Kincaid said quickly.

"Why not?"

"Same reason as yours."

"Then it seems we'll need to postpone the ceremony until one of us finds a safe and secure place."

Kincaid rolled his eyes. "I know a place. It's private, secure, and there's no risk of being interrupted."

"Where is it?"

"I can't tell you."

I sighed dramatically. This guy was a *lot* of work, and I didn't have time for it. "You're really starting to be more of a pain in the ass than you're worth, Kincaid," I growled.

"Esmé, I swear I can't tell you. But I can pick you up and bring you there."

"Fine," I said, pinching the bridge of my nose. There was definitely a headache forming behind my eyes. "I'll just need to pick up a few things from my place, and I can meet you back here in an hour."

I started to get up, but Kincaid seemed nervous about letting me out of his sight, and he reached out to grab my wrist. "What do you need to pick up?"

I glared down at his hand on my wrist, and he wisely let go. "We'll need a knife, preferably one carved from jade, a quill with a silver tip, parchment, and beeswax candles," I said.

"I've got all of that."

I eyed him keenly. "Let me guess, you had a kit ready to go for the ceremony day with Grigori."

"Yes."

I folded my napkin and set it on the table. "Then we should get a move on. And remember to tip Gert generously when you pay the tab."

With that I moseyed out of the bar and waited for Kincaid next to his SUV.

He came out a few minutes later, wearing a rueful smile. "You're lucky I had cash on me," he said, using his key fob to unlock the door.

"No, no," I sang. "*You're* lucky."

Gert didn't accept credit cards and would've made him work off breakfast, which I highly doubted would've involved washing dishes.

CHAPTER NINE
DAY 2

We got into Kincaid's vehicle and headed due west. About ten minutes into the drive Kincaid pulled over to the side of the street, opened up the center console, reached inside to withdraw a sleep mask, which he offered to me and said, "I need you to put this on."

"You're kidding me, right?"

"No."

I turned away from him and opened the car door. I'd walk back to Gert's before I spent one more second with this massively obtuse idiot.

Kincaid reached out and grabbed my arm, his grip tight. "Please," he said. I glared at him. He sighed and added, "I can't reveal where we're going to you. I can't reveal the location to anyone. I'm bound to secrecy."

I growled low in my throat. It was totally understandable that Kincaid might be unable to bring me into a magically protected space unless I was blindfolded, but the part of me that's been clawing for survival in a dangerous world of mayhem and monsters was against going *anywhere* I was unable to see my surroundings and an escape route. So I continued to hesitate.

"I swear, nothing bad will happen to you," Kincaid said, his expression earnest. The son of a bitch.

I rolled my eyes, closed the door and snatched the mask from his fingers. "*Fine.*" Putting it over my eyes, I flattened my back against the seat and concentrated on listening and memorizing any turns that put us on a different path.

I might not be able to see where we were going, but I sure as hell was going to work hard to memorize the path back.

After four rights and two lefts, we entered what sounded like a large-scale garage area. Kincaid's car sounded like it was in a tunnel, and then we sloped downward, no doubt heading for the lower levels. Two more sharp turns to the left, and then another to the right brought us to a stop. "Sit tight for a minute," Kincaid whispered. "And promise me you won't take off the mask."

I held up two fingers in an "I promise" gesture.

He chuckled. "I might be unmentored, Esmé, but I know enough to know that without you vowing it, you'll rip off that mask the second you think I'm out of sight."

I shook my head. Damn this irritating little pissant! He knew just enough to be a total pain in my ass. "*Fiiiine.* I prom—" Kincaid grabbed my hand and held it tight. I sighed. "I promise not to remove your stupid, ridiculous, unnecessary mask."

Warmth snaked its way from my palm all the way up my arm and feathered out across my torso as the promise became bound.

"Thanks," Kincaid said, letting go of me.

I heard the door open and close, and then I waited for what I guessed was about five minutes, maybe a little longer. My door was then opened, and Kincaid said, "Okay, we're good. Take my hand and I'll lead you."

I wanted to grouse about all the theatrics involved in getting to this secret location, but I highly doubted that would help get the sleep mask off any sooner, so I reached out and felt Kincaid's hand, then obediently exited the SUV and allowed him to lead me forward until he stopped and swiveled me around to face the other way. A moment later I heard a *bing* that I quickly realized was an elevator, and my stomach felt fluttery as we ascended to what must have been the length of several stories. The elevator stopped abruptly, and the bell above the doors binged again, then the doors rattled open and Kincaid said, "This way."

He led me out of the boxcar and into a cozy warm space that smelled of musk and cedar.

We continued to walk forward a good ten feet, our footfalls echoing against wood floors, until finally we stopped, and Kincaid lifted the mask away from my eyes.

I blinked in the sudden brightness, but after my eyes adjusted, I discovered that we were in a lavishly decorated apartment, heavy on the dark trim and gray furnishings but impeccably kept all the same.

The kitchen was just off to my right, and in front of me was a large living room with a giant flat-screen TV, with small speakers located throughout the room to give television viewing that special surround-sound effect.

The couch was a sectional, and at one end of the couch cushions there was a slight divot, as if someone spent most of their time sitting in that exact spot watching the boob tube.

The overall setting of the apartment was also decidedly masculine with little in the way of knickknacks, however, on the entertainment unit was a framed photograph of Kincaid and his twin brother when they were probably in their late teens, their arms slung over each other's shoulders, grinning for the camera.

The photo was obviously from happier times.

"Is this your secret Batcave?" I asked, wondering if the detective kept this place hidden from his wife.

"Not exactly," he said, pocketing a key.

And then it hit me, and my eyes widened. I took in the space again, my alarm growing by the nanosecond. "Holy shit, Kincaid! Are you *kidding me?*"

He eyed me crossly. "We won't be disturbed here."

"You mean, your twin brother, *the Flayer*, won't come waltzing on home into *his own apartment?*"

Kincaid put his finger to his lips. "Will you keep it down?"

"Oh, so the neighbors won't hear and alert *Petra's lieutenant?*" I threw my hands up at him, then turned on my heel and headed toward the elevator. No *way* was I going to get caught by Petra's right hand in his own home when the man in question was probably at this very moment looking to hunt me down and murder me.

"Esmé!" Kincaid exclaimed, grabbing my arm and pulling me back. "Just listen for a minute, will you?"

I pulled my arm to free it, but the bastard held tight, so I settled for glaring over my shoulder at him with a lethal stare. "Let. Go."

Kincaid looked desperate. "Just hear me out, goddammit!"

I growled low in my throat. "You have ten seconds."

"Finn isn't anywhere near here. Every Thursday at exactly this time he has a standing appointment that he never misses. We have two hours or more. I promise."

I shook my head, disbelieving not only the story about the standing appointment but the fact that Kincaid would even *consider* bringing me here to perform a ceremony that Finn the Flayer was likely to kill me for participating in.

For his part, Kincaid looked resigned but insistent. "I swear, Esmé—on my life—we're safe here at least until ten o'clock."

I shook my head, seething with rage. Kincaid had just issued a very powerful spell. No mystic, not even an unmentored one, could swear on his or her life and lie. They'd be dead before they even hit the ground, as those words formed one of the most potent and powerful of spells.

So I jerked my arm again, yanking it from Kincaid's grasp and said, "Fine. Let's just get this over with so we can get the hell outta here."

Kincaid blew out a relieved sigh and led the way into the center of the living room.

The blinds were drawn on the windows, so I had no idea how high up we were, or even where we were, and Kincaid made no effort to pull back the fabric and reveal daylight or the view. Instead, he picked up a remote control and clicked it, illuminating the room artificially.

"We can't have those on during the ceremony," I told him.

Kincaid moved to a bag he'd obviously brought up here earlier and began to pull twelve candles out from it.

"I know, but they'll help while we set up."

I pointed to the windows. "We could pull back the drapes."

Kincaid flashed me a crooked smile. "Nice try. I told you I was bound to keep this place a secret, so no dice."

"Whatever," I said, more annoyed than ever.

Still, as Kincaid removed all of the items from his bag, I got them organized on the floor in front of the couch, then sat down on the carpet to cross my legs akimbo before motioning for Kincaid to do the same across from me.

When we were settled, I lit all the candles and motioned for him to douse the lights with the remote. I then closed my eyes and took a few deep breaths, and when I opened them, Kincaid was looking both a little scared and a little excited.

"Have you ever witnessed a mentoring ceremony?" I asked him.

He shook his head.

"Okay. I'll talk you through it as we go. It's pretty simple, but it needs to be precise. It begins with two sacrifices from you; the first is your gift to me."

Kincaid reached into his side pocket and pulled out a small jewelry box. "Here," he said. "I was guided right to it, so I think you'll like it."

I cocked an eyebrow and took the box from him. Opening it, I saw a small gold charm, in the shape of half a heart that gave the appearance of having been broken in two. I stared at it curiously, even as my own powers ignited and began to connect with the trinket. To my eye it gleamed and radiated power, and I actually gasped as I stared at it.

Tentatively I ran two fingers over the top of the charm, and warmth spread into my hand, through my arm, wrapping itself around my torso and neck before concentrating at the base of my throat, and—oddly—around my heart. I lifted the charm away from the box and put it on. It continued to pulse with warmth and, although I didn't quite know its purpose, I knew enough from that immediate connection of its magic to mine that there could not have been a more perfect gift for me.

"Thank you," I said to him, with a bow of my head. "I accept your gift."

The tense set to Kincaid's shoulders relaxed. "Good," he said, looking very pleased with himself.

"Next," I said, setting aside the jewelry box and placing my hands on my knees, "you will need to sacrifice the secrets of your binding spell."

Kincaid pulled back his chin and began to shake his head. "No way."

I nodded in understanding. I'd balked at this step too. "It's required," I said. "As your mentor, I can never reveal what you tell me to another living soul, nor can I ever use it against you, but because you were bound by someone other than me, it's imperative that I know your greatest weakness. There's no way around it."

Kincaid seemed to consider that for a long moment. "Grigori never told me I'd need to do that."

I nodded again. "I'm sure he didn't. If he had told you, you might've changed your mind and requested the gift back. Still, it *is* required for the ceremony."

Kincaid remained skeptical, so, with a roll of my eyes I added, "I swear it on my life."

His mouth opened slightly. Obviously I'd surprised him with that one, but he quickly recovered and said, "Fine. I believe you."

"Good. And if you absolutely don't want to tell me, then you can have back your trinket, and we can get out of here with no hurt feelings or ill will on my part." Of course I left out the part about the fact that if he did back out, I'd someday soon track down the trinket he'd offered me and steal it from him. No way was I ever going to allow such a perfectly matched treasure escape me again.

"I'm not backing out," he said stubbornly.

"Okay then," I said, shifting my position slightly to make myself more comfortable. "Then, whenever you're ready, tell me the details of your binding."

Kincaid cleared his throat and eyed the floor. It was obvious that he was uncomfortable with the memory. "I was bound by a witch who never gave up her name. She was just some old hag who lived down the street from us."

"What year?" I asked, surprised that we'd both been bound by old hags.

"Nineteen thirty-two," he said. I did the math. We were surprisingly close in age, but we both could've passed for our early thirties. Just one of the many minor benefits to being bound. After puberty, the aging process slows way down.

"We'd just lost our dad to consumption," Kincaid continued, "and it was at the peak of the Depression so money was tight. Mom moved us from Omaha to Wichita to live with her sister. The house was small and cramped, and in a crummy neighborhood, but it was better than nothing. The mystic who bound me was this creepy old lady who lived down the street in a house that was even worse looking than my aunt's—"

At this I had to interrupt. "Wait a second. You're telling me a mystic was living in some random poor neighborhood in Wichita, Kansas?" Our kind tended not to mix with the poorest of the unbound. Not when their treasures were so easy for the taking.

"I know," Kincaid said. "Unusual. But it's true. Anyway, as I was saying, this old lady's house might've been a dump, but the garden she kept out back was the envy of the whole neighborhood. She grew every kind of flower and vegetable you could think of.

"Finn and I would walk right past it on our way to the fishing hole every weekend. So one day we're coming back from fishing, empty-handed, and we're starving and worried what our mom is going to say because we'd promised to bring home something for dinner, and as we're walking by the backyard of the old lady, Finn slaps me on the shoulder and whispers that we should raid her garden.

"I didn't want to do it, but Finn said, 'What's the harm? Even if we get caught, it isn't like the old lady can run us down.'"

I smirked, already knowing how this was going to end but enjoying the telling of it anyway.

Kincaid shrugged. "So we snuck into the garden and began filling our pockets with anything we could grab. I was really nervous about the whole thing, so I kept my eyes on the house almost the entire time. Finn was more cocky about it. He didn't seem to care, and he just dug in and filled our knapsack and his pockets. When we couldn't stuff one more thing into our clothes or the knapsack, we turned to leave, and the second we did, the old lady showed up in front of us, only she didn't look like the feeble old woman we both remembered seeing, tending to her yard. She seemed taller. Stronger. And more threatening."

Kincaid swallowed as if the fear from that moment still sat with him. "I don't know how she got behind us to sneak up on us like that, or how she changed into something so sinister, but I remember all my hair standing up on end, and something told me we were in really deep shit.

"Looking back, I think Finn felt it too. Right away, he set down the knapsack and apologized to the old woman, telling her how ashamed he was to get caught stealing from her, but explaining how hungry our family was. During that whole time, she didn't speak a word, she just stared at him with the most..." Kincaid's voice trailed off, and his eyes held a haunted, faraway stare.

"The most what?" I asked when he didn't continue.

Kincaid shook his head, as if he couldn't find the word to describe her expression. "She stared at him in a way that made me think she was going to kill him."

"How did you two make it out alive?" Mystics weren't known for their mercy. Stealing from one was a very risky endeavor, as I knew firsthand.

Kincaid continued. "I think we survived because, right at that moment, things got even weirder. A guy walked into the garden right behind the old lady—"

"A guy?"

"Another mystic. At the time, I thought he was just someone who knew the old lady and was coming to visit, but he entered through the gate silently and came up right behind her in a way that was super creepy. He was walking with a cane, but he wasn't leaning on it; it looked like it was for decoration. Anyway, when he was about ten feet behind the old woman, he lifted the cane high and brought it down, like he was hitting something or someone. He was too far away from us to have hit her, but she reacted as if she'd been beat hard over the head. She fell to the ground, and I remember she was bleeding from a cut on the back of her skull. I also remember Finn and I looking at each other like we couldn't believe what we'd just seen."

"What did this other man look like?" I asked curiously.

"He was a character," Kincaid said. "He had silver hair, like, *actual* silver hair, and he wore an all-white suit, a white eye patch, and a purple ascot. His cane was also striking; it was bright silver, with a huge amethyst crystal at the head."

I gasped at the description. There was only one mystic that could've been. "You're telling me that Vigmar Dobromila was in your neighborhood attacking a low-level mystic?"

Vigmar had been Petra's brother. He'd died under mysterious circumstances when I was fourteen, the year I was taken in by Banzan—the Buddhist monk who became my mentor. Banzan had known Vigmar well but not fondly. He'd spoken about him often, describing him in great detail.

"Yes," Kincaid said in answer to my question. "That's what I'm telling you. Although we didn't know who the hell he was back then. That only came to light later."

"So did he kill the witch?" I asked. I had to admit, Kincaid's binding story was fascinating.

"No," Kincaid said. "She killed him."

I gaped at Kincaid for a good ten seconds. "How?"

"With a wave of her freaking hand, Esmé." Kincaid waved his own hand casually for emphasis.

I shook my head. "It's not possible. Vigmar was even more powerful than Elric. How could this old hag have beaten him?"

"She was more powerful than Vigmar," Kincaid said bluntly.

"Tell me what she did," I demanded. "I want to know everything, from the moment she was lying on the ground, what happened next?"

Kincaid shrugged. "Not much. She put a hand to her head and let out a shriek, and my brother and I reacted. We rushed the intruder; tackling him together, we threw him to the ground. I think we took him by surprise, and I doubt he'd taken much notice of us when he entered the yard because he was so focused on the witch.

"Anyway, Vigmar went down, and I thought we had the upper hand, but then all of the sudden, Finn goes flying through the air and hits the garden shed like he's just been tossed aside by a gorilla. I rolled off Vigmar, about to head to Finn's side, when I felt myself lifted off the ground and thrown ten feet by an unseen hand. I landed a little better than Finn, who had his bell rung, and as I was getting to my feet, I saw the old lady get to her feet. While Vigmar was focused on us, she waved her hand in a zigzag, and all of a sudden, Vigmar's chest… it just exploded."

"It *exploded?*"

"Yeah," Kincaid said softly, shaking his head. "His heart came flying out of his chest, and the old lady caught it barehanded. It was still pumping."

"Sweet Jesus."

Kincaid nodded. "That was my exact thought too."

"Then what happened?"

"The witch pocketed the heart and turned to us. She called us by name, which shocked the hell out of both of us, because to my knowledge she'd never asked us our names, but she called to us and told us to come forward. After watching what'd happened to the guy with the silver hair, Finn and I were too scared not to do exactly as she said. So we got up and walked to stand in front of her, literally shaking from head to toe. She then said that she was grateful we'd distracted her enemy long enough for her to gain the upper hand. For that, she told us, she'd spare our lives, but she couldn't forgive the fact that we'd stolen from her, so she was going to teach us a lesson by cursing us."

"Ah," I said. "The binding."

Kincaid nodded. "She cursed Finn first, and then—"

"What did she bind him with?" I interrupted, hoping Kincaid might just tell me.

He frowned. "Nice try."

I shrugged. "Can't blame a mystic for trying."

Kincaid continued as if I hadn't interrupted. "And then she cursed me. Her exact words were, 'Gideon Kincaid, no fruit shall you bear, even if you plant your seed everywhere. Your branch will be stunted, your tree will grow old, but no child will bear the surname *you* hold.'"

"Wow," I said, totally unimpressed. "That's it?"

Kincaid seemed insulted. "That's it," he said flatly.

"Okay. At least she didn't kill you. And she didn't curse you with anything that's going to get overly in your way, so that's not so bad."

Kincaid's hard stare was unwavering. He seemed ready to yell at me, so I decided to move on. "Now that I know the details of your binding, we can move forward with the actual ceremony."

Kincaid looked away to grab his bag and pull out parchment and a quill, which he handed to me, and while he dug back in his bag for a jade knife, I scribbled down a few lines on the parchment forming the very basics of the mentoring contract where I agreed to be his mentor for as long as he needed me (which hopefully wouldn't be long) and help him navigate the mystic world, teaching him our history, our laws, and enough skills to keep him alive once he fully immersed in our culture. I also vowed to protect the details of his binding, never sharing it with another soul, and I agreed to protect him in those instances where his inexperience might bring him bodily harm.

That last line was the one I was most worried about, but there was no way around it; as his mentor, I was bound to offer him protection.

I then wrote out his part, which was to agree to come into the partnership willing to learn, ready to listen, and accepting of the power dynamic between us. He would also protect any secrets he learned about me and shield me from harm where he could.

It was only a one-page contract, but it was as powerful an agreement as any we had in our world.

When I was done with the text, I formed two signature lines, then passed the contract over to Kincaid so that he could read it over. His eyes darted left to right for a few moments, and then he simply looked up at me and nodded.

"Now what?" he asked.

I leaned forward to arrange the twelve lit candles into a circle that enclosed us in a ring of fire. Once that was done, I lifted the contract out of Kincaid's hands and began to read my part aloud. Once I was finished, I turned to him and motioned for him to do the same. He read his portion out loud and when he was finished, he looked at me expectantly.

"Are you right-handed or left?" I asked.

"Left."

I smirked. "Me too." I was fairly ambidextrous—as most lefties tend to be—but my dominant hand was my left.

Taking up the jade knife, I made a deep incision across my right palm and allowed the blood to pool into a small dish much like the one that Sequoya had used. I then looked up at Kincaid and said, "Give me your right hand."

He held it forward, palm up, and I made the same cut across the surface as I had my own. I was quick with the knife, but I still had to give the guy credit because he barely even winced.

I then offered him the small receptacle, and he allowed several drops of blood to drip into it. Once we had enough for the task, I dipped the quill into the small pool of our combined blood and signed my full name to the contract.

Offering the quill to Kincaid, I expected him to hesitate—I mean, it was a pretty big deal to be bound to someone who's going to order you around for the next couple of years—but he didn't hesitate for a moment. His expression set in determination, he simply dipped the quill into the blood and signed his name.

Even before handing me back the quill, I could feel the marrow in my bones begin to warm. It's a unique feeling when a spell you're tied to becomes activated. You heat up from the inside out, and the more powerful the spell, the more that sort of warmth comes alive. It tingles and dances and spreads rather deliciously throughout your whole body, from head to toe. I love the feeling even though it always seems to come with consequences.

Like being bound to a novice, passing himself off as a cop in the mortal world who also happened to be the identical twin brother of a man so lethal that being within ten feet of him was likely to get me killed.

Still, I enjoyed the small high of the spell while it lasted. Judging by the look of satisfaction on Kincaid's face, he enjoyed it too.

"Now what?" he asked, as the warming sensation began to fade.

I didn't answer him immediately. Folding up the contract, I handed it to him, then I went around the circle and blew out all the candles. When I was done, I said, "We'll wait for the wax to cool a bit, and then we'll pack up and get the hell out of here."

"Then what?" he pressed.

I sighed. Shit was about to get complicated again. "Then we figure out who killed Grigori to close your case, and locate the trinket that was stolen from his house to conclude my business."

Kincaid's brow furrowed in silent question.

I had realized on the way here that, through his friendship with Grigori, Kincaid might have seen the egg either on his person or in his house. My plan had been to wait until we were officially bound to each other—thus able to trust each other—before asking him about it.

"You spent time at Grigori's house, right?" I asked.

"I did. But just a few times."

I nodded. "Do you ever remember seeing a Fabergé egg out on display?"

The furrow to Kincaid's brow deepened. "No," he said, and I felt my hopes fall. "But I did notice he carried a little gold egg around in his pocket. I figured it was his good luck charm."

And just like that my hopes rose from the depths. "Did you find it on him?" I asked. "When the body was removed, I mean. Did you find the egg?" It was possible that Grigori had used up almost all of the juice from the egg, but even if it had one final burst of magic to offer, if I found it and presented it to Elric, I'd still technically be fulfilling my end of his bargain.

"No," Kincaid said. "It was missing. And I know because I checked."

"Why did you check?" I asked.

Kincaid shrugged. "Grigori was my friend. I would've liked to have kept something of his to remind me of him."

I wasn't sure I believed him. "I need to find it, Detective."

"Why?"

"Let's put it this way: Either I find that egg and hand it to Elric, or by one minute past midnight on Sunday, you'll be needing a new mentor."

Kincaid snorted. He thought I was joking. I cocked an eyebrow and pressed my lips together to show him I wasn't. He sobered quickly. "You're serious?"

"Deadly."

"What's so special about the egg?"

"It was crafted by the merlin Peter Carl Fabergé, and it was once owned by Alexandra Romanov, the tsarina, and given by her to Grigori after he used it to save the life of her son Alexi. Or, rather, when the little Tsarevich died, Grigori used it to bring the boy back to life."

Kincaid blinked. "You're telling me that I was within five feet of *the* egg?"

"You've heard of it," I said drolly.

"I have. Finn's been after it for decades."

"I'll bet."

Kincaid chuckled, but it wasn't an especially humorous chuckle. "There isn't much more in this world that I'd love than to deny my brother one of the things he wants most."

"That's telling."

Kincaid shrugged and handed me the sleep mask. "Come on," he said. "Let's get the hell outta here before my evil twin shows up."

I took the mask but studied him for a moment before putting it on. "Someday you're going to have to tell me why there's bad blood between the two of you."

"Or not," Kincaid said, and I felt that his word on that was final. Which was fine. I'd just have to dig up the truth for myself.

Chapter Ten
Day 2

Kincaid and I spent the next two hours at the morgue, and Grigori Rasputin, I noted, was still dead. He'd been the hardest man in history to kill, yet someone had finally finished him off. I almost wanted to hand it to the killer.

Kincaid set up a meeting with the medical examiner—Dr. John Schneider—and the body, introducing me at the meeting as a material witness and consultant on the case.

Schneider eyed me skeptically, but he seemed willing enough to entertain the both of us with the details of Grigori's death.

"He suffered," he began, pointing to the gaping hole in the corpse's abdomen. "They all suffered, but I think this one and one of the women suffered the most."

"Why do you say that?" Kincaid asked.

"Shock set in for two of the victims fairly quickly. It's my educated guess that victims three and four either died immediately from the shot of adrenaline to the heart while they were being eviscerated, or very shortly thereafter. Adrenaline levels in both of them were off the charts, but this character in particular," Dr. Schneider said, tapping the toe tag of Rasputin, "he bled out, and his adrenaline levels were only slightly above normal. Uncanny, really, when you think of it. If I didn't know better, I'd say he'd tried to remain calm while pinned to a chair and his entrails cut out."

"What about the other victim?" Kincaid asked. "The woman."

Schneider nodded. "Victim number two. Yes, her adrenaline levels were also lower than expected. Not quite as low as this man but still well below normal. She would've watched the other two victims expire nearly instantly while she and this man lingered fully conscious, bound to their chairs and suffering significantly."

I had to swallow hard. The details of the murders were especially gruesome. Someone definitely wanted Grigori to suffer both mentally and physically. What I didn't offer the doctor, however, was that we, the bound, have a much different physiology than regular mortals. We age much more slowly, and our reflexes, senses, and immune systems are all significantly more enhanced. In other words, we don't need adrenaline to fuel our reactions, so our bodies all but stop producing it, which means we don't go into the physiological shock that can cause a heart attack or organs to fail in mortals. It would take a lot to kill us, and that's without any special trinkets but we're not immortal and we *can* die. Still, it typically takes an act of supreme violence to do the deed, as the body on the table in front of me attested.

"How long did it take for the two of them to die?" I asked.

Schneider eyed me over his bifocals, his silver mustache pointing down in an exaggerated frown. "Hours," he said simply. Moving over to another table with a white sheet over a body, the ME pulled back the sheet to reveal victim number two, the woman with the long blond hair, Rachel McQueen–Grigori's girlfriend.

Rachel's eyes and mouth were now closed, which was a relief but there was significant bruising around her mouth which I hadn't noticed before. "As you can see here"—the ME paused to point to the corners of her mouth, which were cut and raw—"this makes me think that she was gagged, and she struggled against it, either out of pain or desperation. Probably both. Curiously, I couldn't find a single fiber from the gag in any of her teeth or in her mouth, or in that of any of victim number three or four, but they all appear to have been gagged prior to the stabbing."

What Schneider didn't know was that the gag tied to the dinner guests had been a trinket, so while it would've felt very real to the three of them, there would be no trace evidence of anything material left behind.

"What about this one?" Kincaid asked, pointing back to Grigori. "Did he have a gag?"

Dr. Schneider came back to the table where the mystic lay. "No," he said. "Oddly, he was the last to die but there was no evidence of a gag."

Of course I knew why Rasputin hadn't been gagged. The mystic who murdered him would've wanted him talking, confessing to the location of the egg. What I didn't know was if he'd given up that location.

I studied him while I had the chance, moving my gaze down the body, which had been sewed up rather crudely along the Y incision.

There were scars in all the places you'd expect, given Grigori's history. A round dimple in his forehead and another next to his ear where a bullet to the head had failed to kill him. Three other round dimples dotted his torso, and one long scar ran just under his ribcage, where he'd been stabbed by a woman back in 1916 who'd been angry at the tales of his sexual predation. He shouldn't have lived through that encounter, but he did, and I wondered if that was when the egg had first healed him, which would take the egg down to five uses left.

Scrutinizing the body a little more, I saw that there was the slight but still evident stitching pattern running almost exactly parallel to the stitching the ME had done to his torso.

"You noticed that, eh?" Schneider asked me.

I nodded. "Yes."

He shook his head. "It's uncanny, really. If I didn't know better, I'd say that this cadaver had already experienced an autopsy... that he eventually recovered from."

Kincaid let out a rather forced chuckle. "Bet you've never worked on a zombie, eh, Doc?"

I knew what Kincaid was doing; he was trying to get the ME to agree that no such thing could've possibly happened, but Schneider merely scratched at his chin and shook his head. "I've never had a body on my table present with so many confounding paradoxes. I've noted four wounds that should've been fatal, but none of them—apart from the last—actually was. It's an extraordinary case, Detective Kincaid."

Schneider didn't even know the half of it. Still, we had to be careful here. We couldn't encourage the ME to dig deeper into the mysteries of Grigori Rasputin. It was safer if he simply chalked it up to an unusual case and moved on.

I went back to studying the body, looking for signs that the legendary mystic had had other fatal wounds, but could find only the ones already well-known to history. Well, and the one inflicted the night of the dinner party.

Steeling myself, I eyed the deep gash across his lower abdomen, wondering what had been used to make the cut. It was a precise incision, as if it'd been made with a sharp scalpel—or a jade knife like the one we'd just used for our mentoring ceremony.

Kincaid must've seen me inspecting the wound because I heard him ask, "Any tip you can offer on the murder weapon?"

Schneider sighed like he was weary of having to comment on such things. "You're looking at a surgical-quality implement with a blade at least six inches long."

"That's one sharp knife," Kincaid said.

"It would be," Schneider agreed. "Still, by the aggressive nature of the wound, I would say that the assailant is quite strong, right-handed, and definitely not squeamish. My guess is that he's a hunter."

"Could the murder weapon have come from the vic's kitchen?" Kincaid asked.

"Possibly. But the kitchen knives the CSI team brought in for me to compare are all average quality. There wasn't anything among them that would've been sharp enough or long enough to have made that kind of incision."

"So the murderer brought it with him," I said.

"Most likely. And he left with it too."

"Anything else?" Kincaid asked, his tone impatient. When Schneider's expression registered annoyance, Kincaid clarified. "What I mean is, is there anything else about the victims that stands out to you?"

Schneider shrugged again. "Two things that stand out to me that may or may not be worth mentioning."

"Yes?" I asked.

Schneider walked over to one of the cadaver drawers in the cooler wall and pulled it open. Out slid a bald woman with a youthful face but no hair or brows. It took me a moment to realize she'd been one of the dinner guests. "This woman is related to victim number two—"

"Rachel McQueen," Kincaid said, looking over to the exam table where she lay.

"Yes," Schneider said. "Probably sisters. But this woman had advanced ovarian cancer. She likely had only a few months to live. My theory is that, given her fragile health, even if she were the last person eviscerated, she was the first to succumb."

Kincaid and I traded looks. That was an interesting bit of information, and it gave me insight into another mystery about the crime scene.

Schneider shut the drawer and moved back to the table where Grigori's corpse lay.

"The other thing that stood out to me was that all the guests registered alcohol in their systems, but no one was above the legal limit except for this man. His blood-alcohol was quite high, yet his liver showed only just-above-average alkaline levels for someone who had obviously drunk excessively for many years."

"Why do you say he drank excessively?" I asked.

"Because his blood alcohol level would've put anyone else into a coma, or worse. There's no possibility that he could've been conscious if he didn't already have an extremely high tolerance."

Again, this was part of Grigori's history that was thoroughly documented. He'd been a well-known alcoholic, and I wondered if the egg had in fact been used to repair his liver. I'd have to count at least the chance of that in the number of lives the egg had left to save, which would possibly bring the egg's magical-use count down to four.

Schneider walked to the head of the corpse and sighed as he stared down at what I knew must've been a true enigma to him. "There's so much about this man's case that makes no sense, really. His organs were healthy, and if I'd seen them away from the body, I would've guessed they each came from a much younger individual. And then there's this," he said, tapping the dimple in Grigori's forehead. "See that?" he asked us.

Kincaid and I both nodded. "I'd bet my license that that's a bullet hole," Schneider said. "And yet there's no evidence of a wound beyond this slight dimple. The skull is intact and the brain undamaged. To be honest, I can't account for it."

I looked at Kincaid and made a subtle movement with my head. We needed to go before the good doctor began putting too much together.

He smiled tightly at the ME and said, "Thank you for your time, Dr. Schneider. We'll be in touch if we need anything more from you."

"I'll email you the autopsy reports," Schneider promised.

"Thank you," Kincaid said and led the way out of the room.

When we got to the corridor leading to the parking lot, Kincaid said "We're lucky that Schneider is only a few weeks away from retirement. If he were a little younger, he might start to dig into all the anomalies on Grigori's body."

"And Rachel's," I said.

He glanced sideways at me. "Mystic?"

I nodded. "Quite likely. I doubt Grigori would've taken a mortal for a lover."

Kincaid's face reddened and I found that telling. Switching topics he asked, "What's your take on the murders?"

"My take?"

"Yeah. What're your thoughts on the killer?"

By now we were at the door leading to the parking lot and Kincaid pushed on it, holding it open for me to go through first. "My take is that there was either a whole lotta anger, or a whole lotta twisted sickness involved," I said as I passed him.

"I agree," he said, joining me at my side again.

Squinting in the bright sunshine of the late morning, I added, "I also think that the killer was after the egg, and that may have motivated him to stretch out the murder for as long as possible to make Grigori not just suffer, but also confess to where the egg was."

Kincaid grunted. "We can't assume that whoever murdered Grigori knew about the egg."

"Oh, come on," I said, rolling my eyes.

"I'm serious, Esmé. The killer could've just been a sick son of a bitch who enjoyed torturing people."

"You're forgetting the most important clue though," I said.

"What's that?"

"It had to have been someone Grigori knew and trusted."

We reached his vehicle, but paused in front of it while we talked through the case.

"Why do you think it had to be someone he knew?" Kincaid asked.

"Because no way could someone have gotten into that home if Grigori's guard wasn't down. From everything that I've heard, he was one helluva powerful and suspicious mystic. He would've had wards up on all the windows and doors, and it would've taken someone on the level of Elric or Petra to penetrate them."

"That's a fair point," Kincaid conceded.

"Also remember that not only did someone get inside that house undetected, but they also got the jump on Grigori. There's no other way to explain the complete lack of physical damage to the dining room if it'd been any other way."

"That's also true," Kincaid said. "If Grigori had been overpowered, then there would've been a fight preceding that, and there would've been a path of destruction all around the area."

"Exactly."

"That makes it more likely this was a crime of passion rather than opportunity."

"I disagree," I said.

"Why?"

"Because the egg is missing."

Kincaid puffed out a breath. "The killer probably lifted it off Grigori while he was bound and gagged. He could've simply been searching for valuables when he discovered the egg."

"Nope."

Kincaid frowned at me. "You don't like that theory?"

"No. Grigori wouldn't have had the egg on him during the dinner party. In fact, he would've hidden it as far away from the dining room as possible."

"Why do you say that?"

"Because his guest, what's her name, the bald chick…"

"Sara. Sara Murphy, Rachel's sister."

"Yeah, her. She was dying from terminal cancer. Grigori must've known because no way would he have allowed anyone with a terminal disease near his precious egg. This was an intimate setting with good friends. And you don't hide late-stage ovarian cancer from the keen eyes of a mystic healer. Grigori would have wanted the egg as far away from Rachel's sister as possible."

"I'm still not understanding: Why exactly? Wasn't the egg under Grigori's control?"

"Yes and no. The egg would've detected a significant need in the room, and it would've been difficult for the mystic to have controlled the urge to heal Sara. Especially if he was drinking. I think it was far more likely that well before the Murphys arrived, he hid the egg somewhere far away from that dining room so that he could relax for the evening."

"So maybe he was tortured to give up its location?" Kincaid said.

"I think that's a much more likely scenario."

"Unless he was cut first."

"I have no doubt he was. The torture came by putting him in a position where he knew he would eventually bleed out and die out of reach of the egg, and to put the pressure on, his girlfriend and his guests were also murdered in front of him. The killer probably convinced him that if Grigori gave up the location of the egg, he'd use it to save Grigori's life."

Kincaid frowned. "Or Grigori didn't give up the location of the egg and he died anyway. It could still be hidden in the house somewhere."

"It's not."

"How do you know?"

"Because I did a thorough search of the place before you arrived. It's not there."

"Maybe you missed it."

"I didn't."

"How can you be so sure?"

"Because I'm in the business of locating hidden objects."

Kincaid eyed me skeptically. "Ah, I see. Nothing gets by you, right?"

"Nope."

At that exact moment, four very large men and one Amazonian-looking woman stepped up to surround us.

"Dammit," I growled, taking in the five newcomers who'd just turned me into the world's biggest hypocrite.

For his part, Kincaid seemed just as surprised as I was, but he didn't say a word. He simply stared over my shoulder at a presence I knew was right behind me. And I quickly realized who it was by the quickening of my pulse and a tiny spark of desire. Only then did I also notice that the charm given to me by Kincaid during the ceremony had become warm against my skin.

"Hello, brother," a voice behind me said.

"Finn," Kincaid said with a snarl. "Surprised to see you here and not at my desk, pretending to be someone important."

Finn laughed. "It's amazing what one learns hanging around the police department." Finn the Flayer then reached a quick hand to clamp down on my shoulder, not painfully, but strong enough to promise the infliction of some pain if I dared move. "We need to chat."

"I'm a little busy at the moment," Kincaid said.

"Not you," Finn said, before squeezing my shoulder. "Her. Petra wants a word."

I rolled my eyes and looked dully at Kincaid. "Guess we know whose milkshake brings all the boys to the yard."

The Amazonian snarled at me. Fun.

"Well, I guess it's not your lucky day, Finn," Kincaid said. "She's with me, and I need her so no meet and greet with your boss lady is gonna happen today."

For the next several seconds, it was so quiet you could hear a pin drop.

Which gave me an idea.

With a loud sigh, I looked right at Kincaid before narrowing my eyes, then slid my gaze sideways toward the Amazonian.

He balled his hands into fists, and I knew it was go time. Taking the initiative, he took a step toward his brother, and I used the distraction to whirl in a circle, spinning low and around, which got me out of Finn's grasp. Jerking my left hand produced a small dart from the cuff of my leather jacket, and I poked it quickly into Finn's right thigh.

He didn't seem to notice because he was also in motion, heading toward his brother. He got about two steps before the paralytic hit him and he went down to one knee.

Meanwhile I continued to spin low, which put me temporarily under the arm range of the Amazonian but still high enough to strike her with my leg in the back of the knee. As she began to fall, I gave her a prick with the dart too, right in the lower back. She went down and couldn't get back up.

Vaulting over her, I did a handspring, which brought me right up in front of one of the other goons, who smiled wickedly in my face like he was about to enjoy crushing the life out of me. Reaching to wrap me in his arms for a bear hug, I got my hand up under his chin faster than he'd anticipated, striking him in the neck. His chin collapsed to his chest, and he fell forward taking me with him.

I barely made it out from under him as his entire 300-pound massive frame fell like a giant oak onto the pavement face-first.

Spinning away several more feet, I finally stopped to assess the situation, and discovered Kincaid and Finn locked in a tangle of arms and legs, rolling on the ground.

I began to run toward them when something heavy crashed into my side and sent me flying through the air to land hard against the side of Kincaid's SUV.

For several seconds my head spun, and I slid to the ground as two goons came up and jerked me to my feet.

I tried feebly to fight them, but it was over. That blow had knocked the fight right out of me.

The remaining goon still left standing and unoccupied—and who was also the largest and most intimidating of the group—moved over to Finn and Kincaid and yanked them apart, hauling Kincaid to his feet with one hand and extending the other to Finn.

Finn took it and got up, but his right leg hung limply, which made me smirk, even given my precarious situation.

For his part, Kincaid squirmed in the grip of the behemoth holding him, and he was doing everything he could to get free, from hitting the goon's arm with his fists to trying to kick him in the 'nads.

The only thing that did was piss off the goon, who growled at Kincaid before lifting him off the ground like a ragdoll and shaking him hard.

"Gorch," Finn said softly. "He's my brother. Try not to scramble his brain."

Gorch immediately stopped shaking the life out of Kincaid, who continued to dangle there in the air, wide-eyed and obviously dazed.

Finn swiveled on his good leg and surveyed the rest of his group. Pointing to one of the goons holding me, he said, "Lurch, let Bruno handle her. You help these three get back to HQ. We're going on ahead."

Lurch protested. "We all came in the same car, man. How am I supposed to get these three back without a vehicle?"

"Take mine," he said, tossing Lurch a key fob that the big man caught with his right hand which made him let go of my left arm. Finn then moved to his brother to rummage through his back pocket, pulling up the key to Gideon's SUV.

Even with the keys to the company car, Lurch appeared irritated at having been assigned cleanup duty.

"Hey," I whispered to him.

"What?" he snarled, his eyes eyeing me like a pesky wasp he'd like to smush.

"Want to know how to get out of cleanup duty?"

His frown turned downright menacing. "How?"

I grinned. "By becoming part of the problem."

His brow rose slightly as he tried to puzzle out my meaning, but my free arm was already in motion. I think he caught on about a nanosecond before the dart still in my hand made contact with his chest. Down he went, conscious but paralyzed.

"Goddammit!" Finn yelled, glaring hard at me. "Quit doing that!"

"You mean this?" I asked, turning in to Bruno and jabbing him in the side with the dart. He went down, but he pulled me with him. Still, once I got up, I was basically free. Finn wasn't going to run after me, and Gorch was still holding onto Kincaid. Knowing that Finn wasn't about to execute his brother, I figured he'd be okay if I took off, especially because I had no such assurances for myself.

Turning toward the cover of the woods at the back of the lot, I took two steps, and felt a surge of energy build up behind me.

I ran faster, but it didn't help because a moment later what felt like a thunderbolt clocked me midback, and I was out like a light.

Chapter Eleven
Day 2

I woke up shackled, gagged, and in the hard arms of Gorch, who was carrying me down a long marble-lined hallway. Stirring as I came fully awake, and wincing because my head immediately began to pound, Gorch squeezed tighter, restricting my ribcage and my ability to breathe. This made me squirm even more, and he responded in kind until I couldn't take even a small breath. As stars danced in my vision, I made the smart choice of going limp. Gorch relaxed his grip on me, and I was able to breathe again.

I glared hard up at him, but he didn't even bother to look at me. He simply continued to walk forward, bringing us closer to a well-lit room.

Ahead of us I could see Kincaid, also in chains, being escorted along by his brother, who was dragging his right leg while he gimped down the corridor.

Blinking furiously against the splitting headache, and the brain fog that Finn's magical blow had given me, I extended my left arm a tiny bit, but no dart fell into my hand. Finn had taken it, the bastard. I then squeezed my right arm against my ribcage, feeling my monocle and die there, which brought a sigh of relief. I then did my best to look for a possible escape, but the hallway was empty of any object that could be used as a weapon, and Gorch had me effectively neutralized at the moment.

I'd have to wait and see what was waiting for us in that brightly lit room, but I did *not* have a good feeling.

Finally we got to the entryway, which was guarded by two men who had to have been part gorilla...on steroids. While, not quite as tall as Gorch, the two men were thicker and bulging with muscles. Both of them were also bald, and one actually smiled at me the way a shark smiles at a seal pup.

I set my expression so as not to recoil at the fact that his teeth had been filed into very sharp points.

"Lieutenant," the guard on the right said as Finn paused in front of them.

"Birger," Finn replied with a nod.

"She's waiting for you and wondering what took so long."

"We stopped for pizza."

Birger laughed, and at least his teeth weren't filed into fangs. Looking past Finn at the three of us, he said, "Where's the rest of 'em? Still eating pie?"

"Something like that," Finn said, patting Birger on the arm before moving past him into the room. I noticed that he was taking great pains to hide his limp.

We followed along after him, and once we were beyond the doorway, we entered into a high-domed grand hall, oval in shape and that seemed to be lined with ground pearls. The rounded walls shimmered with mesmerizing opalescence.

There were seating areas all about the room made up of off-white and pearl-colored furniture, and large shag area rugs littered the floor. The space had an atmosphere that was incredibly inviting, and likely intentionally arranged that way to persuade all who entered into dropping their guard.

I had no such plans.

Near the opposite wall next to a second exit was a high-backed throne. Studded in jewels and pearls, it was a gorgeous piece. Next to it, standing sentry was Clepsydra, Petra's high chantress—or priestess, for you mortals. She wore all the trappings of her station, bright white turtleneck which paired nicely with her olive skin, white dress slacks and a long white coat with a large broach bearing Petra's insignia on it.

Given her reputation, I eyed her warily.

Clepsydra is an ancient mystic; one of the very oldest in fact, and had she not made the unfortunate error of being on the losing side in the Great Battle where Petra and Elric first came to power, she would, without a doubt, have been the most powerful mystic in the world.

After the battle when the chantress had been captured, Elric had ordered her slain, but Petra had seen something of a kinship in her, so she'd interceded and spared Clepsydra's life.

Still, Elric had ensured that some of Clepsydra's powers were clipped. Her binder had been murdered in the battle so Elric had rebound Clepsydra with a new and quite-deadly binding spell. If he or Petra ever activated the binding spell, Clepsydra would die on the spot, which of course immediately tamed any urge for the chantress to misbehave.

Even so, clipping her wings hadn't rendered Clepsydra powerless. She was still far, *far* more powerful than someone like me, and likely within the top thirty most powerful mystics in the world.

Not to mention that she was as mean and bloodthirsty as they came. Which made her very, *very* dangerous.

Originally Clepsydra had been enslaved and forced to preform menial tasks for Elric, but when Petra had separated from Elric, she'd taken half his court and Clepsydra with her.

Very quickly thereafter, she'd elevated Clepsydra to chantress—her primary adviser, and the move had solidified the mystic's allegiance to her queen. It was well-known that Clepsydra worshiped the ground Petra walked on for giving her back the dignity that restored the chantress's reputation.

Over the past five hundred years or so, the two had formed a rather dangerous alliance, one that Elric definitely kept his eye on. If Petra ever wanted to take on her husband in a true battle for power, she'd have to do so with Clepsydra's full cooperation—which was a tricky thing because Elric wouldn't go down without a fight, and he'd made it perfectly clear that should Petra and her chantress team up against him, he'd invoke Clepsydra's binding spell, killing her before the day was done.

That kept both Petra and Clepsydra in check. But just barely.

Next to the chantress the throne sat empty, and there was a palpable note of expectation in the air as we all waited in silence for her royal-pain-in-the-assness to arrive, which she did before too long, emerging from the opposite doorway in her signature cream, Greek goddess gown and enough gold bangles and trinkets to sink a ship.

The gown and the gold were meant to show as much skin and as much power as possible, and the effect was perfection because Petra Dobromila Ostergaard was a stunning sight to behold. Petite, slight, and with the grace of a ballerina, she moved with the fluidity of water, gliding into the room, the heels of her golden sandals clicking against the white marble floor.

Her waist-length hair was partially wound with a golden cord to coil atop her head, with enough excess left over to braid midway down her back and swish from side to side as she made her way to her throne.

Alabaster skin, an oval face, big brown eyes, and full lips tinged with deep red lipstick finished off the effect.

"Finn," she purred after she'd slid onto her throne to sit and consider us.

"Petra," he said, placing a hand over the silver pin bearing Petra's insignia which was attached to his shirt, and adding a slight bow.

Petra smiled at him in a way that made me think she liked Finn for more than his flaying skills. After a moment her gaze flickered past him to us. "I see you come bearing gifts."

"Yes," Finn said, stepping carefully forward to the center of the room, which had amazing acoustics. No one needed to raise their voice to be heard loud and clear. "But I'm only bringing you one. The other I plan to keep."

Petra smirked. "Brotherly love. So annoying."

Finn offered another slight bow. "Your continued tolerance of my unmentored twin is much appreciated."

Petra cocked an eyebrow and pursed her lips. It was clear her tolerance was beginning to thin. She then crossed one leg over the other and sat back lazily on her throne. Her attention flickered to me, and I watched with annoyance as her sculpted nose wrinkled in distaste. "Who's this... other one?"

Finn turned slightly to look back at me. As he did so, Gorch lowered one arm and I slid to a standing position, still bound and gagged but doing my best not to show that it bothered me.

"Esmé Bellerose. She's one of Elric's."

Petra pursed her lips and narrowed her big brown eyes. "She's not really his type. But that man will bed anything that moves these days."

Even you, I thought but did not say. Petra was the type of woman you really wanted to bitch slap, but even a cross look from me could get me killed, so I kept my expression neutral.

"Esmé was the last person to see your son before he disappeared," Finn told her.

Petra's back went ridged and she sat forward. "She knows where Marco is?"

In answer, Finn turned to me and motioned to Gorch, who yanked hard on the gag in my mouth.

I worked my jaw a little after being freed of the gag, drawing out the impatience of my host.

"I believe the lady asked you a question," Finn warned.

"Did she?" I asked innocently. "Guess I didn't hear it. What was it again?"

In an instant my right foot felt as if it were on fire. The pain was so intense that I sank to my knees. Gripping my ankle, I pooled some of my essence around my foot hoping it would act as a counterspell, and to my relief it worked; the pain lessened, and I was able to stand up again. Forcing myself to take slow, even breaths, I regarded Petra again. She stared at me with one cocked eyebrow, but she didn't speak. She simply waited.

Knowing I no longer had much to lose and thinking I was already pressed for time, I decided to cooperate. Somewhat. "The last time I saw your son was at his girlfriend's apartment. This was right after it blew up."

"You were there at the time of the blast?" she asked.

"I was."

"Tell me *exactly* what happened."

I laid out the story for her but left out a few key details, which she was keen to pick up on.

"Why was my son in bed and incapacitated?" she demanded.

I inhaled a steadying breath. If I got caught lying, she'd kill me for sure. "Because I had activated his binding spell a few hours earlier."

No one spoke for several seconds, and there was an expectant hush about the room. Next to Petra I noticed that Clepsydra leaned forward eagerly, an evil smile playing its way onto her lips. She couldn't wait for the word from her queen to kill me.

But Petra surprised us all when she said, "How do you know how to activate Marco's binding spell?"

"Your son revealed it to me when he lost a bet in a poker game we played several years ago. As you're probably also aware, Marco is very good at ferreting out information that is often beneficial to someone in my position, and his binding gives me the leverage I need to strike a deal with him now and again."

Petra's mouth quirked, and she tapped the arm of her throne with one elegant, well-manicured finger. "What information were you looking for from him?" she asked.

"It was information that your husband needed," I said. Which was true... in a way.

Petra's eyes narrowed. "What information was that?"

"Private," I told her. "I'm very sorry, ma'am, but I'm bound by the honor of my position to keep Elric's secrets. I can't reveal what Marco told me to anyone but my employer."

Petra scoffed, but even I knew that it was for effect because Petra definitely understood how this game was played. If she killed me outright because I refused to give her information that Elric had sent me to fetch, then Elric would be justified in killing one of her employees, and no way would her husband choose to assassinate a lowly thief in Petra's camp to even the score. He'd aim high, simply to teach her a lesson. It was a risk I didn't think Petra was willing to take.

"So where is my son now?" she demanded.

"I have no idea. And that's the truth."

She scoffed again. "You expect me to believe you based on your earnest insistence? How do I know you haven't kidnapped Marco? Or killed him?"

"It's true that I was with him moments before he was abducted. It's not true that I had anything to do with his abduction."

"And I should believe you ... why?"

"Because if I knew where he was or had anything to do with his kidnapping and I'd been captured by your lieutenant and brought here to stand in front of you, I'd be working pretty hard right now to negotiate something with you for his release, because I'm certain you'd kill me otherwise."

Petra seemed to consider that. With a sigh, she said, "Tell me more about this explosion."

I told her everything I could remember about it, how there was a change in the energy within the room, how it intensified over a period of several seconds before the blast, and how the energy had intensified again just as I released Marco from the spasms.

At the end of my speech, Petra turned to Clepsydra and said, "Sound familiar?"

Clepsydra nodded, her hands bunching into fists. "Rubi."

Petra sucked in a surprised breath. "Hideyo's priestess?"

Clepsydra nodded again. "Yes. And if Rubi's in town, Hideyo is here with her."

Hideyo was head of the East Asian empire. Said to be as ruthless as he was conniving, he never made a move without having taken into account all of the possible outcomes.

In other words, he wasn't stupid. Which meant that grabbing Tic was a calculated maneuver for power.

If it was his priestess, Rubi, who'd blasted a hole in Bree's apartment, that meant that I was damned lucky to be alive and that I could have stumbled into the very beginnings of a war.

Petra looked like she was sucking on a lemon. "Dammit," she swore, getting to her feet to pace the space in front of her throne while everyone else in the room eyed each other nervously.

Finally she stopped and looked directly at Finn. "Find. My. Son," she commanded.

Even I gulped.

"By any means necessary," she continued. "But do it quietly. And bring him back here to me."

Finn said nothing, he simply placed his hand on that pin again and bent at the waist.

Petra turned away and began to walk toward the exit.

"What about her?" Gorch asked, and I wanted to smack him. It'd looked like I might skate out of this situation after all until the three-hundred-pound village idiot spoke up.

Petra paused and turned her head ever so slightly. "Kill her, then feed her to one of my pets to make sure there's no lingering trace of her. We don't need to invite more trouble from Elric."

With that, she was gone.

Finn turned toward me as Petra disappeared through the doorway. Our eyes locked, and I could feel the well of desire spring up, and it made the charm around my neck heat up again. With some deep breaths I was able to quell the worst of the desire, but it was a challenge.

Stepping to Gorch, who still had me by the arm, he said, "I'll take it from here."

Gorch tightened his grip on my arm and I winced. If he squeezed any harder, he'd break the bone. "Petra said I get to kill her."

Finn lifted his chin and curled his lip into a snarl. "Stand down, soldier," he said very softly.

Gorch growled low in his throat, but he released my arm and I rocked on my feet with relief. But it was short-lived.

"Walk," Finn said to me, indicating the doorway we'd entered through.

I looked around the room. Absolutely no one was going to come to my defense. Well, except for Kincaid, who looked ready to murder his brother.

"Not without my protégé," I said, nodding toward Kincaid.

Finn's brow furrowed. "Your what?"

"Hasn't he told you?" I asked innocently. "I'm his mentor."

"Yeah, right," Finn said, taking me roughly by the arm and whirling me toward the door.

His touch sent a bolt of electricity through me and I jerked. Finn dropped my arm, his brow furrowing. He then pointed past me toward the exit. "Move," he said.

He then took his brother by the shoulder and shoved him hard in front of him. Kincaid stumbled into me, but I was able to stiffen against the blow of his body, which allowed him to remain upright and find his balance again. He eyed me gratefully, the gag still wedged into his mouth, and it honestly made me furious that Finn was being such a shit to his twin.

With equal resolve, we began to shuffle back out the way we'd come, this time side by side. When we cleared the oval chamber, Finn called from behind us, "Turn left at the next corridor."

I estimated he was about five feet behind us, and I wondered what I could do to take him down. His were the only other footfalls behind us, and I suspected he thought he could handle the two of us on his own.

Of course, as Petra's lieutenant, he was likely powerful enough to do just that.

Still, I hadn't made it ninety-three years as a successful thief without a bit of resourcefulness; however, Petra's headquarters weren't exactly filled with opportunity. In truth, I didn't even know where the hell we were.

As ordered, we turned left at the juncture and entered a darkened corridor that felt more like a tunnel than a hallway inside a building. Lights overhead illuminated as we approached, then dimmed again as we walked past, while the walls, ceiling, and floor appeared to be cement, and our footfalls reverberated noisily as we walked its length.

There didn't appear to be any doorways off the corridor either, which was odd. It seemed to go on and on, bending ever so slightly to the right and the grade leveling down as we moved along. Before I knew it, the air became damp and cold, and I swore we were now underground.

At last, a giant riveted metal door appeared that looked quite capable of preventing either exit or entrance.

Kincaid and I stopped in front of it and turned slightly to see if Finn would order us through. He walked forward, nudging between us before gripping the lever and hauling it up. He then yanked on the door.

It groaned in annoyance, but light shone into the corridor from the open air beyond.

Warm, humid, dank-smelling air hit us immediately. I wrinkled my nose, and Kincaid eyed me in alarm as the hairs on the back of my neck stood up on end. In front of us was a tropical jungle that looked straight out of the Amazon. Vines slithered to the earth from massive tree trunks, and moss seemed to be growing on every surface. The ground itself was littered with bones—some human, some not, and based on experience, I can tell you that's never a good sign.

To make a creepy scene even creepier, an eerie series of clicks and high-pitched squeaks echoed out from something unseen, hidden by the tangle of foliage.

While Kincaid and I were gawking at the scene, Finn put a hard hand on my shoulder.

At the feel of his touch, aggressive though it was, my heart raced, and I had the intense urge to turn around and collapse against him. With great effort, I tamped the desire down and tried to assess the situation in front of us. No way was this an exit. We were someplace magical. Someplace dangerous.

Finn lowered his lips close to my ear, and I closed my eyes in pleasure. "Word has it that you faced off against Jacquelyn's ruby-throated dragon," he whispered.

"I did," I said, forcing my voice to sound commanding and unaffected.

Finn laughed softly, the sound throaty and exquisitely sexy. "Jacquelyn's a trip. She loves monsters—the deadlier the better—but even she has her limits, or so I'm told."

Finn's grip on my shoulder tightened painfully. "This is where we keep one of her rejects."

At that moment, a twelve-foot-tall spider's leg stepped out of the foliage and pierced a skull lying on the green moss carpet in front of us. And then another leg appeared to crash down on the ground, sending bones flying. Then another leg. And another, until all eight legs and two sets of giant fangs dripping with spittle were in view just beyond the doorway. What light there was, coming from overhead, was blocked out by whatever massive body this creature possessed.

Out of the corner of my eye, I saw Kincaid's head twist and rub hard against his shoulder. Managing to free himself from the gag, he yelled, "Finn! Don't—!"

But Finn the Flayer was already shoving me hard. I stumbled forward, lost my footing, and went down to the ground just as I heard the door slam shut behind me.

Rolling quickly to the side, I managed to avoid being skewered by one of the spider's legs, but even I knew that I stood little chance against this monster unless I managed to free myself from my bindings and improvised a weapon of some kind because I had no trinket on me that could take on something this big and this deadly.

Even before I could come up with a reasonable plan, I had to dive to the side again to avoid the two fangs bearing down on me with alarming speed.

I ran to the opposite end of the monster, away from the fangs and toward what I hoped was its rear. It spun around like a nimble-footed nymph.

I dived again, tumbling in somersault fashion to avoid yet another leg. This time it thundered into the ground so hard, the terrain shook and more bones flew.

For the next several seconds, all I did was weave, bob, dive, roll, and leap in a tight circle, trying my damnedest to avoid getting skewered, but the monster kept coming for me.

And every time I thought I could make it into the coverage of the jungle, a leg or a fang blocked my escape.

But then I noticed something. Where the spittle from the fangs would land, there was a slight sizzle, and a small blue flame would sprout up before quickly flaming out, leaving a charred patch of earth behind.

This told me two things: First, avoid getting splattered by the monster's spittle at all costs; and two, use the obviously corrosive substance to my advantage.

My opportunity came when I darted in a figure-eight pattern and grabbed hold of one of the legs that'd just missed me by a fraction of an inch. The monster lifted the leg, with me still dangling from it, and began to bring it toward its fangs.

Right before the monster could bite into me, I swung forward, raising my hands in front of me and spreading my arms as far apart as the shackles would allow. The chain between the two metal wristbands grazed the monster's fangs with an eerie raking sound, and I dropped again to the ground and rolled away.

Springing up again, I yanked hard on the shackles and the chain broke. My hands were now essentially free, and I was ready to fight back.

As the monster came at me again, I reached for a legbone lying on the ground. Shoving some of my essence into it, I forced it to grow into a staff, then, using it like a pole vault, I managed to raise myself out of the way just as those fangs descended on me. Whipping around, I had to spin in another tight circle, dodging the fangs of the beast while getting closer to one of the legs. I then used the improvised staff like a cudgel, giving the monster's leg a blow to one of the joints, using all the strength I could muster.

As my staff connected, there was a satisfying splintering sound and a screech so loud that I nearly dropped my weapon. The monster sagged dramatically to one side, and when it rose up again, that leg dangled limply. Realizing I'd just discovered a huge vulnerability for the beast, I leapt and rolled forward again, back under the monster's belly, before once again making a strike against the opposite leg.

The beast stumbled and screeched, and it curled its ugly head down toward me, its fangs desperate to sink their length into my flesh. Deflecting those fangs with my staff wasn't easy, but I managed. I then ducked low under that belly again, coming up right next to a rear leg.

Whack! went my staff, and the beast's leg joint crumpled. The monster jerked, its sound of rage and pain rising to ear-splitting levels again.

My head pounded from the noise, but I never once slowed. I just kept striking at those leg joints until it was balanced on only three, and severely limited in its mobility.

By now the monster's massive belly was just overhead, and I could reach up and feel the hairs, thick as corn cobs and sharp as knives, crowding down around me.

I'd have one more strike if I was lucky, and I had to be careful where to place it or this thing would die on top of me, impaling me while also smothering me to death.

With a heaving chest, I gave myself just three deep lungfuls of air, recognizing that I was reaching the point of exhaustion. Sweat dripped down from my hairline into my eyes, and I blinked furiously to see.

As I wheezed out that third and final breath, I spotted a red dot on the underbelly of the monster, and that seemed as good a target as any.

Stumbling forward a few steps, I was able to position myself right under the red dot. The monster must've foreseen my motive, because it attempted to skitter backward, but I was faster.

Using the very last of my remaining strength, I pivoted the sharp point of the staff up toward the red dot, jumping with the effort, and felt my weapon sink into the beast's belly.

It arched up and jerked violently. Far more violently, in fact, than I'd anticipated, and because I was still holding tightly to the staff, I was flipped up in the air a good fifteen feet, smacking hard into a tree.

There was a disturbing crunching sound on impact, emanating from my rib cage in tandem with the *thunk* that sounded when my head hit the tree so hard that my vision closed to a pinpoint of light. I fell in a heap to the ground, feebly clawing at the earth, my left side erupting in pain. Fighting through the temptation to black out, I forced myself to gather my legs underneath me in an attempt to get up, worrying that the monster might still be alive and ready to finish me off. Blinking furiously, I focused only on pushing myself to my feet, managing to slowly rise. I got about halfway to a standing position when the world closed into darkness again and I sank back down to the ground. My body felt like it'd been clobbered by a wrecking ball. I sucked in a deep breath, which gave way to a coughing fit and brought new waves of pain.

I put my hand to my mouth and it came away bloody. The blow to the tree had broken a rib and punctured a lung.

"Fucker," I gasped.

But my various injuries weren't something I could tend to at the moment. I had to get to my feet, because what I didn't yet know was if I'd done the monster more harm than it'd done me. I curled onto my knees and, holding my ribs with one arm, I used the other to push up onto my feet again. This time I was able to stand about as well as a guy on his third six-pack.

Swaying to and fro, I looked dully around, my vision closing to a pinprick and then expanding back out again, over and over, and the effect was making me dizzy as hell. It was also intensely difficult to both get enough air into my one working lung and try not to expand my ribcage. With each breath, the pain seemed to intensify, and I knew that I'd probably lose the ability to remain upright very soon.

At last, I spotted the creature. It was on its back, three of its legs curling inward as small spasms made them shudder.

The makeshift weapon I'd used to impale it had done the trick; a pool of pale blue liquid oozed out and coated a large section of the ground.

Somewhat relieved, I sank back to my knees, even though I couldn't be absolutely positive that I was out of danger yet; I simply didn't have the strength or ability to move away from the scene.

A long time seemed to pass. Maybe an hour. Maybe two, and my condition only worsened. I was having a hell of a time remaining conscious, and there was now a gurgling sound accompanying every breath.

I had to get home to Ember or I wasn't going to survive long enough to worry about what that might mean.

With a substantial amount of effort, I rolled to my knees again, but I couldn't stand. The best I could do was crawl forward in the general direction of the door but that was a substantial struggle. Still, I found the exit far more easily than I should've, given the way the world kept spinning around me every time I lifted my head.

At the foot of the door, I inched my way up to the handle and tried to turn it but of course it was locked, so I reached into my jacket pocket and pulled out my trusty pick.

The effort to pick the lock felt endless. It was so difficult to focus because my vision kept fading to a pinprick and then back out again and I could see my fingertips begin to turn blue from lack of oxygen. My one working lung felt congested and I simply couldn't get the air I needed to concentrate longer than a few seconds. Finally, after what seemed like hours, I felt the lock give way.

"Thank the gods," I whispered. Holding my ribcage with my right arm, I used my left to crawl up the door, turn the handle, and pull. It opened with a rush, and I lost my balance. Falling backward, I didn't even try to fight to save myself. I was too weak, slowly suffocating to death.

The best I could do was brace for impact, and to that, I squeezed my eyes shut and waited for the blow, but something caught me just as I was about to land hard on the ground, and I was then hoisted up into the air.

I coughed hard and wheezed out a cry of pain as I was lifted up.

"Where does it hurt?" a voice asked.

My eyes were closed, and my head lolled on my neck. I could no more answer the voice than I could fight off the arms that were holding me.

"Esmé," the voice called. And that's when I recognized it.

"Kin..caid?" I whispered.

"Yeah," he said.

I opened my eyes a fraction and saw my protégé, looking a bit worse for wear. His left eye was black-and-blue, and his lower lip was bleeding and puffy. His shirt was torn and dirty, and his hair was an absolute mess. He looked like he'd gone a few rounds with Gorch. I coughed several times and gasped for air that barely provided my working lung with enough to live on. "H-h-how..."

"It's been a while since my brother and I went at it, but I managed to get a couple of good punches in and sneak back here. We don't have much time, but I think I know a way out. Can you walk?"

My head lolled on my neck again, and it was all I could do to turn it back and forth a few times. No way could I manage to even stand at the moment.

"Okay," he said. "I'll carry you. It'll slow us down, but I think we can still make it."

My lips quirked upward in what I hoped was an encouraging smile. "I have to… home," I whispered. "I'll die if…"

"Where's home?" he asked.

My mind wanted to reply. I knew it was important, but I was also fading fast, having a hard time staying conscious.

"Esmé," Kincaid repeated urgently. "Where's home?"

"Warehouse," I wheezed then coughed up some blood again. "End of… Pendleton. Old Town North." I managed.

Kincaid gathered me carefully against him and began to walk forward. It reminded me so much of just a few days before when Dex had done the same. Just like then, I allowed myself to let go, dipping my head against Kincaid's chest, wrapping my palm around the charm at my neck. And then I was out like a light.

Chapter Twelve
Day 3

Bright light and the sound of birdsong awakened me. I stirred and felt Ember nuzzle against me. I curled around her warm body and kissed the top of her head. She licked my nose and I smiled.

And then everything that'd happened the day before came rushing back and I sat bolt upright.

I looked around my room for a moment, trying to fill in the pieces between being carried out of Petra's lair by Kincaid and arriving here, but I had no memory of it. I looked down at myself and saw that I was wearing only my tank top from the day before and a thong.

Thank the gods I wasn't naked. I then looked to Ember, who was staring at me with her knowing olive-green eyes, as if she understood exactly what I was thinking.

Truth is, she probably did.

I felt my ribs, gingerly at first, with my fingers. There was no pain or even discomfort. I then put a hand to my head, which felt clear and whole.

All seemed well.

Laying a hand on Ember, I kissed the little divot between her eyes and said, "Thank you."

She licked my nose again.

I got up, shuffled into some leggings and a sweatshirt, and headed out of my bedroom in search of Dex.

When I got to the catwalk, I stopped dead in my tracks. There was an argument happening on the ground floor, and I recognized both voices.

"Shit!" I said, jogging to the middle of the catwalk, where I hopped over the railing, caught the rope, and slid down fireman-style.

I landed dramatically in front of Kincaid and Dex, both of them flexing their arms and curling their hands into fists. Whatever was going on, it was bad, and it was escalating.

"Hello, luv," Dex said in a stilted voice, without turning his gaze away from Kincaid.

Uh, oh. My homeboy was maaaaad. "Dex," I said casually. "How's things?"

"A bit sticky this morning, now that you ask. This bloke thinks he's got the run of the place. Won't leave, even though I told him all's well and he should git."

"How're you feeling?" Kincaid asked me.

My gaze went to him, and suddenly I realized that Dex was in very, very grave danger. If things escalated to an actual fight between the two, there was no doubt my second would be slaughtered.

Forcing myself to remain calm I quickly thought through my options. "I'm good," I told him. "Right as rain. Turns out I just had my bell rung, and all I needed was a good night's sleep."

He considered me with a doubtful frown.

Turning away from him, I focused on Dex. I'd have to get him out of here immediately. "How'd your recon go yesterday, buddy?"

Dex continued to angrily curl his hands into fists and glare hard at the stranger in his kitchen. "Well enough. I've got a lead. I'm headed back to D.C. today."

"No time like the present," I said.

Dex finally turned his head and settled his flinty gaze on me, but he did it slowly, as if to drive home the point that I'd said something out of turn. Which, realistically, I had.

"I could've come to get you last night," he said, his tone cold. "You didn't have to let this mongrel bring you home and expose us."

There was a slight change in the atmosphere, as if the energy in the room began to gather and vibrate around Kincaid. I knew what was about to happen, but I didn't know how to stop it. "Dex," I said softly. "Please. I wasn't in any position to reach out to you last night. I was about done in, and my protégé here," I paused to indicate Kincaid, "risked his life to get me safely out of Petra's lair. We can grant him quarter for a few minutes this morning without starting a third World War, can't we?"

"Can we?" Dex asked, his expression betraying how hurt and angry he truly was. "I know he's your protégé, Ezzy, but we can't have him walking about, knowing where we *live.*"

I gulped. The energy in the room gathered a few degrees more around Kincaid. My heart was beginning to pound, and I didn't know how to save Dex. I probably had maybe only ten seconds to figure that out.

And then, like a miracle, Ember trotted into the room and went right up to Kincaid. Putting her muzzle against his leg, she looked up at him and wagged her tail. And just like that all the tension evaporated.

Dex and I exchanged looks of utter disbelief, while Kincaid bent down and gently rubbed her ears. "She's sweet," he said.

Ember's tail wagged even more enthusiastically, and she doubled down by curling her body into Kincaid and leaning hard against him while he continued to stroke her.

Recovering myself, I stepped forward and grabbed Dex by the arm.

"This way," I said, forcibly escorting him through the kitchen to the rear exit.

"Ez," Dex said firmly, beginning to tug on his arm. "Stop, okay? We need to talk about this."

I let go and turned to him. "I'm sorry, Dex. I really am. I wouldn't have led him here if I hadn't been in really, *really* bad shape."

Dex frowned. Thumbing over his shoulder, he said, "Your detective said Petra's lieutenant picked you two up and then he threw you to *riese spinne*."

My brow furrowed. "It was a giant blue spider."

Dex smirked. "Riese spinne literally means giant spider."

"Ah," I said. "Well then, you know. Anyway, I got my bell rung, and I was barely conscious when he found me. It was all I could do to tell him where I lived before I blacked out."

Dex crossed his arms and continued to frown at me.

I rolled my eyes. "In the middle of fighting off Petra's pet spider, I couldn't very well whip out my cellphone and call you. What could I have said anyway? 'Hey, Dex, I'm somewhere in Petra's stronghold, but I don't know where and, oh yeah, *there's a giant fucking spider currently attacking me!*'"

Dex pouted down at me. "No need to shout," he said.

"Oh, I think there just might be."

"Fine," he relented. "If you had no choice, you had no choice."

I softened too. "I'll make sure he doesn't give away our location to anyone," I said, already formulating a plan.

"Tell him he'd better not," Dex said. "Or I'll have to step in." For emphasis Dex flexed both biceps.

I grimaced. I had to get him out of here before he pissed off our houseguest again and things escalated. "I gotta get back in there," I said, motioning toward where Kincaid and Ember were.

"Yeah, yeah," Dex said heading to the door with me close behind. "I'm leaving, but I need to tell you something."

"What?"

"I stopped off at Gert's last night for my usual nightcap, and she told me all about you being there yesterday morning and she wanted to know if you'd been the one that'd been seen leaving Bree's apartment after it blew."

"What'd you tell her?" I asked as we stepped out into the garage.

Dex flattened his expression as if I'd insulted him. "What do you think I told her?"

"I'm assuming nothing?"

"Correct," he said. "But she did tell me a few things."

"Like what?" I was growing impatient with him, anxious for him to be on his way.

"Like the fact that Bree had been in Gert's place last week, talking to another mystic, a blonde who put on airs every time Gert swung by the table."

I winced. Gert didn't usually tolerate that kind of attitude.

"Right?" Dex said, reading my expression. "Anyway, Gert says that the woman wasn't anyone she knew, but toward the end of the conversation the mystic bursts into tears and Bree had to comfort her."

I blinked at him. "*Bree* gave *comfort* to someone?"

Dex nodded. "That's exactly what I said to Gert and she was as surprised as I was to see it."

"Huh," I said, not knowing yet what to make of the story. "Could be something or it could be nothing."

"Exactly, but I thought I'd pass it on in case it connects to your quest for the egg."

"Thanks, Dex," I said, moving in to hug him fiercely.

He hugged me back and said, "I'll be in D.C. for the rest of the day. You gonna be okay here on your own?"

"I'll be fine," I said, far more firmly than I felt.

Dex kissed me on the forehead, backed away, got in his Mustang and glared at the door leading to inside one last time. I could tell that he was still a little miffed about Kincaid being in our warehouse.

Thank God he didn't know the truth, and thank God things hadn't escalated between him and our house guest because my second would never have survived the battle.

Walking back into the dining area of the kitchen I saw that neither Kincaid nor Ember were there. Moving deeper into the warehouse, I finally spotted them on the couch; Ember was cuddled up against Kincaid while he pointed the remote at the TV.

My breath caught slightly when I realized that the bruises to his lip and his eye were fading dramatically, given the fact that Ember was healing him. Walking toward the pair, I picked up a yellow crystal that Dex had acquired somewhere in his travels. Stepping in front of Kincaid, I handed it to him.

"Here," I said.

He took it and inspected it. "What's this?"

"It has healing properties. Roll it around your face, and it'll take down the swelling."

Kincaid eyed me skeptically, but he reluctantly put the crystal to his face and rubbed it along his skin.

I began to head back to the kitchen and whistled to Ember. "Come on, girl. Let's get you some breakfast."

To my relief, I heard the pitter-patter of her feet behind me and I got her breakfast together, waiting until she'd gobbled it down to then let her out into the grassy, tree-lined courtyard.

Once I was sure she was out of harm's way, I slid a hunting knife I always kept near the back door into my waistband.

My guest was at the mirror hanging on the wall, admiring his face. I walked over to peek at him over his shoulder.

He grinned and held up the crystal. "This thing works great. Can I buy it off you?"

I smiled in return. "Sure."

"How much?"

"Ten grand."

His eyes bugged. "That's a little steep, don't you think?"

I shrugged casually. "Judging by how quickly it healed that ugly mug of yours, I'd say you're the one getting the bargain."

He grinned anew and rubbed his thumb over the surface of the crystal. "Eight grand."

"Nine."

"Eighty-five hundred and we have a deal," he said, turning to me and holding out his free hand.

I took his outstretched palm in my right hand, stepped forward, and thrust the tip of my knife up toward his ribcage, stopping just short of plunging it into him.

He looked down at the knife, and his brow rose in surprise. "Okay, okay. Nine grand it is."

I continued to glare at him. "What're you doing here, *Finn*."

The bastard actually chuckled. "What gave me away?"

I nodded toward his left hand, still holding the crystal, thankful that I had something other than the truth to point to. "No wedding ring. And no tan line to indicate you ever wear one."

Finn nodded, his eyes twinkling like he was quite amused. "So, what do we do now, Esmé?"

"Let's start by you telling me what you're doing here?" I repeated.

"I brought you home and wanted to make sure you lived through the night."

"You didn't seem so concerned with that when you fed me to the itsy-bitsy spider."

He rolled his eyes. "Like I told you: I heard that Jaquelin tested you against her ruby-throated dragon, and you obviously survived. I figured that, after winning against her dragon, the *rise spinne* would be child's play, and, to be honest, I was surprised you had as rough a time as you did."

Anger simmered like hot coals deep in my chest. "Maybe that's 'cause *somebody* forgot to unshackle me."

"Oh, I didn't forget," he said smugly.

The man was infuriating. Poking him a little more with my blade, I asked, "What game are you playing, Lieutenant?"

Finn shrugged, but that amused expression never wavered. "I'm just a boy, standing in front of a girl, asking her not to kill me."

My eyes narrowed, Finn chuckled, and my temper got the better of me. Up went my knee, right into his groin.

Finn let out a bark of pain and doubled over. "Dammit!" he moaned before coughing until his face turned red. "That's dirty pool, Esmé."

"No dirtier than pretending to be your brother so that you could find out where I live, asshole."

Finn waddled over to the couch and collapsed into it. "Seemed only fair," he said with a groan. "You've been to my place, after all."

I pressed my lips together. He sorta had me there. "That wasn't my idea."

"Yeah, yeah," he said, pressing the crystal against his crotch. "I'm sure it was all Gideon. Still, you're lucky I didn't kill you outright for that alone."

The sound of Ember whimpering echoed from the back door. I kept the knife firmly gripped in my hand and said to Finn, "Do not move."

He eyed his crotch meaningfully and continued to wince while holding the crystal against his manhood.

I trotted to the kitchen and let Ember in. She rubbed against me happily and then headed straight for the couch, cuddling up to Finn, no doubt because she sensed his distress.

A wave of jealousy hit me hard. Ember had never, ever helped heal anyone but me and Dex. She was beyond loyal to us alone, and yet here she was, giving her powers away to my mortal enemy. I couldn't figure out why she didn't sense how dangerous Finn was to me, and for that matter, to her as well.

Finn, of course, didn't have a clue about her powers. Even as she cuddled against him, I saw his pained expression lessen, and he lifted the crystal away to admire it again. "Man, this thing works quick."

I nodded, thinking that maybe I needed to cement the idea that the crystal was responsible and not my pup. "Yeah, that thing can work wonders. On second thought, I don't believe I want to part with it." I then held out my hand as if I expected him to give it back to me.

Instead, Finn closed his fist around it. "A deal's a deal, Esmé."

I sighed, as if I was only just realizing the lousy bargain I'd made. "Fine," I said. "But I want the funds today."

"No problem. I'll Venmo you."

Finn took out his phone and I took out mine. The money exchange was fast and efficient, and I worked to hide a smirk at the fact that I'd just sold a worthless paperweight to Petra's lieutenant for nine grand.

Setting aside the phone, I regarded Finn sternly. "Where's your brother?"

He shook his head and shrugged. "Probably out looking for me."

"You let him go?"

"Of course I let him go. He's my twin and I'm not a monster."

"What really happened to your face?" I asked next.

"I needed Gideon's clothes to make you think it was him. He didn't want me to have them."

I crossed my arms. "You're telling me that Gideon did all that damage while he was shackled?"

"No. I unshackled him and then he sucker-punched me."

I cocked an eyebrow.

"Twice."

"So you two are close."

Finn pocketed the crystal and began rubbing Ember's ears. She sighed with pleasure. "He's ticked off that I wouldn't bring him into the mystic fold and that I also actively worked to keep him out. An arrangement you've now ruined."

"Why?" I asked, genuinely curious. "I mean, why wouldn't you allow him to be mentored?"

"Do you really have to ask?"

"Yes."

Finn sighed. "You know what it's like, Esmé. This world is rough, and there's no place for Boy Scouts. My brother's a solid guy. He always does the morally right thing, and in our world, that will get you killed quick. Plus he's a liability for me. If he enters the realm, powerfully evil people—"

"You mean Elric's crew," I interrupted, crossing my arms.

Finn continued as if I hadn't spoken: "—are going see an opportunity, and they'll either kidnap Gideon to use him against me, or they'll mistake him for me, challenge him to a duel, which my hot-headed brother will definitely accept, and he'll be nothing but ash and cinder before he can even pull out a trinket."

I felt my breath catch. I hadn't thought of that.

Finn eyed me knowingly. "Didn't think that through before you went along with the mentoring ceremony, did ya?"

"Not fully."

He nodded. "And now you're responsible for him. He's a newbie and your protégé, and you'll have to spend some time working out a plan to keep him safe. Which is the real reason I fed you to the *riese spinne*. I wanted to make sure you were up for the challenge."

"My second, Dex, and I will look out for him, Finn," I said, irritated that this guy kept gloating over being one chess move ahead of me.

Finn nodded toward the back door. "I like Dex," he said. "It'd be a shame to have to kill him."

My back went rigid. "Is that a threat?"

Finn gave Ember one final rub and stood up. He walked right up to me, getting deep into my personal space while he stared down at me, and to my endless irritation, my pulse quickened, and I felt a renewed lust for him well up inside of me just as the charm burned like a hot coal against my skin.

"It's absolutely a threat, Ms. Bellerose," he whispered softly. "If my brother dies, so does your second."

The look in Finn's eyes was deadly serious, but there was also something else there too, something smoldering and sexual.

The charm around my neck began to pulse, and as it pulsed, it burned against my chest, but I dared not call any attention to the charm.

Still, as if Finn could sense my pain, his gaze dropped to right where the charm lay hidden from view, just under my T-shirt, and he lifted two fingers to gently caress and trace the outline of the charm.

His touch sent a small shockwave through me, and I had to clench my jaw and press my lips tightly together so as not to give myself away.

"Mentor's gift from my brother?" he asked, his voice throaty and lustful as he simply continued to trace the outline of the charm.

I had no idea how he knew the charm was from his brother, but I nodded all the same. I could feel myself on the verge of trembling, so I pressed my arms tightly against my sides and glared hard at him. It was taking every ounce of willpower I possessed not to reach up, take hold of his face, and kiss him with all of the desire welling up inside of me.

The air between us seemed to crackle with intensity, and for one, brief moment I didn't know if our next move would be murderous or ravenously passionate. I inhaled a shaky breath, I wanted to say something to ruin the moment, but I couldn't seem to think of a single thing to say.

Just as I was beginning to give in to the temptation to wrap my arms around his neck and pull him to me, Finn backed up turned and began to walk away. "Take care of my brother, Esmé," he called over his shoulder. A moment later, I heard the back door open and close.

Collapsing onto the carpet as my knees gave out on me, I realized that, even if I found Grigori's egg and began my career working for Elric, as long as Finn the Flayer was in the world, I was still completely, royally, and oh-so-utterly screwed.

Chapter Thirteen
Day 3

Within fifteen minutes I had recovered myself, and the first thing I did was call Kincaid.

"Holy shit, you're alive?" he said by way of hello.

"I am," I assured him. "At least for now."

"Where are you?"

"I found my way back to my place. Where're you?"

"I'm in front of my brother's building, looking for him. After he threw you to the spider, he hauled me further down that tunnel to an exit near the 395 underpass. Once we got there he tried to swap clothes with me, which I didn't appreciate. I got in a few solid punches before he did his magic-spell shit, and the next thing I knew I was in my driveway, dressed like Finn, with no idea how I got there."

I smirked. Finn had been right about what his brother might be up to. "We need to meet," I said.

"Okay, where?"

I glanced around the warehouse. Since Finn the Flayer now knew where I lived, and Dex believed that Gideon Kincaid was the guy who'd been here, I probably needed to sync up that pesky loose end before it became a problem. I couldn't risk that, at some later date, Dex discovered that

Gideon had no clue where our warehouse was. So, with a reluctant sigh, I gave him our address.

Kincaid showed up within ten minutes, which was telling, because, although Finn was right that I'd been to his condo, I still didn't know its exact location. Gideon's prompt arrival told me that Finn lived closer than I would've guessed.

"Hey," I said when he arrived. "Come on in."

He entered, and immediately Ember got off her spot on the couch to come and sniff him over. She must not have liked what she smelled because she immediately turned tail and headed back to the couch, where, after getting comfortable again, she made a point of staring at Kincaid like she resented his presence.

It was an interesting reaction for sure, and I didn't quite understand why she was so affectionate with one twin but not the other.

"Tell me what happened to you after Finn tossed you into that hellhole," Kincaid said once I'd invited him to have a seat on a loveseat, opposite the couch.

I took up the spot next to Ember. "Once I got free of the shackles, which was no small feat, mind you, I beat the spider to death with a leg bone."

His eyes widened. "For real?"

"For real."

"Shit," he said, casting an appreciating look my way. "Finn's an asshole. How'd you get out of there after that?"

"I'm a thief, Gideon—I can call you Gideon now, right? I mean, we've been kidnapped together so I think that puts us on a first name basis."

He smirked at me. "Gideon is fine," he said. "After all, you're my mentor now."

"Groovy," I said. "Anyway to your point, by profession, I'm a thief and getting past locked doors is how I make my living."

He nodded. "Got it. Just don't do any of that in front of me."

"Or what?" I said. "You'll *arrest* me?"

"Definitely," he said, and there was no humor to his tone.

I shook my head. "Man, you really are a Boy Scout, aren't you?"

His brow lowered and his head tilted, as if he'd heard someone call him that before. Maybe several times.

I decided it was best to change topics. "We need a plan," I said. "Your brother's gonna figure out I'm not dead fairly soon, and I need to find Grigori's egg before my boss kills me."

"Right," he said. "We need a lead."

"I think we should start with the crime scene. I want to look around with fresh eyes."

Kincaid's expression turned suspicious. "You want to look there for the egg again."

"No," I insisted. "It's not in that house. I would've found it on my first pass if it had been. It's too powerful to escape notice."

"So, what is it that you hope to find?"

I stood up. "I don't know, which is why we need to look again."

Kincaid got up too. "Fine. Let's take my car."

We arrived at Grigori's not long afterward. It was an absolutely beautiful spring day, but I didn't let it distract me. Once Kincaid had cut a knife through the crime scene tape and unlocked the door, the smell was the first thing to hit us, and it packed a hell of a punch.

"Jesus," I whispered, putting my arm across my nose. "They removed all the bodies, right?"

Kincaid nodded and stepped across the threshold ahead of me. "The city removes the bodies, but the estate is in charge of cleaning up the crime scene. It was a messy one, so there's going to be some residual body fluids left behind to stink up the place."

I gagged, recovered, and looked at him. "How do you do this for a living?"

"You get used to it," he said and motioned me inside.

I kept my arm over my nose and moved into the front hallway, keeping my gaze on the floor simply to have a moment to prepare for the sight of anything grisly.

Behind me, Kincaid shut the door, then came to stand next to me. I lifted my eyes to him, and he nodded toward the hallway in front of us. "The quicker we get to it, the quicker we can leave," he said.

I nodded, dropped my arm, and lifted my gaze. The hallway was darker than I remembered, and the house was still and quiet—almost too quiet. There was a sense of something emotionally heavy having taken place here, which of course it had, however, even if I hadn't known anything about Grigori's murder, I'm sure I would've sensed the taint of evil in the air. It permeated every crack and crevice, making the task at hand all the more unappealing.

Still, Kincaid was right; there was no sense lingering in the hallway, so I traversed its length to move quickly past the dining area and into the kitchen.

Oddly, when I entered the kitchen, the most pungent of those foul odors wafting through the house lessened by a noticeable degree.

I paused at the kitchen island and looked around. Something felt out of place, but I couldn't put my finger on it. The area itself was uncluttered and tidy, with everything exactly where it should be.

I turned in a circle and looked about, but nothing jumped out at me. I then walked to the fridge and opened it to peer inside, finding it well-stocked mostly with meats and cheeses.

Closing the fridge, I looked around again, wearing a frown.

"What?" Kincaid asked me.

I sighed. Whatever I felt I was missing wasn't materializing. "Nothing," I said. "Come on, let's check out the rest of the house."

Kincaid and I spent the next hour looking in every nook and cranny for anything that might be a clue. The only thing I found of interest was hidden between Grigori's bed and his nightstand, as if it'd fallen there. It was an ancient book written in Old Gaelic that dated back to the end of the tenth century. There was a receipt stuck to the second to last page. The vendor was a rare book shop in D.C. I wasn't familiar with it, which meant it wasn't mystic-owned.

The total at the bottom of the receipt showed that Grigori had paid a little over four thousand dollars for it.

And he'd paid cash.

My eyes widened at the total. Why would the mystic have spent four grand on a book he could've easily stolen?

I frowned as I thumbed through the text. I didn't speak Old Gaelic . . . I didn't even speak Middle or Modern Gaelic, but I knew that Dex's mother had been born and raised in Ireland, so maybe he'd be able to parcel out a few words just to decipher what the book was about.

I glanced toward Kincaid, who was currently rummaging through Grigori's closet. His back was to me, so I pulled out my monocle to have a look at the text through the crystal.

The old relic gave off very little magical energy. Just a trace coming from the center of the book, which, honestly, could've been Grigori's essence as a makeshift bookmark.

So it wasn't a trinket, and yet Grigori had paid over four thousand dollars for it. Why?

Glancing one more time toward Kincaid to make sure his back was still turned, I slipped the book into the inner pocket of my leather jacket, then swirled my finger over the bulge and whispered, "Hidden from sight, hidden just right, let no one sense the text in flight."

Edging over to a full-length mirror, I looked at my reflection. I could feel the bulge of the book, nestled inside my pocket, but there was no visible sign of a book hidden there.

Kincaid came out and spotted me looking toward the mirror. "Anything?" he asked.

I turned and shook my head. "Nothing."

He nodded, and yet he didn't seem to want to take my word for it because he then moved to the bed and pulled up the mattress to have a look under it. I thanked my lucky stars because he for sure would've found the book if he'd started with the bed rather than the closet.

A bit later we made our way back downstairs to the hallway.

"Satisfied?" Kincaid asked me. He looked more than ready to leave the house.

I began to nod but then caught myself as something that'd been niggling at me finally bubbled up to the surface.

"Hold on," I said, grabbing his arm and turning toward the kitchen.

"What is it?"

"Follow me," I instructed. It was better to show him than tell him.

Kincaid followed me, and once we were in the kitchen, I looked again at all the clean counters, the empty kitchen sink, and the stove, which was free of pots and pans.

"Where's dinner?" I asked him, motioning to the counters and the stove.

"Where's dinner?" he asked, looking annoyed. "You thought I'd have dinner waiting for you?"

I pointed again to the counters and the island. "Not for me, Detective, for Grigori and his guests. When they were murdered, they were seated at the table, right? And their wine glasses all had fresh pours, and yet there's nothing here to indicate that they were about to eat."

Kincaid's brow furrowed, and he glanced around the kitchen with renewed interest. He then went to the fridge and opened it, poking around at the contents while he was at it. "You're right," he said, closing the door. "There's no dinner for the dinner party. And no appetizers or dessert either."

"So why would they all sit down in front of empty china with full glasses of wine, ready to eat unless they *believed* that dinner was on the way?"

Kincaid shrugged. "They could've been waiting on a delivery."

I scowled. "For a dinner party?"

He shrugged. "Maybe the caterer was late, and when they got here, maybe they knocked, and no one answered, so they left."

I shook my head and moved to the back door, which was just off the kitchen. Looking through the window, I said, "I don't think the caterer was late. I think he or she was right on time and Grigori let them in, assuming they were in here preparing a meal. And when he and his guests sat down, the caterer came out and surprised them with a spell that froze them in place, then killed them, one by one."

Kincaid again looked around the kitchen, which had a door leading to the dining room. He moved to it and looked out at the empty chairs, stained with blood, and the elegant tablecloth, also stained, while the remnants of the china that wasn't collected by the CSI team still sat on the table.

"So your theory is that the caterer did it?"

"No," I said. "My theory is that someone posing as the caterer did it."

Kincaid stared at me for a long couple of seconds. "Huh," he said.

"Huh, what?"

"Huh, you just got us our first clue, Esmé Bellerose."

I smirked. "You should give me a badge."

"Don't push it."

Kincaid then moved to the sink and pulled open the cabinet door. Reaching under it, he extracted a trash can, pulled out a pair of black latex gloves from his pocket and began to poke through the contents. "There's nothing here but a fresh bag, and my team wouldn't have put in a new lining if there'd been trash in the waste can, and we'd needed to bag it for evidence."

"Right. Your team's not the cleaning crew."

"Damned straight," he said, setting the trashcan back under the sink. He then stood back and surveyed the kitchen, his lips pursed in a frown. "We've already canvased the neighborhood. On the night in question, nobody saw anything unusual besides a silver Mercedes in the driveway, and we've already traced that to the Murphys."

"Grigori's guests?"

"Yeah."

I motioned to the back door. "There's an alley that runs right behind the house. The caterer-slash-killer could've parked there, and no one would've been the wiser."

Kincaid moved to the back door and peered out. The alley was maybe twenty-five feet to the left of the door.

"Damn," he said, stepping back from the window. "I missed all of this on my initial search of the house." He looked at me appraisingly. "Good job."

"We're not home free yet," I reminded him. "We still have to confirm that there was a caterer scheduled to show up here that night."

"I've already got a warrant for Grigori's phone records. I should have those results sometime today. I'll be able to trace any number he called."

"Good. That's good," I said, lifting my elbow to sniff at my jacket. "In the meantime, I gotta get home for a shower. The stink in this house is starting to leave its mark."

Kincaid and I headed to the front door, which he opened and allowed me through first. I waited while he resealed the door and locked it, and we both turned to startle at the sight of Elric Ostergaard standing at the base of the steps.

"Oh, shit," I whispered.

"Hello, Esmé," Elric said ever so pleasantly. "How's the quest coming?"

My eyes darted around the front yard and past the gate to the street. No one else was about. Elric, it appeared, had come alone, and the distinction between his wife sending a posse of big, thuggish mystics after Kincaid and me compared with Elric, who'd simply shown up on his own, wasn't lost on me. It emphasized how frighteningly powerful he was.

As if I needed the reminder.

"Elric," I said in a far more casual tone than I felt. "What brings you by?"

The mystic took one step forward and looked pointedly at Kincaid. "I believe I asked my question first. And when you answer, you also might want to tell me what you're doing in the company of my wife's lieutenant?"

"He's not Petra's lieutenant," I said quickly. "This is Gideon Kincaid. Finn's twin."

Next to me Kincaid stepped forward, his expression triumphant as he whipped out both his badge and his gun. "Elric Ostergaard, I've been trying to track you down for a long, long time. You're under arrest for—"

My hand clamped down hard on Kincaid's arm, and I jerked him backward. "Do. Not. *Speak!*" I hissed. Turning back to Elric, I added, "Gideon is assisting me with the quest."

Elric cocked an eyebrow. His disappointment in me was evident. "My employees do not fraternize with the police. You *know* this, Esmé."

"You're trespassing," Kincaid barked. "And you're under arrest."

I slapped him on the arm. Hard. To Elric I said, "I know this isn't an ideal partnership, Elric, however, without Gideon's contacts, locating your trinket will be significantly more difficult."

Elric blinked lazily. "You're a thief, looking to join my organization, and you can't even locate the trinket you promised me?"

"I can," I insisted, careful to make my voice ring with confidence. "Given enough time, I certainly can. But you've given me only four days to bring you a trinket your organization has actively been looking to find for the past century. I'm close, Elric. Allow me to use the resources available to me or lose the egg forever."

In that moment, my head snapped back from an unseen blow that spun me around and dropped me to my knees.

From the ground, my cheek burning from the blow, I watched Elric take two steps closer. "Are you really stupid enough to threaten me, Esmé?"

"Okay, that's it!" Kincaid snapped, and he began to move in Elric's direction, his gun raised. "Put your hands above your head, Ostergaard!"

I opened my mouth to yell at him, but it was too late. Kincaid was suddenly hurtled into the air and thrown back against the house with such force that it stunned me—to say nothing of what it did to him.

For his part, Elric stood stock still, but then he raised one finger, pointing it toward Kincaid, and a series of high-pitched clicks emanated out from Elric in a wave pointed directly at Kincaid.

He stood there, pinned against the wall of the house, his mouth agape, his expression pained, and the gun dropped out of his hand to clatter on the wooden porch.

The clicks became louder, and even though Elric's finger wasn't pointing at me, I could feel a vibration emanating from the sound reverberating through my solar plexus.

And then Elric spoke. "Esmé," he said casually, "did you know that the sperm whale can emit sounds that reach two-hundred and thirty decibels?"

"Elric…" I said, desperately trying to think of the words that might save Kincaid's life, and maybe even my own.

But Elric wasn't interested in anything I had to say. "The sound waves are so powerful that they can be heard by other sperm whales on the other side of the planet. They can also, literally, vibrate a man to death."

The clicking grew louder still.

Kincaid's whole face registered the pain. His eyes widened, sweat broke out across his brow, his limbs shook in spasms, and his complexion was so pale that he looked already dead.

I stood up and bowed at the waist to Elric. "I need him." When I dared to look up, I saw that Elric's gaze had shifted to me. "He's an unmentored, lowly mystic working for the APD. I hardly think you'll miss him."

"But that's exactly why you shouldn't kill him. It'll only draw APD's attention to you and your organization."

Elric smiled cruelly. "There won't be enough left of him to draw attention."

Kincaid's body began to vibrate violently against the side of the house. Elric would shatter Kincaid into a million pieces if I didn't stop him soon.

"But the Flayer would find out," I said, still trying to reason with him. "And that would start a war. Do you really want that?"

Elric shrugged, his attention still on Kincaid. The clicking intensified. "Petra's errand boy is no match for me."

"Of course he isn't," I said. "But he's a match for any of your employees, and trust me, Finn the Flayer wouldn't come after you. He'd just cripple your organization, slow business, and cause some vulnerabilities. And with Hideyo in town, is this really the time for skirmishes?"

Elric took his gaze off Kincaid and eyed me critically. "Who told you Hideyo is here?"

"Petra's cha—" I caught myself. I was entering very dangerous waters mentioning Clepsydra to Elric. He'd want to know how I came to be in the company of Clepsydra and I'd have to confess to him about being with Tic when he was abducted and Tic was the reason Elric and Petra were at odds. Still, I didn't see how it could be avoided. Clearing my throat, I tried again, using Marco's well-known nickname. "Tic was kidnapped. He might even be dead. My sources tell me that Clepsydra and Petra sense Rubi's handiwork in the air."

Elric rolled his eyes. "A rumor, no doubt, begun by the two of them."

I shook my head vigorously. I was running out of time to convince Elric, and I didn't know how much longer Kincaid could hang in there. "It's not a rumor. I was there when he was abducted. I was in the apartment when it blew. I felt the force of the energy that caused it. Only someone as powerful as one of the Seven or one of their advisers could've pulled it off."

Elric eyed me critically again. "What were you doing with Petra's mutt?"

"He's a source. At least he was. But I swear to you, *on my life*, Elric, he was taken from his girlfriend's apartment by a hostile force of immense power."

Elric considered me for a long, long time, and all the while the clicks echoing from his finger pummeled Gideon unmercifully.

But then the mystic's finger dropped, and the clicking abruptly stopped. Kincaid slithered down the wall to the floor and was so still that I feared he might already be dead.

"You have thirty-nine hours, Esmé. I want that egg."

With that, Elric disappeared from sight. Blinking, I looked about the small yard, but there was absolutely no sign of him, which made me shudder. For all I knew he could be anywhere, waiting and watching, and he'd probably used *my* pen to abracadabra himself from view. The bastard.

Moving over to Kincaid, I rolled him onto his back and checked his pulse. It was faint but present. Still, he did *not* look good, and as if to emphasize that point, his nose began to bleed.

"Shit, shit, shit!" I swore. I didn't know what to do. Kincaid was in bad, bad shape. He was covered in sweat head to toe, both his ears were bleeding, along with his nose, and his breathing was ragged and shallow. I felt his forehead and he was blazing hot, as if he had a very high fever. What's more, the skin under his fingernails was beginning to turn blue.

If I didn't find a way to help him, he'd die right here on this porch. Grabbing my cell, I called Dex.

"Ezzy," he said.

"Dex!" I was so relieved he'd picked up the call. "I need you. Now. And I need any emergency healing trinkets you have on you."

There was a pause, then, "Where?"

I gave him Grigori's address.

"I'm on my way."

"How long?"

"Half-hour. Maybe less."

I looked at Kincaid, unsure if he even had that much time to spare. "Make it less."

Chapter Fourteen
Day 3

Dex arrived with a screech of tires. He took one look at Kincaid and whistled. "What'd you do to him?"

"It wasn't me," I said, motioning for Dex to help me get Kincaid to the car.

"Who?" he asked, moving quickly to Kincaid's side.

"Elric."

Dex sucked in air through his teeth before he bent down, took out a bronze charm in the shape of a serpent winding its way up a staff, and placed it inside Kincaid's shirt. "He's lucky to be alive then."

"If we don't get him home and convince Ember to help him, he won't be so lucky," I said, moving around to Kincaid's feet while Dex hoisted the detective's torso up off the wood floor of the porch.

Dex eyed me skeptically as we made our way down the steps, but he didn't say what I knew he was thinking, and that was that Ember had only ever healed me and Dex. Well, she'd also healed the Flayer, but Dex didn't know that. That's what'd given me the idea, in fact.

Still, even if I begged her, she might not feel inclined to heal Kincaid, and given her reaction to him earlier, I had a bad feeling about how it might go, but I had to try.

Together we moved down the path and through the gate, toward Dex's car. Along the way I glanced up and down the street nervously, unsure if Elric was still nearby.

After opening the door to the backseat, I got in first, pulling Kincaid's feet lengthwise as Dex pushed his torso into the car. Once he was fully sprawled out on the backseat, I used the two seatbelts to strap him in, then checked the charm Dex had laid against Kincaid's heart. It was warm to the touch. I also checked Kincaid's pulse, and it had definitely improved.

"Thank the gods you had this thing on you," I said.

Dex nodded. "I keep it with me anytime I'm far away from Ember."

The charm was a moderately good healing trinket, a strong level-four-and-a-half. What it lacked in power it more than made up for in longevity. We'd had the thing for over two decades, and we'd used it on occasion when we needed help staying alive long enough to get back to Ember.

The charm had been a level-six when I'd first lifted it off the mystic who'd owned it previously, and its power had diminished only a degree and a half, which said a lot about how powerful it might've been when it was first conjured.

Once I was sure Kincaid wasn't going to die on the way back to the warehouse, I joined Dex up front. It was while I was buckling myself in that I felt the bulge of the book I'd pinched from Grigori's bedroom.

Taking out the book, I held it in my hands for a moment simply staring at it.

"New trinket?" Dex asked, pulling away from the curb.

"I found this hidden in Grigori's bedroom."

Dex took one hand off the steering wheel to lay it on the book, his gaze far off. "Not getting much in the way of trinket vibes from it, Ezzy. Sorry."

I nodded. I already knew it didn't possess any strong magical qualities, but Grigori had definitely prized it. "He paid four grand for it," I told Dex. When he eyed me in surprise, I held up the receipt. "He got it from a rare book dealer here in town."

"Wait, he paid for it? Why'd he do that when he could've pinched it on his own?"

"I have no idea. The only thing I can think of is that he didn't want to risk calling attention to himself."

Dex nodded. "Which means there's something in there not worth taking the risk for."

"That's what I'm thinking," I said, thumbing through the pages. "It's written in Old Gaelic, so I can't make any sense of it, which is why—" I stopped speaking abruptly.

Out of the corner of my eye, I saw Dex glance at me again. "Which is why, what?"

My hands began to shake while I held the book, staring at a page dead center in the text with a colorful drawing. I felt sick to my stomach and panicked all at the same time.

"Ezzy?" Dex asked when I didn't answer him and simply kept staring at the page. "Ezzy, what is it?"

I turned the book so that he could see the drawing. He glanced at the road ahead, then back to the book, and then he braked so hard that I shot forward and nearly banged my head on the dash.

Dex seemed startled by his reaction and turned to look back at Kincaid. I did too, and we were both relieved to find him still strapped in tightly against the back seat with a bit more color in his cheeks.

Dex let his foot off the brake, but he moved us to the curb and parked, then he motioned with his fingers for me to give him the book. I did, and he gazed at the drawing for a long, long moment before he looked up at me. "Shit," he whispered.

"It's what I think it is, isn't it?" I asked him, my voice quavering. "Even though we can't read the words, that's Ember, right?"

The drawing was elaborate and detailed. It depicted a red dog with a lean body and long legs, proudly sitting in the middle of a ball of flame as the spectral image of a phoenix rose up behind the dog.

"Yeah," Dex said, his voice grave. "Yeah."

I stared out the windshield, not knowing what to do. I wondered who else might've seen this book either before or while it was in Grigori's possession. Was he the only one who'd connected the dots? Was that why he was here in Alexandria, which, given Elric's power and political reach, was one of the most dangerous places in the world for the old mystic?

In the pit of my stomach, I knew that it was. Grigori had been hunting for the phoenix, and he'd discovered an old text that told him *exactly* what to look for.

"What do we do?" I asked so softly, I didn't know if Dex had heard me.

My partner handed me back the book, wiped his face with his hand, and pulled away from the curb again. "We translate it, then we burn it," he said.

"You speak a little Gaelic, right? Could you parse out some of this?"

Dex frowned and adopted a brogue. "I speak a wee bit of it, lass, but not enough to make any sense of that. It's Old Gaelic. You'll be wanting someone more familiar with the old way of speaking."

"And it'd have to be someone we could trust," I added.

Dex turned to me. "Don't say—"

"Ursula," I said, beating him to it.

"No," Dex said, turning his eyes back to the road and gripping the steering wheel so tight that his knuckles turned white.

I sighed dramatically. "Then who? Who, Dex, can we both trust enough not to use what's in this book against us, and who's capable of translating it?"

"There's got to be someone else," he insisted.

"I'm all ears," I told him.

"Someone unbound, maybe."

I nodded. "Yeah. Someone unbound. Let's just put an ad on Facebook and see who responds, shall we? And I'm sure no one in the mystic world will be at *all* curious why we're so interested in a translator of Old Gaelic text."

"Ezz," Dex said.

"I'm sure it won't take long, after all. A few weeks or so to sort through the *hordes* of people who'll surely respond."

It was Dex's turn to sigh heavily. "You done?"

"Are you?"

Dex nodded and offered me a crooked smile. "Yeah. All right. I'll take the book to her. But you know what she'll want in return."

"I do. And I'm sorry, but this is too important. We *need* to know what the book says. And then we need to know everything about the shop that sold it. And then we need to wipe the memory of anyone who has seen the pages. And that includes Ursula, so make sure that's a part of the bargain."

"I will, I will," he said. Then he glanced at me again. "Could you at least *pretend* to be a little jealous?"

In spite of the panic currently gripping my heart, I managed to smile genuinely at my second. Laying a hand on his shoulder, I said, "Don't you *dare* fall in love this time, you hear?"

Dex laughed. "You know I will. But only for a day or two."

Ursula would absolutely demand a quid pro quo, and we both knew what she'd demand of him. Ursula's addiction was passion, and she was crazy about Dex. She pined for him something *fierce*. Were I not in the picture, I often wondered if the two of them would've paired up.

Ursula was significantly older than the two of us—we both thought she was at least four hundred and fifty years old. And even though she was a gorgeous, platinum-blond Brigitte Bardot look-alike, her powers weren't especially powerful for a mystic her age. Around her neck she wore a golden locket, given to her by a former lover who'd been so sated by Ursula's "attentions" that he'd given it to her freely. Everyone knew that the locket was Ursula's secret for longevity.

And, to my knowledge, no thief had ever tried to lift it off her because she was such a valuable resource for thieves like us. She knew a great deal about a great deal, she spoke and read at least a hundred languages—both old and new—and she could fashion a love potion so powerful that slipped into the drink of an unsuspecting mystic, someone like me could easily sway the poor fool to part with a prized possession.

By going to her for help, I knew that poor Dex would have to give in to one of Ursula's love potions, which would render him nearly useless to me for at least a day or two. But it was both a risk I needed to take and a resource I was willing to exploit in this time of crisis, because I knew that Ursula could definitely translate the text, and to spend an evening (or two) with Dex, she'd be willing to submit to an amnesia spell, ensuring that she'd never remember what she'd translated from the book.

And even though Dex was putting on a good front, I knew damned well that getting a little sumpin' sumpin' from Ursula was hardly a hardship. He'd be wined, dined, and well-ridden, then sent home with nary a scratch.

I was about to say as much to him when a new and terrible thought entered my mind. I looked again at the book and felt another shiver of fear.

"Ezzy?" Dex asked. He'd obviously noticed my sudden distress.

"What if..."

"What if what?"

"What if whomever killed Grigori wasn't after the egg. What if they were after the book?"

Dex's lips settled into a firm frown. "That would be trouble. *Real* trouble."

I took a breath and turned back to the page in the book with the illustration of Ember. Impulsively I pulled at the page, intent on shredding it into teeny, tiny pieces before we got home, where I would promptly set the pieces on fire.

But the page didn't tear or rip out from the spine, and hard as I tried, I couldn't so much as wrinkle it. "What the hell?" I demanded.

"Give it here," Dex said, pulling up to a red light. I handed him the book and he tugged on the page, but it held firm. A look of surprise flashed across his face before he yanked harder. The page resisted. Dex clutched the entire page in his fist and gripped the spine hard and tried to pull them apart, but even though all the muscles in his neck and arms bulged, the book remained solidly whole.

A honk from behind alerted us that the light had turned green. Dex handed me back the book and hit the gas. We bulleted forward, and I glanced again in the back seat to make sure Kincaid was still secure. "Easy," I said softly, aware that my partner was furious that something as fragile as a piece of paper—and an ancient one at that—could stand up against his brute strength.

I saw him glance at the back seat too. "Sorry. We're almost home. I'll give it another go when we get there."

We arrived at the warehouse, and I went ahead to unlock the door while Dex got Kincaid out of the car. Gideon was still out of it, but Dex had him mostly upright and half-dragged, half-carried him across the threshold. I led the way to the couch and helped Dex ease the detective down onto the cushions.

Checking his pulse and the temperature of his skin, I was relieved to find that his pulse was at least steady, but he was still hot to the touch.

"Can the trinket cure him?" I asked Dex while pointing to the serpent and staff charm laying on Gideon's chest.

Dex shrugged. "It might. But it'd take a month. Maybe longer."

"That is time I do not have," I growled. "Ember!" I called, and she appeared from the stairwell, carrying the blanket she liked to be covered up with at night. Tail wagging furiously, she came to me and shoved her head into my legs before turning in a half-circle to lean against me, still holding the blanket firmly in her mouth.

I wrapped her in a hug, then pointed to Kincaid. "He needs you."

Ember dropped the blanket, and her tail stopped wagging. She turned away from facing Kincaid to curl against me again.

"Ember, please," I begged. "*I* need *him*."

But the pup was having none of it. She steadfastly refused to get up on the couch next to Kincaid. And even when I sat down next to him and patted the cushion, she refused to come close.

"Ouch," Dex said. "She's being a picky Sheila, eh?"

I frowned. "I was afraid of this."

Meanwhile Ember was already gathering up her blanket and trotting over to the love seat opposite the couch to curl up with a sigh and eye us moodily.

I rubbed my brow, trying to think of a way to convince her to lend her magical energy to Kincaid. All I needed was for her to lie next to him, and her energy would naturally flow into him, healing him much faster than the bronze trinket. And then an idea struck me, and I felt my shoulders sag, because I knew it was probably the only plan that would work.

But Dex couldn't be in on it, which meant he couldn't be here.

I offered him the book. "Take this to Ursula and have her translate it. Then do whatever you have to do to destroy it."

"The whole book?"

"Yes."

Dex was about to take the book from me when I had another thought and pulled it back. "Hang on," I said. Holding the book between my palms, I whispered, "Treasure trove of hidden secrets, return to me should fingers poach it."

Dex eyed me skeptically. "A comeback spell? Really, Esmé?"

I shrugged. "If it falls into the wrong hands, they might realize it's not a trinket per se, and forget to deactivate any comebacks."

"I'll make sure to keep my eye on it just in case," Dex said drolly, holding out his hand for the book.

I gave it to him and then had yet another thought. "Say, Dex," I said, reaching behind my neck to undo the clasp for the charm that Gideon had given me.

"Say, Esmé," he replied, mimicking me.

I handed him the trinket. "What're your thoughts?"

"It's not really my style," he said with a grin.

"Come on, tell me what its power is."

Dex bounced the charm in his hand, his brow furrowed as he studied it. He then looked up at me and said, "Whoa."

"Whoa? What's whoa?"

"Ezzy, when I'm holding this and looking at you, I feel nothing. Not even a hint of attraction."

I smiled. "That's what I though—"

"You could be a lump of sludge," Dex said, waving his hand in a circle at me. "A hairy goat. A warty toad for all I care."

"Got it," I said stiffly.

Looking me up and down and back again, he said, "It's like you're a big beefy ogre. I feel nothing for you, Ezzy. *Nothing.*"

I snatched the charm out of his hand. "*Noted*, Dex, thank you."

Dex blinked and shook his head. "And now I'm back to fancying you."

I rolled my eyes and put the charm back on. "Poor boy," I said, grinning.

"Where'd you pinch it from?"

"I didn't, it's Kincaid's mentor's gift."

Dex crossed his muscled arms and cocked an eyebrow at me. "Okay, out with it. Who're *you* fancyin'?"

I felt heat sear my cheeks. "What, me? No one."

Dex slid his gaze to the couch. "No one, eh?"

I puffed out an exasperated sigh. "Oh, come on, Dex. He does nothing for me."

The cocked eyebrow remained.

"*What?*" I snapped.

"Proteges gift only what will best serve their mentors in the moment. You know that. How's a repelling trinket going to serve you right now?"

"Duh," I said. "It's like you've just met me. The whole reason I applied for the job at SPL was to finally have the chance to rid myself of the binding curse. This charm is obviously going to allow me to roam freely without the fear of being swept off my feet and dumped again while I work off my contract with Elric."

Dex's brow came back to neutral again. "Right. Forgot about that. Well, that should do the trick because, I mean, Big Doodle and the twins didn't even twitch when I held that thing."

I laughed. Big Doodle and the twins were Dex's nickname for his... well, *you* know.

Placing my hands firmly on his upper arms, I sang, "Say hi to Ursula for me."

He chuckled. "Pass. She's so jealous of you, she's likely not to help us if I do."

I chuckled. Ursula and I were fine whenever Dex wasn't in the picture.

Dex pointed to Gideon. "What do you want to do with him?"

"Leave him. We'll just let the serpent and staff trinket work its magic, and hope that it heals him sooner rather than later."

Dex eyed our houseguest suspiciously. "I know he's your protégé now, Ezzy, but he feels like trouble to me. Mark my words, he'll land us both in hot water if we're not careful."

I patted him on the arm and offered him a mocking grin. "There's that enthusiasm that I know and love. Now go find Ursula and call me the minute she's through translating the book."

Dex shook his head but didn't protest as he turned and left the room. I waited until I heard the roar of his Mustang pulling out of the drive before I moved over to Kincaid and began to search his pockets. He was still quite hot and unconscious, which was worrisome.

After checking all the pockets in his jacket and the front of his jeans, I rolled him carefully onto his side and found what I was looking for. "Bingo," I said, tugging his cell out of his back pocket.

Turning the screen to his face, I managed to easily unlock his phone and was scrolling through his contacts when the screen lit up with an incoming call from someone named Trish.

There was a photo attached to the caller ID, and I stared at the lovely face of a pale woman with brilliant blue eyes, long white-blond hair, and a smile as sweet as an angel.

She stared into the lens of the camera with such a look of trust, and my gaze darted to Kincaid on the couch for a moment as a pang of something hot and unwelcome flashed in my belly.

I shook my head and looked back toward the phone, unsure where the sudden jolt of jealousy had come from. I had no romantic feelings for Kincaid, but the second this beautiful woman showed up on his phone, I was feeling all those terrible insecurities that came with every relationship I'd ever been scorned from.

It was so weird. Especially since I'd never experienced a single moment of jealousy where Dex was concerned. So why was I having a reaction to this Trish woman now?

The phone stopped ringing then, and a few moments later a text came in from the same number.

Gid, are you planning on working late tonight? Need to know about dinner. Call home soon, okay?

I frowned and looked again at Kincaid. "So, Trish is Mrs. Kincaid, huh?"

I tapped my finger against the side of the phone, unsure what to do with the text message. Should I leave it alone or respond? It was clear to me that Kincaid wasn't going anywhere for at least several more hours, maybe even days, and I didn't want the missus to start calling around trying to find her husband, so I decided to take the risk and respond.

"Sorry," I said, tapping out the word as I spoke. "Working late on a case here. Can't talk. Will call when I can." I then scrolled up to see how Kincaid usually signed off with his wife, and saw a few texts where he ended with "L U."

"Blech," I muttered. "The man can't even spell out the word love? Or send a heart emoji? Lame."

Still, I didn't want to break the pattern, so that's how I ended the text before sending it.

Once that was done, I went back to Kincaid's contacts and found who I was looking for, then placed the call.

It was picked up on the fourth ring. "Gideon?" came the wary greeting. "This is a surprise."

"No, it's Esmé. Your brother is critically injured. You need to come to the warehouse."

There was a long pause, then, "Why aren't you loaning him whatever trinket healed you last night?"

My gaze went to Ember and I had to think fast. "Because I sold it to you."

"The crystal?"

"Yep."

There was another pause, and I could tell Finn was suspicious of the call. "How do I know this isn't a trap?"

I turned the phone toward Kincaid and snapped his picture, then I texted it to Finn before putting the phone back to my ear again. "Satisfied?"

"On my way."

The line disconnected and all I could do was wait.

Finn arrived ten minutes later, and he brought the useless "healing" crystal with him. "Where is he?" he asked as soon as I opened the door.

"On the couch," I replied, drinking in the sight of him.

He breezed past me and I could feel the charm around my neck heat right up, but fortunately I didn't feel compelled to strip naked and throw myself at him.

I'd take my victories where I could.

I tucked the serpent and staff trinket into my jacket pocket after having just taken it from Gideon, then I followed behind the lieutenant, watching him go right to his brother. He stared down at him with a rigid posture for a moment before laying his hand on Gideon's forehead. "He's burning up."

At that moment Ember trotted over to Finn and leaned against him while she wagged her tail. Finn stroked her head absently and focused on me. "How long has he been like this?"

"About an hour. I couldn't move him after he was attacked without Dex's help, and it took him a half hour to get to us."

Finn placed the crystal on his brother's chest. "How do you activate this thing?"

I stepped forward and held my hand out. He placed it in my palm and I put my lips to the crystal, pushed some essence with some specific intention into it and said, "Trinket, trinket come to light, awaken now to save a life."

The crystal lit up with a bright yellow glow, but it held absolutely no healing properties whatsoever. But Finn didn't know that, so I handed it back to the lieutenant and he put it back on his brother's chest again.

Meanwhile Ember was still leaning against his legs and wagging her tail, waiting for him to notice her. Finn looked around and eyed the loveseat.

I moved there quickly and waved him back to the couch. "Sit with your brother. Let him know you're near."

Finn's face was creased with worry, but he didn't argue. Moving to Gideon's feet he lifted his legs, sat down and allowed his brother's calves to drape over his lap.

Just as I'd hoped, the second Finn sat down Ember hopped up onto the couch next to him and wiggled her way onto Finn's lap too. "Hello, girl," Finn said, rubbing her muzzle. "Be a good pup and get down now, eh?"

"Let Ember stay," I said casually. "She kept me company last night and I swear it helped me recover faster. Just having her near brought me comfort."

Finn laid a hand on Ember's back and she squirmed to lay half her body on Finn and half against Gideon.

I didn't care where she settled as long as she was physically touching Gideon. Even a paw on his leg would help him heal.

Sitting back on the couch, Finn regarded me, his expression curious and far too sexy for my liking. As he gazed at me the charm grew hot again against my skin. A well of desire rose up but I was able to tamp it down again, and I didn't think I'd ever been more relieved in my life to have a trinket to help stave off the worst effects of my binding spell.

"How did he get like this?" Finn asked.

"Elric," I said without any further explanation, because what other explanation would he need?

The Flayer's brow lowered and his lips pressed into a thin line. His hatred for my boss was palpable. "What spell did Ostergaard use?"

"Don't know. I've never seen anything like it, but he said something about the sound waves from a sperm whale being able to vibrate a man to death."

Finn muttered an expletive. "That would explain why Gideon's core temp feels like it's on fire."

"It would," I agreed.

Narrowing his eyes at me, he said, "And where were you when all this was going down?"

"I was trying to convince Elric to spare your brother's life."

"What beef could Ostergaard have with Gideon?"

I sighed. "The second he spotted Ostergaard, your brother whipped out his badge and yelled, 'Hands in the air, Ostergaard! You're under arrest!' Quelle surprise, Elric felt disrespected."

Finn frowned at his unconscious twin. "Idiot."

"Yes. But I'd say he paid a fairly high price for being so obtuse."

Finn pinched the bridge of his nose and sighed. "How did you guys bump into Ostergaard anyway? The guy lives inside his headquarters."

"He found us."

"Where?"

I felt my shoulders tense. I didn't trust Finn. Not even a little, but I was worried that if I didn't answer him, he'd pick up his brother and take him away, and I wasn't yet convinced that Gideon would make it without Ember's intervention. "At the scene of a crime," I said, vaguely.

Finn frowned. "Grigori's?"

"Yes."

"So Elric's looking for the egg, huh?" Finn asked.

"Duh," I said. "Same as Petra, I assume."

"Duh," Finn said, echoing me. "But that's not my mission."

"Right. Tic's your mission."

"He is. And you're still the only solid link I have to that little mystery."

"I don't know what else I can say that I haven't already told you."

Finn sighed. "What intel did the little bastard give up to you the day he was abducted?"

I drummed my fingers against my knee, considering what I should tell him. "He gave up Grigori's location."

Finn grunted in agreement. "Marco's always been good for solid intel, but it bothers me that Grigori was here for at least a month and I never got word of it."

"He was careful," I said.

"Not too careful if Marco found him."

"They'd met before when Marco was seven and he and his father were making their way back from Prussia. Marco recognized Grigori, but Grigori didn't recognize Marco."

Finn grunted again. "But why would Grigori risk coming here of all places? D.C. would be the most dangerous place in the world for him."

"Maybe he liked the sight of cherry blooms in springtime."

"Oh, I think it was quite more than that."

I eyed him curiously but he didn't elaborate. Instead, he reached out and felt Gideon's hands. "He's better," he said. "Cooler."

Gideon responded to his brother's touch by jerking and letting out a small moan. Ember startled and jumped off the couch. She then went into a deep stretch followed by a good shake of her body and I could tell there'd be no getting her back onto the couch to settle against Gideon again.

So, when Finn wasn't looking, I focused on the crystal on his brother's chest and pulled my essence back from it.

The light illuminating the crystal winked out.

Finn picked it up. "What happened?"

I shrugged. "I think your brother took all the juice it had left to give."

He frowned, and cut me a suspicious look. He knew he'd been hoodwinked out of nine grand.

I offered him another shrug with my palms up. "A deal's a deal."

"Or a steal's a steal," he said.

Ember trotted toward the door leading to the courtyard, and I got up to let her out.

When I came back to the love seat, Finn had already gotten his brother to a sitting position. "I think he's recovered enough to move now," he said. "I'll take him to my place. There's a trinket or two there that'll help him get the rest of the way back to normal."

I nodded. "Good plan. Do you want help getting him into the car?"

"Nah," he said. "I got it. Oh, and you can keep this."

Finn tossed me the crystal dud, and I reached out to catch it. A second before it landed in my palm, I heard Ember's warning bark from the courtyard, but it was too late. As my hand closed around the trinket, a bolt of energy hit me like a sucker punch, and in an instant, my world went dark.

Chapter Fifteen
Day 3

I jolted awake in the front seat of a vehicle alone, with something taped across my mouth, and hands and legs bound by a golden cord.

"*Mutdahuck?!!!*" I swore. Well, would've sworn if I hadn't been muzzled. Looking around frantically, trying to get my bearings, I quickly realized that I was in a parking garage, currently stuck in an SUV sitting in front of an elevator.

"*Hinn!*" I growled. "*Matsonohamitch!*"

Even though I'd been knocked completely out, I felt no worse for wear. And my head and thoughts were clear. Which meant that whatever spell Finn had hit me with had only been set for stun.

The bastard had obviously repurposed the crystal I'd sold him the second my back was turned to let Ember out. Seething with rage, I tried to pull out of my bindings, but they were as strong as steel. I then tried reaching up to remove the tape across my mouth, hoping to say a counterspell to free myself, but the cord around my wrists wouldn't allow my hands to rise past chest level. I then resorted to twisting and squirming, trying to figure out how to get out of the SUV if I couldn't do more than wiggle.

The problem was that I was still locked in by the seatbelt, which was holding me fast against the seat, and try as I might to depress the release to unclasp the thing, I couldn't get it to budge. Finn had obviously enchanted it too.

Frustrated and furious, I leaned back against the seat and yelled, "*Essole!*"

The door opened abruptly, and Finn stuck his head inside. Wearing a smile, he asked, "Who's an asshole?"

What followed was a lengthy stream of muffled yelling that was all but unintelligible. But I think he got the gist.

"Whew!" he said, when I paused to breathe heavily through my nose, trying to gather enough air to go for round two. "Feel better?"

If looks could kill, that son of a bitch woulda been stone-cold dead. And I mean dead-dead. The kind of dead that even Ember couldn't bring him back from.

"Yikes," he said, reading my thoughts, but I could tell that I didn't really scare him.

Good, I thought. *Underestimate me. That'll be fun for you.*

Finn crossed his arms and continued to stand there expectantly.

I rolled my eyes and grunted, "Uht?"

"Will you cooperate if I undo your bindings?"

I simply glared at him in reply.

He sighed dramatically. "Esmé, come on. You have no play here. I can leave you in the car for as long as it takes to make sure Gideon is okay, or you can agree to behave once I get the bindings off and invite you upstairs to keep vigil with me."

"Ers Mmmer?!" I demanded. If he'd left Ember in the courtyard or worse, brought her here, I really would kill him.

"Your pup is safely back inside the warehouse," he said. "I let her in from the courtyard after I'd settled you and

Gideon in the car. She wasn't especially happy with me, but she didn't tear me to pieces, so I think we're good."

Mollified that Ember was safe, I took another couple of seconds really thinking through my options. The problem was that Finn had caught me completely off guard. I had nothing on me save a low-level location trinket, lockpick, voice-concealing die, the monocle, and the serpent and staff healing trinket, which meant that I had no weapon available to me except my wits.

Reluctantly and with an irritated grunt, I nodded, holding up my wrists so that he could undo the rope.

Finn ignored the gesture and said, "Your solemn vow that you'll cooperate, and not attack me or run away if I let you out of those?"

I rolled my eyes again. Why was he being such an asshole about this? And, more important, why the emphasis on my not running away? What was it exactly that he wanted from me?

It wasn't like I could ask him with the tape over my mouth, and I doubted he'd give me a straight answer anyway. So, simply to move things along, I offered him my bound hands and nodded.

The second I put forward my hands, though, Finn enveloped them with his own. In the instant his skin touched mine, another bolt of energy surged through me and, had my mouth not been taped shut, I definitely would've gasped.

Desire curled like smoke through every part of me, so intense that my eyes watered. Finn caught my gaze, his irises swelling to all but obscure the hazel of his eyes, and I thought I'd drown in those dark pools if he held onto my hands for much longer.

Numbly, I continued to nod my head, and warmth flowed outward from our hands to continue to draw out the smoke of desire like a backdraft.

Finn stepped closer, hovering just above me, so close that I could feel the warmth of his body. Against my chest the half-heart charm burned like a hot coal, and the more I became aware of its uncomfortable heat, the more I was able to back away from the lustful urge to strip Finn the Flayer naked and have my way with him.

Still, it was damned hard to pull my hands out of his grasp once the heat from the binding agreement between us had dissipated, but I managed.

What I couldn't hide were the physical effects his touch had had on me. Sweat had broken out against my brow, my skin felt flush, and my breathing was ragged and strained, hampered by the tape across my mouth.

If Finn noticed, he said nothing. Waving a finger toward the twine around my wrists and feet, they fell away, releasing me.

He then reached out with that same finger, moving a lock of hair out of my eyes.

The move was a caress that was altogether unexpected, and again the charm around my neck burned hot.

Finn allowed his hand to fall and then he stepped back. I reached up and pulled the tape off my mouth, hissing at the pain but grateful for it, because it also helped snap me out of a dangerously tempting moment.

"This way," Finn said, turning his back to me and walking toward the elevators.

I was so grateful that he opted not to linger in the doorway of his SUV. If he touched me like that again, I'd rip off the charm myself and treat him like a bull in need of a ride at the rodeo. As it was, when I got out of the cab, I had to grip the door tightly before I felt my legs were sturdy enough to carry me. I wanted to blame it on the aftereffect of that knockout punch Finn had given me when he'd repurposed the crystal. But I'd be lying to myself if I did that.

We rode the elevator up, and I made sure to stand against the far wall opposite Finn, eyeing him warily lest he attempt another move like the one he pulled a few moments before, but he stayed on his side, patently ignoring me.

We got as far as the second floor when the left pocket in my jacket began to vibrate. Finn eyed me curiously as I dug out the phone.

"Shit," I said, when I looked at the display.

"Trouble?"

I held out the phone to him. "Probably. This is your brother's phone. I forgot I still had it on me."

"Trish," he said, grabbing the cell from my hand and swiping to answer the call. "Hey babe," he said. "Sorry I didn't call sooner. It's been a hell of a day here. I'm knee-deep in a case. You okay?"

I blinked. It was amazing how easily Finn slipped into the persona of his brother.

"That's great," he continued, never making eye contact with me. He stared at the ground, as if he were self-conscious of the fact that I was listening. And I realized that I suddenly felt like a third wheel, and that tingle of jealousy that I'd had when I first saw Trish's face appear on Kincaid's phone reemerged.

I stiffened my posture and focused on keeping a neutral face, but inside my chest a green-eyed monster was coming to life.

Meanwhile Finn was speaking softly to Mrs. Kincaid—as if he were the one married to her. It upset me more than I could say, certainly more than it should've.

"Yeah, I'll have to pull an all-nighter, sorry," he was saying. "No, don't worry about bringing dinner to the station.

I'll grab a burger around the corner. You get some rest, and I'll be in touch later, okay?" Then, "Great. Love you too."

Finn tapped at the screen and pocketed his brother's phone just as the elevator stopped and the doors pinged open. "What?" he asked when he saw that I was staring at him.

"You do that like you've had practice at it." My tone was way more accusing than it should've been.

Finn shrugged and moved out of the elevator. "I've been impersonating my brother for years," he said casually. I followed right behind. As we entered the hallway leading to the kitchen and living room, he added, "Plus, it's not like I can send him home looking like he does. He'll need to heal here for the night before I can release him back to his wife."

"You say that like he's your prisoner."

Finn paused to look at me over his shoulder. "Isn't he?"

A cold chill traveled down my spine. *Shit*, I thought. *I'm his prisoner too.*

I said nothing and waited for Finn to take the lead again, which he did, and I followed, studying him the way I'd study a mark.

Kincaid and the Flayer were identical in nearly every way, however, when Finn walked, it was with an air of confidence and authority that, frankly, his brother lacked. Finn moved through space with the stealth and grace of a panther, and his was the kind of stride that I would've noticed immediately if I were actually out in the world surveilling him. His was the kind of easy, nearly carefree gait that actually amplified rather than hid a person with immense skill and power. If he'd been on my list as a possible mark, one look at that walk of his and I would've scratched him from my list.

I didn't tango with men like Finn the Flayer. It's how I stayed alive to thieve another day.

We entered the living area, and I was thrilled to see the blinds open but shocked to see that early evening had fallen. I'd been sitting unconscious in Finn's Escalade for longer than I'd thought. Still the view through his window told me all I needed to know about our location.

Finn's condo was only about a half-mile away from my warehouse, but in a *much* nicer ZIP code. Ember and I had even run past this place many a time when we were out for our runs and craved a jog along the scenic route. I suspected the penthouse, with its view of the Potomac, was worth more than my entire warehouse.

I guess being Petra's lieutenant paid well.

I followed Finn to his bedroom—a room I hadn't been allowed to explore on my previous visit, and which was absolutely gorgeous in its cool gray and white tones (with nary a spot of yellow in sight).

Lying on his back against the European pillows was Gideon who was shivering so hard his teeth were rattling. He surprised me by being awake. This must've been a new development, because Finn paused midway into the room to consider his brother.

He then walked to the headboard, rubbed Gideon's forehead, and said, "You dumb bastard. What the hell were you thinking taking on Elric Ostergaard, of all mystics? He could've killed you, ya know."

"Ffffffuck yyyyou, Fffffffin," Gideon snarled, and with great effort, he lifted his hand to slap Finn's away.

Finn seemed hardly insulted. Instead, he simply stared at his twin in a quizzical way and nodded, as if in silent agreement with Gideon's rebuff.

Still, Finn picked up a crystal wand lying on the bed next to Gideon that was maybe six inches in length, glowing a turquoise blue. Placing it on Gideon's chest he said, "Don't let this roll off again. You need to keep that close."

Gideon glared at his brother, and there was an anger in his eyes that was honestly surprising to see. With trembling fingers, he took hold of the crystal and flung it away. It hit the wall and shattered into several smaller pieces as the blue glow winked out.

I held my breath waiting for Finn's reaction, which I assumed was going to be fury, but he surprised me when he quite calmly said, "I've got a few other healing trinkets I can lend you, Gid, but that one was the best I had on hand. I'll get you another if you promise not to break it."

"Ffffffuck yyyyou, Fffffffinn," his brother replied.

Even given Finn's calm demeanor, or perhaps because of it, I was worried that the situation might escalate, and Gideon would be the worse for it. So I extracted the serpent and staff trinket from my pocket and stepped forward to place it in Gideon's hand.

"Here," I said.

Without turning his head, Gideon's eyes roved to me. "Wwwwhat're yyyyou doing here?"

"Saving your ass. Again," I said with a smile.

Gideon looked at his brother, then back to me. "I ccccan take him."

"Of that, I have no doubt. But how about we get you feeling stronger first, eh?"

Gideon lifted his hand to stare at the bronze trinket I'd placed there. "Wwwwhat's this?"

I closed his open palm around the trinket. "It has healing properties. Maybe not as strong as that wand you just smashed, but it should have you feeling back to about fifty percent normal by tomorrow. Which, by the looks of you, would be a forty-nine percent improvement."

A tiny hint of a smile crept to the edge of Gideon's lips. "Dddon't tttry to bbbbutter me up," he said.

"Pfffft. As if."

I started to take away my hand when Gideon caught me by the wrist and pulled my hand closer to look at the red marks still present from the golden cords his twin had bound me with.

With an even more venomous look in his eye, he glared at his brother. "Sssstttop tttying her up!"

Finn smirked. "Maybe she likes it."

A tiny, delicious shiver traveled down my spine. "Don't flatter yourself, Flayer," I snapped, covering my desire with a little sass.

Finn merely shrugged, and sighed, "Desperate times…"

Gideon tugged on my hand again. "Dddddon't let himmm ppppush you arrrround."

I smiled gamely at him. "I can take him."

Gideon twisted his mouth into something that was either a grimace or a smile, squeezed my hand, and let it go. Holding onto me looked like it'd taxed him significantly. "Wwwwhat abbbout the ccccase?" he asked next.

"Esmé has agreed to work with me on that," Finn said.

I was about to protest when I remembered that I was now bound to cooperate with the lieutenant, and I'm pretty sure he'd led me to believe that he'd only meant coming up here without murdering him, not about working the case to retrieve Tic for Petra.

Still, Finn had also agreed to cooperate with me, and Grigori's murder and Tic's abduction could well be the same case. As unappealing as it was, it made sense in a way to team up. Especially if I had a death wish, which, by the looks of the past three days, apparently I did.

With a nod toward Finn, I said, "That's true, Detective. You heal up, and your brother and I will solve Grigori's murder."

Gideon's gaze moved slowly but deliberately back to his brother, and the deep-seated anger returned to the cast of his eyes. "Nnnno," he said defiantly, and the idiot actually tried to sit up.

I pushed him gently back, which was easy because he was a mess. "I'd rather have you, Gideon, but you're in no shape to help me right now, and as your mentor, it's within my power to insist that you stay put."

Gideon's gaze shifted to me again, and this time there was a crease of worry along his forehead. "Ellllric," he said hoarsely.

I knew what he meant. He was worried that if Elric knew I was working with Petra's lieutenant that he'd definitely kill me, and he'd likely try to kill Finn.

Nodding toward where Finn was standing on the opposite side of the bed, I said, "He looks just like you. In fact, he'll need to pass as you to hunt down any leads we come across."

"Ah," Gideon said, and I noticed he was trembling just a bit less, which was a very good sign that the serpent and staff trinket was working. "Yeah, Ffffinn's good at passing as me. Ain'tcha, big bbbrother?"

My brow furrowed and my gaze traveled to Finn, who had moved to a wing chair, where he sat casually, staring at Gideon, but I swore there was tension crackling in the air between these two.

Still, Finn reached to the pin with Petra's insignia attached to his shirt. "Here," he said, removing it and laying it on the nightstand. "If anyone comes looking for me, you're going to have to pass for me too. Show them that, tell them you're working on a lead to find Marco and that you need some privacy. They should leave you alone as long as you flash that like you do your badge."

Gideon eyed the pin and curled his lip up in that snarl again. "I'll nnnnever sssssay I'mmmm you."

Finn smiled, but no humor reached his eyes. "Never say never, Gid."

Knowing that if I didn't separate the brothers there'd be trouble, I snapped my fingers a few times and said, "Gideon, get some rest. Finn, let's go."

Walking out of the room without a word I headed straight to the elevator to wait for Finn, expecting it to be a few moments, but he surprised me by reaching over my shoulder to press the elevator button.

Apparently he wasn't big on long goodbyes.

Which was telling.

After the doors of the elevator closed and we were on our way down, I said, "What's between you two, anyway?"

Finn stared at the door. "I was Mom's favorite."

I laughed but caught myself, unsure if he was actually making a joke or not. Finn wasn't smiling, and there'd been no hint of humor in his reply. "Come on," I said. "Seriously."

He turned a hard gaze toward me, but I wasn't especially deterred.

"Okay," I said, my tone teasing. "I'll just ask your brother later."

Finn's expression changed in a nanosecond, and it was as if I was looking at Elric when he had me pinned to the chair. Reflexively I even braced for a punch.

"Don't you fucking dare," he said, his voice barely above a whisper.

I held his gaze but was worried I'd lit a fuse best left cold. "Fine," I said. "But geez, Lieutenant, I'm not your enemy, okay?"

The doors pinged and parted and I moved to walk out, but Finn stepped in front of me turning to face me and block my exit while also holding the doors open. "Let's get one thing straight, Esmé Bellerose: As an employee of SPL, you are *definitely* my enemy, and I am currently under orders to kill you."

Standing so close in front of me was enough to reignite that deep lust between us. The charm around my neck immediately heated up again, but so did the desire to embrace Finn and kiss him until I lost myself. Still, the charm managed to quell the worst of the temptation, and with squared shoulders I met his gaze without blinking.

"You can't kill me, Finn," I said with a snarl. "I'm your brother's mentor, which, under the law, makes me a person you're *obligated* to protect."

"Who's gonna tell on me?" Finn asked. "You think *my brother* is gonna file a complaint with Ostergaard, who's then gonna come looking for me? Get real. I could kill you and no one would give a shit. Least of all your boss."

He was absolutely right, of course, but I still wanted the feel of his naked skin against mine. I took another deep breath and focused on the heat coming off the charm, which helped keep my head clear. "Fine. I'll leave it alone," I said, if only to end the argument.

The tension between us evaporated and, satisfied, Finn pushed away from the doors and rolled his arm in an "after you" gesture.

I walked past him with my nose in the air. "Jesus, does *everybody* want to kill me this week?"

Finn chuckled. "I hear Jacquelyn wants first crack."

I waved tauntingly over my shoulder. "She already had her turn. And I won."

We reached the SUV, and before I could lift the door handle, Finn reached around to do it for me. His whole body pressed close, and in an instant I was aflame with desire again. Even the heat of the charm wasn't strong enough to quell that desire, and without thinking, I turned to face him, saw him looking down at me with those gorgeous hazel eyes, and the next thing I knew, I was pressing myself against him, my breath coming quick and my fingers curling around the sides of his jacket.

Somewhere in the deep recesses of my mind, I could hear myself screaming to let go, back away, and get into the car, but the desire for Finn was overwhelming. He flooded every sense I had and chased out all good reason and rationale.

It even took me a moment to realize that he'd wrapped his arms tightly around me and was lowering his lips to mine. I closed my eyes and surrendered, overcome by the wanting desire of him.

Just as his lips touched mine someone shouted, "Lieutenant!"

We both jumped. Finn released me and I fell back against his car, breathing heavily. He quickly stepped away from me as well, looking over his shoulder for the source of the voice.

A muscularly sculpted, young mystic stepped forward, wearing a sheepish grin. "Sorry, sir. I...didn't mean to interrupt."

Finn squared his shoulders, his face a mask of granite. "Sipowicz," he said. "What're you doing here?"

Sipowicz cleared his throat, glanced at me, turned red, then stared at his feet. "Petra sent me. She's been trying to reach you, but you're not answering your phone."

Finn stared at the young man like he wanted to punch him. "I'm busy."

Sipowicz gulped. "Yes, sir, but she *wants* to *see* you."

Finn sighed heavily, and a long silence filled the garage. At last he turned to me and held up his key fob. "I have to deal with this."

My eyes widened. "You're...you're going to meet Petra?" My concern wasn't misplaced. If Petra got wind that I was not only still alive, but hanging out with her lieutenant as well, she'd likely give the order to have both of us executed, and while I kind of liked Finn's chances, given his reputation, I didn't especially like mine.

"I have to," he whispered, his mouth set in a firm, grim line. "Sipowicz has already sent the message that you're still alive, and that he caught the two of us..."

He didn't need to finish that sentence.

"Will she punish you?" I said softly, trying not to let Sipowicz overhear.

Finn reached for my wrist using two fingers and turned my hand palm-face-up. Dropping the key fob into my hand, he said, "She will. But that's nothing new. I'll meet you as soon as I can."

Finn then turned and held out his hand to Sipowicz.

"What?" the junior mystic asked.

"Keys."

Sipowicz's expression registered surprise. "Uh..." he said. "Lieutenant, I just got this car. She doesn't even have fifty miles on the odometer yet."

Finn waved his fingers in a come-on gesture. "Give 'em up, Sip."

Reluctantly the younger mystic dug into his pocket and offered Finn his key fob. Finn snatched it out of Sipowicz's palm, and the pair moved toward a bright red Corvette.

Knowing that I needed to check in with Dex and not wanting to wait around in the garage for any of Sipowicz's pals, I hopped into the front seat of Finn's Escalade and followed the pair around the cement pylons of the parking garage to the exit, which was up a ramp to the street.

I had to wait for the gate to lift to follow the red Corvette up the ramp, but I was still fairly close when I saw something ejected out of the sports car. I gasped and barely had time to react, pulling hard on the wheel and narrowly avoiding hitting the body tumbling along the pavement.

"*What the fuck?*" I exclaimed, focusing on the rear view mirror. I couldn't tell if Sipowicz or Finn was the person who'd been knocked out of the car.

If it was Finn, he was likely banged up and in need of help. If it was Sipowicz, he was likely dead and beyond any help.

Right about then my phone rang. The caller ID said it was Gideon. "Hello?" I asked, picking up the call.

"Follow close behind me," Finn said.

"What the hell happened?"

"Sipowicz had a prior engagement," Finn said smoothly.

"Is he dead?" I asked, glancing in the rearview mirror again, but I could no longer see the mystic behind me.

"I doubt it. Probably a little bruised, but he'll heal."

"Why?" I asked next. I couldn't understand why he'd done that.

"Because you don't defy an order from the boss," Finn said. "She gets even unless you give her a reason not to."

"What're you going to do?"

"Give her a reason not to."

I thought about that for a minute. "If you find Tic, she no longer has a reason to want to kill you or me."

"Bingo. And for the record, she wouldn't kill me. She's definitely interested in killing you though."

"She'll have to get in line."

"Esmé?"

"Yeah?"

"You've got a shadow on your six."

My gaze flew to the rearview mirror for a third time. Sure enough, a big, black F-150 was several car lengths behind, weaving in and out of traffic, and gaining ground. Fast.

"Friends of yours?" I asked.

"Yep. We're probably less chummy these days, but they're trouble for sure."

"What do I do?" I asked, glancing all around for a place to hide and finding nothing. Not even a side street.

"Follow my lead," he said.

I was about to ask him what that meant when the Corvette bulleted ahead.

"Dammit!" I swore, hitting the speaker function on the phone before shoving a tiny bit of essence into it, whispering, "Stay put," and sticking it on the dash, where the phone would hold like superglue until I released it. I then gripped the wheel with both hands and punched down hard on the gas.

The tires squealed and the car rocketed forward. I had to focus intently as I wove through the early evening traffic, doing my best to catch up to the Corvette.

Finn's maneuvering was tighter and more controlled than mine, which was a given since he was driving a sleek sports car that could turn on a dime and I was driving an Escalade which was basically a tank that turned like the *Titanic*.

Still, with significant effort, I managed to keep within a few car lengths of Finn, but I also wasn't able to shake the big-ass truck following behind us.

"What's the plan here, Lieutenant?" I called out through gritted teeth when I narrowly missed sideswiping a minivan.

"Just keep on my six, Esmé," he said. "We're almost there."

I tightened my grip on the steering wheel in frustration and glanced again in the rearview. The F-150 behind me was gaining ground and would be within spell-casting distance in a few moments if I didn't do something to lengthen my lead.

Searching the road ahead for an opportunity, I spotted a city bus stopping for a lone pedestrian who was waiting at a bus stand. It was the perfect opportunity.

Moving over to the far-right lane, I rolled down the window and shot out some essence and yelled, "Wrong bus, wrong bus, step it back, don't make a fuss!"

The lone man at the bus stop approached the open doors but then suddenly stopped, looked up at the bus in confusion, then stepped back and waved the bus on.

Meanwhile I was still hurtling toward it, and I gripped the wheel even tighter, waiting until just the right moment.

"Esmé!" I heard Finn yell through the speaker. "What the hell are you doing?"

I didn't answer. Instead, I put my entire focus on aiming directly for the bus. The distance between us was closing with lightning speed. Behind me, the truck on my tail also picked up speed, quickly coming to within spell-casting distance.

"Come on!" I shouted.

And then, like a miracle, the bus's brake lights went out, and it began to pull forward.

I was three car lengths away and still aiming for the center of the bus.

"*Esmé!*" Finn yelled again. "*Talk to me!*"

I ignored him. "*Move*, you son of a bitch!" I yelled at the bus.

I didn't know if I'd have room, or if the maneuver would work, but it was too late to turn back now, especially with the truck on my tail, closing in fast.

The rear end of the bus came up so fast, and still I waited until the view of it filled the entire windshield before I did anything to veer off my current trajectory.

With less than a few feet between me and the back of the bus, I pulled hard on the wheel, cranking the SUV to the right, wedging the vehicle into the narrow space between the bus and the sidewalk, but there wasn't quite enough room, and the SUV lurched as two wheels jumped the curb.

The SUV was now tilted slightly, but I wasn't about to let off the gas. But then another complication appeared in the form of a lamppost with my name written all over it if I didn't do something quick. Squaring my shoulders, I kept the pedal to the metal, filled the cab with more of my energy and yelled, "Faster, faster, avoid this disaster!"

The SUV picked up an extra burst of speed and zipped through the pocket of open space between the front of the bus and the lamppost, and with only an inch to spare on either side of me, I managed to emerge from the pocket unscathed, pulling hard on the wheel again, only this time correcting to the left, putting myself directly in front of the bus.

Behind me there was the sound of metal scraping metal, and I grinned as I saw in the rearview mirror that the truck chasing me hadn't calculated nearly as well as I had. I held my breath, hoping it would crash and burn, but the son of a bitch driving it somehow managed to avoid crashing, fishtailing for a bit until it could correct course again.

"Fucker!" I shouted at the view in the rearview, continuing to press hard on the gas.

"Catch up!" Finn yelled.

"Doing my level best, Lieutenant!"

"There's a right turn coming up," Finn said, ignoring my tone. "Be ready."

My palms were sweaty against the wheel, but I pointed the car directly toward Finn's the same way I'd driven toward the bus.

"Three streets away!" Finn yelled. "You're going to have to take your foot off the gas now, Esmé! Don't brake and let them know what you're planning!"

I glanced nervously into the rearview mirror. The F-150 in pursuit was again closing in fast. "They'll be within casting distance!" I shouted.

"Kiener's at the wheel," he said quickly. "His range isn't great. You'll make it."

"They'll see you take the turn, though, and know that's where I'm heading!"

"No, they won't! You're two streets away! Don't pay attention to me. Just turn where I've pointed you!"

The red Corvette suddenly whipped to the right, sliding down a street that was one away from where Finn had directed me. The move gave me a moment of indecision. Had I misunderstood? Was I supposed to turn where he had?

"Keep going!" Finn shouted, and I knew then that he'd pulled down a side street hoping to lure the truck off my tail.

I did as he told me to and passed his street, then took my foot off the gas, slowing down slightly right before my turn came up.

Behind me I saw the F150 slow down too. The Corvette could be seen in my side-view mirror racing down the street like a rabbit luring a greyhound, daring Kiener to come after it.

I came up to my turn faster than I'd anticipated and had to hit the brakes to avoid tipping the Escalade over as I made the maneuver. Still, I felt two wheels come off the pavement, which caused me to shoot my right arm out and command, "Steady!"

The two wheels dropped, and the SUV shot forward.

"Keep going, and don't stop until you're through the gates!" Finn yelled.

"Gates? *What* gates?!" There was nothing in front of me but open road.

Finn didn't respond. I looked over to my right and could see between the open lot on the right that his car was still racing ahead, parallel to mine, and behind him came the F-150, which meant they cared more about nabbing Finn than nabbing me.

"Thank God for small favors," I muttered.

"What?" Finn asked through the speaker.

"Nothing! Except they're on your tail now."

"Thank God for small favors," he repeated back to me with a hint of sarcasm.

"Better you than me when it comes to your own people, Lieutenant."

"Yeah, yeah. Just focus on getting the hell through the gates."

I stared into the darkness of the road ahead. There were no streetlights in this part of town, but I could still see the Corvette and the chase car, roaring down a parallel path from mine.

Turning my attention back to the road in front of me, I realized it'd begun to curve left, taking me away from the parallel path with Finn. I was feeling a bit anxious about that, but then a sign reflected in my high beams signaled that the end of the pavement was just ahead. I tried to brake but ended up fishtailing, barely holding it together as the SUV jumped onto the dirt road, hitting every giant pothole and divot, making my bones rattle.

Working hard, I fought with the steering wheel to stay in control, turning into each swirl and pumping the brakes until finally the front and back of the Escalade were heading in the same direction again.

I moved ahead cautiously but at the fastest speed I could still maintain control.

"Esmé!" Finn suddenly shouted into the silence of the cab.

I jumped. "What?"

"Watch out for the dirt road. It comes up quick."

I glared at the phone. "Gee, thanks for the head's up."

"Can you see the gates?"

"No!" I yelled. The tension in my shoulders from gripping the wheel and trying to navigate the bumpy dirt road at a faster-than-comfortable speed was intense.

"They'll be in front of you any minute. When you go through them—"

Finn's voice cut off as an insanely loud noise echoed from my phone's speaker.

"Finn?!" I yelled, my gaze pingponging between the phone and the road ahead. "*Finn!*"

But he didn't reply, and I couldn't take my hands off the wheel to check and see if my phone had died—or if he had.

"Dammit!" I swore, pressing the accelerator a little more aggressively. I needed to get to the end of this road so I could pull over and figure out what had happened to Finn.

At almost the exact moment I had that thought, two insanely high metal gates attached to a twenty-foot wall lit up in my high beams. "Whoa," I said, hitting the brakes again.

The gates were shut, and Finn hadn't told me how to get them open, so I eased to a stop in front of them, hoping to spot a call box or mechanism or something.

As I was about to throw the SUV into park, there was a beeping sound from the dash, and a red light began to blink. I squinted at it, and then my attention snapped back to the windshield as the area beyond the gates lit up like an evening game at a baseball park. That was promptly followed by a series of large gears turning and the sound of metal grinding on metal, and then the gates begin to part.

"Cool," I whispered, throwing the gear into D again. I didn't waste any time zipping forward when the gates were barely wide enough to allow Finn's SUV to pass. They closed behind me with a loud clang as soon as I was through.

On this side of the gates and the wall, a surprise awaited. "A junkyard?" I said to myself.

But not any junkyard. All around me were piles and piles of discarded trinkets in every kind of shape and size you could imagine.

And the piles weren't small. Each was at least thirty feet tall. There were musical instruments, clocks, rocking horses, toys, vases, furniture, staffs, canes, hourglasses, music boxes, broken mirrors—large and small—tapestries, paintings, sculptures and, very oddly, what looked to be a miniature replica of the Statue of Liberty.

"Wow," I said, parking Finn's car and opening the door to get out. The temptation to have a closer look at what was a thief's wet dream was overriding any sense of caution.

Although the former owners of all this trash might've been convinced that their things were dead of magical powers and worth discarding, sometimes something really precious got sent to the trash heap because the user wasn't very good at bringing out the magic.

Reaching into my jacket pocket, I pulled out my monocle and looked through it. The pile in front of me emitted small pockets of faint green light but most of it was junk. Moving my gaze slowly up, I searched for anything emitting a light in the emerald category, not expecting to find anything but it was still worth looking.

So I was absolutely gobsmacked when at the top of the pile, I spotted a radiantly brilliant aqua green light that pulsed with power. Only levels above ten were that color.

"Whoa," I whispered.

Behind me, and still attached to the dashboard, my cell began to ring. For a second, I hesitated even considering answering it because of the view through the monocle, but then I remembered that Finn had been in a crash and might need my help. Growling, I swung around and reached inside the cab to whisper, "Let it go." I caught the cell as it fell off the dash. "Finn?" I asked urgently.

"Yeah," he said. "Sorry. Petra sent a crew in a second car that caught me off guard."

"How's the Corvette?"

"It's seen better days. Did you make it through the gates?"

I lifted the monocle with my free hand, drawn by the brilliant bright light at the top of the pile in front of me. "I did. I'm assuming this is where Petra sends all her discarded trash?"

"It is. I'm headed your way—"

"In the Corvette?"

"No," he said simply. "I'll be in the F-150."

So he'd dealt with Kiener. Or maybe the other crew's truck if they also drove F-150s. The man was a legit badass.

"Stay in my vehicle until I get there. Under no circumstances are you to leave the car, understood?"

I continued forward to the base of the large pile in front of me and lowered the monocle. Scowling, I asked, "Why? Don't want me to get tempted by some bits of trash that still have a little life left in them, Lieutenant?"

There was a pause, then, "Esmé, are you out of the Escalade?"

I rolled my eyes. "Of course I'm out of the Escalade! I'm a thief, and you've just opened the gates to Disneyland."

Finn's voice lowered in volume, almost to a whisper. "Don't move," he said. "Esmé, I mean it. If you're out of the car, stop and *do. Not. Move!*"

My brow furrowed. Was there a defense system in place that I hadn't recognized?

The moment I had that thought, I felt the hairs on the back of my neck stand up on end. Behind me I heard movement. Something sounded like it was slithering over the ground, and it came at me fast.

The slithering continued while I held perfectly still, barely breathing, because whatever was coming up behind me was very, very large. At last, the slithering stopped. Right behind me.

Chapter Sixteen
Day 3

I could feel the enormous weight of the creature, hovering just behind me, like an oppressive force, but I dared not move or make a sound.

"Esmé?" Finn whispered. "If you can hear me, tap the phone with your finger."

I tapped the microphone with my index finger very softly.

"Good. You're still alive. If you want to stay that way, hold still."

Now I've been in tricky situations before. I've faced creatures that would literally scare the shit out of you, but this thing behind me was releasing some sort of energy that was hard to explain. Not only was every single fiber of my being on high alert, but I was also petrified in a way that didn't feel natural. My heart was pounding in my chest, and I had to work at keeping it to a rhythm that wouldn't give me a heart attack while also waiting to feel the bite, or the sting, or the slice of whatever Hell had coughed up behind me, but the moment continued to drag out, and I had a feeling the creature was enjoying playing with its prey.

And then something appeared out of the corner of my eye. It landed gently to the right of me, maybe two feet away.

I refused to turn my head to get a better look at it, but whatever it was, it slowly edged forward, and I realized it looked like a bony finger, riddled with long thorny hair and ending in a bulbous, pulsating red tip with a stinger the size of my forearm, curved down toward the ground.

It tapped the earth in a way that suggested thoughtful impatience, and at the clear sight of it, I felt a shudder threaten to shake me right out of my still-as-a-statue posture.

With significant effort, I swallowed the scream that was slowly working its way up my windpipe. The terror taking over my entire nervous system was like a physical force, pressing on me, worming its way into my psyche.

My breathing was shallow and quick. I felt the urge to close my eyes away from that pulsating stinger, but I was literally too terrified to take my gaze off it.

In the back of my mind, I knew what I was looking at. The stinger belonged to a creature called a cruellion. One of the deadliest monsters ever to have cursed the world.

There were said to be only three in existence, but I'd not heard any rumors that either Petra or Elric actually kept one as a pet.

If memory served me, cruellions were as tall as a dragon, long as a python, and deadlier than both creatures combined. They were keenly intelligent, ugly as sin, and enjoyed toying with their prey before injecting them with a poison that was said to light every nerve ending on fire, and keep them alive and aware while the creature slowly ate them... sometimes over a period of days.

No images existed of a cruellion. Everyone who'd ever gotten close enough to snap a photo had never been seen or heard from again. Still, they'd been thoroughly described by the very, very few who'd managed to see one at a distance and lived to tell about it.

With a long black body that sported both hair and scales, it slithered like a snake but had two boney arms and humanlike hands but each finger was tipped with a bulbous red stinger.

I'd met a mystic once who'd had a brief encounter with a cruellion. He was missing the bottom half of his right leg. He'd described to a group of eager listeners how he'd managed to wedge himself into a hole that the cruellion hadn't been able to fit through, but it had been able to reach its arm in and sting him with just the tip of its longest finger. It'd kept trying to get at him for hours, and the mystic suggested that just that initial sting had felt like being injected with acid and set on fire. Even after the cruellion had grown bored and moved on, the pain had continued, and finally the mystic had cut off his own leg simply to end the unceasing agony.

I remembered walking away after listening to the mystic, thinking he was a teller of tall tales and doubting his story, but one side glance at that stinger and the palpable fear that the creature behind me was pumping into the atmosphere told me that the old man had understated his encounter.

"Esmé," Finn said, jarring me out of my nightmarish thoughts "Is the creature nearby?"

I dared not even whisper a reply. Finn would simply have to interpret my silence for confirmation.

"Tap the phone once for yes, twice for no."

I tapped the microphone.

"Shit. Can you make it back to the Escalade?"

I tapped the mic twice. The cruellion was between me and Finn's SUV, and that stinger was just a few feet away. I figured I'd get less than that distance on my sprint back to the vehicle.

In the background I could hear the sound of Finn's truck picking up speed. "I'm on the way," he said. "Stay with me and don't move."

A clicking sound cut through the silence of the night. Low and insanely eerie, the sound rose up from a deep, guttural place, vibrating through the atmosphere and rippling along my skin. Accompanying it was another series of slithers, and four more talons appeared to my right, all tipped with the pulsing boil of poison and a long sharp stinger.

The sight was too much to take so I closed my eyes and held my breath. It was all I could do not to tremble and faint. I'd never been so afraid in my entire life, and even though much of that fear was no doubt created by the cruellion's own magic, it did nothing to help me reason my way out of the abject terror coursing through my veins.

And then, just as suddenly as both the clicking and the slithering had started, they stopped.

For a long moment nothing happened, and then I realized that the terror I'd been experiencing was beginning to wane. I mean, yeah, I was still scared shitless, but I wasn't close to passing out in fear.

Had the cruellion gone? Had it slithered away to find other prey?

I thought about the giant wall and the metal gates behind me, and realized that they weren't that tall to keep unwanted guests out, but rather had no doubt been constructed to keep the cruellion *in*.

When I couldn't stand the uncertainty any longer, I opened my eyes to look... and came face to face with a hideous sight.

In front of me was a mouth large enough to bite me in half, and teeth that were at least six inches long, which peered out of leather black lips and nose shaped like the snout of a snake.

Amphibian eyes ogled me, and then the leather black lips pulled back to expose lots more jaggedly sharp teeth, and I realized the cruellion was grinning.

It'd gotten me to look.

I realized my mistake far too late, and another bolt of fear hit me like a ton of bricks. If I hadn't been so firmly rooted to the spot, I probably would've gone flying backward.

The cruellion rose up in front of me, gathering all ten of its poisonous talons, splaying them sideways before beginning to curl its body toward me. It wouldn't use just one stinger to do the deed. It'd use all ten, and I'd be stung from toe to head. No way would I survive that, but no way was I likely to die quickly either.

The cruellion's jaw parted, and a spittle of drool dripped down its leather jaw to fall with a plop at my feet.

It was hungry.

My mind was racing to find a weapon, anything that might buy me a few seconds or allow me an escape, but I had nothing at hand. It struck me as somewhat ironic that the one thing that would've come in handy—my magic pen—was with Elric now. That bastard had all the luck.

The cruellion hovered maybe six feet above me for a few more seconds, then it began its descent, slowly, almost elegantly, and I couldn't take my eyes off it.

Just before it grabbed me up and stung me from stem to stern, a horn blasted loudly, and an engine roared from the road leading in.

The cruellion's gaze pivoted to the right, and I dived left without ever looking toward the gates.

Gravel crunching under large wheels came frighteningly close, and still I didn't look back. I just focused on running for my life.

The clicking behind me told me that I should probably run faster.

A stinger landed in the dirt not even a foot in front of me, and I twisted just in time to avoid a twin headed toward my chest.

Another stinger landing nearby pivoted me farther, and I realized that the cruellion was blocking my escape back to the Escalade.

Instead, it was directing me to the pile of trinkets where the aqua light of pulsating energy had told me an insanely powerful trinket lay, which gave me an idea. Make it to the top of the pile and pray to the gods that the trinket was something I could use to transport me beyond the reaches of the cruellion.

I made it to the base of the pile of junk, sensed something whooshing through the air behind me, and dived to my left.

A stinger landed in the pile, kicking up trinkets, while behind me, Finn continued to lay on the horn and charge toward us.

The roar of his engine never let up, and I clawed and spun my legs up the pile, losing ground several times while I pivoted to the left, trying to get far enough away from the creature to avoid any more stingers.

Again and again the creature clawed after me, but it too seemed hampered by the slippery slope, and for all its swiftness, still wasn't able to climb as fast as I could amid the loose footing of discarded trinkets.

I made it up to fifteen, then twenty, then twenty-five feet, very close to the top of the pile, while behind me I heard the scrabbling of the cruellion and shuffling of trinkets. It seemed to my racing mind that the beast was falling farther and farther behind.

But then I reached for what I thought would've been a solid handhold—the leg of a chair sticking out of the pile—but as I grabbed it, the whole chair came loose and tumbled down on top of me, sending me sliding back toward the cruellion.

Even with flailing arms and legs, I slid down a good ten feet, which I knew without even needing to look had put me within striking distance of the creature. While still attempting to reverse direction, I braced for the inevitable sting I knew was only a second away.

And that's when I heard the roar of Finn's truck surge forward, followed by a thumping sound that shook the pile of trinkets and sent more of them raining down on my head.

Risking a look down, I saw the cruellion on top of Finn's hood, draped there while its own hideous form writhed wildly on its back. Finn shoved the truck into reverse, backed up with a punch to the gas, and turned the wheel hard to the left.

The F-150 rocked violently as it careened in a semicircle, but then Finn hit the brakes, and the cruellion flew off the hood, crashing into another pile of trinkets. Meanwhile I clawed and crawled for purchase, at last finding some, and began to make my way up again. No way did I trust that the cruellion was going to be so easily dissuaded from coming after me again, even with the current distraction of Finn engaging it in a game of demolition derby.

I managed to gain another five feet or so when I chanced another look back. The cruellion had recovered itself and was wearing its wickedly grotesque smile. It was currently slithering with tremendous speed toward Finn's truck, stingers out and ready to engage.

Finn was backing up, his head craning to look behind him while chancing a glance at the approaching beast. His expression was grim. He and I both knew he was as good as dead. No way could his Escalade outrun the thing as he swerved and rocked around the piles of trinkets, each meter taking him farther away from the gates. Even inside that cab, the cruellion would get to him.

With renewed urgency I scrambled up the pile, sweat pouring off me as I fought for every foot. At last I crested the heap and even without my monocle immediately spotted the thing that'd been emitting the powerful radiant light because it glowed bright enough for even my own eyes to see.

Sticking out of the junkpile was the hilt of a sword. Without thinking I reached for it, pulling the sword from the pile. As I pulled it free and held it aloft, a movement at my feet caught my eye, and I realized the scabbard that accompanied the sword had dropped at my feet. As I gripped the sword, warmth enveloped me, surging down my arm, radiating every fiber of my being with raw courage. The magic set fire to the fear, chasing it out of my chest like the noon sun, scaring off shadows.

Turning to look down toward the bottom of the pile, I saw a horrible sight: the F-150 was backing up, narrowly missing a pile of trinkets while heading straight toward another pile, with the cruellion on top of the hood, where it raised its grotesque hand above the windshield before punching it straight through the glass.

A surge of fury roared through me as I watched the cruellion murder Petra's lieutenant, who'd definitely saved my life just moments before. The fury intensified filling every fiber of my being until it finally released itself in a carnal challenge that was by far the loudest sound I'd ever emitted.

It did the job though. Momentarily pausing its murder of the Flayer, the beast turned its big disgusting face toward me.

At that exact moment, however, the backend of the F-150 slammed into the pile of trinkets, and an avalanche of sorts took place, with once-enchanted treasures raining down on both the truck and the cruellion, burying them in a smaller pile of junk.

That pile then moved like churning water and the cruellion emerged, its eyes trained on me and those terrifying lips parting into an evil smile to reveal more of those hideous teeth.

I knew I should've been afraid—terrified even—but rather than paralyzing fear, only courage coursed through my veins. I smiled back at the creature, hungry for the fight.

I waited as it slithered quickly out of the pile it'd created and headed my way with eager speed. Arriving at the base of the pile of trinkets I was standing on it began to slither its way up again.

In my hand the sword felt alive and light as air. It was easily two and a half feet long and literally gleamed with bright unbridled power. I felt more alive holding it than I'd ever felt in my life—its magic was insane.

Shouting another war cry, I bent down to pick up the scabbard, then threw it at the cruellion like a gauntlet in challenge before leaping off the top of the pile, ready to meet the cruellion head-on.

Everything that happened after that moment felt like time slowed down. The cruellion reared up, opening its gaping maw and exposing a double row of razor-sharp teeth. Its two boney arms tipped in stingers extended toward me, triumph in its eyes.

The sword moved of its own volition, sweeping downward in a long arc while my body twisted to the left, twirling in the air away from the beast's clutches. As I spun in the air, I felt the sword make clean contact with the beast, but the speed of the arc never lessened. I heard a series of popping sounds as the blade cut through each digit, sending the bulbous sacs of poison and their stingers flying.

A moment later, I landed sideways on the pile, ten feet from the bottom. Flipping my head to clear the hair from my eyes, my gaze landed on the cruellion, staring at the stumps of its bleeding fingers as if it couldn't believe what'd just happened.

Another surge of power coursed through me, and I charged again toward the beast.

It saw me coming, and the constant clicks it'd been emitting changed in frequency and tone. They went from a menacing, dangerous cadence to a high-pitched frightful rhythm, and before I knew it, the beast had twirled in a circle and was spinning backward down the heap of trinkets. It reached the bottom well ahead of me, and it slithered with blinding speed over the ground toward parts unknown. With a final leap, I made it to the ground myself and began to chase after it, but it was far faster than me. After a bit I stopped and stood defiantly, sword still clutched in my hand while I stared in the direction the beast had fled. My chest was heaving and sweat lined my brow, but I felt oddly invigorated and ready to fight a dozen cruellions.

"Holy shit!" I heard from right behind me.

Startled, I spun around, raising the sword defensively.

Finn put up his hands in surrender. "Hey, easy, it's just me."

I lowered the sword. "You're alive," I said, more statement than question.

Finn nodded. "Ducked just in time."

I pointed the sword toward a nearby digit from the cruellion. "It's wounded but not dead."

Finn nodded, and for the first time I could see that he was looking at me warily.

"What?" I asked, then froze as I had a sudden thought. "Is it behind me?"

"No," Finn said. And then he pointed to the sword. "How... how did you get that?"

I relaxed and pointed again with the sword to the top of the trinket heap. "It was up there sticking out of the trash. It was the only weapon I could find."

Again, Finn nodded. "Yeah, no, I know it was up there. What I'm asking is, how did you free it?"

My brow furrowed. "Free it? You mean, like, pick it up?"

"Yeah."

"Uh... by grabbing the hilt and pulling it out of the heap."

"It just came free?" he asked. And his tone was incredulous.

"Dude," I said. "What's with you? The sword wasn't stuck. I just plucked it out of the trash."

Finn swept a hand through his hair and then he looked around, as if wary of the return of the cruellion. "We need to go," he said. "Come on."

"Okay," I said, holding tight to my weapon. "But I'm keeping the sword."

"Duh," Finn muttered, turning away.

His response really surprised me. No way would Petra's lieutenant simply allow a treasure like the sword to be taken away unchallenged. Still, there was no sense arguing the point when a deadly beast was still lurking about.

And then I had an alarming thought and glanced toward the gates. They were closed, thank the gods. A cruellion unleashed upon the world of the unbound would've been cause for immense alarm.

With a sigh I followed after Finn, pausing to pick up the dyed-black leather scabbard, embossed with gold filigree from where it'd landed when I threw it off the pile of trash, and resheathed the sword, using the cord that attached at both ends of the scabbard to strap it to my back.

We reached the Escalade, which was still idling exactly how I'd left it. Finn and I got into the cab and he adjusted the seat to allow for his longer legs, then pointed the SUV away from the gates and hit the gas.

"Didn't you say we need to go?" I asked.

"Yep," he said, picking up speed and swerving between trinket piles. "There's a secret exit at the back of the yard. We can't chance an escape out the front gates again. It's ripe for an ambush."

We wound our way across the junkyard, both of us scanning the area for any sign of the cruellion. "Keep that sword handy," Finn said as we cruised around one particularly large pile.

I gave him some side-eye. "You gonna make me take it on all by myself again?"

"Damned straight," he said, with a hint of a grin.

I glanced down at the sword, which I'd set at my feet. It really was a thing of beauty, with a silver blade, golden hilt, and a grip made of twisting black onyx, studded with pearls, and finished off with a pummel of three stacked golden blocks, also studded with onyx and pearl. "I can't believe you guys tossed this," I said, lifting the sword to eye-level to marvel at the craftsmanship and attention to detail. "The jewels on the hilt alone would make it worth keeping, not to mention the fact that it's still got a whole lotta life left in it."

Finn puffed out some air. "You could say that."

"What's that supposed to mean?"

"You really have no idea what you're holding, do you?"

I lifted the weapon. "It's a sword. I'd guess it's circa late sixth to early seventh century, probably Anglo-Saxon or Vendel. Whoever infused it knew what they were doing. The thing's got a mind of its own."

"It's actually fifth century, and it was infused by Merlin the great."

My jaw dropped. He was joking. He had to be. "Come on," I said, turning my gaze again to the windshield to scan the area for any sign of the cruellion.

"I'm not kidding."

I rolled my eyes. "You're telling me this is Excalibur?" I said, holding the sword up again, which was definitely too small and too light to be the famed sword. "Unless Arthur was built like a woman, no way would this sword have fit his palm."

"It's not Excalibur," Finn said, never taking his gaze from the windshield. "It's Lunatrabem."

I stared at him, mouth again agape. "Hold on," I said, pushing back against the notion. But then I had to consider that it actually made sense. Lunatrabem—Moonbeam—was made by the same mystic who'd created Excalibur—Merlin the Great.

Legend had it that Lunatrabem had been given as a wedding gift to Guinevere by the old mystic.

Since the legend of Excalibur as a sword of might and power far exceeded that of Lunatrabem, which was thought to be nothing more than a decorative totem to the queen, almost nothing existed in the history books about its use. Or its power.

But we mystics had heard of it. Even though Guinevere was no warrior, legend still had it that Lunatrabem was every bit the feminine equal to Excalibur.

And while the unbound had heard stories that Guinevere had entered a convent upon King Arthur's death and lived out her days as a servant of God, we mystics knew that she'd entered the convent pregnant with King Arthur's child, a boy named Longinus, bound and taken under the wing of Merlin who raised the child in the mystic world.

Legend also said that upon Guinevere's death, Lunatrabem was placed into her headstone by Merlin at the request of Longinus, who knew that if the sword ever fell into the wrong hands, such as loyalists of Morgana, the free men and women of the world would be in grave peril.

Since no one but Guinevere's descendants knew where she and King Arthur were buried, the whereabouts of the sword were lost to time.

Turning to Finn again, I asked, "How the *hell* did Petra come into possession of Lunatrabem?"

No way could any descendant of Guinevere's allow the sword to fall into Petra Dobromila Ostergaard's hands. Certainly Elric never would've allowed it, because with Moonbeam in her exquisitely lethal hands, there would be no limit to the wreckage she could forge.

Finn dipped his chin and looked at me with half-lidded eyes. "Sigourney Astoré," he said. "Direct descendant of King Arthur and Guinevere."

I gasped. "Tic's *father?*"

"Yep."

I turned to stare out the windshield, stunned by the series of revelations, so it took me a minute to note that we were approaching a huge rock wall at the base of a bluff with no clear sign of an exit. Still, my mind continued to grapple with the knowledge that Petra had been in possession of Lunatrabem for all these years and hadn't wielded it against Elric and his forces to gain control of the continent. The idea was unfathomable to me. Why had she held back?

"Why would your boss toss this in the trash heap?" I demanded, holding tighter to the ancient, magical weapon.

"She didn't toss it," he said. "She put it there for safekeeping."

"Safekeeping?" I repeated. "Safekeeping from whom?"

Finn tapped a button on the top of his console, and a section of the rock wall began to move to the side, exposing a hidden tunnel. "From thieves like you," he said

I blinked at him. None of this made sense. "If Petra had the sword, why didn't she just use it to reign over the whole territory?"

"Because she couldn't," he answered, accelerating forward quickly when the wall had opened up enough to let us through.

"Why?" I pressed while Finn braked long enough to press the button again and close the exit, all the while keeping a nervous gaze on the rearview mirror.

When we started moving again, he finally answered me. "Because, until about ten minutes ago, Esmé, it was stuck in two tons of stone. You're the first person in fifteen hundred years to wield it freely."

My jaw fell open for a third and final time, and for the next several minutes, it remained that way.

Chapter Seventeen
Day 3

Finn drove us along the darkened tunnel, and the tense set of his shoulders didn't relax until we were at least a quarter mile away from the exit.

At last I found my voice. "So what does it mean that I was able to free the sword?"

Finn sighed. "I don't know," he admitted. "Other than it makes you the protector of the realm."

"And by the realm, you mean Tic," I said, with no small hint of irritation.

"Yep," Finn said.

"Son of a bitch," I muttered, setting the sword to lay against the seat. "Leave it to Marco to drag me further into Petra's politics and make things extra sticky with Elric."

Finn snorted. "Having possession of the sword wouldn't be something I'd be broadcasting, Esmé. Especially not to Elric. He'd kill for it."

"For sure he'd kill for it," I agreed. And then I had a thought. "What if I just gave the sword to Tic? I mean, it's rightfully his anyway."

"Marco tried for years to pull that thing out of the stone. If it belonged to him, it would've released itself into his grasp long before now."

"Still," I insisted. "What if I just handed it over? I mean, he'd be bound to keep it safe, right? He wouldn't be able to sell it or trade it, and it'd help him put up a defense against his mother and Elric should either one of them decide he'd be better off hanging out with his dead father."

"Petra would use Marco's possession of the sword to declare war on Elric. She'd send him up against her husband in a duel and, even armed with Lunatrabem, it's supremely doubtful that Marco would come out the winner. Elric would then rightfully hold possession, and *that* wouldn't be great for any of us."

"Least of all you," I said. As Petra's lieutenant, Finn would have to represent her in any battle or duel against Elric.

"Least of all me," Finn agreed.

"So what the hell am I supposed to do with it?"

"I suggest you keep it close until we find Marco, and then keep it very, very well-hidden."

I eyed Finn skeptically. "You won't tell anyone I have it?"

"Who would I tell?"

I rolled my eyes. "I dunno, maybe your *boss?*"

Finn chuckled. "She's the last person I'd tell. Besides, right now Petra's trying to kill me."

"Oh, yeah. Almost forgot. Why is that though?"

Finn shrugged. "She ordered you dead, and here you are alive and in my company. Sipowicz would've sent video over before he even made us aware that he was in the parking garage and, if I know Petra, which I do, the second she saw the video, she became convinced I've turned traitor."

I grimaced. "What'll you do?"

"Same as before. Find Marco and show Petra that I was just being strategic by enlisting your help."

"That'll work?"

Finn shrugged again. "It's all I've got at this point."

We came to the end of the tunnel and I thought we were going to drive out, but Finn braked and put the SUV into park.

"What's the plan?" I asked.

Finn lowered his window. "The plan is to make sure we're not heading into a trap."

I glanced out the windshield again at the faint light of the night beyond the tunnel. Nothing moved or looked suspicious, however, I thought his suggestion was wise.

He made a soft whistling sound, and something from the shadows fluttered into view. Finn stuck his arm out of the window, holding out two stiff fingers as a makeshift perch.

What I thought was a bird landed upside down on his fingers, but as I looked more closely, I quickly realized that the small creature was a bat.

I have a thing for bats. I find them fascinating—cute even. This little guy was no exception. He made a few high-pitched squeaking sounds, and Finn brought his hand with the bat carefully inside the cab. "Binks, meet Esmé. Esmé, Binks."

I smiled. "Hey buddy," I cooed, craning my neck to look at the bat's face. "You're a cute little guy, ain'tcha?"

That got me a squeak.

Finn pointed to the glove box. "There're some dried cherries in there. Would you fish a few out for him?"

I did as he asked and pulled up the bag, handing over three to Finn so he could feed the little bat.

Binks chomped hungrily on the cherries until he'd had his fill. Then Finn lifted his fingers to eye level and said, "Okay, buddy, you know the drill. Scout the area and come tell me if anyone's out there, okay?"

Finn moved his hand carefully through the window again, and the bat took off.

We sat in silence for a bit, my mind still whirling with the implications of having drawn Lunatrabem out of Guinevere's headstone, which'd no doubt been buried under a pile of trinkets obscuring it from view.

"How did you see the sword anyway?" Finn asked, breaking the silence.

"It was sticking out of the pile," I said cautiously.

Finn frowned. "That pile was thirty feet high. How the hell could you see it from the ground?"

"You sound like you doubt my story."

"I do doubt your story. I put the damn sword there myself and made sure it couldn't be seen from the ground."

"Hid it in plain sight, huh?"

"Yes," he said simply.

I shrugged and then decided to give him a version of the truth. "The cruellion boxed me in, and my only move was to make it up to the top of the pile. I had no idea there was a sword of power up there, I just wanted to get to the top and hopefully stay out of the beast's reach. When I got there, I tripped over the hilt, and noticed it was a weapon I might be able to use, so I pulled it free, and you know the rest."

Finn made a grunting noise, and I could tell my story was plausible. No *way* was I going to mention the monocle and the radiant light the sword had been giving off. To further distract him, I changed topics. "Do you think the sword might be the reason Tic was abducted?"

Without looking at me, Finn replied, "I do. Or at least it was *a* reason."

"Did Marco know where you guys hid the sword?"

"No. If Marco knew where the sword was kept, he would've auctioned off the information to the highest bidder, and trust me, cruellion on guard or not, he would've made a hefty profit for that information."

"Then who knows that Tic is the direct descendant of Arthur and Guinevere and would've abducted him to try to get to the sword?"

"There aren't a lot of mystics left alive who *would* know. Petra made sure to kill anyone who could've been suspicious of Sigourney's connection to the realm. And even she only ascertained the truth when she discovered Arthur's crest on the underside of Sigourney's foot."

I nodded. "The famous King Arthur birthmark."

All true descendants of the realm were born with a birthmark that began as a red blob, but over time it would morph into a golden dragon—the crest of King Arthur.

"Yep."

"I'm assuming Tic has a birthmark too?"

"He does."

"Where?"

"He's also got one on the underside of his foot. That's why you'll never catch him barefoot."

I actually *had* noticed that about Tic. Even on the hottest summer days, that man was always wearing shoes and socks. I'd always chalked it up to one more weird thing about a weird little man.

"Could Tic's girlfriend have known?"

"Bree?"

"Yeah."

Finn shrugged. "I doubt it. The last time Petra checked Marco's birthmark, it was still red and only hinting at the shape of a dragon."

"She *checks* his birthmark?" The idea was a bit too Oedipal for my taste.

Finn smirked. "She does. The more it reflects the crest, the more in danger Marco is of being discovered as Arthur's descendant. The last thing Petra wants is for Marco to end up being murdered over it."

"I never knew she cared so much about her son," I admitted.

"She doesn't. She cares about sticking it to Elric. She uses Marco to needle him because she knows she can get away with it. Elric's not going to murder Marco and start a war. He's not going to let Petra think it bothers him enough to do that."

I agreed. Elric didn't need that kind of headache. "But if Elric found out that Marco was a descendant of the realm, all bets would be off, right?"

"They would. There are still plenty of powerful mystics willing to unite behind the descendant of Merlin's favorite king."

I sighed. "Then who could've known?"

"Beats the hell out of me."

I tapped my thigh with my index finger, trying to puzzle it all out. "The bigger question is, what does Grigori Rasputin have to do with any of this?"

Finn shifted in his seat, his gaze steadily looking out the windshield, but he seemed to be having an internal argument with himself.

"What?" I asked.

Finn scowled, as if he'd just decided which voice won the argument in his mind. "Grigori was making a power play."

"Meaning?"

"He was here, I suspect, because he was after something that we took from him a year ago."

"Something you took from him?" I asked carefully. "Are you talking about the egg?"

"No," Finn said. "Last year, a source of Petra's discovered Grigori might be in London. We deployed five of our best thieves to retrieve the egg. Only one survived. Grigori killed the other four. He managed to sneak off with the egg, but not before our thief took something of great value to him and something of immense power. Something he'd been using the egg to create."

My brow furrowed. "Using the egg to create? What does that mean?" As far as I knew, Grigori wasn't a merlin.

"It means, he was using the egg to build himself a succubaen."

I sucked in a breath. "Holy shit!"

Succubaen were illegal in the mystic world, which wasn't much of a deterrent, but the actual act of creating a succubaen *was* sufficient enough to deter even the most earnest mystic—or merlin—from attempting to create one.

Derived from an ancient dark magic, a succubaen was a trinket that quite literally killed you while also giving you one clue to discover the thing you most desired. Every time it killed you, the succubaen rose up a level or two, depending on how powerful you were at the start. If you were able to come back from the dead, you'd have just one clue toward the thing that you most desired. You could use that clue to try to suss out the location of the object of your desire or the answer to your quest, but if you didn't succeed, you'd need to use the succubaen all over again and risk not coming back from the dead.

I'd once whimsically entertained the idea of creating a succubaen to find the mystic hag that'd bound me, but the problem with that was that I didn't yet possess the magical skills it took to craft such a powerful trinket, and the fact that every time a succubaen took your life, if you managed to be revived, you came back a little less sane and forever lost a part of your soul to the dark magic side of our realm, a place of significant evil and destruction.

Still, succubaen had long been thought to be the ultimate gateway to discovering the exact location of the phoenix, but it would literally take six or seven lives to receive enough clues to track her down, and at the end of those lives any mystic still standing would be a slave to dark magic, which is why none of the Seven had ever tried it. The sacrifice wasn't worth the prize.

In fact, after the last Great Mystic War, the Seven had formed a pact—bound by magic—never to create a succubaen for their own purposes or force one of the mystics in their courts to use it on their behalf. As such, anyone caught creating or using a succubaen was executed on the spot. They were that dangerous.

But Grigori had thought it worth the risk and he'd had both the magical skill to create one and at least six or seven lives to spend to find not only Ember's exact location, but also what to look for once he discovered my warehouse.

So now I understood what had brought Grigori Rasputin to a city where he might easily be discovered. No doubt he'd figured out who'd stolen the succubaen from him and wanted it back, but the most recent clue it'd likely given him was where to locate the book that identified the phoenix as an ember-colored dog. By being here the old mystic was killing two birds with one stone.

"You think Grigori was here to steal back his own trinket?" I asked Finn.

Finn's gaze lifted a bit as he stared out the windshield, and mine did too. A fluttering movement had caught both of our attention. Binks was back.

"I do," he said, rolling down the window and sticking out his hand again.

"How much power had he given the trinket when you stole it from him?"

"He'd brought it up to level five, give or take," Finn said, just as Binks landed in his hand, upside down again.

"So Grigori had used up, what? Two to three of the egg's lives to get the succubaen to that point?"

Finn nodded. "Two for sure, maybe a third. But that would've left him with only one or two egg uses left."

"Where's the succubaen now?" I asked, hoping like hell it was behind us in the junkyard.

Finn didn't answer me. He simply fed Binks another cherry. The bat took the treat, greedily gobbling it up, issuing several squeaks as he did so.

Extending his hand out the window again, Finn said, "Thanks, buddy."

The bat flew off and Finn rolled up the window, putting the Escalade into drive. "The coast is clear," he said.

We began to drive out of the tunnel when I pressed Finn for an answer to my question. "I'm assuming the cruellion is guarding the succubaen. Like the sword, it's also buried in a pile of junk, right?"

The sword had been the only thing my monocle had recognized as holding any kind of power, but there'd been acres of trinket piles back there, so Grigori's trinket could well have been buried in one of the hundreds of other heaps I hadn't looked at through the crystal.

"It's somewhere safe," Finn said.

"Good," I said, intending to drop it.

But then I had another, quite terrible thought. The memory of the little glass cruet with the stopper on Grigori's mantle came back to me. I remembered looking into it and seeing the mystic who'd bound me while hearing the beginnings of what I knew would be a clue to discovering her.

I then remembered being sucked down a very dark hole as the succubaen had demanded my essence for the knowledge, and I'd resisted, so it'd knocked me out flat for several hours.

I hadn't realized it until that moment, but I'd been looking into what *had* to have been a succubaen. Nothing else made sense.

And when I'd awakened, the succubaen had been taken. My blood ran cold.

"Finn," I said, my voice barely above a whisper.

"Yeah?" he asked, distracted as he navigated the road in front of us with his lights off.

"I think Grigori was working on a replacement."

He took his gaze off the road to eye me sharply. "What?"

"When I was in Grigori's house, right before your brother arrested me, I discovered a little trinket on his mantel that took me down a rabbit hole where the object of my deepest desire was shown to me like a carrot on a stick. It started to pull too much of my essence out of me though, so I resisted. Strongly. That's when it knocked me out cold for several hours. When I came to, it was gone."

Finn stomped on the brakes and we skidded to a stop. For a moment he stared ahead, blinking several times before he simply asked, "What'd this trinket look like?"

"It was a little green-glass cruet about yay high," I said, using my hands to show him. "It had a golden stopper and a swirl on the side of the glass. It didn't look like much more than a cheap knickknack until I pulled out the stopper and looked inside."

Finn closed his eyes and allowed his head to fall the steering wheel. "That son of a bitch," he said softly.

"So he *was* working on a replacement," I said, a little surprised by his reaction. It was logical that Rasputin had tried to replace the succubaen. As long as he had the egg, that should've been seen as a likely possibility, but with only one or two uses left of the egg, it wouldn't have been strong enough to point toward the phoenix. But it *would* have been strong enough to point toward the book in the rare bookstore, which would be a significant clue.

Finn lifted his head and hit the gas again. "It's not a replacement," he said, surprising me. "It's the same trinket, Esmé. Different time. Different place. But the same trinket our thief took from him in London."

"What do you mean the same trink—" And that's as far as I got before I understood. "Gideon," I whispered.

"Yep."

"He gave Grigori, his future mentor, a gift that would best benefit him."

"Yep."

"But how could your brother get past the cruellion?" Not even Finn had come out the winner in that head-to-head.

"The succubaen wasn't kept in the junkyard," he said.

"Then where was it kept?"

"My place, which, once upon a time, I told Gideon was his place, which gave him full run of the penthouse, and all of its hidden stores."

"Why the *fuck* would you hide a succubaen in your own home?!" I shouted. His recklessness was astonishing and particularly frightening given the personal stakes for me and Ember.

Finn ignored my tone, answering calmly. "Cruellions are powerfully magical beasts with intelligence that rivals humans, and a life force that far exceeds it." Thumbing over his shoulder toward the junkyard behind us he added, "That brute—who, mind you, is only an adolescent—has been looking for a way out of the junkyard for half a century. If it'd discovered the succubaen, it could've given enough of its essence to have the trinket show it a way out without leaving the creature dead."

"Holy shit," I said.

"Yep."

"Where are we going?" I asked as Finn raced down the road, barely swerving in time to avoid hitting a tree.

"My place."

"Why?"

"To either find the succubaen still in its place in my storeroom or murder my brother if it's not."

"I like that plan," I said. I'd murder Gideon myself if he'd allowed a trinket powerful enough to reveal Ember's location to fall back into the hands of one of the only mystics in the world with the skills and the tools to find her.

But then I had another thought. "Wait, how can we go back there when Petra's goons are probably scoping it out for any sign of you. And me."

"I know a back way in," Finn said, adding, "I have to talk to Gideon and ask him if he took the trinket from Grigori's house after discovering you out cold."

"He didn't."

Finn cut me a look. "How do you know?"

"I came to before your brother discovered me."

"Son of a bitch," Finn grumbled again. But then he seemed to brighten. "Wait, when you woke up it was gone?"

"Yeah. And when your brother and I went back to search Grigori's house for clues, it was still gone, and I know because I looked." When Finn narrowed his eyes suspiciously I added, "Dude, I swear."

Finn shook his head but focused on the road again. "The part of the story I didn't yet tell you, Esmé, was that before our thief could make it back here with the succubaen, he was intercepted by another mystic from a rival house who took it from him. Do you know what happened to that guy?"

"Let me guess...you and he became besties, and you spend each Friday night braiding each other's hair?"

"I tracked him down and challenged him to a duel for it," he said, ignoring my sarcasm. "Winner take all."

"I'm assuming you took all."

"Yep. Including his head."

"Who was this unfortunate opponent?"

"The guy you replaced," Finn said, eyeing me meaningfully.

My eyes widened. "Ah. Not sure if I should thank you or jump out of the car."

He chuckled, the hardness of his expression melting away. "In here with me or out there with Petra's forces in pursuit? Hard to say which one's safer."

I glanced toward the window as my heart raced and the charm at my neck started to heat up. *Out there,* I thought. *For sure, out there.*

We arrived about a half-hour later several streets away from Finn's condo and very close to my warehouse, in fact.

After parking in an alley behind a noisy bar and a three-story apartment building, he turned to me. "Stay put. I'll be back soon."

I clamped my hand on his arm as he was about to get out of the car. "You think I'm not coming with you?"

Finn slid his gaze to my hand, still grabbing firmly to his arm. I held steady. "I'll move faster alone," he said.

I let go of him because the charm was starting to burn my skin. "Doubtful."

"I'd prefer to speak to my brother in private."

"And I'd prefer to question him with you. Besides, Flayer, we agreed to cooperate with each other, remember? We're bound by that."

The lieutenant frowned. He knew I had a point. "Fine. If you can keep up, you're welcome to join me."

I unbuckled my seatbelt, grabbed Lunatrabem, opened the car door, and hopped out. When I turned toward Finn again, he'd vanished.

With an irritated sigh, I slung the scabbard across my back, then pulled out a small coin envelope from the secret pocket in my jacket. Opening the lid carefully, I tipped out what to most would look like a dried butterfly of blue and gold. Cupping the creature carefully between my fingers I lowered my lips to it, breathed out a warm breath, and whispered, "Seek out Finn the Flayer."

The butterfly's wings opened, and it crawled to the edge of my index finger. Taking flight, it fluttered far faster than any mortal butterfly would, and I had to run to keep up.

Before long I was working up a good sweat, which felt awesome. I hadn't worked out in days, and my body was itching for a good run.

Finally the butterfly stopped at a metal door, fluttering just outside it. I tried the handle, but it was locked. "Of course," I said, extracting my lockpick. It took me only thirty seconds to pick it, which meant that Finn was in fact cooperating by not enchanting it more heavily.

After holding the door open for my fluttery little friend, I followed it into a pitch-black tunnel. Reaching behind me, I pulled out Lunatrabem, which gave off a glow that mirrored the glow of the moon. Using its light, I moved forward cautiously.

The tunnel was interesting; it seemed to follow an old track of some kind that was too small to be railroad tracks but just the right size for a cart—perhaps one constructed a century or two ago that allowed builders to send construction materials to the center of the city without clogging up heavily congested streets.

It was hard to tell how long the tracks went on, or where they led, and I didn't follow them to the end because after about a quarter-mile, my butterfly made a hard right at a steel ladder that led upward. I had to partly sheath Lunatrabem, but the exposed blade was just enough to give off the light I needed to make it to the top of the ladder and step off onto a platform that formed an enclosed space with another door.

Moving to the door, I opened it a crack and peeked out, amazed to find myself in what appeared to be the lobby of Finn's condo. Pulling the door a tiny bit wider showed Finn, standing confidently in front of the bay doors of the elevator.

Quickly I sheathed Lunatrabem the rest of the way, coaxed my butterfly back into her envelope, and stepped out of the door into the lobby just as the elevators binged open.

Finn stepped in, and I was right behind him.

"Hey," I said as we both turned to face the closing doors. "Come here often?"

If Finn was surprised to see me, he didn't reveal it. "Took you long enough," he muttered, but there was also a noticeable quirk to the edges of his lips.

"Yeah," I said, inspecting my nails. "I stopped for coffee."

We rode up to the floor just below the penthouse, and Finn stepped in front of me to lay a hand on the elevator panel, mumble something, and the boxcar stopped. He then reached into his jacket and pulled out a small, black coin purse with elaborate embroidering on the sides. Bending down, he held the purse close to the doors before opening it up. A puff of smoke drifted out of the purse and appeared to be sucked through the cracks of the door.

Finn stood and we waited in silence, and while we waited, I'll admit that I was damned curious about his trinket. About three minutes ticked by before the puff of smoked wafted back through the cracks, where it floated up to Finn's face and began to mold itself into a three-dimensional replica of his front hallway, then his living room, then the kitchen, bath, and both bedrooms. Every detail was present, like a ghostly hologram unfolding a tiny gray dollhouse.

When the puff of smoke displayed the master bedroom, Finn swore and shook his head. It was obvious to see why; there was no sign of Gideon on the rumpled bed in the master bedroom or in the guest room or in either bathroom.

Grabbing the smoke with his hand, Finn shoved it like a solid form back into the coin purse, and then he waved his hand at the elevator panel again. The boxcar moved, and one floor later, the doors parted and we stepped out into his condo.

The place was eerily quiet, and neither of us said a word as we sent our own mystic senses out into the space looking for any sign of trouble.

While I'm sure both of us trusted his little trinket to warn us of intruders possibly lurking about, neither one of us wanted to take any chances that it'd missed something.

After many cautious moments of waiting, watching, and feeling out the space, I began to relax the set of my shoulders, and noticed Finn did too.

At that moment my cellphone rang. I jumped, which was embarrassing, and Finn looked annoyed. "Why isn't that thing on silent?" he barked.

"It was," I said. Only one person could override the silent feature with an incoming call. "Dex," I said, holding the phone to my ear. "It's not a good time."

"We're in trouble, Ezzy," Dex replied urgently.

I stiffened. Glancing over at Finn, I was relieved to see that he was too preoccupied with investigating his condo to pay any attention to my phone call. "Tell me," I said very, very softly.

"Ursula translated the book," he said. "It's a history of the phoenix, and it's the only text I've ever heard of that describes her as a living, breathing shapeshifter. She's been a dragon, a bird, a lioness, and, as you know, a red hunting dog."

"What else did it say?"

"It said that the phoenix is able to grant her immortal powers to any mystic she either chooses or is forced to choose; proximity is the only requirement. It also says that she will bond with only one mystic at a time, and it is always up to the phoenix which mystic she chooses to bond with. For that mystic, the phoenix will gladly give up her own life, so if she is captured by an enemy combatant, it's best to kill the mystic she's bonded to, then cage and enslave the phoenix for the rest of eternity in order to gain immortality."

Much of this information about Ember, I already knew, but to hear it spelled out so succinctly in a book turned my blood to ice. I thought about the scene in Grigori's dining room. What if he'd revealed the contents of the book to the mystic slowly torturing him and his guests to death? What if whomever murdered the Russian now knew that the phoenix wasn't a bird, or a trinket of some kind, but a living breathing creature bonded by love to *me*.

"Fuck," I whispered. "He tortured Grigori. He could know what the phoenix *is*."

"Right. That's what I'm worried about too."

I glanced in the direction where Finn had gone and heard rustling that sounded like he was rummaging through a closet. "Hold on a sec," I said to Dex, then fished inside my jacket again and came up with my one magical die. Holding it close to the microphone, I mentally wished upon it and waited to feel its warmth spread out to envelope my lips before I said, "Can you get home?"

"I can," Dex replied. "It'll take me a little bit, but I can."

"Find a way to destroy that book and take Ember away, someplace far from here. And don't stop running until you hear from me."

"I will," he assured me. "But Ezzy..."

"What, Dex?"

"Promise me I'll hear from you."

I closed my eyes and leaned my head against the nearby wall. "I promise I'll try," I said.

That was all I could give him, which wasn't nearly enough, but at the moment, it honestly was all I had.

Chapter Eighteen
Day 4

I found Finn in his bedroom staring angrily at the bed, which was empty but rumpled and showing the imprint of someone having lain on top of the cover for a bit.

"Where do you think he went?" I asked.

"Home. He thinks it's the one place I won't go."

I eyed him curiously. "Why would he think that?"

Finn didn't answer. Instead, he held up a small, dark blue box with a lid. Opening the lid, he revealed a velvet pillow with its own imprint pushing down on the material. The outline of a small vase exactly the size and shape of the cruet that had been on Grigori's mantel revealed itself.

"I put a comeback spell on it when I first took possession and just tried to recall it. It's not coming back, so whoever has it has it tied to something able to resist the spell."

I smirked at him. Was he really that naive? "Hate to break it to you, Flayer, but any thief worth her weight could've countered your comeback spell. In fact, I would've done that before leaving Grigori's place."

Finn cocked an eyebrow at me. Damn him, he was so striking that even when he was looking crossly at me, he was still sexy as hell. "Is that so?" he said in a way that said I might be the one who was naive.

"It's so," I said, crossing my arms. I was confident in my ability to hold onto the objects that I stole.

Finn walked over to his chest of drawers and rooted around in the topdrawer, pulling out a pair of gold cufflinks emblazoned with Petra's insignia. Bringing them over to me, he said, "Do your best."

I laughed. He had to be kidding.

His expression said otherwise.

"Okay," I said, snatching the cufflinks out of his hand. Turning away from him, I closed my hands around them, feeling them out for magical energy which felt fairly powerful and sent my thieving mind racing with envy. Inserting my own essence onto their surface, I felt along their every groove and commanded them to remain with me. I then tucked them into the magical pocket of my jacket, which would give the illusion to Finn that they were no longer in the bedroom.

Turning back to him, I smiled and held out my hands to display that they were gone. "See?" I said. "Easy peasy."

"Uh-huh," he said, swirling his index finger in a circle. "Why don't you have a look in the drawer?"

The small weight of the cufflinks in my jacket suddenly vanished. It was so sudden and so surprising that I actually reached into my coat to be sure they were gone.

Finn crossed his heavily muscled arms, nodding over his shoulder toward the chest of drawers.

Curious and a little put off, I walked over to his dresser and pulled open the topdrawer. There were the cufflinks, neatly resting in a velvet lined box.

To make sure it wasn't simply a duplicate set, I took them out and felt their energy. There was my essence, still clinging to the gold surface, but now I could sense an even stronger essence curling over my own to retake possession.

Sensing that energy did two things: one, it made me realize that Finn the Flayer was far, *far* more powerful than I'd given him credit for; and two, his energy mixing with mine, even on an innocuous pair of cufflinks, was causing the charm at my neck to burn almost as hot as my sudden desire for him.

I dropped the cufflinks back into the drawer and shut it quickly. "Neat trick," I said.

"And that was just a pair of decorative cufflinks," he said. "Imagine how strong a claim I could put on an object I really treasured."

As if for emphasis, Finn walked right up to me and reached with one finger to trace the outline of the charm under my T-shirt.

I couldn't help but suck in a small breath of surprise and desire.

Finn's touch was light, sensual, and full of promise. "This gift my brother gave to you was also part of my personal collection."

I put my own hand up to block his and cover the charm. It was the only thing standing between me and certain death, that much I knew. Without the charm, I'd be unable to withstand the attraction I felt for Finn. Hell, even *with* it I might be circling the drain.

Taking a deep breath, I stepped back, glaring hard at Finn. He'd have to fight me for the charm. It didn't matter if it'd once belonged to him; by right and by mystic law it was now magically bound to me.

"It's *mine*, Flayer."

Finn sighed. "So it is, Esmé. So it is."

We stood like that, staring at each other for a long moment, and I couldn't tell if we were about to rip each other's clothes off or haul out weapons and begin to duel.

Both options actually turned me on.

Finn took a step closer to me, and I still didn't know which way this would go, but I stood my ground. He lifted his hand slowly toward my neck, his gaze boring into mine, and I tilted my head back, exposing my throat, my breath coming quick. I wanted him so much, I didn't think I could stand it. His hand closed around the back of my head, and he gently pulled me the last foot between us, all the while stroking the base of my throat with his thumb. The charm burned and burned against my chest, and I knew I was so close to ripping it off and giving in to the unceasing yearning of the moment.

Finn's eyes grew black with desire, and I'm sure mine mirrored his. He lowered his lips to my throat, and when I felt their touch, I whimpered.

With trembling hands, I began to reach up to twine my fingers into his hair, dying to feel the touch of those black locks. I was intensely aware of the nearness of the bed. I wondered if we'd even make it the three feet to it.

The second my hands touched his scalp, Finn reached around my waist and pulled me against him. My eyes rolled up and my lids closed, the sensation of falling into a deep, deep hole making me feel unsteady on my feet. I was aware that I was trembling. I was aware of the heat of his skin against mine, the taut muscles of his chest, the bulge at my thighs. I was aware of the building tension in the energy around us, mixing with the air, curling its way through every pore and crevice of the room—a thousand volts alive like serpents, ready to strike...

A sudden and jolting alarm cut through my muddled thoughts and without even thinking, I took hold of Finn around the waist, and using every ounce of strength I possessed, I pulled him sideways with me five steps before throwing both of us to the floor on the other side of the bed.

KABOOM!—came the explosion, even before we hit the floor.

Debris blasted in all directions, furniture splintered, stuffing erupted, glass shattered, and clothing flew. I landed awkwardly, half under Finn, my body twisted and tense, attempting to brace against the worst of the detonation.

I heard him grunt when we hit the floor—hell, I heard myself grunt too, and then I felt his arms wrap around me as he rolled over and tucked me underneath him while shielding me from the worst of the carnage.

As debris settled onto the floor all around us, I clung to Finn with my eyes squeezed shut, selfishly grateful he was shielding me from the downpour of rubble and debris.

And even while the air around us clouded with a dusty haze, Finn pressed up on all fours, lifting himself off of me and twisting himself side to side to shake off what he could.

I looked up at him, his hair now white, completely coated in dust, and his hazel eyes ablaze with fury.

In a singular move, he was on his feet, whirling around to face the aggressor, but the smoky haze in the room was too thick to see through.

With effort, I also got to my feet. My ears ringing loud enough to block out all other sound. I saw Finn's lips move; he was saying something, but I couldn't make out what. He waved his hand in front of him, and the air around us began to clear. And then Finn formed his hands in the shape of a ball, splaying his fingers and creating a bright blue pulse of energy that emanated out from his palms as raw power gathered between his hands, and he readied himself for battle.

Forgetting all about Lunatrabem strapped to my back, I stepped up next to him, also taking up a defensive stance.

Focusing my own essence, I too formed a circle with my hands, infusing the air between my own palms with a green ball of energy.

By trade I'm more escape artist than soldier, however I've been known to be fairly scrappy when cornered, and there was no way I was abandoning Finn in this fight—not after seeing what the mystic did to all his other victims.

So I tensed and made myself ready for the attack I knew was sure to come while I watched Finn's lips move as he spoke some magical words to clear the foggy air. It was then I noticed that the thick cloud surrounding us wasn't solely created from dust and debris, but rather seemed to have a magical quality to it, intent on obscuring our view.

Finn also seemed to recognize this because his left hand came away from the ball of energy he was forming, and he waved it at the thick cloud while repeating the clearing spell again with more earnestness.

But the obscuring cloud remained. And rather than being battled back, whomever was behind the cloud began to charge the air with electricity again. My eyes widened. I had a feeling we were at the center of the bull's-eye and there was no way we could survive a direct hit.

With mounting panic, I dropped my hands, the ball of my essence winked out, and I grabbed Finn by the arm, tugging him sideways as hard as I could, away from the center of the gathering energy. Surprised, he stumbled for a step, and I kept pulling. The energy all around us continued to charge, and I could feel my hair stand up on end, and all the nerves along my skin were alight and tingling. Our attacker was drawing any energy they could out of the atmosphere to create a deadly bomb that would explode in our faces at any moment.

Finn tried to shake me off, and I screamed a warning at him. Yanking hard on his arm I pulled him with me away from that bullseye, but he was so focused on the foe in the room that he barely acknowledged me. Desperate, I let go, twirled around to his front, and tackled him around the middle, shoving him back.

Caught off guard again, Finn stumbled and I felt him grunt when his back hit the wall. The pitch of the energy gathering around us had reached a note that was so intense, I thought my already belabored eardrums might pop.

In the moment that I thought we were surely about to perish, I encircled my arms around him, hugging him tightly and that's when I heard him yell something, the sound of his voice barely resonating above the ringing in my ears and the piercing buildup of energy. But then there was a sudden *whoosh* of air, he lurched the both of us sideways, and the world went dark as we once again fell to the floor.

I panted for air twice, maybe three times, before there was another *KABOOM!*, but this time I felt only a slight percussion, as if something had blocked the most violent aspect of the blast.

Underneath me, Finn moved. I felt the rumble from his chest under my fingertips and knew he was speaking, but I didn't know if he was speaking to me or uttering a spell. Taking a few more deep gulps of air, I managed to say, "I can't hear you. The blast... I can't hear." I could only hope his ears weren't as affected as mine.

His hands came up to gently cup my face, lifting his forehead to rest it against mine. It was a whole other level of intimacy between us, and the absurdity that it was formed in the immediate aftermath of our nearly being blown to bits didn't feel nearly as insane as it should have.

For a long moment we both just lay there, gasping for air. Then finally Finn wrapped his arms around me again and sat up slowly, carrying me with him. He spoke again and a light came on, illuminating an enclosed and obviously blast-proof room, absolutely chock-full of treasure.

"Whoa," I said, sitting up a little taller to take it all in, my thieving nature already making scoundrel plans.

Finn cupped my face again and turned it toward his. *Don't even think about it*, he mouthed.

I grinned. In spite of everything going on in that moment, a bit of levity managed to sneak through.

Finn moved me off his lap, got gingerly to his feet, and held out his hand for me. I took it and allowed him to help me up as well. By now the ringing was lessoning, and I could almost hear him when he began swearing at the closed door in front of us.

It took me a moment to realize that he wasn't swearing at the door, but rather the mystic beyond it.

"I told you," I said, hearing my own voice as a muffled thing, reverberating inside my skull. "I told you what this mystic is capable of. This is the same thing he did to Bree's apartment."

Finn turned to look meaningfully at me. *You did*, he mouthed with a nod.

"Do you know who it is?"

He shook his head and appeared troubled. The mystic had caught the both of us off guard, but I wondered—even if Finn had been prepared—would he have been a match for this violent intruder?

The kind of power the mystery person was exhibiting was enormous. It was the kind of power that could be generated by only the most talented among us, and to have it unleashed against me—twice now—was enough to take stock of the risky nature of my mission. Facing Elric without having secured the egg was perhaps not quite the worst-case scenario I'd thought it to be.

"We need to get out of here, Flayer," I said, the ringing in my ears finally quiet enough to hear above it. "The floor of your penthouse is probably unstable and the whole building could come down."

Finn shook his head. "I own the building. I had the penthouse's floor reinforced just in case the place met a catastrophic event."

I stared at him in wonder. "You were *expecting* that?"

He shrugged. "I'm Petra's lieutenant. It's my job to expect the worst-case scenario."

I shook my head then looked around. "What do we do now?"

Finn pointed toward the back of the large room before stepping past me in that direction. I walked behind him, trying my best not to eye the merchandise. (I failed miserably, of course.)

When we got to the back of the room, Finn swept a hand over the wall and a doorway appeared, revealing nothing of the darkened room beyond. He bowed slightly at the hip in an "after you" gesture.

I didn't move.

"It's safe," he said.

I waved at the opening. "Then you go first."

He dipped his chin. "And leave you here with all this temptation? Not likely."

Damn. He'd read my mind. "There's a lot of stuff here that could probably help us," I said.

Finn pointed over my shoulder to the sword strapped to my back.

"Oops," I said, pulling it out of the scabbard to hold it aloft in front of us. It glowed that same white moonlight, and I marveled at its power once again. "I'm not used to having a weapon like this handy. My usual tactic is to make a run for it."

"No judgment here," Finn said. "Whoever that is out there caught me by surprise too."

Finn continued to stand next to the exit, waiting for me to cross the threshold. With a sigh, I sheathed Lunatrabem and stepped forward into an area about fifteen-by-fifteen which was very dimly lit, but which also appeared to be the landing to a staircase leading straight down. Turning back to Finn to ask where it led, I watched him snap his fingers and the doorway disappeared, leaving me all alone on the landing. "Son of a bitch!" I yelled, moving to it to pound on the brick wall.

I stopped pounding real quick when I heard a deep, menacing growl reverberate up from the stairwell.

Whipping around, I pulled out Lunatrabem, plastered my back against the door, and held the sword aloft. Its glow helped chase away the fear of whatever it was that was obviously readying for an attack.

From the stairwell, there was a loud *whump* somewhere below, maybe two flights down, the noise very much like something heavy plopping onto one of the steps. A moment later, another *whump* sounded, and the floor under my feet vibrated from the impact of something very big and very heavy.

Shaking my head in frustrated fury I muttered, "Fuck you, Flayer. I will soooo get even with you for this."

The glow from my sword wasn't bright enough to illuminate the staircase beyond about the fifth step. With the back of my heel, I kicked the wall behind me out of both anger and frustration, but no magic doorway appeared with Finn to back me up. "I am gonna *kill* him," I vowed, gripping the sword with both hands and readying for battle.

Another *whump* sounded, and a whole new series of growls followed. There was nothing for me to do but wait,

Finn's betrayal burning a hole in my chest. It was stupid, I know, but goddammit, I'd started to develop some true *feelings* of kinship for the asshole, and again he'd tossed me into an enclosure with a ferocious and probably hungry monster before slamming the door behind me to lock me in.

"Asshole!" I spat.

Whump! came another footstep. This one far closer than I thought it should've been.

And then right below my sightline, something sparkled in the light.

Or rather, two somethings.

Like eyes.

I flexed my knees, ready for some gymnastics and fencing, and watched as the two eyes rose very slowly, but all around them it was black, and I wasn't able to see the creature clearly.

But it saw me.

It began to growl again, and I felt the hairs on the back of my neck stand up on end. My mouth went dry when I realized the eyes were about seven feet off the ground. Whatever it was, the creature was massive.

The rumble from the beast's throat continued, and then I saw that it must have black fur or skin, because its fangs and front teeth suddenly appeared in a snarl as if black lips had pulled back to reveal them.

I swallowed hard and didn't move, still holding my glowing sword out in front of me and praying that the beast recognized the weapon as something dangerous to itself.

Another *whump* sounded on the staircase, and the beast inched into the dim light of the room and my sword.

"Easy, boy," I whispered as it began to reveal itself. I squinted into the darkness, trying to discern its features. Standing at least ten feet tall, it seemed to be a cross between a hyena and a bear, covered in thick, black fur, with a square snout and very large teeth. Big, beady amber eyes bored into mine, and I also sensed a keen intelligence there.

The growls stopped as it sniffed the air—probably looking for the scent of fear, but the sword was giving me courage and the beast would find no scent of fear here. Meanwhile the hairy creature inched its way up another step.

More of it came into the light, and I could tell I was in for a battle. Gigantic paws as big as dinner plates planted themselves on the staircase. They were attached to long limbs and powerful hindquarters.

The more the beast came into view, the more of a resemblance to a hyena it showed. Mentally I sorted through the contents of my pockets, trying to recall if I had any kind of a treat I could throw at it to distract it for the second or two it would take for me to take a running leap past it to the bottom of the staircase ... where I didn't know what else may lay in wait. For all I knew, the now-hidden doorway behind me was the only entrance or exit.

The beast came up another step to rest one paw on the landing. "Easy there, big fella," I said. "You don't want to tangle with me. I'm far too thin to offer you much of a meal, and you're likely to get hurt if I prick you with this sword."

The beast's eyes narrowed, and I swore it understood some of what I said. As if to tell me what I could do with my threats, it put the other front paw on the landing.

By now it was only fifteen feet away, and I could smell the thing clearly. It was a musky scent but not unpleasant. Also its fur glistened, as if it'd been well cared for even given the darkened environment.

The beast's jaws opened when it emitted another growl, and I spied a pink tongue and molars the size of my thumbs.

"Come on, buddy," I said in what I hoped was a coaxing tone. "I don't wanna hurt you."

The beast hardly seemed deterred but probably thought it was cute that I was worried for his safety.

He did pause the menacing growling routine for a bit as he came all the way up onto the landing, inching forward cautiously to give me a few good sniffs. "That's it," I encouraged. "See? I'm harmless. We could be buddies, right?"

The beast lifted his head away from me and rose up to his full height. By now he was practically towering over me, and I raised my sword accordingly. Whatever the outcome between us, it was bound to be messy.

His eyes narrowed again, and now I could see the full scope of his predatory instincts.

"So be it," I told him, bracing for the battle about to unfold. Gripping the sword as tightly as I could, I held it aloft and opened my own mouth, ready to emit a battle cry, when the wall behind me abruptly disappeared and I fell into Finn's arms.

Straightening me up again, he put a hand on my arm and snapped, "Hey! Put the sword away!"

I jerked my arm away and moved as if I'd trained with a sword all my life. I whirled in a circle, twirling the sword away from Finn, spinning around to raise it aloft again as I faced both him and the mammoth beast on the steps. "*Where the fuck did you go!*" I shouted.

The beast's growl reverberated loudly, and it lowered itself down into a crouch, ready to spring itself at me and gobble me up in one bite.

Finn moved quickly to get between me and the beast. "I had to secure the door from the bedroom and pick up a few things," he said calmly, his hands splayed out in front of him to show me he meant no harm.

Meanwhile the beast continued to crouch and growl, and we had ourselves a little standoff.

"Boris," Finn said loudly, as he turned his head to glance over his shoulder. "It's okay, buddy. She's a... friend."

I wanted to roll my eyes but thought it wasn't a good idea to take my gaze off the big, bad, beastly Boris.

"What is he?" I asked, nodding toward Boris. "Some kind of bear-hyena hybrid?"

"He's mostly hyena," Finn said. "But a little bear curious."

I offered him a heavy-lidded expression.

Finn chuckled and relaxed the tense set of his shoulders. Behind him Boris stopped growling but remained crouched and continued to glower at me.

"He's a bearena," Finn explained. "You've never heard of them?"

"Nope," I said, irritated that he was making jokes when I'd nearly been a hyena/bear-curious appetizer.

"His name is Boris and he's harmless," Finn said.

"He doesn't look harmless."

"Well, he is. At least to anyone who means me no harm and has no intention of stealing my treasure."

"Ah," I said, suddenly nervous about the scoundrel thoughts I'd had earlier. "So he's your pet."

Boris stopped glowering at me and looked at Finn, and I swear his expression said, "Is she *serious?*"

"No," Finn said, glancing over his shoulder at Boris again. "He's definitely *not* a pet. He's a companion and a protector."

I continued to hold my sword defensively. "How about I lower my weapon as soon as he stops looking at me like a late-night snack."

Boris snarled at me, as if to suggest I wasn't the boss of him.

Finn held up his hands again. "Sorry," he said to me, "but he doesn't work that way. You're gonna have to lower your weapon first."

I stood stubbornly still; my sword still raised just to show Boris that he wasn't the boss of me either.

"Guys," Finn said, turning sideways so he could pivot his head back and forth between us. "Seriously. We don't have time for this. You're both gonna have to back down."

With a heavy sigh, I lowered the sword three inches. Boris rose from his crouched position ever so slightly. I lowered my sword another inch. He rose another inch, and it went on that way for a good thirty seconds, until we were both standing straight but still tensed and ready for action.

"That's better," Finn said. And then he moved toward me, wearing a charming smile that made my insides feel squishy. My breath caught at his nearness, but then he turned his back to me and opened the door to the treasure room again. "Boris," he said gently. "Dinner's ready. If the door to my bedroom gets breeched, take out anyone who tries to enter."

The bearena ambled forward and brushed his muzzle against Finn's chest for a few moments before heading into the treasure room. A few seconds later, we heard the sounds of teeth grinding on bone.

Finn then turned to me and held up a bejeweled, golden trinket in the shape of a pocket watch that made my eyes water it was so lovely.

"For you," he said.

My heartbeat ticked up but then I grew suspicious. "Why?"

"You saved my life back there. Twice. I figure I owe you."

I held out my free hand and Finn lowered the watch into my palm, curling my fingers around it with his own. "It requires a simple dose of essence to be activated."

"What does it do?"

"It slows everything around you down," he said. "But careful how you use it. If you employ it at the wrong time, it could slow things down you'd rather have sped up."

I looked at his serious gaze and understood what he meant. In a moment between life and death, dying slowly wasn't a good way to go.

"Ready?" Finn asked me.

Pulling my hand out of his grasp, I said, "I'm still mad at you."

"I know."

Pocketing the gift, I stepped forward before redirecting myself to turn in a circle and thrust Lunatrabem upward, stopping just short of Finn's throat.

The bastard didn't even flinch.

Still, I narrowed my eyes and glared hard at him. "You ever lock me in a room with a deadly beast again, and I will find a way to make you pay, Lieutenant."

The corners of Finn's mouth quirked in a hint of a grin. "I have no doubt you will, Esmé, but how about we worry about that *after* we deal with the problem at hand, eh?"

I stepped back, sheathed Lunatrabem, and waved him toward the stairs. "After you."

I followed Finn down the stairs, which proved difficult because he moved fast and there were a *lot* of stairs.

At last we reached the bottom of the staircase, which deposited us into a long, dark room where Boris obviously spent most of his time. There was a huge rubber tire lying in the middle of the room with big claw marks on it, another hanging from the ceiling like a swing, and a giant rubber ball next to what was likely the gnawed-on remains of a bison's leg, not to mention a big king-size mattress on a low platform where the bearena slept.

"I turned angrily to Finn. You keep him down here in the dark all day and night?" This setup was my worst fear for Ember.

"He prefers it," Finn said easily. "Bearenas are nocturnal and they abhor sunlight."

And then something else occurred to me. "If Boris guards your treasures, how did Gideon get past him?"

Finn looked chagrin. "Boris has a soft spot for Gid. Drives me nuts, but the two used to play catch together down here."

"Used to?"

"Gideon doesn't come around much anymore, unless he wants to steal a trinket or two."

Tension had crept back into Finn's voice as he spoke about the trouble between them, letting me know I was beginning to tread on thin ice if I continued to pursue the subject at hand.

Lest he leave me down here in this dungeon-esque space, I decided to switch back to the bearena. "Where did Boris come from?"

"He was a gift from Petra," Finn said, leading the way across the room.

"She's *quite* generous." I couldn't quite keep the sneer out of my voice.

"She is when it suits her," he said, and I remembered that Petra was currently trying to kill us. Or maybe just me, but she was also certainly intent on bringing in Finn, and probably not for coffee.

When we reached the end of Boris' lair, Finn pulled on the big metal latch of another door and deferred to me to go through first again. All I had to do was cock an eyebrow and he chuckled. "Right," he said. "Forgot. Okay, this way, your highness."

I rolled my eyes and followed him through the door. We came out from Boris' lair into a tunnel I recognized. "This is how we came in," I said, noting the door that led to the lobby and the elevator of his building to the left of us.

"It is," Finn said.

I eyed him warily. "You nervous about me knowing the secret back entrance to your bachelor pad?"

"Not nearly as nervous as you'd be encountering Boris if I wasn't around."

It was my turn to chuckle.

With that we set off, and I had time to think about the two explosions back upstairs in Finn's condo. Pointing to the ceiling, I asked, "How bad was the damage, do you think?"

"Bad enough that it's going to take me a long time to rebuild," he said, irritation evident in his speech.

"Why though?" I asked as we walked side by side.

"Why though, what?"

"Why target you?"

He eyed me curiously. "What makes you think *I* was the target?"

"Um… other than it being *your* home? Gee, I wonder."

"It could've just as easily been you the mystic was after."

"*Me?*" I asked incredulously. "What makes you think this renegade was after me?"

"Well, it is the second time you've been hit by this guy, right?"

"True, but the first time we know for sure he was after Tic."

"Do we?" Finn asked. "Maybe he was after something he believed Marco had and maybe now he thinks that *you* have it, because, after all, you definitely have something else of supreme value in hand right now."

I tried to cover the fear that the mystic might know about Ember by reaching over my shoulder to tap Lunatrabem's hilt. "You mean this."

"Yep. But you and Marco would be the only ones who could wield it which still makes it worth abducting you."

I scoffed. "If I'm one of the only mystics that can wield it, then in my hands it'd be useless to whoever's after it. I'm not fighting anybody else's battles for them. I'm only gonna fight my own."

I walked a few more feet in silence before I realized that Finn was no longer at my side. Turning to eye him over my shoulder, I asked, "What?"

His expression was deadly serious. "Trust me in this, Esmé: Anyone can be made to do anything if the cost of not doing that thing is too high."

"What's that supposed to mean?"

"It means that your enemies could easily exploit your vulnerabilities to use you to meet their own selfish and evil needs."

"What if I have no vulnerabilities," I said, trying to bluff my way through a sticky conversation.

"Oh, you have them. Everyone does. For you, it's probably your second, what's his name... Dusty?"

I gave him a half-lidded look. He damned well knew my second's name. "Dex."

"Yeah. Him. He's got an obvious weak spot for you, and that could be exploited for as long as he's alive. Which, if I were your enemy, I'd make sure was a very long time."

Finn didn't even realize the half of it. Dex could absolutely be used against me, and if anyone ever realized what

Ember meant to me, there isn't anything in this world I wouldn't do to protect her.

As I stared at Finn, however, I felt the tension grow between us, and it left me feeling exposed and vulnerable. "Are you my enemy, Finn?"

He shrugged. "I work for Petra. You work for Elric. Which means that I'm not your friend, and you'd be wise to remember that."

As hard as that was to hear, I knew it was a truth I definitely needed to be reminded of. Finn wasn't my friend; in fact, as long as he was Petra's lieutenant, he was far closer to being my actual enemy.

The two moments of intimacy between us aside, in this one endeavor, we were reluctant allies at best, and we'd be that only for as long as it took to discover where Tic and the egg were. The second Tic was found and the egg was claimed, all bets were off.

I looked Finn the Flayer over with a different eye as he stood a few feet away. He wasn't his brother, and I needed to see him for the powerful, deadly mystic he was if I was to survive the next twenty-four hours. "I'll remember," I said, turning my back to him to carry on with the walk.

CHAPTER NINETEEN
DAY 4

We reached Finn's car about twenty minutes later. When we emerged from the tunnel back above ground, the sounds of half a dozen sirens echoed through the streets.

After getting into the Escalade and pulling away from the curb, Finn wound his way carefully north toward the sound of the sirens, and I understood that he wanted to see the extent of the damage for himself.

We came upon an alley that allowed us to peek through the buildings surrounding Finn's condo and look directly at the penthouse.

Or what was left of it. The section of the penthouse where his bedroom had been was an open, gaping hole. It was a miracle we'd even survived.

"Son of a bitch," Finn muttered, gripping the steering wheel until his knuckles turned white.

I could appreciate his fury. If anyone caused that kind of damage to the warehouse, I wouldn't stop until I'd tracked them down and exacted some deadly revenge.

Bree's apartment had suffered far worse than Finn's condo, but then, Bree's apartment had been in an old building and her floor definitely hadn't been reinforced.

"Who's capable of causing *that*?" I asked.

Finn kept his gaze on his building. "Besides your boss?"

I rolled my eyes. "And yours?"

"Any one of the remaining Seven for sure," he said. "And maybe a few of their lieutenants or advisors."

"Could *you* do that?" I asked.

Finn inhaled a deep breath and let it out slowly. "Yes. But it'd take just about everything I have."

I nodded. The energy needed to gather enough power to cause that kind of wreckage—while impressive—was also extremely draining.

"It's probably why he hit us only twice and stopped," Finn continued. "No juice left for a third strike."

"How did this mystic even know we were in your condo?"

Finn turned to me. "How did you know when your targets were or weren't home?"

I grinned. "I have mad skills."

Finn grunted. "Any reasonably good thief does."

I looked again toward the building. "So you think our mysterious mystic is a thief?"

"Given how stealthy he's been—hitting Grigori when he least expected it, then getting to Marco at Bree's, and now attacking my place. Yeah, I'd say this guy's spent some time thieving, for sure."

Finn's attention was momentarily diverted to something to the right of his building. "Shit," he muttered.

I looked and saw a black SUV making its way down the street, headed in our direction. Finn pressed on the gas and zipped deeper into the alley.

"Did they see us?" I asked, knowing that the SUV likely belonged to Petra's crew.

"We'll find out in a second," Finn said.

At the first opportunity to turn right, he did, and looped back around the block, zigzagging his way through traffic and steadily increasing his speed.

"What're you doing?" I asked when he took another right that would lead us directly back the way we'd come.

"Circling back."

"*Why?*"

Finn didn't answer. Turning right yet again, he cut the lights, and increased his speed even more. By now we were flying along the same alley we'd come down to inspect his building.

Ahead of us, a set of taillights illuminated the gloom. Finn took his foot off the accelerator and, to my relief, we began to slow down.

"One of yours?" I asked, nodding to the car far ahead.

"Looks like it."

"So Petra's still on the hunt for you."

"Don't kid yourself, lady. She's still on the hunt for *you*. At this point, I'm just an errant employee, needing a reprimand."

"What'll she do to you if she catches you?"

Finn glanced sideways at me. "She'll force me to kill you in front of her, and then she'll send me to bed without any supper."

I felt the blood drain from my face when I realized he was only half-kidding. Tapping the scabbard of Lunatrabem, I said, "Even though I carry the sword? She'd still be willing to kill me even though I'm now the appointed guardian of her son?"

Finn turned his gaze toward the taillights up ahead again. "Better to kill you than allow you and the sword to fall into the wrong hands, Esmé."

"That's comforting."

He shrugged. "So let's avoid that scenario, shall we?"

"That probably includes not following behind your gal's henchmen," I said, waving toward the car ahead.

"Yep," he said, and to my immense relief, he took yet another right, and we began to move perpendicular to Petra's patrol.

For several minutes, all either of us did was check the Escalade's mirrors for any sign of a tail, but nothing suspicious showed up in the rearview.

"Now where?" I asked as we were once again headed north.

"I'm following a hunch."

I wanted to ask what hunch, but Finn didn't seem like someone who wanted to make a lot of small talk, and I could respect that. We rode in silence for about fifteen minutes before the area began to look familiar and I understood exactly where he was going.

"What do you expect to find at Grigori's?" I asked when we were just a few blocks away.

"Answers," he said cryptically.

I rolled my eyes again but left it alone. I'd figure it out once we got there.

When we rolled down the street, my breath caught. "It's gone," I whispered.

Finn stopped several houses away from where Grigori's house had once stood. In its place was a burnt-out hollow husk of charred wood and scattered debris.

"Would your guys have done this?" I asked.

"No," Finn said, and then he surprised me by asking, "Would Elric?"

I shook my head. "No. There'd be no reason that I could think of why he'd destroy the place."

"Not even if he couldn't find the egg?" Finn pressed.

"Trust me, he has other trinkets. I mean, yeah, he'd love to add Grigori's egg to his collection, but I doubt he'd succumb to frustration just because it wasn't readily available to him."

Finn nodded. "You're right. This isn't Elric's style."

"But it is the style of the mystic who keeps blowing up places we've been to."

"You mean places *you've* been to."

I nodded toward the ruined structure. "For someone who claims not to have been here, you seemed to know exactly how to get to the place."

"I've driven by," Finn claimed. "That's all."

"Why?" I asked curiously.

"Just checking up on my little brother," he said.

"And when did you drive by?" I asked, sensing there was something else Finn wasn't telling me.

He sighed. "The day you and Gideon discovered Grigori's dinner party, I may have swung past this place."

I sucked in a breath. "What time were you here?"

"Right around noon. I watched Gideon ring the doorbell and wait for somebody to answer. When no one did, he left."

"Hold on, so you knew that Grigori Rasputin was in town?"

"No. I only knew that some drunken old mystic was willing to mentor my brother. I planned to shut it down on the day of the ceremony, but Grigori got himself killed before I had a chance to identify him."

"What I don't get is why you'd block every attempt your brother made to get himself mentored. Don't you know how dangerous it could be to him over the long term? Untrained magic is dangerous to both the mystic and the public at large."

Finn tapped the steering wheel. "It'd be even more dangerous to have him enter our community, Esmé. Besides, knowing how determined he was, I'd offered to mentor Gideon myself. That way I could've kept him both reined in and safe."

"Then why weren't you? Mentoring him, I mean."

Finn turned, glaring eyes to me. "Because *you* beat me to it."

I recalled our conversation in the tunnel leading away from Boris' lair; about how I could be manipulated if the wrong person gained control over someone I loved. I doubted there was a power-hungry mystic out there who wouldn't see the opportunity to mess with the novice and possibly naive twin brother of Petra's lieutenant.

Just to show him I wasn't intimidated, I rolled my eyes and got us back on topic. Waving to the burnt-out wreckage of Grigori's former home, I said, "Whatever this mysterious mystic was looking for, they either found it and burned the place down so that nobody could figure out what they'd been looking for, or they didn't find it and got frustrated."

Finn pulled up to the opposite side of the street and parked. Leaving the motor running, he stepped out of the SUV and began to walk toward the wreckage, which was spooky and dark with only the light from a streetlight a few meters away.

I debated staying in the car or chasing after him for about twenty seconds, and then hopped out of the car and crossed the street myself.

I stopped next to Finn, who stood at the front gate, which was covered in charred smoke and hanging on only one hinge. He put up his hand, fingers splayed, and closed his eyes. I waited while he muttered a few words and watched the rubble carefully, after recognizing that Finn was invoking his comeback spell.

If the cruet was in the rubble, I doubted it had survived the explosion, but knowing the power of the vessel, I also knew that some of the fragments would still hold some charm and would likely rise from the rubble unless pinned underneath.

So I waited and watched, feeling and admiring the sheer power emanating from Finn. As he commanded the remnants of the cruet to rise from the ashes, his essence wafted off him in big sexy waves, and dammit if it wasn't a gigantic turn-on.

The charm below my shirt seared into my skin, and without thinking, I leaned a little closer to him, pulled by the insanely strong attraction I felt for him—especially in that moment.

It was then that something really, really weird happened: I felt my own essence gather, unbidden, and it rose in power by several degrees more than I might be able to manage on my own. It pulsed with new life, as if some secret, hidden part of me had been harboring a well of energy that had previously been held just out of my reach.

This extra burst of energy then shifted sideways to meld with Finn's. It wasn't like the melding of our energies when he'd had me tied up in his car. This was different. Significantly so. It was like getting a boost in amplitude from an unknown source, then lending that source to Finn to wield it as he would.

And the feeling was also igniting a spark of passion that I was once again slave to.

A wave of pleasure rose with the wave of new energy, mingling with it, tagging along as it bonded with Finn. I closed my eyes, concentrating on resisting the urge to turn to him, rip off my clothes and his, then have my way with him. The charm once again seared my skin, this time more intensely than it ever had before. A battle was taking place for control over my will, and I felt like a bystander to that battle more than an actual participant.

And still the energy of our combined essence ratcheted up in power until the air was practically crackling with it. It was so similar to the feel and vibration of the energy that built right before it exploded back in Finn's condo, but this didn't seem lethal. Well, at least not to me.

I began to lose myself in the swirl of our energies, dancing all around us. It almost felt like I was falling, so I opened my eyes to try to anchor myself, and that's when I saw the remnants of Grigori's mantel, fireplace, and part of his chimney rise out of the rubble.

I realized abruptly that that had been the last place I'd seen the succubaen and I was mesmerized by the sight of such a large and heavy structure lifting effortlessly out of the debris.

I looked over at Finn and saw that he was looking intensely back at me. We were both engulfed in a flame of aqua blue energy, my green mixing with his blue, and it was gorgeous. As gorgeous as the light coming off Ember when I looked at her through my monocle.

But there was more. I swear I became aware of Finn's thoughts. Not in specific words, per se, but I sensed that I could feel what he felt while he was looking at me: a note of surprise, of empowerment, and of attraction. It mirrored everything I was feeling, but it was distinctly separate and masculine.

And I realized that if I could sense what he could, then he could no doubt do the same.

I think he also realized it, and at the exact same time we broke off from each other, causing the chimney and fireplace to crash back to earth with a loud rumble.

"What the hell was that?" Finn whispered as we continued to stare at each other.

"I have no idea," I admitted. "But I don't think we should ever do that again."

"Agreed."

I clenched my hands into fists, once again at war with myself. There was nothing I wanted more than to mingle my energy with Finn the Flayer, but I couldn't admit it. Especially since he had agreed.

To my relief, he broke off eye contact, turning away from me to kick open the gate and stride up the short walkway directly into the rubble. I followed but kept my distance.

Using the flash from his phone to light the way, he moved to where the remains of the chimney lay and shuffled the ash, soot, and brick with his foot. "Did you sense it?" he asked.

"The succubaen? No. But the mantel was the last place I saw it."

"Explains the chimney," he said, kicking at a brick.

"What now?" I asked.

Finn sighed, and it was such a reluctant, heavy sound. "Now we go talk to my brother. He was in no shape to go anywhere but home, so that's where we're heading."

I nodded. I was out of other ideas of where to look too.

Finn began to walk back toward the Escalade, and I followed.

"Should we call first?" I asked.

"Nope. And don't you dare send him a text that we're coming."

"Wouldn't think of it," I said, lowering the hand that'd been reaching toward my back pocket where I'd tucked my phone. I'd actually been ready to do just that.

A short time later, we arrived at a neatly arranged suburban home with precisely trimmed shrubbery, a perfectly manicured lawn, and tastefully elegant touches.

A lone bench sat under a giant oak tree off to the side of the yard, and a tire swing hung from a nearby limb of that same tree.

Gideon's home was a surprise: I'd expected something closer to his brother's place—all sleek wood and midcentury modernism. But this was elegant and homey. It was nice.

We headed up the brick-paved walkway and stopped at the front door. Finn raised his hand to eye his watch and scowled. "My watch stopped."

"Probably from the blast," I said. I reached for my phone to check the time before we knocked, when the door opened abruptly and there stood Gideon, wearing sweats and a long plaid robe, looking mad enough to murder the both of us.

"What the fuck are you *doing* here?!" he whispered harshly to his brother.

"We need to talk, Gid."

"Do we?"

"Yeah."

Both men glared hard at the other, and it wasn't a pleasant thing to watch two identical twins staring venomously at one another.

"You look better," I said, trying to break the ice.

Gideon slid his gaze to me, narrowed his eyes in warning, then went back to having a glaring contest with his brother.

"Detective," I said softly, unwilling to back down. "It's about the case."

He stood there clenching and unclenching his fists, his gaze still firmly on his brother. "I've told you never, ever to come here again, Finn."

"Gideon?" a woman's voice called from somewhere deep in the house. "Who's at the door?"

I saw both men stiffen, which was a surprise, given that I would've expected only Gideon to startle at the sound of his wife's sleepy voice calling to him from the stairwell.

His eyes held such hatred in them as he stared at his brother that I thought he might punch Finn in the face. Still, what he said was, "It's just Officer Stanton, babe. He's here to brief me on the case. Go back to bed, okay?"

"Brett's here?" she asked, on an apparent yawn. "Does he want coffee?"

"I don't know," Gideon said, his expression practically double-dog-daring Finn to reply. "Stanton, would you like some coffee?"

Finn opened his mouth as if to respond when Gideon spoke for him. "No, honey, he's good. I'll take the meeting outside so you can get back to sleep, okay?"

"But you're sick, sweetheart. Does Brett know you've had food poisoning?"

"He's just briefing me. I'm not going to work until I feel better. I promise."

"Okay," she said, but remember that Keaton's window is open, and you know what a light sleeper he is, so keep it to the side of the house, okay?"

Gideon's eyes closed as if she'd said something painful, while Finn pressed his lips together and looked as if he'd just been hit in the gut. Meanwhile, my head swiveled back and forth between the two brothers, utterly puzzled by their expressions.

Gideon stepped back inside and closed the door slightly, preventing us from seeing his wife up the stairs. "We will, Trish. Go back to bed. I'll be there soon."

He waited a bit—probably to see if she'd turn and do as he suggested, and then satisfied, he stepped out onto the porch and motioned us toward the driveway.

We followed behind him, and I could see how he was still struggling to walk, his whole frame straining under the weight of standing upright.

Ember had definitely rescued him back from the brink, but her limited time with him had brought him only so far, and the trinket I'd loaned him could do only so much given that he'd had it for less than a day.

I glanced at Finn and saw a pained expression on his face as he too watched his brother struggle.

Gideon would have to recover the rest of the way on his own, which I had no doubt he would, but it would take time, and any thoughts I might've entertained about bringing him along to finish the rest of this quest abruptly ended when I watched him labor the twenty-five feet to the driveway.

We followed him all the way around the house, then down the drive to the detached garage, which lent a lovely view to the backyard, where flower gardens were neatly trimmed and free of leaves, and a soccer net was set up at the far end.

When Gideon finally stopped underneath a basketball hoop, he turned to face us. "Spill it," he said.

Finn asked him, "Where's the pin with Petra's insignia that I left you with?"

"Don't know, don't care," Gideon said stubbornly, but I saw him press his hand against the pocket of his robe and immediately knew he was lying. I also thought that maybe it served Finn right for impersonating his twin at the police station.

"Why do you need it back?" I asked, if only to dispel the tension. Plus, it wasn't like any of Petra's goons were going to suddenly bow down to Finn if he paraded around with it clipped to his jacket.

"Gideon can't be walking around impersonating me with that thing," Finn said, glaring at his brother. He thought he was lying too. "It'll get him killed."

"Like I said, I don't have it, don't want it, and when you find it, you can shove it up your a—"

"It's probably in the rubble," I said quickly, stepping to Gideons side and placing a hand on his arm. I needed to ease the tension before this friendly tête-à-tête escalated even more. "I'm sure you'll find it when you sort through the debris."

Gideon, however, eyed me sharply. "What rubble?"

"My condo blew up," Finn said easily.

Gideon blinked at him. Then he looked at me and blinked some more.

"It was the same mystic's essence that was used to blowup Bree's place," I explained. "Somehow he found out we were there and blew your brother's bachelor pad to kingdom come."

"With you in it?" Gideon asked, his eyes still wide.

"Yes," Finn said simply. Then he bumped me gently with his elbow. "This one helped get us both into the trinket room before the second blast though, and good thing, or you'd no longer be a twin."

Gideon worked his jaw in a way that suggested he wasn't sure if that was in fact a good thing. "Boris?" he asked next.

"He's fine. And so is the trinket room, which I see you've been pilfering from."

Gideon ignored him and turned to me again. "Did you get a look at the guy?"

"No," I said. "Too much debris in the air. Whoever he is, he's a powerful son of a bitch."

"Any ideas who it could be?" Gideon asked next.

"Plenty," Finn told him, without elaborating further.

"That's helpful," Gideon sneered.

"You'd know all about helpful, wouldn't you, Gid? Like how you helped yourself to the most valuable possession in my trinket room?"

Gideon's brow furrowed. Giving a subtle wave toward me he said, "You've got another one just like—"

"Not that!" Finn snapped. For the first time he reacted angrily toward his brother, and I found it telling on several levels because I believed they were referring to my charm, and if they were, then the thief in me *definitely* wanted that other half, mostly because it would likely give me double the power to ward off my attraction to Finn.

"The glass bottle in the leather box?" Gideon said next, looking surprised by Finn's reaction.

"Yes. That," Finn said, anger still wafting off him in waves. "You have *no* idea what you've unleashed, little brother, by sending that thing out into the world."

"Didn't seem that powerful to me," Gideon replied, crossing his arms and puffing out his chest. He was back to being difficult.

I sighed. "Gideon," I began, laying a hand on his arm to get his attention. "The cruet you took and gave to Grigori is a succubaen. Do you know what that is?"

Gideon tore his gaze away from his brother to look at me. "I've heard the term. Doesn't it mean that using one will kill you?"

"Yes," I said. "Which is one of the reasons they're illegal and why there are almost none left in the world. But Grigori created one, using the egg to raise himself from the dead each time he gave up his life to bring the trinket up a level or two."

"Why?"

"Because the succubaen would eventually lead him to the phoenix."

Gideon uncrossed his arms. "*The* phoenix?"

"Yes," I said.

"That thing *actually* exists?"

"It does," Finn said.

"Supposedly," I countered, trying to throw a little smoke around the subject. "It's more legend than fact, but most members of the Seven believe it's real."

For the first time since opening the door to us, Gideon's expression registered regret. "I needed it, and it was the one and only trinket in the room that pulled on me for an appropriate gift for Grigori." He then eyed his brother and said, "Plus, you weren't using it, so I figured it was safe to give away."

"I wasn't using it for good reason, you idiot!" Finn snapped.

Gideon stood up a little taller, which was a struggle for him, I could tell. "You got a lotta nerve calling *me* names here at *my* home, *Flayer*."

Finn took a deep breath and sighed. With a nod, he said, "You're right. Still, Gideon, you don't understand what you stole from me. That thing is dangerous. Especially in the wrong hands."

"I already gave it to Grigori. It's probably still at his house."

"It's not," I said. "We checked."

Gideon turned angry eyes to me. "You entered my crime scene without authorization?"

"Nope," Finn told him. "We stayed on the sidewalk."

"Then how do you know it's not there?"

"There's not much *there* there anymore, bud. Grigori's killer blew that up too," Finn said.

Gideon swept a hand through his hair. "Jesus," he said. "What the hell?"

"This guy is out of control and as lethal as one of Elric's death spells," I told him. And then I turned to look at his house meaningfully, spotting the soccer net and the swing set. "Maybe you and your family should think about relocating for the night. Maybe even for the next couple of nights."

Gideon's eyes widened, but then he followed my gaze to the house, and specifically to the soccer net.

"I think that's a good idea," Finn said, backing me up.

Gideon turned to his brother, "Can't you just assign some of your goons to watch the house for a couple of days?"

"I would if I could, bro," Finn replied. "But Petra's not letting me play with her toys right now, so we're all on our own. How about taking your family to the lake house?"

Gideon ran a trembling hand through his hair. "This is so fucked up," he whispered.

"It's only for a few nights," I said. "Until your brother and I can identify who's behind all this."

Gideon shook his head slightly but then changed that to a reluctant nod. Glancing up at me again, his brow furrowed. Pointing over my right shoulder, he asked, "What's that?"

I reached up to tap my hand against Lunatrabem's hilt. "New toy."

"Did my brother give it to you?"

"More or less. We can save that discussion for later. What we need to know now, Gideon, is how you first came into contact with Grigori."

"Why?" he asked stubbornly.

I wanted to punch him. But then I remembered that I could basically tap him on the shoulder and he'd probably fall over, he was still so weak. "Because no one else could've gotten the cruet from Finn but you. And what better way to lure it out of the trinket room than to set up a mentorship between you and a willing mystic who'd been in hiding for a hundred years?"

Gideon's brow furrowed, and I could see that he was trying to put the pieces together. "I interviewed him," he said.

"You interviewed him?" his brother repeated.

Gideon ignored Finn and focused on me. "One of Grigori's neighbors was murdered."

I frowned. "Who?"

"A guy that lived three houses down from Grigori."

"Wait, there were two murders on that street in recent weeks?" I asked.

"No. This guy was murdered in his bookshop. He was a rare books dealer."

That confession went through me like a hot knife. Now I understood how Grigori had learned about the book that would lead him to the knowledge that the phoenix was a rust-colored dog.

"How was he murdered?" Finn asked, unaware of my alarm.

Gideon continued to direct his answers to me. "His throat was cut."

I winced. "If he was murdered in the bookstore, why would you interview Grigori?" I asked, trying to tie it all together.

"The guy's sister shared the house with him. I asked her if anyone had been acting suspiciously around her brother, and she mentioned that one of their new neighbors gave her the creeps. She said he seemed overly friendly with her brother and was always trying to get himself invited over, so I checked it out and met Grigori."

"You took him off the suspect list?" I asked.

"He had an airtight alibi. He was playing a Russian card game in D.C. at the time of the murder. Half a dozen people swore he was there."

"How did you know he was a mystic?" I asked next.

Gideon simply stared at me for a moment before answering. "He took one look at me and called me 'Flayer'. Scared the shit out of him, I think. I knew then that he was a mystic, because only one of our kind would've known my brother's nickname." With a sneer toward Finn he added, "It took me an hour to convince him I'm nothing like my brother."

"Ah," I said, understanding that Grigori must've thought he hit paydirt when he discovered Petra's lieutenant had an unmentored twin. "Don't tell me, let me guess; when he discovered you'd never been mentored, he offered to take you under his wing right then and there."

"He did," Gideon said.

I nodded and looked knowingly at Finn. His mood seemed set on simmering anger.

"So what did Grigori tell you about the guy at the bookstore?" I asked next.

"He said that he knew the owner only casually, and that they'd shared a love of rare books. He said he'd been to the shop only once to check it out, and he'd purchased a book for which he showed me the receipt. He also said he'd only been trying to be neighborly when he popped over for a visit."

I felt another jolt of alarm. Gideon had probably seen the book that I'd taken from Grigori's place and didn't have any idea how vulnerable the contents made me.

"When was the bookseller murdered?" I asked next.

"About a month ago."

"Ever figure out why he was murdered?" Finn asked.

Gideon glared at him, as if the question were a challenge to his detective skills. "No."

"I do," I said.

The brothers eyed me expectantly.

"The succubaen's last clue before Petra's thief stole it must've led Grigori here to that bookstore. There must've been something in the shop that would lead to the next clue to find the phoenix."

"The receipt," Gideon said, referring to the one I'd found at the back of the book. "Grigori bought a book from the shop."

I nodded. I felt I could talk about the book because it was safely in Dex's hands, about to be destroyed.

"Throw in the fact that Grigori must've known that Petra's thief was the one that stole the succubaen and he had more than enough reason to come here, poke around and leave no witnesses," I said with a pointed look at Gideon.

"You think he murdered the bookstore owner?" he asked.

"I'd bet my warehouse on it. Who better than a mystic to create an airtight alibi for murder?"

Gideon's expression became troubled. I could tell he was reconciling the fact that he'd thought Grigori was his friend and a good guy as far as mystics go, only to realize he'd been played by a murderer.

"That still begs the question of who, besides Gideon, knew Grigori was even in town," Finn said.

And that's when I put two other clues together. "Besides Marco, his girlfriend, Bree, knew."

"Why is that important?" Finn asked me.

"Dex spoke to Gert this morning—" I paused to look at Finn, "You know Gert, right?"

"Who doesn't?"

"Right. Anyway, Dex said that Gert had just heard about Marco going missing and that Bree had been killed in an explosion. Gert told him that a few days ago, Bree had been in Gert's bar with a mystic she didn't recognize. Some blonde who was putting on airs."

"How does that link back to Grigori?" Finn asked me.

"Gert knows every mystic in this town and nearly every mystic who comes to visit. The only mystic she wouldn't recognize is someone who'd never been here. Someone of low rank. Someone who'd probably been in hiding with her lover. And no one puts on airs more than an American expat from Europe."

"Rachel McQueen," Gideon said, putting it together.

I nodded. "I think that Bree and Rachel were working together. They had to be. Grigori never would've allowed anyone into his home—including a caterer if they weren't thoroughly vetted first. Rachel had to have been in on plotting Grigori's murder. I'll bet you my warehouse again that she let in the murderer posing as the caterer. Grigori probably never entered the kitchen to check on dinner. Rachel would've done that and announced everything going smoothly when they all sat down together."

"She was in on her own murder?" Gideon asked skeptically.

I shook my head. "She never dreamed she'd be murdered. Which is why her sister was also there. I think Rachel was hoping to benefit from Grigori's tortured confession of where he had hidden the egg. I think she'd been promised that one of the uses of the egg, once it was found, would go to her sister."

"So Bree was the mystic who bound and murdered the four?" Gideon pressed.

Again I shook my head. "No. Bree wasn't even remotely skilled enough for something like that. She and Rachel would've been working for someone who was though. And that mystic also left no witnesses behind."

"You're saying that someone trying to get to the egg and the succubaen recruited Bree and Rachel."

"That's exactly what I'm saying."

"What does any of this matter, though?" Gideon asked. "So what if this unknown mystic is trying to get the phoenix. I say, let him have it. The world might be safer when every mystic on the planet isn't hunting and killing for it."

Finn and I both chuckled in a gallows humor sort of way. "You're not getting it, Gid," Finn said. "Whoever gains the phoenix becomes the most powerful mystic in the world. And throw in Lunatrabem—"

"Luna what?" Gideon asked.

I tapped the hilt of the sword over my shoulder. "Tic is a direct descendant of King Arthur and Guinevere. This was Guinevere's sword. The second-most-powerful sword ever created, next to Excalibur, which is still missing and likely never to be discovered again."

"We think that Marco was abducted because someone knew that he was a direct descendent of the realm, *and* that he knew where to find Lunatrabem," Finn said.

"How'd you get it?" Gideon asked me again.

"I pulled it out of a junkpile."

"Wasn't Guinevere's sword also sunk into stone?"

"It was," I said, allowing Gideon to draw his own conclusions.

"Petra and I hid Guinevere's headstone in our junkyard," Finn explained. "A couple of times we tried burying it at the base of a twenty-five-foot pile of discarded trinkets, but it always rose to the top, exposing the hilt to the sun, so we left it where it was.

"Then a little while ago some of my coworkers got the stupid idea to come after us, so I directed Esmé to hide at the junkyard. I joined her after I dealt with the reconnaissance patrol and watched her pull Lunatrabem out of the headstone like a knife from butter."

Gideon's eyes widened, and he looked at me with surprise. "What does that make you now? Part of Petra's crew?"

"No," I said firmly.

"Maybe," Finn said.

I glared at him. I would never, ever work for Petra. Besides, she'd definitely kill me before offering me a job.

"But if you have the sword, why is finding the phoenix such a big deal?"

"They won't stop at just getting their hands on the phoenix, bro. Once they have it, they'll be able to use it with the succubaen to obtain all the world's most powerful weapons, including Lunatrabem. All they have to do is desire a weapon or a trinket and the cruet will show them step by step how to steal it. Eventually, they'll acquire Lunatrabem, Excalibur, the Trident, Skofnung, the Bow of Anubis, the Bolt of Zeus—"

Gideon put up his hands. "Okay, okay, I get it. They'll get the mystic world's most deadly weapons. What good would that do one guy against the armies of the Seven?"

I smirked. It was amazing how naive Gideon Kincaid was. I said, "If you were in one of the armies of the Seven and a new mystic came onto the scene, possessing not just the phoenix but every supremely powerful weapon ever magically created, who would you follow? Petra? Elric? Hideyo? Radcliff? Vostov? Mostafa? Vala? Or would you pledge allegiance to the newly minted immortal? The mystic who couldn't be killed and had all the fun new toys."

Gideon worked his jaw for a bit, thinking that over. "I'd follow the immortal with the toys."

"Exactly," Finn said. "And if you stuck to your pledge for one of the other Seven, you'd face off against a growing army gobbling up troops from all across the globe."

"This guy's power would grow exponentially in a New York minute," I said.

"It'd be war like no other," Finn added. "And you, in handing over the succubaen, were the spark that lit the fuse, Gid."

The color drained from Gideon's face. "Holy shit," he said, and he looked like he might be sick. In fact, he took a step back and stumbled. I reached out, but Finn was quicker. He caught his brother, waited until his twin was steady again and said, "Take Trish and the kid to the lake house. Don't move until I tell you it's safe. If you don't hear from me or Esmé, assume the worst has happened and go into hiding. Change your looks, change your hair, do whatever you have to do to not look like me and stay alive. Oh, and Gideon, never, ever, *ever* look for a mentor again."

We left Gideon standing in his driveway, pale and sweaty. I felt bad for him, in spite of all the trouble he'd caused. He'd had no idea what offering his mentor a simple gift would set in motion, and his own twin had kept him in the dark about the dangers lurking in his trinket room.

In my opinion it was far more Finn's fault than Gideon's, but assigning blame wasn't going to get us anywhere. We had to find a new lead that would take us to the cruet. But where to look? What could possibly point us in that new direction?

As Finn drove us away from Gideon's house, I fiddled absently with the charm that Gideon had given me. It was warm under my fingertips, no doubt activated by Finn's nearness, and it was soothing to feel it pulsing with energy. I'd have to figure out a way to deactivate Finn's comeback spell, even though it wasn't likely to work on the charm now that the trinket had been a part of the mentoring ceremony. Mentor's gifts were protected from that kind of trickery. It didn't matter that Gideon had stolen the charm before giving it to me. By right and by law it was mine but that didn't mean I trusted Finn not to snatch it back sometime in the future.

As Finn turned left out of Gideon's subdivision, a sudden thought bulleted into my brain. "Oh, my god!" I whispered, sitting up straight.

"What?" Finn asked, his gaze immediately traveling to his rearview and side mirrors.

"I know where to find the cruet!"

He cut his gaze to me. "Where?"

Chapter Twenty
Day 4

A couple of hours before dawn we pulled into the empty parking lot, circled the building, and parked on the far side at the back door.

From here I could easily see my warehouse, all aglow, just a half mile or so away.

I'd called Dex on the way and told him where we were going. He'd sounded both surprised and worried. He'd then told me to be careful, stay safe, and that as soon as he was finished digging a hole to toss Grigori's book into and cover it with concrete, he'd be off with Ember. I was relieved he was taking measures to hide the text. Above all, he couldn't be caught with both it and Ember as he fled town.

"You're sure about this?" Finn asked, pulling me from my thoughts.

I turned to see him staring moodily at the building in front of us. "Not in the slightest."

"I don't like it. Feels like a trap."

"Probably is."

He sighed again. "Fine. Let's get this over with."

We got out of the Escalade and moved quietly but quickly to the back door. Finn tried the handle—of course it was locked. He began to gather a ball of energy, probably to blast it opened, so I laid a hand on his wrist. "Allow me."

He stepped back and I dropped to one knee, pulling out my trusty lockpick. I worked at the door for all of twenty seconds when I heard a click, and the latch gave way.

We moved inside, and I was surprised to find the place lit. Pointing to the overhead light, I whispered, "Is there somebody here?"

He shrugged. Pulling out his coin purse, he held it in front of him, whispered the words to activate it, and a ball of smoke rose from the trinket and shot off down the hallway in front of us.

We waited for a minute or two in silence, both of us straining to hear any sounds that might indicate we weren't alone in the building, but only the steady sound of the ventilation system came back to us.

The puff of smoke returned in a hurry, stopped in front of Finn, and began to unfold a mini model of the building we were in. It displayed an incredible amount of detail, and my thieving mind was already working on a plan to steal the coin purse from Finn.

What can I say? My true nature sometimes gets the best of me.

"No one's here," Finn said softly.

I nodded.

Even though we both agreed that it appeared we were alone, no way were we about to take a chance by talking at regular volume.

Finn motioned for us to move forward, and we began to make our way down the hallway. At a juncture, I led us to the right, remembering the way from just two days before, which was hard to believe since so much had happened between then and now.

When we came to a set of double doors, I paused to peek through the window just to make sure there was no movement about. There wasn't.

Finn pushed the doors open and we strode in.

I went right to the back wall and pulled open a drawer. A naked dead woman, bald, with features frozen in a silent scream stared up at me with cloudy, sightless eyes.

I shut the drawer quickly and pulled open another one. It was even less pleasant.

"Yikes," Finn said over my shoulder, wearing a look of repulsion. "That is *nasty*."

I shut the drawer. "Probably a car accident. At least he went quick."

"How do you know it was a he?"

"I don't. But I'm not gonna pull the drawer back open to check, okay?"

Finn grunted and moved to the right to pull open a drawer himself. Frowning down at the occupant, he said, "I guess this one was in the car too."

I slammed that drawer closed. "Will you please focus?"

Finn smirked. "The unbound die ugly."

I glared at him impatiently. "Grigori has to be in one of these drawers..." Taking a chance, I pulled open a drawer at shoulder height, and Grigori Rasputin rolled out. "Bingo!"

Finn came over to stand next to me. He was taller, so he could better see the body on the slab. "Wow."

"I know. His death wasn't so pretty either, right?"

"No. It wasn't. But that's not what I was referring to."

"What were you referring to?"

Finn reached up and moved Grigori's arm. It dropped down to swing in front of my face. I pushed it back up and noticed that Finn had stepped back and was admiring the cruet that had knocked me on my ass in Grigori's living room a few days earlier. "You were right," he said.

I gave in to a grin. "When you activated the comeback spell, I wondered if it would come back to you or Grigori, because he became the rightful owner of it when your brother gave it to him."

Finn nodded. "Clever."

He opened his jacket and began to pocket the cruet when I grabbed his arm to stop him. "What're you doing?"

Finn's eyes narrowed as he looked at my hand on his arm.

I didn't let go. No way in hell was I allowing him to walk out with that thing.

"I'm taking back what's mine," he said evenly.

I released his arm and stood back, taking up a defensive stance, purposely blocking the exit out of the morgue. "No."

Finn pushed the cruet into his inside pocket and regarded me like I was some minor inconvenience he had no desire to trifle with. "I beg to differ, *Thief.* No *way* am I going to hand over the key to finding the phoenix to one of Elric's minions."

I reached up and unsheathed Lunatrabem. "Well that's a shame, because you're definitely not walking out of here with it, Flayer." I'd fight to the death for that thing. If he used it and survived, he'd know that Ember was the phoenix, and I'd be as good as dead anyway.

Finn stood tall and held out his palm. A ball of blue energy formed. "Who's gonna stop me, Esmé?"

"I don't want it for myself," I said, realizing how quickly this could get out of hand. "I want to destroy it."

Finn regarded me for a long, long moment. "You think I'll use it."

"Yes," I said.

"If I was gonna to use it, I would've done that already."

"It's more powerful now, and you know it. Grigori has probably charged it to a level seven or eight by now. All you'd have to do is come back from the dead *once* and you'd know exactly where to find the phoenix. And something tells me you've got a trinket or two in that hidden room of yours that could easily handle pulling you back from death."

The ball of blue light in Finn's palm grew two sizes larger. "I told you I'm not going to use it."

I lifted Lunatrabem, holding it with both hands out in front of me, knowing we were likely moments away from killing each other over a stupid trinket. But I absolutely couldn't back down and allow the succubaen to continue to exist in the world. It was one more thing threatening everything I held dear. "No one's going to use it, Flayer. No one. And if you think it through, you'll agree. As long as that thing exists, the threat to both Petra's and Elric's courts exist."

"It'll be safe enough with me," he said.

I let out a mirthless chuckle. "You mean, just like it was safe with you before your twin waltzed into your trinket room and stole it? *That* kind of safe, Flayer?"

Finn continued to study me silently. I watched him closely for any sign of a sudden move, but his expression was blank and his body perfectly still. I couldn't read what he was thinking, and that made me nervous as hell.

Still, I held onto the sword and allowed its power to run through me, giving me courage. I'd faced down a freaking cruellion with this weapon. I could sure as hell face down Petra's lieutenant.

Couldn't I?

Abruptly Finn dropped the hand holding the ball of energy. I braced, tightened my grip on the hilt, and readied myself for the blow...but it never came.

"Fine," he said as we stood there in the cold of the room, no longer allies.

I blinked. "What do you mean, 'fine'?"

"Fine, Esmé, have it your way. I'll allow you to destroy it."

I narrowed my eyes. I smelled a trap.

Finn began to reach inside his coat again and I changed my stance, bringing the sword up to stand like a baseball player at bat. "I'm warning you, Lieutenant," I growled.

"I know," he said, continuing to pull at his jacket.

I remembered the crystal he'd repurposed into a sucker punch, and it infuriated me that he'd try that trick twice and think I wouldn't be ready. "

Finn withdrew the succubaen and held it up, wiggling it at me. "Ready?"

I pressed my lips together and ground my jaw. I was going to kill this fucker for sure if he messed with me.

Finn bent forward like a softball pitcher and tossed the cruet toward me. It flew high toward the ceiling, and I was caught between aiming Lunatrabem at it or at Finn, because I knew he was about to blast me the second I swung at the succubaen.

So I let the cruet fall and kept my eyes on Finn. It could crash to the ground for all I cared. I could destroy it after I'd dealt with him.

Out of the corner of my eye, I saw the succubaen descend, closer and closer to the floor. In my hand, Lunatrabem began to hum, and the white moonglow coming off it filled the room with power.

"Hit it!" Finn yelled.

But I didn't take my eyes off him. Instead, I waited to hear the succubaen crash. The second it did, I'd charge Finn.

My attention was so focused on him that it caught me by surprise when he stared in shock at the floor. As if he'd just seen something he couldn't believe.

And then I realized that I hadn't heard the sound of glass striking tile. The cruet must have fallen to the ground by now, right?

Why hadn't I heard it?

Taking a chance, I allowed my gaze to dart to where the succubaen should have been and saw it suspended in midair, just resting there as if it had landed in the palm of an invisible hand.

And then it was like the atmosphere itself, curled invisible fingertips over the small glass cruet, hiding it altogether.

I looked up at Finn, thinking he was doing it, but he was staring at the spot where the succubaen had disappeared in surprise too. A moment later, he seemed to put the pieces together, because in an instant he gathered a ball of energy and yelled at me, "*Esmé, duck!*"

He didn't have to tell me twice. I dropped low, twirled in a tight circle, spinning away from the spot, while still holding Lunatrabem aloft. Finn unleashed his ball of power, and a silent shockwave hit the spot where I'd just been standing.

There was a cry of pain, and something was thrown through the double doors into the hallway beyond.

Before I could fully take in everything, Finn was in motion, running to the doors and barreling through them. I sprang forward, right behind him.

In the hallway we searched the floor but saw nothing. A tingling feeling of doom entered my mind as I surveyed the corridor. I had an idea about what'd just happened, but I didn't yet want to admit how stupid I'd been.

And because I knew I'd been duped, I took another risk. Finn was in front of me, moving forward slowly, holding another blue ball of essence, ready to unleash it.

But with no target to aim at, I knew he was likely to miss. Changing hands with Lunatrabem, I reached into my jacket and pulled out my monocle, covering it with my hand the best I could, and allowing only a peephole to see through.

I then held it up, looked through it, and saw the unmistakable green outline of a ballpoint pen that hovered in midair by an unseen form about fifteen feet in front of us, hugging the wall and lurching forward.

"To the right!" I shouted.

Finn glanced at me over his shoulder, and I tightened my grip on the monocle, pointing to where I'd seen the green smoke. "There!" I urged.

Finn moved so fast, it was hard to capture it all. The blue ball of essence shot forward and struck the wall exactly where I'd been pointing.

There was another grunt of pain and the sound of a body being thrown against the opposite wall.

Finn and I charged forward, following the sounds. We got about ten feet when an explosion sent us hurtling back, landing together in a heap on the floor.

I held onto Lunatrabem, but only barely.

Finn had unfortunately taken the brunt of the blow. He lay on the ground, clearly stunned but trying to shake it off. I scrambled to my feet, knowing that I couldn't wait for him, and stumbled forward, raising my hand to look through the monocle again and seeing that whisp of green smoke turn the corner at the juncture.

I put on a burst of speed. I couldn't let the succubaen leave the morgue. Rounding the corner, however, I saw the door to the back entrance open, seemingly by itself.

"*Sequoya!*" I shouted.

The door slammed shut.

"Goddamn *bitch!*" I hissed.

I ran at the door at top speed. Behind me I heard footsteps but didn't slow down. Right before slamming my shoulder into the door, I moved Lunatrabem to my side to keep it out of the way.

I hit the door and bounced off, my shoulder burning from the pain of taking the full force of the blow. With a shaking hand, I tried the handle. It'd been locked by magic because the knob was still warm and wouldn't even wiggle when I tried to twist it.

Thinking fast I backed up a foot or two, raised Lunatrabem, and brought it down on the door handle, slicing through it and the steel door like a knife through paper. The handle dropped to my feet with a clatter, and I kicked the door open.

"*Esmé!*" Finn shouted. He was a few steps behind me, but I wasn't slowing down.

The rage of being made a fool of was almost more than I could stand. That whole conversation in the conference room when Sequoya told me Elric wasn't happy with my offering was a ruse to get me to cough up something even more valuable that she could then keep for herself—and I'd fallen for it. I'd offered her one of the most precious trinkets I had: my ballpoint pen. She'd never passed it on to Elric, using it instead to follow me to Grigori's and very likely stealing the succubaen from my palm while I lay unconscious. Had Finn not invoked the comeback spell, she never would've needed to steal it back from us.

And, Sequoya had no doubt loaned out the pen to whomever blew up Bree's apartment and Finn's condo. I knew she wasn't capable of that kind of destruction, but it didn't mean that I still wasn't going to kill her over it. The fury welling up inside me was almost blinding. I was going to cut down Sequoya like the tree she was named after.

Stumbling out into the parking lot, ready for battle, I stopped abruptly when I saw the souls gathered there.

"Ezzy!" Dex cried out.

I stared at him as if I barely recognized the man who'd been my loyal second for all these years.

Dex was in horrible shape. His face was bludgeoned and bruised, one of his orbital sockets looked broken, which caused his left eye to swell completely shut. Blood dribbled out of his obviously broken nose, and his jaw was a mass of purple, bloody bruises.

His lower lip was fat and bleeding, and he was hunched in a way that told me his ribs were fractured, and possibly his right arm.

Battered, bruised and broken, he still managed to hold my gaze with his one good eye.

"Dex?" I whispered, belatedly seeing the two goons on either side of him, holding him up.

I recognized both of them, and I felt sick to my stomach. On Dex's right was Gorch, the bruiser who'd taken on Gideon and me in this very parking lot two days previous, and the Amazon warrior who'd been there as well.

Finn's footfalls rushed up behind me and stopped just as abruptly. "What the fuck?" he exclaimed.

I began to look over my shoulder to confront him when Dex again called out, "Ezzy!"

My gaze flew to him and saw that he was motioning toward his right. When my eyes traveled there, I think my heart stopped. Muzzled, leashed, and struggling for all she was worth was Ember. Holding tight to that leash was

Sipowicz, the young muscled-up little shit who'd come to the parking garage to tell Finn that Petra wanted to see him. Ember tugged hard on her leash, trying to get to me. She whined and barked with the effort and Sipowicz yanked hard on her leash, choking her as he pulled her back.

Seeing my beloved pup muzzled and restrained like that turned my blood to ice but that was immediately dispelled by a rage even hotter than before. I gripped Lunatrabem tightly, ready to murder every single enemy in this parking lot to save Ember and Dex. Taking a step toward Ember I was stopped in my tracks when right in front of me emerged Sequoya, her lip bloody but a triumphant look in her eyes.

I blinked in surprise at her sudden appearance, and she seemed to realize that she'd become visible again too, because she looked down at herself, then clicked the silver pen in her hand in near panic. But she remained visible.

Preparing to end her I said, "Like I told you, you treasonous bitch, it wears off in an hour and you can't use it more than once a day."

Sequoya reacted by casually clipping the pen to her jacket before producing a dagger with lightning speed. Her expression turning to a smug smile, she cooed "Hello, love. Shall we have a bit of sport for the pen?"

I raised Lunatrabem high when a sharp voice rang out from the shadows. "Don't even think about it, Thief!"

Sliding my gaze slightly to the right I saw the owner of that familiar voice step out of the shadows.

"Clepsydra," Finn said behind me. He sounded almost relieved.

But I knew there was no reason to feel hopeful—our number was up.

"Flayer," she purred, walking into the light of the streetlamp illuminating the parking lot. Strapped to her back was the Bow of Anubis—the very weapon that Elric had stripped her of a thousand years ago.

From her wrist dangled a rope, and Clepsydra pulled violently on it, yanking another form out of the shadows.

Into the light stumbled Tic. He looked feverish and weak. The wound at his chest just below his collar bone was weeping through a dirty bandage, and tears streamed down his face from pain or fear—it was hard to tell which.

His hands were tied together by the rope, and Clepsydra reeled him in like a prized fish.

Sequoya backed away from me and walked to Clepsydra's side, cuddling up next to her, she kissed her lovingly on the neck, then placed the succubaen neatly in Clepsydra's outstretched palm.

"Petra will kill her for this," Finn said softly.

"Petra will be the first to die," I told him. "Right after us, that is."

I could see her plan so clearly. Obviously she'd recruited Bree to spy on Tic and she'd heard from Bree that Marco had played cards with Grigori Rasputin. She'd then put a tail on Rasputin, following him to the bookstore. Knowing that Finn had an unmentored twin brother he was highly protective of, she'd killed the bookstore owner, triggering a police investigation which had sent Gideon to interview Grigori. Clepsydra had then used Bree to recruit Grigori's girlfriend, Rachel, with the promise of saving her sister's life once the egg and the succubaen were recovered. No doubt it was Clepsydra who'd told Bree to promise this to Rachel, which explained why Gert had seen Rachel crying in the bar. I thought it likely that Clepsydra had told Rachel to suggest that Grigori mentor Gideon, triggering Gideon to present Grigori with the succubaen, which of course Clepsydra knew about.

And then, with a naive and trusting Rachel's help, Clepsydra had entered Grigori's home on the night of the dinner party and murdered them all. But even after torturing the Russian mystic and his guests Clepsydra had been unable to locate the egg or the succubaen. And I knew that because the chantress had then sent Sequoya to use my pen to follow me, thinking I might lead them directly to either prize. As I lay unconscious on the floor at Grigori's house three days ago, I'd unwittingly given up the succubaen, and I knew Clepsydra didn't yet have the egg because if she did, Petra and Elric would already be dead.

Once she'd secured the succubaen, Clepsydra had launched another part of her plan by killing Bree and abducting Marco in order to redirect Finn away from Petra's court. The lieutenant was the only mystic who could protect Petra from the chantress. With Finn distracted and out of the way, Clepsydra was free to organize her mutiny, recruiting Sipowicz, Gorch, and the Amazon and carry on the search for the egg.

But she was hampered by the fact that Finn had invoked his comeback spell, causing the succubaen to disappear again. So Clepsydra had kept Sequoya on our tail, and I had no doubt Elric's assistant had spied on us when we were outside Gideon's house and she'd followed us here, obviously guessing that I knew where the succubaen was.

The rest of Clepsydra's evil plan was to recover the succubaen, ambush and murder us then do the same to Petra using an arrow from the Bow of Anubis which was well suited to the task as the arrows themselves were magically infused to literally find the heart of their targets. And when she allowed her arrows to fly, Clepsydra would be far out of spellcasting range, avoiding the risk that Petra might see her coming and invoke the chantress's binding spell which would kill her instantly.

Adding a new and opportunistic angle to Clepsydra's plan was Lunatrabem, which was why Dex and Ember were here. The chantress thought she could threaten them to control me, and once Petra had been dealt with, Clepsydra could force me to wield the sword against Elric, distracting him while she unleashed her deadly arrow from afar. But if I refused to cooperate, Clepsydra could kill me and force Marco to engage Elric with Lunatrabem in my stead.

Once Elric had been killed, she'd be freed her from her binding spell and then nothing and no one could stop the chantress as she used the succubaen to acquire every other trinket and weapon she desired, including the phoenix and Grigori's elusive egg.

As I stood there in the parking lot what I didn't know was if Grigori—in his tortured state—had confessed to Clepsydra what he'd read in the rare book he'd purchased, that the phoenix was an ember-colored hunting dog. Namely, *my* ember-colored hunting dog. With Ember leashed and muzzled here in the parking lot, I had to assume there was a strong possibility that he had.

One glance at Finn told me he'd put much of Clepsydra's plan together too because his expression was murderous fury.

He stepped forward several steps to the right and in front of me, gathering a large ball of energy, preparing for battle.

As he came forward toward her, Clepsydra's expression turned gleeful. Dropping the rope before stepping on it to make sure Tic didn't sneak off, she produced an arrow from the quiver strapped to her back, nocking it expertly in her bow.

"Oh, Flayer," Clepsydra said with an amused smile. "You never disappoint."

No sooner had she gotten that sentence out of her mouth than Finn unleashed his ball of essence. I thought for sure the chantress had met her doom, but in that same instant Clepsydra took aim and let the arrow fly. It met Finn's bundled essence at the midway point and the impact of the two caused a violent explosion that knocked me back several paces.

When I'd gained my footing again, I saw that Finn was no longer standing. Instead, he was on his knees, the arrow sticking out of the center of his chest and blood pouring down his shirt.

"*No!*" I screamed, rushing to his side. I tried to hold him up as he began to wilt to the ground, but Finn's complexion quickly drained of color and he crumpled to the pavement. There his eyes closed, blood dribbling from his mouth and with a gurgled sigh he breathed his last.

Panicked, I looked up, seeking help but my gaze landed on Clepsydra, who'd nocked another arrow and was pointing it directly at me.

I got to my feet drawing Lunatrabem up and close to my chest. Clepsydra could unleash her arrow but I knew it was no match for one of Merlin's swords and the blade was wide enough to protect most of my vulnerable heart.

In reaction to my protective stance, the chantress grinned and it infuriated me that she was so tickled by the carnage she was unleashing. Swiveling her aim she pointed the arrow again at Finn, waiting.

But Finn didn't move and the seconds ticked by while everyone watched the dead lieutenant closely.

After nearly a minute, Clepsydra pivoted her aim once more, this time pointing it at Dex but keeping me locked in her gaze. "Move away from the lieutenant," she commanded.

I did as I was told, keeping the sword over my heart and my gaze trained on her.

"Check for his pin," she said to Sequoya.

Sequoya skipped happily to Finn and my lip curled into a snarl. I mentally vowed to hurt her before I too breathed my last. The mystic squatted down and pulled on Finn's shoulder, looking for the lieutenant's pin that I knew he no longer had because it was currently in my jacket pocket where I'd tucked it after pinching it easily out of Gideon's pocket with him none the wiser.

Staring down at Sequoya as she rifled through all of Finn's pockets, I began to suspect I knew what magical powers that pin actually had.

At last Sequoya stood, kicked Finn's body and announced, "He's not wearing it."

Clepsydra smiled in triumph and Sequoya skipped back to her side, gazing adoringly up at her. "Now what," she asked.

"Now," she said, eying Lunatrabem and Tic meaningfully, "we take out the rest of the trash." Before the final word was out of her mouth, Clepsydra unleashed the arrow trained on Dex.

"*Noooooo!*" I screamed, running toward him. But before I even got two steps, Dex jerked forward, pulling out of grip of the two warriors guarding him. He looked down at the arrow, sticking out of his chest that'd pierced him clean through. He too crumpled to his knees, his gaze agonized as it met my own. And then his eyes went sightless and he fell forward face first.

Ember let out a heartbreaking howl as she pulled and struggled against the leash held by Sipowicz who yanked hard on the leash and kicked her with his knee.

Meanwhile Gorch and the Amazon laughed at the smacking sound Dex made when he hit the pavement.

I'd stopped running toward them the second Dex had sunk to his knees. Tears stung my eyes and my heart hammered in my chest as a fury so powerful engulfed me that I felt my essence build and gather toward my hands holding tight to the hilt of the sword. My energy mingled with Lunatrabem and I turned toward Clepsydra.

She nocked another arrow and took careful aim. At that exact moment, out of the corner of my eye I saw Sequoya draw her knife again and come at me from the side.

The arrow and Sequoya would each deliver a deadly blow to me at the exact same time and I knew I couldn't fend off both of them no matter how fast I moved.

So I used the only option I had left, hoping it would be to my advantage. Shoving my hand into into my pocket, I wrapped my fingers around the pocket watch Finn had given me, pushing some essence into it as I tightened my grip. In the next instant, everyone around me was moving in slow motion but I was moving at what felt like normal speed, which meant I was *actually* moving far faster than anyone around me.

Bolting forward I began to race toward Clepsydra who had unleashed her arrow. I saw it coming at me moving fast but not fast enough for me to knock it from the air. Lifting Lunatrabem high, I ducked away from Sequoya on my right, and was about to bring my sword down on the arrow when from my left Ember appeared right in front of me, blocking the arrow from view.

I gasped as her body flew past me slow enough to appear to be floating. Before I could even comprehend what was happening, a terrible cry echoed across the parking lot and in almost that exact instant the tip of an arrow exploded out of Ember's side.

Dropping my sword, I caught my beloved pup before she landed on the hard pavement and she went limp in my arms. As I fell into a crouch, I stared down at the life fading from Ember's eyes and it was like a part of my soul shattered into a million pieces.

Behind me there was a rush of movement and somewhere in the very recesses of my mind I realized that the sound of footsteps nearing me was far faster than it should be given how the pocket watch had slowed down time. Next to me, Lunatrabem hummed. Without thinking, because I couldn't even form a coherent thought, I reached for the sword, let go of Ember and twirled to a standing position to face Sequoya, wielding her dagger and coming at me fast.

Around her neck a medallion glowed brightly. "Two can play at that game, Thief!" she yelled as she leapt in the air ready to bring down her dagger into my shattered heart. Lunatrabem came alive moving of its own accord, blocking the blow just in time.

Sequoya's body, however, knocked into me but I twisted quickly and threw her off. She landed gracefully and turned again toward me wearing a ferocious expression.

I stared at her dully for only a moment until the warrior's power of Lunatrabem flowed into me and blocked out the pain of losing everyone I loved in this world.

I raised my sword to counter her blows, backing away from her in calculated steps that brought me nearer to Tic and Clepsydra.

It was a purposeful maneuver. Sequoya struck at me again and again and each time I easily defended myself, luring her in. When we were within feet of Tic and Clepsydra, I unleashed the restraint I'd placed on Lunatrabem and the sword danced in my hand, coming up in an arc as Sequoya brought her dagger down.

My blade cut through her wrist without even pausing.

Sequoya stood in front of me, staring in stunned horror at her dismembered limb. I waited until she lifted her gaze to look into my murderous eyes before fully unleashing Lunatrabem. The sword jerked up and sideways, slicing right through her neck.

Freed from the magic of her pendant, Sequoya's head and body began to drop slowly and separately to the earth. Snatching my ballpoint pen from her jacket, I whirled in a circle and cut through the rope attaching Tic to Clepsydra.

Marco's eyes widened in slow motion when I grabbed his hand, shoved the pen into it and used his thumb to click the plunger. He disappeared from view. While I still had hold of him, I pivoted him toward the nearby patch of woods, giving him a small shove in the process.

I then focused my full attention on Clepsydra. But then something weird happened. In the blink of an eye, she stopped moving in slow motion or rather, I stopped moving with lightning speed.

Finn had warned me that the effects of the watch would be short-lived.

Still I held the element of surprise and I didn't waste it when I stabbed Clepsydra through the heart while she watched her lover's head fall at her feet.

I then turned to face the rest of the group, hearing the sound of the chantress's dead body hit the pavement with a thud.

The Amazon warrior and Gorch rushed toward me. I waited patiently, standing with Lunatrabem held at ease by my side.

Three feet from me they both reached out with hands curled into claws, ready to rip me to pieces. I cut off all four of their arms at the elbow. I then twirled neatly in a circle, cutting them both in half.

A dozen meters away, Sipowicz stood stunned and shaken. I thought about how cruel he'd been to my beloved Ember, how he'd muzzled her, yanked on her leash, kicked her with his knee, and ultimately had allowed her to get loose to save me which had killed her in the end. All that anger began to well up inside my chest as I stared at him across the lot.

He read my expression correctly when he turned to run. I hitched Lunatrabem's handle up above my shoulder, caught the hilt deftly, stepped back to use the sword like a spear and launched my weapon. It flew as straight and true as one of Clepsydra's arrows.

Sipowicz didn't even make it ten steps.

A moment later I walked over to him and pulled the sword from the center of his back. I then moved over to where Clepsydra lay, pale and lifeless. I waited and sure enough color returned to her and she sucked in a sharp breath.

Before she had fully recovered herself, I bent down and snatched the broach with Petra's insignia from her shirt. "How many lives will it give?" I demanded.

The chantress stared up at me in panic, the wound at her heart already sealed shut but she was still weak and feeble. Clutching at the ground—no doubt in search of a weapon, she refused to answer me.

"Fine," I said. "Have it your way."

I raised Lunatrabem, ready to end her as many times as it took to actually *end* her when she raised her arm and gasped, "Thief, wait! Listen to me! I'll use the succubaen to find the egg and the phoenix! Together we can join forces and rule the world!"

I lowered the sword, considering her. No doubt she thought I was mulling over her offer, but really I was thinking how pathetically ironic it was that, at one point in the past ten minutes, she'd had the phoenix, the succubaen, Lunatrabem and the key to finding the egg all within her evil clutches and she'd blown it so magnificently that it shamed her as a mystic and Petra's chantress.

For her part, Clepsydra stared up at me with wild, panicked and then hopeful eyes. I hardened my gaze, letting her know the truth before I even spoke it. "No deal," I told her.

A moment later, I was the only living being in the parking lot.

Chapter Twenty-One
Day 4

I went to Ember first, sinking to my knees at her side, the pain of seeing her lifeless was nearly more than I could bear. Letting out a sob, I pulled the arrow from her side, broke it in two and threw it away, feeling the urge to murder Clepsydra all over again.

Tears slid down my face as I stroked her soft fur, praying to feel the rise and fall of her chest, but no sign of life emerged. Gently I placed Clepsydra's broach on her shoulder, pushing a bit of essence into it, but while I waited for it to activate, it remained stubbornly cold.

Desperate, I reached into my pocket and pulled out Finn's lieutenant's pin. I laid that on her shoulder, waiting and hoping, but nothing in her stirred.

It was then that I knew for certain what I'd long suspected; a trinket's magic wouldn't work on Ember. She was immune to their curative powers.

With a sob, I hugged her to me, kissed the top of her head, then lay her back down again.

Brokenhearted, I stood up and brought the pin and broach over to Dex. Standing over him I pulled the arrow from his back and turned him over. He had no pulse, and his complexion was pale and gray.

Opening his palm, I wrapped his cold fingers around Clepsydra's broach, again trying to activate it, but it was empty of power. The broach had held no more than one life to give, which made sense given the threat to Petra of Clepsydra's considerable powers.

Throwing the broach across the parking lot, I then placed Finn's lieutenant's pin into Dex's palm and the second it touched his skin it activated on its own. I watched him for a moment and when he sucked in a breath, I let go a relieved sob. I stroked his hair and called his name but he was still unconscious. I looked to his wound which was very slowly starting to heal. I kissed him too and moved off to see to Finn.

He was lying on his side in the fetal position, his skin also pale and a pool of blood surrounding him. After removing his arrow, I dug through his pockets and came up with the key fob to the Escalade. I went to the SUV and drove it from its spot in the parking lot over to where he lay.

With considerable effort, I loaded Finn the Flayer into the cargo space of the Escalade, and then I went back to Ember and knelt down.

Gathering her in my arms, I rocked her for a bit, feeling her body grow cold. Slowly I got to my feet and carried her over to Finn's car, placing her in the back seat and covering her with my jacket.

I bent forward to kiss her cheek one last time, then closed the door and headed over to Dex again.

Squatting down, I felt for a pulse and let out a breath of relief when the throb of his pulse, steady and strong, beat against my fingertips. His eyelids fluttered, then opened, and he stared up at me in confusion. "Owwww," he moaned.

I stroked his temple, careful to avoid his swollen eye.

Only the mortal wound on Dex had healed. I lifted his hand and felt the pin. It was cold to the touch, and I knew that its powers were also limited. "Can you stand?" I asked him.

"No," he grunted. "Not yet."

"We have to go, Dex," I said, looking anxiously toward the eastern horizon. The first whisps of dawn were starting to streak across the sky. Even on a Saturday I didn't think the morgue would remain closed. Focusing back on Dex, I said, "Can you try to get up, honey? I don't think I can get you into the car myself."

"Ezzy, I can't," he gasped.

"Stay here," I said, moving off to the car. There I placed the pin in Finn's palm hoping and praying that it activated again but it remained cold as a stone.

"Dammit," I swore, leaving the pin in his hand. I then got in the Escalade and drove it over to Dex. Keeping the engine running, I came around to stand over him and pulled him up by the arms to a sitting position. He winced and gasped in pain, but I had to continue to hurt him a little in order to get him into the car and away from here. Crouching down next to him I managed to get my shoulder underneath his arm. "Help me as much as you can," I told him.

Dex grunted sharply several more times as I hauled him to his feet. I felt terrible about causing him even an ounce more pain, but I didn't have a choice. The parking lot would be descended upon by both the bound and the unbound any minute, and we had to get out of there.

As I was easing him onto the lip of the tailgate, he hissed through his teeth and asked, "Can you fish that book out of my waistband? It's digging into my ribs."

I blinked but quickly felt along the back of his jeans and discovered the rare book that revealed all of Ember's secrets. I threw the text into the front seat, cursing it under my breath.

"I was in the courtyard...about to mix the cement...when Clepsydra...showed up," Dex wheezed, leaning heavily against me and gasping for air. "They walloped me pretty good...but they never found the book."

I nodded, not even wanting to think about that cursed thing, and then managed to ease him gently down next to where I'd laid Finn.

"Oy! He's dead, Ezzy," Dex complained, when he realized he was staring into the sightless eyes of Petra's lieutenant.

"I know," I told him. "Hang tight, okay? I'll do everything I can to get you home and healed soon."

"Where's Ember?" he asked, right before I closed the lift gate.

My voice was horse when I said, "She's in the back seat."

Dex nodded. "Good," he said, his eyes fluttering closed again. "I was worried they'd hurt her."

I did a little cleanup in the parking lot, crying quietly while snatching several trinkets littering the scene then got into the front seat of the Escalade and wiped away my tears. The whole process had only taken two to three minutes and I would've skipped it but it had to be done. There were some trinkets I couldn't leave behind.

Starting the engine I bit my lip and shook my head, willing myself to stop the tears. I had to keep it together because I had a lot to do in the next hour or two.

Using the Escalade's stored location navigation system, I plotted a course and made my way through the nearly empty streets as dawn broke.

Because traffic was light between 5 and 6 AM, I arrived at my destination in under an hour. Parking at the curb, I got out and made my way to the front door. Raising my hand to knock, I thought better of it and went around to the back door, which was lined with windows for a better view of the lake.

Through them I could see Gideon sitting in a chair by the fire, wearing a robe and slippers, and looking so exhausted that I wondered how he was even awake.

I rapped on the glass of the back door ever so lightly and watched as he startled, bringing up a gun, ready to shoot at the first sign of trouble.

When he looked toward me, I waved to him, and he shook his head as if to clear away his surprise, then came forward and unlocked the door.

"Esmé, what're you doing here?"

"I need the egg," I said simply.

Gideon stared at me and didn't say a word.

"Gideon," I said firmly, holding out my hand. "Give it to me."

"How did you know I had it?" he whispered, while his eyes darted around the yard, no doubt suspecting a trap.

"I didn't know until about an hour ago," I told him. "It was when I realized that Grigori wouldn't have had it anywhere in his house with him being so close to finding the phoenix. He would've especially not had it nearby when his girlfriend's terminally ill sister arrived for dinner.

"And wherever he hid it, Grigori would have to trust that no one would think to look there. Who better to give it to than Finn the Flayer's twin; an unmentored Boy Scout who hated his brother and the mystic elite enough to never reveal to anyone that he was holding the egg for safekeeping."

Gideon offered me the hint of a rueful smile. "That's pretty close to how he put it," he said before moving to a backpack, hanging on a hook by the fire.

I watched as he dug through the contents, retrieving a small gold box, maybe three inches square. He brought the box to me, handing it over right before he also pulled out the serpent and staff trinket that I'd lent him.

Placing that in my other hand, he said, "I feel well enough to give that back to you. Thanks for saving my life, Esmé."

Pocketing the trinket, I weighed the gold box in my left hand, feeling its heft. "This is solid gold?" I asked, only then noticing the embossed double-headed eagle on the lid of the box that was the seal of the House of Fabergé.

"It's heavy enough to be. Grigori told me that the egg would be safe from lending its power randomly if it was kept in that box."

I opened the lid, revealing a velvet pillow with a perfect, golden egg nestled in its center. I badly wanted to touch the egg, but I didn't dare. Closing the lid, I wormed it into the secret pocket inside my jacket.

"What're you going to do with it?" Gideon asked.

"I'm going to use it to save two lives."

"Good, because Grigori told me that's all it has left."

I nodded and turned to leave.

"Hey, hold on a sec! Whose lives?"

I glanced over my shoulder. "Mine... and an ally's."

Gideon stiffened. "My brother?"

"In the car."

The tension in his shoulders relaxed. He opened his mouth to ask a follow-up question, but I cut him off.

"Get some rest, Gideon. Stay here for a couple of days until I tell you it's safe to return home. You and your family won't be in any danger here."

With that I left him and got back to the task at hand.

After giving the serpent and staff trinket to Dex, I drove all of us back to the warehouse. Parking the Escalade in the garage was no trouble because the double doors had been blown clean off, which was no doubt Clepsydra's work when she'd come looking for me and Finn and found only Dex and Ember in the courtyard.

Fishing the rare book from the floor of the front seat, I tucked it into my own waistband, then moved to the rear passenger door and opened it. The sight of Ember's still form was like another gut punch all over again, and I bit back the sob threatening to burst out of my throat. With the greatest of care, I lifted her out of the back seat and carried her inside. Cradling her in my arms, tears streaming down my cheeks, I walked through the warehouse all the way to the opposite end and over to a door that was always kept locked. Reaching out to the door handle, I pushed a bit of essence into it and it unlocked, turning in my hand.

I pulled open the door to a set of stairs and I carried Ember down, hugging her still form tightly until I reached the basement level.

"Illuminate," I said at the bottom of the stairs. Three crystal cathedrals glowed with soft yellow light and lit the space enough to allow me to see where I was going.

I walked with Ember forward to a fireplace set in the middle of the room. Dex and I had built it. At the time, I'd wondered if it was worth all the labor, but now I was grateful for the effort.

Getting down on my knees in front of the brick, I placed Ember in the center of the hearth, then removed the book from my waistband and placed it just behind her. I didn't know if my plan to rid the earth of its presence would work, or if it was even necessary at this point, but I had to try.

I sat back on my heels, bending forward until my forehead touched the cold stone floor, and sobbed tears of fear and denial and longing and regret.

Finally, the thought of Dex in the back of the Escalade pulled me from the depths of my sorrow, and slowly I got to my feet, bending low once more to gently stroke Ember's muzzle before heading back upstairs.

Getting Dex out of the SUV proved just as difficult as getting him in, but with the use of the wheelbarrow we'd used to shuffle bricks into the warehouse to build the fireplace, I was able to move him into the living room and eventually maneuver him onto the couch. He was almost totally out of it, which was probably a good thing.

Next I headed into the trinket room and sorted through the various treasures there, coming up with three trinkets that, combined with the serpent and staff trinket, would take away a lot of the pain Dex might be in and help him feel more comfortable while his wounds healed.

After activating all three additional charms, I laid them on his chest, and within the few minutes it took to fish out a blanket and pillow for him, I saw that the look of discomfort that'd etched itself onto his features had relaxed, and he was now sleeping soundly.

I turned then to stare toward the back door leading to the garage. I knew I was taking a chance by not helping Finn but I couldn't risk having him witness what was about to happen to Ember.

With a heavy heart I turned my back on the door and headed down the stairs again. Ember's body was still lying where I'd left her, and I sat on the floor akimbo to stare at her unmoving form. Soon a small wisp of smoke rose from the hole where the arrow had pierced her heart.

More tears leaked down my cheeks.

A moment later, my beautiful, beloved companion burst into flames.

The heat was so intense, I had to get up and take a few steps back, and it proved to be the remedy for ridding the world of the clue that would've identified her. The edges of the book turned black before the whole text also went up in flames.

I waited until the fire had died down and there was nothing left of her but ash and cinder, then I went back upstairs and into the garage once again to where Finn lay dead in the back of his Escalade.

I opened the golden box and placed the egg in Finn's cold hand. Immediately it grew warm and I stepped back, waiting and watching for it to work its magic.

For several moments nothing happened. I reached out and felt the egg. It was still warm and I began to worry that perhaps the lore about the egg being able to bring someone back within twenty-four hours was wrong, and I'd inadvertently left this last task for too long but then Finn's body twitched and a second or two later, he gasped for air.

Letting out a sigh of relief I crawled into the Escalade next to him and stroked his hair. Something tender welled up within me then but I was too emotionally fragile to examine it, so I pulled my hand back and waited for Finn to move again.

"Hey, there," I said when he stirred. "Welcome back to the land of the living."

Taking the egg from him, I tucked it into its box, then pocketed the treasure before helping Finn as gently as I could into what I hoped was a more comfortable position, laying him on his back and moving a pillow that I'd brought with me under his head.

"Where am I?" he muttered, as if the effort to speak was exhausting.

"Someplace safe," I told him. "But I'm going to move you to an even safer location where you can rest up for a couple of days and fully recover, okay?"

Finn muttered something unintelligible. I took that for an okay.

After getting back into the driver's seat, I used the navigation system once more to plot my course.

We arrived at Gideon's tidy suburban home a mere twenty minutes later. I helped Finn out of the car, which was much easier now that he was alive again, and he took one look at where we were and said, "No fucking way."

"Fucking way, pal."

"Esmé, I can't stay here."

"Your brother's at the lake. I told him to stay there for a couple of days. He'll never know you were here."

Still, Finn resisted when I tried to get him to walk to the back door with me. "It's either here or the mean streets of downtown D.C.," I snapped impatiently.

"I can't stay with you?"

"No," I said firmly. That was absolutely out of the question.

He sighed and allowed me to half-carry, half-guide him inside.

After getting him settled on the couch, I said, "I'll be right back."

A moment later, I reappeared with Lunatrabem. Leaning the sheathed sword against the stone fireplace, I said, "I need you to store this with Boris in your trinket room for a while."

Finn's features crinkled in surprise. "You're giving me the sword?"

"I am definitively *not* giving you the sword, Flayer. It's *my* sword and remains my sword until I die or give it willingly to

Tic, which I'll likely never do because he's … Tic. But I need to store it someplace safe for now."

"And you think I'm someplace safe?"

"Oh, you're definitely trouble. But, at present, you're the only kind of trouble that's not actively trying to kill me."

Finn smiled, and I felt that unmistakable chemistry between us crackle to life. "You're safe with me, Esmé."

"I'd better go," I said before things turned to wearing less clothing and making poorer choices.

"I'll be in touch," he said, "as soon as I clear things up with Petra."

"You do that," I said, turning to go.

"What happened to Marco?" he asked, stopping me. "Is he dead?"

I sighed and didn't turn back around to face him because I couldn't. I'd given Marco the pen, and he'd disappeared into the unknown. He'd been wounded and weak, but I had no doubt he'd survived and would find someplace safe to recover too.

"Besides me, Flayer, Marco's the only one who made it out of that parking lot alive."

There was a moment of silence between us as Finn took that in. "Your second?" he pressed.

"Is recovering from an arrow to the back. I used your pin for the deed, you know the one you gave your brother and which you didn't tell me had lifesaving powers."

"You're a thief, why would I tell you that?"

"Good point."

I took another step toward the door, and he asked, "What about your dog?"

I stiffened, pausing once again. Then I simply shook my head, not trusting myself to speak.

When Finn didn't say anything either, I began to make my way to the door again.

"Esmé?" he said when I put my hand on the door handle.

I paused for a third time, waiting.

"I'm sorry. She was a sweet pup."

With that, I fled the house.

Later I sat in front of the fireplace, staring at the pile of ash, a cup of lukewarm coffee in my hands. I'd barely taken more than a few sips, and I was so tired that I felt like the walking dead, but I had to stay awake.

Just as my lids were becoming too heavy to keep open, the ash in the fireplace stirred.

Immediately I set the coffee aside and leaned toward the hearth. "Please," I whispered. "Please, please, Ember. Come back to me."

The ash stirred again, as if my voice had caused a bit of excitement. Hope broke open the darkness of my despair, and fresh tears slid down my cheeks. From the ash there was a tiny squeak, and eagerly I leaned forward a little more, but I didn't reach inside the hearth. I had to be patient. She had to choose.

At last the ash parted, and a tiny, copper-colored newborn pup wormed her way out of the blackened cinders. A happy sob escaped my lips, and I quickly tamped it down, trying not to make another sound, but it was so hard.

Before my eyes, the newborn magically grew in size and matured until she resembled a puppy about five weeks old. Opening emerald green eyes, she blinked at me and wagged her tail.

I held my breath, my hands clasped together in silent pleading.

And then, on wobbly limbs, she trotted happily forward and leapt off the lip of the fireplace into my welcoming arms. "Oh, my baby," I whispered, covering her in kisses. "You came back to me. You came back!"

"Ezzy?" I heard Dex call from the top of the stairs. "Is it Ember? Is she born again?"

Ember let out one tiny, perfect bark, and I laughed and buried my face in her fur. "She is, Dex. She's back."

"Did she choose you?"

"She did!" I shouted, overjoyed.

"Thank the gods," he said.

I'd learned from the mystic who'd cursed me that, as the phoenix, Ember could choose to be reborn—or not—but she could also choose the shape she wanted to live her next life in, *and* who to spend that next life with. If she'd emerged from the ash and had ignored me, I would've had to set her free to find her way to a new companion, and that, quite literally, would've killed me.

The fact that she'd leapt into my arms and was now covering me with wet sloppy kisses told me in no uncertain terms that we were once again paired for as long as we both should live.

Carrying her upstairs, I placed her on the floor at Dex's feet. She sat down clumsily as she stared up at him. "Hello, luv," he said to her, his one good eye leaking a tear.

She got up and moved over to his leg, rubbing against him and letting out a little whine. He looked at me, unsure. "I don't want to pick her up," he said. "She's so tiny. I might drain her."

I looked from Ember to him and said, "Let her be the judge, Dex."

Still, he hesitated, settling for gingerly crouching down, which I could tell caused him significant pain. The healing trinkets I'd given him had helped to mend him a bit, but he still had a long way to go. "Hello, little one," he said, smiling from ear to ear, and giving her a good rub. "It's been a very long time since your mum had to raise a puppy," he said before looking up at me and adding, "Hasn't it, Ezzy?"

Ember had been killed only once before: ninety-three years earlier, my father had brought to our home—in a part of Bolshevik-controlled Ukraine—a beautiful red dog who'd been terribly wounded, as if she'd been in a horrific battle. Her fur was singed, her skin was slashed, two of her legs were broken, and pain radiated in waves through her trembling form.

My uncle, a doctor, had been called upon, and he'd looked her over, telling us there was nothing that could be done to save her. Still, I wouldn't allow my uncle to shoot her, as he'd suggested, and insisted on holding her through the night, praying that she somehow would survive. Close to dawn, the dog had died in my arms.

And even after she'd stopped breathing and had turned cold in my arms, I'd continued to hold her, rocking her back and forth, forlorn and inconsolable at her loss for reasons I couldn't explain.

In the morning, Dad had lifted her from my arms and taken us both outside, laying her on a blanket under the shade of an oak tree. He'd then gone to the shed and brought back a shovel, telling me that we'd dig her grave together. We both took turns at the task, and I realized later that my father had wisely seen that it was important for me to participate in the ritual of her funeral.

Just when we'd finished digging the hole and were about to wrap her in the blanket and ease her into the earth, Ember had burst into flames. We'd both been so shocked by it, jumping back so as not to get burned. Later, when my uncle came over, Dad had told him all about it, but he kept telling us it wasn't possible.

My father had left me to fill the hole back in. There was nothing left of Ember but cinder and ash, and he told me I could scoop in those remains as I filled in the hole.

I did as he'd instructed, but I hadn't touched her ashes. Something had told me not to. And for the rest of that afternoon, I'd sat under that tree in front of those blackened cinders, waiting for something but I couldn't say what.

An hour before dinner, the ashes had stirred, and a few moments later a tiny puppy had emerged. I'd yelled for my father and uncle, who'd come running, and we watched in utter amazement as Ember in the form of a newborn pup had wormed her way out of the ash. As we stared in stunned silence, the pup had matured a few weeks in just a few moments, and then she'd trotted straight over to me and barked up happily. I'd swept her into my arms twirling us in circles, filled with a joy that made me want to dance on air.

I'd stopped twirling when I nearly bumped into an old woman who'd stepped out from the shadows. Haggard, bloody, and obviously gravely wounded, she'd limped into our yard and stared at the scene, taking it all in as if she knew exactly what'd happened.

Seeing her wounded, my uncle had rushed toward her to help. She'd raised her hand and he'd made a terrible sound, then dropped to the ground, dead.

When his brother fell, my father had also rushed forward, only to die right on top of my uncle.

Stunned and frightened beyond description, I stood there trembling, holding my new puppy and waiting for the woman to kill me too. But she hadn't.

Instead, she'd stepped forward eagerly, reaching for the puppy in my arms, but Ember had growled and barked at her, and the mystic had immediately abandoned the effort to take her from me. It was then that she'd regarded me with a loathing that was hard to quantify. She began speaking something that sounded like a nursery rhyme, but at the end of it, my whole body became warm and tingly.

She'd then said these words to me: "The phoenix belongs to you now, child. She will turn you immortal if you wish, but she herself can perish like any mortal. If she should die in your care, see that she reaches a hearth, and allow her to make her choices. Her first choice will be to be born into this world again, or not. Her second choice will be the shape to live in while she walks or flies among us. And her third choice will be to pick the companion to bond her life with. She may choose you again, or she may not, so steps must be taken to protect and care for her, lest she fall into the wrong hands."

With that, the hateful hag had disappeared back into the shadows, never to be seen or heard from again.

Shaking off the memory I stared down at Ember sitting at Dex's feet, and smiled genuinely for the first time in days. I also felt a well of gratitude tighten in my chest. It was the honor of my life to know the phoenix had chosen me twice now.

"Raising a pup will be fun," I said, giggling when Ember tried to climb up on Dex's lap to lick his face.

He finally relented and picked her up with his one good arm. "Do we have anything for her to eat?"

I sighed, glanced at the clock, and said, "I have a delivery to make and then I'll bring her back a burger. We can get some puppy chow in the morning."

Dex looked at me with a furrowed brow. "I should come with you, Ezzy."

I shook my head. "Not a chance, pal. Stay here. Guard Ember. If I don't come back, run."

I drove Finn's Escalade over to SPL Inc., parked at the curb, got a special package out of the back and approached the building. It was well past 11 PM, but I knew there'd be people inside.

After pressing the buzzer and announcing myself, the door clicked open, and I walked into the spacious lobby. The guard on duty, a sharply dressed woman with long red hair widened her eyes at the sight of me, but didn't hesitate to point me to the elevators. "Mr. Ostergaard is waiting for you on the eighteenth floor."

I nodded and moved to the elevator. The doors opened as I approached. I stepped inside and saw that the button for the eighteenth floor was already lit.

Leaning against the wall, I closed my eyes and gathered my courage, which would've been easy if I'd had Lunatrabem with me, but no way would I *ever* enter SPL headquarters with that sword in hand.

The bell above the doors binged, and they opened to reveal the man himself, standing casually in an empty foyer wearing an unreadable expression.

I stepped out of the elevator and greeted him with a nod.

"You've been busy," he said.

"I have."

"You killed my assistant," he said next.

"I did."

He took a deep breath, assessing both me and my responses. "Lunatrabem?"

"No longer in my care."

Elric laced his fingers together in front of him. "That is…unfortunate."

"It is. But I brought you back a consolation prize." With that I stepped back into the elevator and grabbed the Bow of Anubis and its quiver of arrows, bringing both into view and setting them against the wall.

The faintest trace of a smile flashed across Elric's lips.

"The succubaen?" he asked next.

"Another casualty," I said. Using Lunatrabem, I'd smashed it into pieces before leaving the morgue's parking lot.

Elric nodded knowingly. He'd no doubt discovered the shattered pieces when he'd gone to retrieve Sequoya's body.

"Do you have the egg?"

"You know I do."

"True," he said.

Reaching into my pocket, I took out the golden box, carefully handing it to Elric. "I believe it has one life left."

Elric took the box, opening it and removing the egg. He then held it up to eye level for a closer inspection before placing it back into the box, closing the lid and considered me.

"Esmé Bellerose," he said. "Welcome to SPL Inc."

Printed in Great Britain
by Amazon